Till the *Fat Lady's Sung*

Terry White

Pen Press Publishers Ltd

Other titles by the author
WITH GENTLY SMILING JAWS
TRESPASSERS WILL BE MUTILATED

First published in Great Britain by
Pen Press Publishers Ltd
25 Eastern PLace
Brighton
BN2 1GJ

ISBN 978-1-906206-63-5

Printed and bound in the UK by
Cpod, Trowbridge, Wiltshire

A catalogue record of this book is available from
the British Library

Cover design by Jacqueline Abromeit

To Hilda with Love,
and thanks for her patience.

With thanks to Diana, Corina, Maureen,
Lyn, Jane and Joanna, and to
Terry Darlow for his support.
Special thanks to my daughter-in-law Claire
who found the time to proof read as well as coping
with two young children.

Prologue

The minute hand on the Town Hall clock jerked forward to register four minutes past two in the morning. Holding a folded sheet of paper, the black-robed figure of the Town Clerk moved to centre stage. The light on the top of the television camera winked red and the milling throng of local government scrutineers, assistants, constituency workers and other political aides in the body of the hall fell silent.

The Town Clerk cleared his throat, hoped like hell that the knot in his tie hadn't slipped and nervously smoothed down the hair his wife had carefully plastered across his bald patch to prevent reflections from the battery of lights, which momentarily focused the nation's attention on the statistics he was about to reveal. His voice when he began to speak was fractionally high.

"I, James Arthur McHugh, being the returning officer for the Sheringford constituency, hereby give notice that the following is the total number of votes cast for each candidate in the General Election." Blinded by the glare of the lights in his eyes, he held the piece of paper at arm's length, cursing the myopia that at the previous election had sent him stumbling base over apex up the steps on to the selfsame stage in full view of ten million viewers. That incident and the sniggers and suggestions of excessive elbow-lifting that followed it had compelled the donning of his 'distance' spectacles today.

"Peter Anthony Adams..."

The voice-over television pundit murmured, "Liberal Democrat."

"...two thousand one hundred and twenty-seven votes."

A few orange flags waved and a sprinkling of cheers drifted across the microphones but Peter Anthony himself showed no emotion – he knew he had lost. The camera switched from the close up on the rictus grin of another five-year political exile to the returning officer.

"Barmy Earl Welly..."

"Raving Loony Party," whispered the voice.

"...one hundred and six votes."

A figure dressed in black with the pancake white face of a mime and shiny red Wellington boots capered around for a few seconds until quelled by a Medusian glare from McHugh.

"Kenneth Alun Davies..."

"New Labour." The voice-over had a hint of expectancy in it.

"...eight thousand four hundred and sixty-eight votes."

There was a stunned silence punctuated by a few gasps. A ragged cheer broke out from a tight knot of red rosetted figures clustering at the apron of the stage. The thin, sharp-faced man in the off-the-peg grey suit, red tie and huge rosette clasped his hands over his head in a victor's salute and beamed all round, but in spite of the television commentator's observation that "this could be a shock result, a twelve percent swing could give Labour this once safe Tory seat", the performance lacked total conviction. James McHugh tightened up his voice.

"Sir Gwaine Lissett..."

"Tory," murmured the pundit.

"Poofter!" called someone from the crowd secure in her anonymity.

Taut vocal chords seized McHugh with a bout of coughing, endearing him to nobody, especially the anxious TV producers waiting to push on to Merthyr Tydfil, and provoking from a tall aristocratic-looking cove standing stage right with a hauteur as high as his forehead hissed instructions to "get on with it, man!"

James gathered himself together and gargled, "Eight thousand five hundred and thirty-four votes."

The aristocratic crust stepped forward and flapped a limp arm towards the TV camera. The cheers that greeted the announcement were muted, an expression of relief rather than triumph. The TV pundit, disappointment in his voice, reported to the nation that the Tories had held Sheringford but with their majority slashed from six thousand to less than a hundred. The scene switched to the Mechanics Institute in Merthyr Tydfil and Sheringford slid out of the nation's consciousness. Its moment of glory in the spotlight was over – or so it believed.

For a small group of people, however, intently watching a twelve-inch black and white television, borrowed for the night, in the upper room of a shabby terraced house, a carbon copy of all those along the street and in the other South London streets surrounding, the figures were those that they had been waiting for.

"The bastards are going to get in by a fucking landslide." The speaker was a tall, well-dressed man of about thirty-five, his intelligent face showing no emotion, the words dropping like marbles onto a sheet of glass. He tapped his teeth with the pencil with which he had jotted down neat records of the voting figures, a gesture of deliberation rather than disappointment. The alert, elderly man with the half-moon spectacles nodded agreement.

"Gives us just the opportunity and time we need to get our man into position."

"And we know where to start, now," murmured the tall man. His smile didn't reach his eyes.

* * *

Personally I couldn't have cared less; stuff the lot of them, I was thinking. All those little red, blue and yellow dots on the BBC's great election swing-o-meter flickering on the bar television of The Frog and Nightgown were only of passing interest to me. As the Sheringford result came through I vaguely noticed that Scales, Smallwood, Charlie and the other two girls were slowly merging into the furniture. So, as my election night experience drifted towards an alcohol-fuelled, peaceful, comatose end, my last thought was 'Big deal, but it won't change my life.'

How wrong can you be!

Chapter One

Sheringford dozed sleepily after lunch in the warmth of
the April sun. The occasional rook clapped its way across
the clear blue sky, listlessly applauding the early arrival
of summer. Radiant heat shimmered from the mellow
stone of the more dignified buildings. The four square
Town Hall, the old Court House and the Town Gaol
cheerfully bedecked with rusty manacles, chains and leg-
irons of a bygone era, the fifteenth century grammar
school sporting birching block and leaded light windows,
the square tower and lichen-stained buttresses of the
church of St. Stephen-neath-the-Willows and The Star
Inn lurching alongside the Old Bath Road, its stables
housing not two hundred stage horses these days but
table lamps with tasselled shades and avocado with
prawns. The breeze wafted stronger effects from the slit
windows and arched doors of the Gothic horror
dominating the east end of the long market place. The
Tolliver Grimshaw Memorial Gentleman's Urinal seeped
pungent ammonia into the afternoon air, such that even
the bronze nostrils terminating the long powerful nose
of Tolliver Grimshaw himself seemed to flare more
disdainfully than ever as he stood, eyes arrogantly gazing
in perpetuity over the town he had ripped off for forty
years. With foot thrust forward, frock coat swept back
and hand firmly on his wallet, or so the locals claimed, he
posed proudly on his plinth. The sculptor, denied his
stage payments, had deliberately accentuated that by
which friend Tolliver was more infamously reputed, and

the tight Victorian trousers boasted a bulge that wouldn't have shamed a bull elephant.

Around the back lays and alleys tucked out of sight behind the front streets, the crumbling weathered brick of the artisans' cottages reflected both their jerry built structure and the warmth of the sun.

I wandered idly down Bull Street a contented man; hands thrust in pockets, sun on my back and relaxed in sweatshirt and jeans, I was half-listening to the murmur of a high-flying aircraft, probably from Heathrow, America bound. I scanned the sky for a vapour trail but the vault was devoid of even a single trace of white. My thoughts returned to street level, considering how I was going to fill in the time for the next two hours whilst awaiting reunion with my loved one. Sinking a pint or two amid the horse-brasses and copper kettles of The Highwayman Bar in The Star was one possibility but the weather was so beautiful it would be a shame to waste it indoors; just to stroll through Sheringford, letting the sun warm me through, mind ticking over in neutral, was much more appealing.

It had been a somewhat heavy morning, a bit of a busman's holiday in fact, spent crawling into cobweb-festooned roof spaces framed with beetle-riddled oak, probing flaking weathered stone work and jumping on sagging trembling floors. More a labour of love than a matter of choice but when the bugle sounded one was expected to get on parade. At least shinning up ladders had enabled me to get an eyeful up Fleur Fullerton's skirt – but even that small consolation was muted by the stoutness of the knickers she wore. A sailmaker from a ship of the line couldn't have stitched more formidable garments. Her poor bloody husband must really be in the doghouse these days, having to assault that lot. Charlie had prudently worn jeans, thank God. Randy old Nesbitt, the Borough Surveyor, hadn't been seeking divine guidance when he kept casting his eyes heavenwards either.

The ascetic female from The Historic Buildings Society, all angles and pince-nez, made copious notes as she plunged instruments into softened wood and crumbling mortar, pursing her thin lips and squinting down her nose muttering, "This will never do!" and "What a tragedy!"

She kept asking me if I thought 'it' would collapse, whatever 'it' was she was filleting at the time.

'How on earth would I know?' was the truthful answer. Most of the 'its' in Sheringford had been standing for over three hundred years and I supposed that sooner or later 'it' would collapse; everything would in time. The question should be when, not if! But my answer would still be the same. Still, as Charlie had trundled me out as an experienced civil engineer, I had to say something, so I compromised with expressions like "Very dodgy", "Structurally unsound" and "Becoming unstable". The woman seemed to be satisfied with these and copied them down assiduously in her notebook.

The Save Old Sheringford Committee members had then pushed off to continue their meeting over lunch, happily leaving me to my own devices. Hence the contented strolling around the ancient streets of this pretty and historic town, just taking the air without a care in the world.

It could well have continued that way if it hadn't been for a small stone lying on the pavement in front of me. It's strange how one tiny incident can change the course of history, even life. You know the sort of thing, a butterfly flaps its wings in Outer Mongolia and the result is total chaos in New York. Well, it wasn't quite as spectacular as that, but for me it certainly changed many things.

Transformed momentarily by the sight of it into England's World Cup striker, I took a hop and skip forward and swung a casual kick. Moon in his deceptive lazy style casually picks his spot, sends the goalkeeper the wrong way and hammers home the winning goal. My thick-soled trainer caught it clean and true, a lovely shot, right in the meat. The stone rocketed across the pavement, ricocheted off the road's surface and finished spangling and whanging round the spokes of the front wheel of what I noticed, with a stab of alarm, was a bicycle being ridden by a formidably large lady. Whilst she was wobbling, trying to get her bike back under control, I recognized her and my alarm grew. Mrs Hartley-Worthington was the wife of the local vicar, a doyenne of local society and, more to the point, a member of Charlie's Save Old Sheringford Committee.

Shocked out of my reverie, I hopped anxiously on one foot, shaking the other as if to withdraw its previous kicking action.

"Terribly sorry," I called. "I just..." I gestured feebly at the dangling foot, hoping that perhaps she wouldn't notice it was attached to me by a leg.

Minerva Hartley-Worthington was a formidably large, hairy woman with a tweed-covered face and tweed-covered legs. When we had first met, I formed this awful mental picture of her stripped to the buff and shrouded in tweed from head to toe; her body hair woven into a form of Harris combinations. The Reverend Percy would have her dry-cleaned once a week, paying extra for her to be done whilst he waited and getting her re-textured each month.

Our one and only meeting had taken place the previous week at one of Charlie's SOS dinner parties up at Prinknash Keep. I hurriedly recalled that I had been seated opposite the vicar, a gentle little soul, but that Mrs H-W had arrived late and had been placed well away from me – on purpose, I suspected. Notwithstanding that, and under the present tricky circumstances, just to be on the safe side and cover all possibilities, some sort of disguise would not go amiss in case there were future encounters. Thus, to accord with the one-legged hopping performance, I gave her my Long John Silver, closing one eye and twisting the face into a 'Har Jim Lad'. Not that Mrs H-W was able to focus her attention on me for the present, with her bicycle bucking and squirming all over the road. However, she was not a noted member of the local hunt for nothing and, calling on years of experience with recalcitrant horses over ferocious fences, with a mighty heave of her meaty thighs she restored the errant transport to its original course, flashed me the sort of look she bestowed on members of the hunt who were careless enough to ride over hounds, and pedalled past.

I grasped the gist of her feelings towards this encounter from an expression left hovering in the warm, still air which sounded like 'Blasted new-town yobbo'.

Well it certainly wasn't 'Good afternoon, Mr Moon, nice to see you again!'

She obviously hadn't recognised me; that was a relief. I watched her large tweed-covered behind disappear round the corner, muscular calves pumping the pedals, and, shielding my eyes from the sun, scanned the street for any other potential hazards. There were none visible, but to be on the safe side (again) I reversed my original direction away from Mrs Hartley-Worthington and, hunching my shoulders, walked briskly upwind from the odour of Jeyes Fluid floating from Tolliver's pissoir, and headed for The Highwayman's Bar in The Star Inn.

An hour and three pints later I wandered back into the High Street. The High Street of Sheringford was once a place where banks and building societies came to die on top of the bones of bankrupt businesses that had predeceased them. For years the ancient market town had been slowly and remorselessly strangled to death by the coils of traffic around its throat.

The bypass, completed a couple of years ago, had effected an instantaneous reversal of the mortification process, and, with the release of the traffic ligature, the life blood had begun to flow back into the town and regenerate the cells of trade and commerce. The place was definitely on the up. There was one strange thing about the town centre: apart from a few spruced-up shop fronts, there were no new buildings. It looked just as it would have done fifty or even a hundred years earlier. Keeping a wary eye open for Mrs Hartley-Worthington, I contemplated the shops and businesses with an alcohol-fuelled pleasure. It was thriving again, a busy little centre of commerce, a draw for shoppers and traders alike; a place to which people were attracted and civic pride attached. A warm feeling for the place began to build in my breast. The new industrial estate on the southern edge of the town and the influx of people over-spilling from the cities into the new estates around it had clearly made their contributions. The pale faces of the women and the trendy clothes of the children showed the many who were newcomers. Mellowed by three pints of Trubshawes real ale, I gazed around with some pleasure at the scene of quiet prosperity; the feeling grew into that which lurks within the breast of all good British stock, a desire to do something for those you think should have something done for them but in reality who just wish you'd piss off and leave them alone.

I still had time to kill before my rendezvous with Charlie so I looked round for something useful to do to help my fellow citizens. I don't normally do this, but when pleasantly mellow I get these warm feelings for my fellow man – in the widest sense of the word. The street was deserted. No blind old ladies ready to be dragged

6

protesting across a busy thoroughfare and marooned on the side alien to them: no handicapped person to be hauled up a flight of steps in their wheelchair to a platform from which they couldn't get down after you'd gone. It was very disappointing.

Whilst jingling the change in my pocket I had an idea. At least I could help the local economy by spending a pound or two and I could do with something more solid than just a liquid lunch. Maybe a small bar of chocolate – no point in being too rash at this stage, a gradual build-up of capital injection made for better founded growth than a sudden deluge.

Spotting 'Thos Tugwood Newsagent and Confectioner' on the corner thirty metres away, I changed direction by a degree or two to starboard and set course for Thos Tugwood's shop with the intention of purchasing a little stomach lining.

It occurred to me, and simultaneously to the said Thos Tugwood, that Thursday was half-day closing in Sheringford – at two o'clock prompt. My watch indicated exactly two o'clock, give or take a few seconds, so I increased my pace towards Thos' door which I could see still bore a small cardboard sign suspended from a cord stuck to the glass by a plastic sucker. The sign read 'Open'. I could also make out through the shop window a shadowy form approaching the selfsame door from the opposite direction and from the nervous agitation of the figure I deduced that it was probably Thos himself and not a departing customer. I also deduced that it was moving towards the door with the determined intention of reversing the little cardboard sign on its cord to announce to the outside world that from thenceforth for the remainder of the day, Thos Tugwood, Newsagent *extraordinaire* was 'Closed'.

The heel of his hand rammed the bolt home a split second before my final lunge connected with the door handle. The door shivered but remained closed. An almost orgasmic expression of glee lit the ancient's lined face, exposing a brace of rather badly made false teeth set in bright purple gums. He rotated the notice six inches in front of my nose and the word 'CLOSED' (in Gill Sans capitals, about thirty-six point) appeared through the dusty glass. He could not be serious. I tapped with a fingernail on the glass and pointed to my mouth, making munching motions. He pointed to the notice indicating quite emphatically that punters were now excluded. The case being made clear, he pulled the blinds and shuffled back across the Stygian shores of his sealed shop, leaving an unproffered seven-sided coin clutched in my hot hand.

"You stupid, un-commercial, dozy old goat!" I bawled at the now reflective glass. Jesus Christ, that was typical of this one-horse town. Didn't they know what business was about these days? One almost had to apologise for wanting to thrust one's filthy money into some traders' tills – if one could actually get into the blasted shop in the first place. The British shopkeeper had no idea, no idea whatsoever; no wonder the place was such a rundown dump, it deserved to be. I glared round, daring anyone to contradict but the populace, at least its only representative within earshot – a pale boy attached by a long lead to a scruffy looking hound scratching itself lazily behind one ear – stood unmoved and uncaring. For his studied unconcern he collected the remainder of my frustration. The glare riveted him to the spot.

"If I let you have them I'll have nothing left to sell to other customers," I mimicked in the whinging tones of the corner grocer, wagging a finger under the kid's nose. "Bloody Hicksville, that's what this town is – you go and tell your dad that."

The kid counter-attacked: "I'll tell my dad you asked me to go with you and do rude things..." His bold-eyed stare neutralised my glare. "... and he's a big bastard," the kid added to complete the one-two. A tricky low blow the first one.

"I never suggested anything of the kind, you little sod." Defensive caution took over from irritation; one had to treat that kind of threat carefully these days. A clip round the ear was not an acceptable riposte in the socially aware society in which we existed today. Prosecution for assault, grievous bodily harm or, depending on the local police's failure to meet current targets, attempted murder, could result from such a reaction. If that was not sufficient deterrent, then accusations of child molesting and paedophilia could easily follow. If I managed to escape ten years in the pokey, plus a lifetime on some sexual perverts' register, at the least a huge bollocking from the magistrate about 'taking the law into your own hands' plus a massive fine beckoned. Whose law was it anyway? I asked myself. Was it the magistrates'? Was it the police's? Was it Parliament's? No it bloody well wasn't, it was our, the people's, law, so all this about 'taking the law into your own hands' was a load of cobblers. It was our law in the first place.

I was just fulminating to myself about this and my attention was temporarily distracted from the kid. He was still standing there holding his ground and had drawn the mangy mongrel closer for protection.

"Up yours, skinny," quoth the kid, refocusing my attention on him.

I weighed the alternatives again in the balance of pride but although the kid's last observation had shifted the weights substantially on to the 'Fat Ear' side of the scales, it was not quite sufficient to tip them that way. A diplomatic withdrawal was called for.

"And yours, spotty." This shaft struck home, pubescent acne speckled his forehead. I nodded at the kid, trousered the orphaned coin, shrugged my shoulders in half amusement and continued down the street.

A small mechanical shovel was squeezing itself between Monsieur Paul – 'Hairstyle de Paris' – and the 'Mother Wouldn't Like It' boutique, up a narrow lane between the two. I brightened, the possibility of watching a hole being dug offered, on current showing, one of the more exciting opportunities for the afternoon.

On the right-hand side, stretching from the rear of 'Mother Wouldn't Like It' for about a hundred and fifty metres, as far as I could judge, was a high, rusty, corrugated iron fence, too high to see over from the narrow road. On the opposite side of the road, ancient terraced cottages leant against each other like drunken sailors reeling out of a dockside tavern.

The excavator swung right and lurched through a ramshackle gate in the fence and I, following its tracks, did likewise – safe, I assumed, from any further encounter with Mrs Hartley-Worthington.

Fronting me was a number of large derelict buildings, some basically little more than sheds, and others which had obviously been used in the past for some industrial or manufacturing process. A faded sign painted on the gable of one of the structures proclaimed: 'Joshua Grimshaw and Son Est. 1852 – Barrels, Casks and Drums of All Kinds'. So this was the old Grimshaw place. I looked around with interest. The 'Son' must have been friend Tolliver; it had been Tolliver's industry that had brought Sheringford its prosperity around the turn of the century, just as his balls had originated the number of long powerful noses that could be seen cutting the wind along the streets today.

The excavator disappeared along the cracked concrete roadway between two sheds, I hastily sprinted after it. All the buildings were old and well past the end of their useful life. Rusty pipe work, containers of all sizes, broken asbestos cement sheeting and glass lay scattered about on all sides. The wood of the sliding doors was rotten, but each door had been secured by a new-looking padlock, a forlorn and belated attempt to discourage the vandals who had turned the place over years before.

The site on which the old works stood was huge; the effect on the town of such a major employer closing down must have been devastating. As far as one could judge the place must have folded fifteen to twenty years ago at least, and the site had stood derelict, untouched and, I realised, hidden behind its corrugated iron hoarding for the intervening years – no use to anybody as the town followed it into decline.

The excavator squealed to a halt beside an old battered tipper truck with no identification, against which a beefy man in oily blue overalls was leaning, smoking a cigarette. Neither of the two men noticed me and after exchanging a few words, the driver extended the booms that gave the digger stability and making sure that they were firmly jacked on to the ground, began to load the truck with scrap metal. Clouds of rusty dust filled the air and all my excited anticipation rapidly dwindled to zero. Watching two rogues nicking scrap was more likely to lead to a black eye than anything profitable, so with a feeling of disappointment, I moved away to return to the gate. As I strolled back, the germ of a possibility entered my mind and just for interest I decided to pace out the limits of the site. It turned out to be roughly square and bounded at the rear, away from the town centre, by another road which obviously had been the main access to the works. On the third side a tree-lined, steeply sloping bank fell away to the River Shering forming the boundary, and a high fence concealed the dilapidated outbuildings on the fourth side from the rear of the High Street shops. A quick calculation showed that the site area was about four acres – I couldn't remember the metric conversion to hectares, was it two point two or was that litres to gallons? Perhaps I had better bull up on metric measurements of area, after all, it was a lot simpler.

Apart from its seclusion, there was one other curious thing about the site. Approximately halfway along the boundary at the rear of the High Street property the fence turned sharply in to the site for forty paces, turned at right angles and continued for twenty paces and then turned back out towards the previous boundary line. In the small enclave of land so contained rested a rather badly proportioned, small stone building with slate roof gaping to the blue sky. Where the roof slates were missing, split and rotten rafters could be seen. Its windows were boarded over with plywood sheets bleached and delaminated by the weather. The rainwater gutters and down pipes were cracked and clumps of purple buddleia flowered proudly from crevices in the flaking yellow stone walls.

Whoodling softly from their perches above the rotting cornices, pigeons puffed their feathers and blinked gently in the afternoon sunshine amongst the crumbling pinnacles. The whole building exuded chromatic warmth that completed the picture of natural tranquillity and remorseless decay.

The long thin profiles of the windows and the decoration of the surrounding stonework were evidence that here, snoozing in the twilight of its life, lay an old chapel. It obviously pre-dated the factory by decades, maybe centuries and equally obviously it had been derelict well before the factory. There was a narrow gap between two of the High Street shops bounding the chapel site, I presumed access to the chapel had been gained via an ancient alleyway that lay within that gap.

A needle stabbed my conscience. I glanced hastily at my watch.

"Jesus Christ!" Time had flown. I had spent an hour and a half wandering round and now I was going to be late.

12

I began to hurry back across the site towards the gate, when a faint stirring within the nether regions told me those three pints of Trubshawe's wished to make a reappearance. It was a good half hour's drive back to Prinknash Keep from Sheringford even under the pressure of a bursting bladder and to the best of my knowledge, there was no other public convenience in the town apart from Tolliver Grimshaw's grotesque amphigory – and that was in the opposite direction to my point of convergence with Charlie.

Ah, yes, Charlotte. The conscience twinged again for a different reason. Was it right, I asked myself, for a close personal friend – okay, live-in lover but my intentions were honourable – of the Secretary of the Save Old Sheringford Society even to contemplate development within the bounds of that self-same Sheringford he was supposed to be assisting his beloved to save? Were Catholic priests even able to consider that God did not exist without suffering dire penances, or scientists that matter could both be created and destroyed? Well, the earth was not flat nor was it the centre of the universe and previous acceptance of these matters indicated that movement was possible within even the most intransigent breast – given time. A convincing argument but, I recalled ruefully, only after a certain amount of burning, hanging, flogging and torturing of the original proponents. Better not to think too much about it just yet, just concentrate on the problem to hand.

A quick glance around confirmed that the lee of the corrugated iron fence adjacent to the gate was not overlooked and therefore, stepping forward to face the fence, I unzipped and commenced operations.

Now I don't think that even people who were not Marcus Moon supporters would claim that I was one of life's pushers, one of those forever driven forward faster so that the peripheral pleasures become merely an unrecognised blur flanking the urgent pursuit of success. My progress to ambition permitted frequent stops along the way to smell the flowers and the present short interlude was both figuratively and metaphorically such an occasion. The sun's rays filtered through my cotton shirt, wrapping a soothing shawl around the shoulders; the bees hummed in and out of the cow parsley, the birds twittered softly in the stunted sycamores and the sweet smell of Catmint wafted over. Life felt good at the moment, the high spot of the afternoon so far and with Charlotte still to follow, marvellous.

Contemplating what the remainder of the day held, my mind was miles away in our bathroom at Prinknash when padding, panting and snuffling noises intruded off stage rear, breaking my nicely developing train of thought just at the stage when I was loosening up the soap immediately prior to a body contact soaping of Charlie under the old-fashioned shower. Two large, black Labradors – bitches, I discovered later – had suddenly lolloped round the gate and, noses to the ground, sniffing away happily, were rapidly making a beeline in my direction.

I twitched nervously with alarm and rapidly took stock.

Now I had a Moon plan to cope with dogs, all dogs from the minute Yorkshire terrier to Rhodesian Ridgebacks. Well, perhaps not quite as far as Rhodesian Ridgebacks, or even Dobermans, but certainly up to your average Great Dane and even black Alsatians. This plan was based on three fundamentals: one, never show fear – hence the caution about including the Ridgebacks and Dobermans which scared the shit out of me; two, never allow the dog to get behind you; and three, if possible, stand still and persuade the dog to approach by making friendly noises.

My problem, however, in my present situation was to

solve fundamental number two, because unless I was very quick, the dogs were certain to come up behind, poking their noses into nice smelly parts – *my* nice smelly parts – and with a cold wet nose up your bum one was not in a strong position from which to exert the mastery over dumb animals required in fundamental three. A final effort concluded the micturating part of the activity, but the dogs were now very close. I glanced over my shoulder to assess the position and at the same time gave a sharp jerk on my zip. A small piece of thread from the inside of my jeans was engaged in its teeth. It jammed. I cursed softly.

The dogs, startled by the sudden movement, sheered off and circled warily. Turning to face them, I put fundamental three into operation.

Crooning softly, "Here, my boys, come to Uncle. Don't be frightened" to the apprehensive animals, I clicked the fingers of one hand whilst tugging feverishly at the zip fastener of my gaping flies with the other trying to work the thing down again to free the jam. There was a sharp intake of breath from the direction of the gate and looking up, I beheld Mrs Hartley-Worthington, bicycle supported by one hand, clasping the other to her mouth as if inserting an exceptionally large gobstopper. Her horrified eyes were boggling with the stunned incredulity of a dowager Duchess discovering an Irish fiver in her change at Harrods.

I straightened up, twisting my face hastily into my Long John Silver impersonation again, but before I could explain she gave a strangled squawk.

"Flossie, Daisy, to heel at once!" And with her eyes riveted on my flies, she gathered herself together and rasped out in tones usually reserved for the leadership of the Hunt Saboteurs Association.

"You bestial brute – you absolute bounder – how dare you molest my dogs, you filthy animal! Flogging would be too good for people like you – you're sick. What you need is an operation to render you safe so that decent creatures can be secure on this earth. You should have been doctored at birth. I shall have you before the local magistrates of which, I will have you know, I am the Chairman, and I will have you locked away, you unutterable swine! I shall remember you, have no doubts about that. Pah!"

And with a final snort of disgust, she swung a hairy leg across her machine and pushed off rapidly up the narrow road with the two puzzled dogs trotting obediently in her outraged wake.

"No, hang on a minute," I called, "you don't understand..." I ran to the gate to call her back and explain – not that that was going to be easy, but under the circumstances, it seemed much the lesser of the two evils regarding her opinion of my character, but she only pedalled faster. I contemplated chasing her up the lane but with my flies still agape, I decided that far worse conclusions might be drawn from such behaviour by even fair-minded people, let alone the local bench – although a plea of insanity would have something going for it. And so I reluctantly withdrew back behind the fence to loosen the zip. By the time I was decent again, Mrs Hartley-Worthington and pack were hull down on the horizon.

I shrugged. It was some consolation that we probably would not meet again at least for a long time, and in that event if she challenged me, I would just deny all knowledge of today's events. It was hardly likely that she could bluntly accuse me of buggery or bestiality or whatever it was she thought I was attempting with her dogs, either in public or at a Prinknash dinner party. Feeling somewhat ruffled and indignant, I gathered the shreds of my self respect together and repaired at a swift jog to my rendezvous with Charlie outside The Boot and Flogger.

She was waiting beside the car, impatiently tapping a neatly-shod foot on the pavement. Pleasure momentarily overcame my apprehension. By God, she was a fine striding girl, very sexy when angry, a real turn-on. She saw me approaching and her lips set into a firm line. Oh Christ, it must be later than I thought – my watch had developed a tendency to lose of late. I realised with a sinking feeling that 'loin girding' was called for and if I hadn't been preoccupied with thoughts of Mrs H-W's dogs, I would have prepared for it – but it was too late now. I welded a grin across my face.

"Where on earth have you been? I've been standing here for nearly half-an-hour waiting for you! It's too bad, we shall be late for tea now and there were some people coming I wanted to meet, really Marcus!"

I harrumphed and harr'd a little, realising that I was totally without the defence of an explanation; the truth was out of the question, and as I had failed to foresee the fourth ice age on the hurried walk back, a suitable melting white lie had not been prepared. From past experience it was fatal to try instant improvisation – Charlie tore that sort of thing to shreds in seconds.

I flung in interest and flattery as a stop gap – it sometimes worked. "And how was your meeting, 'Light of my Life'?"

"You've been drinking in the pub all afternoon, haven't you, Marcus Moon? You've got that rigid, flushed, glazed look that always gets pasted on your face when you get pissed."

Stone me, I thought, that's a bit of a nasty one. That, in fact, is going to take some replying to. To deny being in the pub amounts to virtual acknowledgement that I look rigid, flushed and glazed when pissed. She will also want to know where I *have* been. If I tell her, and Mrs H-W relates encountering a mad animal abuser in the town on the same day, the ubiquitous Charlotte, being very

17

well equipped between the ears, as well in other equally useful and desirable parts, will definitely put two and two together and make four. It was safer to deny being rigid, flushed and glazed even when pissed and therefore, by implication, let her assume that the afternoon had been whiled away in the boozer – a quick decision. Yes, that was much safer and a known quantity. I would receive a standard bollocking Mark Three – Drunken Lovers for Use On – and be sent to Coventry for the rest of the day – perhaps less if I was ingenious. I could put up with that no trouble at all. Any other reply led into unknown territory – jungle country. The presentation and tone of the reply was equally important – any foot-scuffling, voice-wavering or eye-shiftiness and exposure would be immediate. Even initial throat-clearing was dangerous, it had to be shot straight out without hesitation, unrehearsed, firm and positive, yet treated with sweet reason. I drew a discreet breath, prayed that the voice wouldn't crack and launched off.

"I do not get rigid, flushed and glazed and with one or two minor infractions, I do not get pissed. A few jars of home-brewed real ale in convivial company serve merely to heighten my perception of the activities of mankind and bring to the surface those hidden fellow feelings that lurk deep within this affectionate bosom."

The stony silence that followed this was broken by a snort of derision. I thought for a moment I had overplayed it, but after a brief pause, Charlie walked round to the other side of the car, climbed into the driver's seat and sat there waiting. I frowned a little, everybody seemed to be snorting at me today – perhaps the pollen count was high. Sensing that the interrogation was over, I relaxed. She was going to drive, so that little exchange appeared to have gone off without too much of a hitch. Hidden by the car roof I puffed my cheeks and I blew my breath out slowly.

It was all a matter of positive thinking and firmness. Women appreciated masterful men, secretly liked their menfolk dominant. It was just a question of experience and after five years of paradise with Charlie – Doctor Charlotte Prinknash – I had finally cracked it. As I squeezed my six-foot-two into the MG, I permitted myself a faint smile – very faint under the circumstances but nevertheless a superior twitch of the lips. Charlie was engaged in fitting the key into the ignition so I was safe. Shoulders squared and mouth fixed into a straight line, I settled back into the seat. There was only the Mark Three bollocking to follow and I could think of other things whilst receiving that – feigning rapt attention to every word, of course. This was vitally important, otherwise the bollocking would be immediately and indisputably upgraded to a Mark Two and that was a much more serious matter, cutting off activities pleasurable, sexual and erotic for a period undefined. I might even develop the soap theme a little further if I had time before we reached the Keep, otherwise that would have to be played off the soap dish when the opportunity arose – as it would, as it most certainly would. I composed my face into a picture of attentive contrition.

Five years ago I had gone with friends to a Sloane Ranger function in somebody's flat. Late in what had turned into, as the gossip columnists termed it, a 'lively evening', just as I was demonstrating to a group of equally smashed revellers the Moon Pivot, a new dance step I had invented which consisted of rotating on one heel with your eyes closed and a pint of beer on your head, I had been caught off-balance at the crucial moment by a spinning shoulder and precipitated head first into the surrounding tables. My next recollection was of a splitting headache and, on separating the eyelids, beholding not twelve inches from my own sandpapered orbs, a pair of the most beautiful deep violet eyes I had ever seen. What was more, they were filled with concern and set in a face that would have launched a Trojan war. There was something vaguely familiar about that face but nothing sprang immediately to mind to provide background perspective against which to set it.

The surroundings were unexpected too; a brief exploratory glance revealed a large double bed in a cheerfully decorated little bedroom with sunshine pouring through the window. The realisation that it was daylight had registered only slowly, as did the fact that whereas I was in bed, she was not. I had struggled to sit up but waves of sickness rolled over and I sank back onto the pillows.

The eyes were still fixed upon mine, studying them carefully and I felt my pulse being taken. My instincts pushed back the nausea that surged as I concentrated. There was a question to ask, a vital question. I struggled to form the words and she bent to catch what I had to say.

"Put that bloody sun out and come to bed." It had been a croak of bravado; I couldn't have raised even a smile.

She had laughed, however, and that had finally sealed matters there and then. It was a delightful laugh, throaty and yet light and it showed beautiful even white teeth and lovely crinkles round those eyes.

"You'll live," she chuckled but I wasn't listening – by then I was in love. It was as if I had been hit with a velvet sledgehammer. I had closed my eyes and gone back to sleep – secure in the knowledge that all was now well in the world.

When I awoke again the headache had abated to a bearable throb, but the sun had gone from the room. I could hear someone singing and the rattle of crockery from a distance. I had felt happy and contented; it crossed my mind that the vision may have been a dream, an unconscious figment of deep desires brought on by the blow, and a brief stab of disappointment passed through me, but somehow I knew it wasn't and she would return as perfect as I thought she was.

My fingers explored the lump on my forehead, feeling the long strip of plaster. I pressed gently and winced, the lump felt hot and sore. Little flakes of dried blood adhered to my fingertips so I must have been cut.

I had gingerly climbed out of bed to look in the dressing table mirror. Ghastly! Pale-faced and eyes glowing like two hot coals in the snow. The plaster showed white against the red and purple swelling just above my right eyebrow and although somebody (presumably my as yet unknown angel of mercy) had washed off as much blood as they could, there were dark brown encrustations round the edge of the plaster and in the creases of the eye socket. I realised that I had been undressed and left only in my underpants which, although clean the previous evening, were a bright fluorescent orange: thirty pence from the Oxfam shop. They had a blue Donald Duck on the rude bit – well, it makes a talking point if you're stuck for something to say with a new friend. I shuddered now at the thought. I was looking round for the rest of my clothes when I heard that throaty chuckle again. Spinning round – a careless movement that sent my eyeballs swirling and set the room in violent motion again, I saw her standing in the doorway watching.

I had grabbed desperately for the duvet to cover Donald Duck. She laughed again.

"I'm not worried if you're not. I'm a doctor – and a Disney fan." She had paused and looked at me quizzically. "You don't remember me, do you, Charlotte Prinknash, we were at university at the same time?"

The penny dropped at once: that was it, I remembered instantly, she had been an ethereal figure I had once admired from afar, but as we had moved in different social circles, afar was as close as I had got in the short time our residences coincided.

"Marcus Moon," I had croaked, wondering whether to release the bedspread and hold out my hand, thus giving her another flash of the fluorescent knickers. I decided against it and tried a smile instead.

"Yes, I know. I remember you," she had murmured. "You were the one who shaved all the fur off the Vice-Chancellor's poodle and painted it in Arsenal colours."

"Doncaster Rovers." The correction slipped out without a thought.

"Ah yes," she said softly, "it was that that upset the Vice-Chancellor the most, wasn't it?"

I groaned inwardly, it was not an auspicious memory on which to build what I had determined was going to be The Relationship of the Century.

"I don't support them now," I offered.

"It's all right, I don't have a dog." She gave me a smile – a full, straight-look-in-the-eye smile. I closed my eyes, happy again.

She had allowed me to stay in the spare bedroom for three days until she was satisfied that there was no concussion, keeping me gently at arm's length. I returned a week later for her to remove the five stitches with which she had sutured the wound, took her out to dinner and, growing increasingly cheesed off with having to keep returning to my own flat for clean shirts and pants – now ninety pence from 'Young Executive' – moved in permanently three months after that.

I glanced across at her out of the corner of my eye. She really was gorgeous, shining dark hair framing an oval face, violet eyes with their long lashes fixed on the road ahead. She was nibbling a lower lip, her perfect white teeth trying to hold her full mouth into a line of rigid disapproval. Unconsciously, I had turned to study

22

her in a more obvious way and whilst I was thinking how I liked neat white teeth nibbling things, she became aware of my scrutiny. Too late, I saw her mouth tighten and the slight hardening of the muscles along the side of her jaw, but at the same time her eyes began to crinkle round the laughter lines as she struggled to maintain her severity.

"You fool, Moon," she burst out laughing, "what on earth have you been up to then – and don't try to deny it because I'll get it out of you one way or another."

"What on earth do you mean?" I assumed an air of injured innocence.

"You gave in far too easily, that's what I mean, and that also means that you have something to hide – and if you have something hidden, some nefarious little activity you have been indulging in on my home territory, then I jolly well want to know what it was – or is. So come clean and it will be all the better for you."

"It?" My mind conjured up delicious thoughts as to how 'it' could be 'all the better' for me. It was pretty good for me already and it was not easy to imagine major improvements. It also gave me a chance to regain the recently lost initiative. I continued after a pause.

"Can you be a little more specific about the betterment of 'it' that you're proposing – you haven't been down to that discreet shop off Fulham Road where they sell those little black satin knickers and suspender belts again?" Here I gave what I imagined was a lustful leer, screwing up my eyes as they did in French films – maybe it was all the Gitanes smoke, I must practise it a bit more.

"No I have not," she snapped. She glanced sideways at me. "Have you got something in your eye?" Her voice had a note of concern in it so I quickly abandoned the sexual red herring for an ophthalmic one.

Dragging out a large, somewhat off-white handkerchief, I clasped it to an eye.

"It's nothing," I murmured, hoping to convey the impression that my eyeball was being scarified, "just a bit of grit, I think. If I just sit quietly and let the eye water naturally, it will probably wash it out."

Charlie shot me a suspicious look, she knew me too well, but it was difficult to get an eyeball to eyeball confrontation whilst she was driving the car and I had my face turned away from her with the nearest eye now covered by a large grey cloth, and without a direct look into my face, she could not be sure whether I was bluffing or not.

Time must be bided and patience exercised. Sooner or later she knew my guard would drop – sooner rather than later with a little subterfuge. She drove in silence for a further five minutes, seemingly concentrating on the road ahead. A few things needed to be sorted out in her mind following the afternoon's 'Save Old Sheringford' committee meeting in the Town Hall. The whole thing was beginning to get out of hand. Successful, yes, but taking on the government was not a relaxing occupation.

* * *

For six months now, Save Old Sheringford had been an increasingly frustrating obstacle to the government's plans. From small beginnings initiated by local councillors and townspeople, its ranks had swelled rapidly to include the bigger land owners and farmers, three Members of Parliament, the County Council and the main national preservation and conservation societies. By its sheer energetic resistance, it had further attracted to its orbit a large number of the many other pressure groups lurking in the mansards and wainscoting, the hedges and fields, and the pools, ditches and rivers.

Charlotte appreciated that the problem stemmed from the population migration of the late Seventies when, to

24

ease pressure on the overcrowded, cramped, unsanitary conditions of urban Southwark, Lambeth, Islington and North Kent, Sheringford had been designated as an overspill town.

'My old man said follow the van' sang Marie Lloyd, and follow it they did from the dingy, graffiti-covered walls of London to the alien environment of Wiltshire's green rolling hills. Coaxed from the tottering tower blocks conceived by the politicians and planners of the Sixties and braving the hail of precast concrete cladding panels, flashings and other architectural impedimenta showering into the streets, they were stuffed into the sterile new housing estates built to the south-west of Sheringford with all the subtle sensitivity of an ice-cold enema.

From day one there existed the mutual hostility with which the 'old towners' and the 'new towners' regarded each other. Integration, that smooth word that slithered from the lips of the sociologists and public relations men, coined from the mathematicians for whom it worked on paper, did not take place. It never would and the politicians, who never intended that it should, checked new electoral registers anxiously. However, the implantation of an industrially orientated workforce into a rural community required more than just houses and schools; the people, the breadwinners, needed somewhere to go to win their bread. Jobs had to be provided otherwise contented voters soon became discontented moaners drifting rapidly into 'Don't Knows', 'Don't Cares' and 'Get Stuffeds'. So with more public money, factories were built adjacent to the housing estates, raw materials and fuels fed in, finished goods trucked out and bread won – the perfect equation.

Unfortunately, as Rabbie Burns put it so aptly, "the best laid plans o' mice and men gang aft a-gley" – or, as

Marcus Moon so eloquently expressed it in the modern idiom, "The status quo has an inbuilt resistance to being buggered about". Put quite simply, it doesn't like it, and having spent centuries achieving a harmonious balance, the 'status quo' takes massive umbrage when this is rudely upset and a-gley it gangs. However, the active agent of this ganging was not the 'new towners' themselves but an unforeseen by-product of their bread winning. The fumes from the factory chimneys rising into the atmosphere dissolved into the moisture-laden clouds borne up by the prevailing South Westerleys and precipitated themselves as a weak acid rain wash over the fabric of the town. The stuff ate into the age-old monuments of historic Sheringford with the enthusiasm of mites into green cheese.

The Georgian Society, The Council for the Preservation of Historic England, The Historic Buildings Society, Save Britain's Heritage and sections of the inhabitants of Wiltshire met in fulminating committees to write stinging letters of protest to nobody in particular. But worse was to follow. Politicians of whatever persuasion are but transient beings, a fact comfortingly clear to most mortals except the politicians themselves, and the great swing-o-meter in the British Broadcasting Corporation had reached its perigee for the Tories just as the first factory opened.

Five years later New Labour came to power and on the crest of the private enterprise wave that followed, in surfed those overseas industrialists with their eyes on the British labour market. Nippon Kansun, the huge Japanese engine manufacturers impassively eyed the British mainland as a political base for their thrust into the European Union and the newly elected government drooled like Pavlov's dogs.

Incentives were dangled, promises made, unions placated and studies done. Tens of different sites throughout the length and breadth of the British Isles were examined, assessed, reported on and evaluated. Short lists were drawn up, tax concessions drafted and investment grants proposed.

The Department of Trade and Industry finally prepared its recommendations for the Secretary of State to present to the Cabinet prior to the announcement to the world of this coup for Britain.

"It appears," concluded the Secretary of State for Industry, back muscles twitching nervously as he sensed the tightening of grips on the concealed daggers of his Cabinet colleagues, "that the choice of site lies between Washington in County Durham, Bridgend in South Wales or Cumbernauld in Scotland." He paused carefully, sensing the wind, awaiting some reaction. The others eyed each other surreptitiously, not wishing to be the first to respond, preferring to counter rather than initiate; but nervous lest the first blow be decisive and deprive them of the kudos that must attach to the choice. One of the bolder spirits wound up his vocal chords and opened his mouth...

The Prime Minister looked across at his political advisor, who nodded.

"Sheringford," said the Prime Minister.

The observation was stillborn in the bolder spirit's throat. The SS for I's eyes narrowed. "I beg your pardon, Prime Minister?" Being directly opposite him he had heard quite clearly the first time; the question was merely to gain a few seconds thinking time. His First at the LSE had been in political science.

"Sheringford," the PM repeated, "that was one of the alternatives, was it not?'

"Yes, but we excluded that location some time ago."

"Well, put it back – at the top." The SS for I hesitated, all his instincts told him that whatever the logic for locating this factory elsewhere, there was a strong smell of some deal cooked up between the 'ruling' clique that he was not aware of. He nodded agreement and cynically awaited the foreseeable outburst from the Cabinet members less politically attuned than him.

The Honourable Member for Glasgow Bridge was the first to blow his top. "Ye canna da that, Prime Minister! All the studies and technical appraisals show that any one o' the others far outstrips Sheringford as a feasible location!"

He met the cold blue eyes of the Prime Minister's political advisor; they softened slightly with a touch of sympathy for his sodding stupidity. The advantages and disadvantages of his presence in the Cabinet, and as a political ally, were reassessed in a nano-second by the computer-like brain and his position confirmed but shaded further towards the cut at the next reshuffle.

The PM replied steadily: "Sam, what do Washington, Cumbernauld and Bridgend all have in common?" And before he could reply the PM continued, "And which is the closest marginal seat which we lost but had the biggest swing towards us at the last election?"

Sam goggled, his pink protuberant eyes bulging with embarrassment.

"Precisely, Sam, the first three are all rock-solid Labour which we could never lose, but Sheringford..." The word hovered in the air.

Sam clung on by his finger tips. "But are we sure that Sheringford wants it?" he persisted.

The PM sighed and sat back. Sam really was off message these days. "*We* want it Sam, that is the important thing, *we* want it; and if we want it then we shall persuade Sheringford that it wants it as well."

The other doubters, deciding that discretion was the better part of survival, kept their own council for the time being. 'He who fights and runs away lives to fight another day.' And there would be plenty of other days and other times and other ways in which influence could be brought to bear.

There being no other dissenters, the matter had passed into the official record and Sheringford revealed as the hot favourite for the Nippon Kansun forge and foundry project.

Indignation, fulmination, realisation and organisation had followed in that order. Spearheaded by David Prinknash with Charlie as organising secretary, the Save Old Sheringford Group had eventually got its act together. The forecast fume output of the foundry had been the catalyst that triggered the reaction, converting the enthusiastic but ineffective SOS into a formidable conservationist lobby.

By May, through vigorous campaigning in the West Country, discreet Front Bench support and constant unremitting lobbying in Westminster, it was generally acknowledged that SOS had become a powerful, effective political force. Some ministers were reported as saying both privately and publicly that it was becoming a thorn in the government's flesh

Speeches by the Secretary of State for Industry had of late indicated an element of 'head-down keeping' under the constant bombardment. There was even mutterings that the proposals were principally for discussion as a White Paper rather than a committed intention. The government was forced to concede that it would hold a full Public Enquiry into its proposals together with whatever else the public thought should be done. The opposition seized upon the alarm and disarray in government ranks to stick the knife in at every opportunity and twist it in the wounds.

The whole affair was a growing embarrassment to the government in general and New Labour in particular.

* * *

Charlie had had to spend more and more of her spare time away from the hospital to organise and direct these activities and to my astonishment, was tackling the job with relish and full enjoyment. I had been amazed at the financial acumen she had developed, the raising of funds and planning their best strategic use was by no means an easy matter and yet Charlie had undertaken this with skill and success, as witnessed by the amount of money that was being collected and expended to hire halls, print posters, publish pamphlets and maximise publicity. The media, both press and television, had given and continued to give Save Old Sheringford good support. Being guaranteed to sniff out and encourage any promising troublemakers and give them maximum coverage at any time, SOS was absolute grist to their mill.

The one thing that puzzled me about SOS was the constituents of the main committee.

"They're all lightweights, Charlie," I kept telling her. "Why don't you get some of the real heavies to front it up? You have enough of them giving support. You need a real tough hard man – or woman..." I had added hastily, seeing her brows beginning to knit "...as Chairman, somebody who will pull the whole shooting match together and lead a much better directed campaign than you have at present. When I see some of that lot on television I begin to despair, it all looks so amateurish and disorganised. I'm surprised you're having the success you obviously are, but I tell you this, if it wasn't for you the whole thing would fall apart. Only last week they had Colonel Corrigan-Croot on that current affairs programme with Jeremy Thingummy and every time he was asked anything resembling a penetrating question he either harrumphed like a love-sick hippo or bellowed like a prospective gelding at the first clench of the vet's teeth. Totally pathetic he was, absolutely useless, no idea of the meaning of a persuasive argument. You need somebody with commitment, wholehearted, full-blooded commitment."

There was a momentary silence whilst she considered this. "But many people are involved and work hard for us, they have to have some representation." She had been slightly irritated by my observations.

"There is a major difference, dear heart, between involvement and commitment."

"Just words." She shrugged the remark off.

"No," I retaliated, "not just words. Think of bacon and eggs: with bacon and eggs the hen is merely involved but the pig is wholeheartedly committed. You need a pig or two, not a bunch of clucking hens."

You know how it is with these things: a casual comment, a few words tossed carelessly into a conversation and months later when, as a consequence, you're struggling up to the armpits in deep shit, you wished you'd kept your bloody mouth shut. This was such an occasion. Charlie had laughed it off at the time and replied that in her view perhaps it was its lack of professionalism that was making it successful – "people feel that it's genuine, you see, and not just some cooked-up pressure group. The support of the Society for the Preservation of Rural England, the Georgian Society, Save Britain's Heritage and the genuine conservationists also helps a lot."

Neither of us was really convinced by this argument, but by unspoken consent we had agreed to let the matter rest. It came back to her now as she drove. I was right – they did need somebody, someone who could take a share of the front running with conviction and relieve some of the burden on her. She would then have the time to direct their efforts in a more concentrated, less fragmented way. Unfortunately, nobody immediately sprang to mind who could fill that bill. The locals didn't have the political clout, the members from other societies were too busy with those, and her father's health did not permit him to take on such a full-time demanding role – hence her involvement. Old Lissett, the local MP, did not have the time – or the dedication for that matter. No, they needed a national figure or a dynamo; thought would have to be given.

She glanced to her side, the large handkerchief was still obscuring my face but unbeknown to me the spotlight had switched back and I was about to be dealt with.

With the handkerchief as a shield, I had gradually relaxed and began to think of other things. Tomorrow was lunch with an old friend and client, Bob Barclay, and although Barclay's lunches usually took up all afternoon and sometimes most of the evening, leaving most of the participants with a grade one hangover, they were always good fun – and Barclay might be very interested in what I had to tell him. I was beginning to savour the anticipation when a low whisper broke into my thoughts.

"It's a tiny little blue thong."

The content and implication of this remark took some time to displace thoughts of Barclay's lunch in my cerebral matter, but when they did, it was like an Exocet missile hitting the brain. Once the message had penetrated, a great flash of enlightenment blossomed forth and my whole interest suddenly became focused on one of the few subjects dearer to my heart than eating and drinking. Although the brain picked up and responded to the message, it was a few microseconds slow in transmitting the correct response to the mouth and vocal cords, so what was probably intended to sound like, 'Stone me, we're in for a good night then' or some such equivalent reply, came out as a totally incoherent, "Ahh wah ahh an."

She glanced round at me with that intimate coy little girl look that is second nature to all feminine women and although by no means the most devastating weapon in

32

the female armoury, it is far superior to any male counter measures. I turned to face her to rearticulate my reply, removing the handkerchief from my eye at the same time. In a trice she fixed me with twin violet lasers straight through the old corneas to the brain. I knew I had been tricked instantly, and that she had read the flash of guilt that passed across my face like a lightning streak fixed on photographic emulsion, before she turned back to look at the road.

Her left hand dropped to the gear lever, she executed a smooth change-down to set the car up for the sharp turn into the drive up to the Keep, the seat of David and Angela Prinknash whose ewe lamb Charlie was. The drive was long and wound through lush woodland opening out just before the house to neatly fenced paddocks and open, rolling countryside that stretched down to the River Shering, glinting silver in the late afternoon sun, three miles away. She kept the car in third gear to control its speed and to give me time to complete my story.

"I had a... an encounter... well actually two encounters with a colleague of yours," I began. She didn't respond, knowing that I was prone to understatement and more was to come. I took a deep breath.

"Do you want the good news or the bad news?"

"Both."

"Well, the bad news is that Mrs Hartley-Worthington is now firmly convinced that I am 'into dogs', taking the worst possible connotation of the phrase, and possibly sniffing the saddles of vicars' wives' bicycles also, but the good news is, I don't think she recognised me in the different surroundings of Sheringford."

I gave her an outline of my afternoon's activities, concluding with the incident with the two Labradors but avoiding any reference to the site.

She shook her head slowly. "My goodness me, I can't leave you alone for ten minutes without you getting into trouble," she grinned. "If she comes to dinner again, which is quite possible, you'll have to grow a beard or eat in the library. I need Mrs Hartley-Worthington's support for SOS, she's the Chairman of the local bench and Regional Director of the Women's Institute. More important, however, her brother is James Hartley-Worthington, Permanent Under-Secretary at the Department of the Environment."

The car slid to a halt in the loose gravel, we climbed out at the side of the house and walked round to the front door. As we passed through the hall towards the superb Hepplewhite staircase, she glanced over her shoulder.

"I don't suppose you'll be interested anymore today in wispy blue whatnots, having already slaked your lust on the animal kingdom?" And she ran up the stairs chuckling to herself. I was slow to react and give chase and by the time I made the upper landing, she had locked herself securely in her room. I contented myself with a nominal pounding on the door and a stream of whispered intentions as to what I would do with her and Johnson's Baby Oil that night, getting so excited in the process that I had to go and lie on my bed for fifteen minutes and ponder again fruitlessly what it was about Doncaster Rovers that had so infuriated the Vice-Chancellor of my University, before I was decent enough to go down for dinner.

Chapter Two

On the same evening, and at the same time as I was leaning forward to savour the fine bouquet of David Prinknash's 1945 Warre's Port and get a look down Angela Prinknash's magnificent cleavage in the mellow, oak-panelled dining-hall of Prinknash Keep, ninety-five miles away at a dingy hall in South London, Deirdre Plant also leaned forward, her strong legs braced apart, her meaty thighs indented by the edge of the red baize-covered trestle table, her skirt stretched tight across a muscular bottom. In a voice that had shied many a Metropolitan police horse, she was laying into her audience.

"...but we are not doing enough, sisters and brothers, we are not doing enough in our work, we are not doing enough in our spare time, we are not doing enough in our homes, we are not doing enough in our unions and we are not doing enough in our politics. Remember the thesis provokes the antitheses. Only through destruction shall the phoenix rise, only through chaos shall the new order emerge. From the clash a new synthesis will be born, a new society will spring forth where each will be the equal of her sister and brother and all will hold the highest place together."

Her voice became confidential. "And how, you are asking yourselves, shall this be brought about, how can change take place, how can the new order emerge, how can a classless society rise from the ashes of feudalism? I know that each of you is saying to yourself, what can I do? What part can I play in this groundswell to restore true socialism to the people of this country, wrenching it from those false Tories who call themselves New Labour? Well, this afternoon you have found out."

She turned and stabbed her finger at the two people sitting on her left, a large slab-faced woman with grey skin, a severe shingle hairstyle and a bulbous nose; and next to her a cuddly teddy bear of a man with round owl glasses, rosy pink cheeks and a thick crop of grey curls that surrounded his large, pendulous head like a halo.

"Helga Gundelach of the Lambeth Co-operative Workshop and Professor Hugh Acklem-Dite of Sussex University have presented to you the theories of Marxist-Leninism, modified by the tenets of Trotskyite thinking to interlock with the aim of ultimate socialism, and I am sure that we have all been refreshed and regenerated by their dedicated idealism. It is a lesson to us all and a cornerstone of our movement."

The two persons nodded. Professor Hugh Acklem-Dite beamed broadly, his eyes crinkling up behind his glasses. This sort of guff was ambrosia to him, the intellectual theories would or could work and what their effect would be on the masses was quite irrelevant. To him the people were clay to the potter, a formless soft grey inert mass which should and could be moulded, pressed, squeezed and forced into whatever form he, the potter, decided was best. He was free to change his mind at any time regarding what that was. He would do so, however, with a smile on his soft gentle face and a twinkle in his eye and if tens of thousands went to their deaths each time just to ensure that the masses fitted his revised theories, so be it. He could hardly wait to try them out.

Helga, however, was more pragmatic. Her life was a perpetual conflict between, on the one hand, her passionate desire to articulate a radical new psychological theory for socialist women based on feminist principles and, on the other, a nose that grew larger and even more purple the longer she held forth in argumentative discourse. She covered her nose with her hand, a defensive gesture, jerked from her introspective study of face creams and heavy make-up by Deirdre's sudden refocusing of the metaphorical spotlight back onto to her. She gave a grunt which could be taken as acknowledgement or confirmation, and returned to continue wrestling with her current problem: should she wear make-up? On the one hand to do so could be misconstrued as supporting the idea that it was necessary for women to be made up solely in order for them to attract a mate; an idea which was total anathema to Helga. But on the other hand, whenever she got involved in a heated discussion her nose always swelled and turned purple, which distracted the attention of those she was trying to convince away from her argument and on to her hooter. God (if there was a god), life was difficult she sighed to herself. Envying Deirdre's seemingly unshakeable, positive beliefs and direction, she decided to put aside her problem for the present and concentrate as Deirdre continued with her passionate peroration, conviction ringing from every syllable.

"But we must not forget that all historical developments are basically due entirely to economic phenomena and, therefore, to influence future history we must penetrate the fragile, cold, soulless citadels of capitalism and the false tenets of New Labour, attack them with the pure heat of our revolution, melting their foundations, destroying their structure, demolishing their stability and..." She paused for effect, her eyes flicking over the motley assembly and then with her fist hammering the table, she shrieked at full decibels: "...and Bring-Them-Crashing-Down." She paused again, somebody blew their nose rather loudly, but nothing else broke the silence and so, slightly disappointed, she continued in her normal shout: "Not just down, but first to their knees and then to the floor and then to the earth itself and then... then, sisters and brothers, then..." Her voice dropped so that the audience had to strain to catch her words – a carefully calculated effect learnt at the Socialist Organiser's Training School, "...then we bury them." Her voice rose in crescendo. "And from the eye sockets of their rotting corpses will spring the True Socialist Movement."

She stood upright, eyes glaring, neck muscles so tense that her head looked as if it was supported on two flying buttresses.

The last glimmering of dusk forced its way through the grimy wired glass of the skylights and flickered on the weary grey paint. The cracked and stained cream wall tiles clung to a high-level deep green cornice, seemingly as a last effort to prevent themselves sliding down the wall to oblivion on the rough wooden boards that formed the cover for the old swimming pool. A whiff of chlorine pervaded the gloom. The lower levels of the hall were illuminated by three rows of bare forty-watt bulbs shielded by yellow plastic, plate-like shades which seemed to intensify the approaching darkness rather than relieve it.

Silence hung momentarily in the dusty air; feet shuffled nervously and a few people coughed. A pale-faced girl in the front row wearing a crumpled shirt and brightly-coloured peasant skirt started to applaud and this was picked up in a desultory manner by a couple more women. The remainder of the four dozen or so audience scattered throughout the hall expressed their appreciation of this rousing, climactic speech, calculated to unleash the pent-up fervour of dynamic revolution in the breast of the oppressed peasantry of West Lambeth, by sitting in a stunned silence. The nose blower gave another blast like the last trump, followed by some revolting sucking noise as further mucus precipitation caused extra problems.

Deirdre glared in his direction then slowly resumed her seat, lowering those muscular buttocks onto the bright orange curved plastic chair.

What a bloody disaster! It had all gone wrong after promising so much. Shit, shit, shit, and shit. Up to the last night all had gone smoothly, almost perfectly, and then those stupid bloody bitches of sisters had screwed it all up, and screwed her up as well just when she was making the big breakthrough.

Except Suzie, of course. Suzie had come because she was a caring kind of person – there she sat on the end of the front row, eyes shining in response to Deirdre's rally cry. Simple Suzie. Deirdre glanced at her and then back at the platform. The hostility had been manifest the moment Hugh Evans and his mob had seen the turnout. She could feel it now growing stronger. Shit, shit, shit. What a dump in which to die before she'd ever had a chance, and it wasn't her fault, which made it worse. But they wouldn't care about that. Her angry gaze took in the depressing scene.

The rows of empty folding chairs gave a mute response to Deirdre's impassioned appeal, the ringing tones intended to penetrate the hearts and minds of the listeners had been absorbed and swallowed by the appalling acoustics. Only the front five rows had any occupants and of these less than one third had shown interest in the event they were attending. The others were dozing fitfully, reading the Sporting Life or staring blankly into space, picking or scratching at various parts of their unwashed bodies.

The crudely painted banner strung above the stage proclaimed in white capital letters on blood red canvas: 'THE SOCIALIST ORGANISER'S SOVIET REVOLU-TIONARY PARTY OF GREAT BRITAIN (WEST LAM-BETH BRANCH)'. Underneath the banner, five people sat on plastic chairs behind the trestle table. Each had a hand-printed, folded cardboard name card in front of them which also bore their respective positions in the Lambeth Branch of the Socialist Organiser's Soviet Party. The one in the middle carried the inscription 'Deirdre Plant – Chair'. The one in front of the pale-faced man to her far right with thin, mousey hair plastered down across a dome-shaped skull, deep-set, migraine eyes, sunken cheeks and a long, pointed, spotty, very red nose, said 'Ernest Goad – Treasurer'.

It was he who now rose to his feet. He had a thin, high, reedy voice.

"Brothers and sisters, you have responded as we your comrades, spearheading the fight, believed you would. Our Chairperson has given us a magnificent lead and it is now up to us to support her with our heads held high and our banners flying; to crush the running dogs of imperialism, but primarily to sweep away the traitors of New Labour who have usurped our socialist creed with their false promises, their capitalist lies and their city cronies..."

"Ey you, Rudolph," demanded a truculent looking, pasty-faced youth in the second row. He had a bone-ribbed forehead and narrow, closely-set eyes.

"We've been doing fuckin' flyin' picketin' for free weeks now and we come for our money."

"Fumping the fuckin' fuzz," echoed his mate, a member of the same anthropoid tribe, sitting next to him.

Ernie riveted them with his burning black eyes, nose now flaming more brightly with anger.

"When the revolution comes, Comrades," he hissed, "when the revolution comes – and it is not too far away now." His voice rose. "We shall not only thump and bash them, we shall hang them from the lampposts, shoot them on the street corners, cut them down in the fields, pursue them in the mountains and hound them in the valleys until they are eradicated from the face of this earth. The gutters will run red with the blood of the tyrants as their crimes against humanity are paid for, and through this blood we will purify..."

"I fought we was goin' to get our fuckin' money tonight, din' I?" persisted the anthropoid youth, "and me mate did an' all, din' he?"

Ernie's thin lips tightened and there was a silence as his eyes found and fixed those of his heckler.

Whilst Ernie fulminated against the traitors of New Labour, another problem was starting to manifest itself for Deirdre. She had had a bit of an upset stomach that morning and had swallowed a couple of 'blockers' as a safeguard. Slight bubbling in her nether regions suggested that their effect was wearing off. Pressure was building up to threatening proportions. She squeezed the cheeks of her ample buttocks together and bit her lip, hoping that Ernie's oratory would come to a speedy end so she could slip out to the Ladies'. It was a forlorn hope. Ernie was convinced his oratory moved people: it usually did – out of earshot – so he droned on. Perspiration began to form on Deirdre's forehead and she leant forward in a desperate gamble to relieve the pressure. Fortunately for her, but not for her immediate neighbours, it was only gas.

She crimsoned and hastily pushed her chair back, scraping it hard on the floor to disguise the noise. The other occupants of the platform feigned ignorance but made it more obvious by deliberately looking everywhere except at her. Those closest to her could be seen holding their breath.

The anthropoid from the second row shouted, "Whistle it again, luv, the tune's familiar but I can't remember the words!"

The Treasurer waited with increasing irritation until the coarse laughter died down, whilst Deirdre squirmed with embarrassment, and then he continued with his eyes still on those of the anthropoid youth.

"Comrades," he raised his eyes to cover them all. "Comrades all, violence is only one of our weapons. We must use the Capitalists' own system to defeat them. The traitors in Downing Street have not done that, they have treacherously linked arms with them. We must take New Labour and their Tory allies and strangle them with their own evil system. Thrust their necks into the noose of our revolution, make them stretch their throats across the blade of change – and to do this we require your full support. We need your ears, your eyes, your voices, your money, your hands, your hearts, your whole beings..."

The anthropoid's brow grew even more furrowed as one word of this diatribe penetrated the dense structure of his skull, wandered around the vacuous spaces within like a lost soul before finally attaching itself to one of the few centres of stimuli occupying that bony concretion

"Ere Rudolph, you're not coming up for another fuckin' sub, are you?"

A note of desperation crept into Ernie's voice and it wavered slightly as he ploughed on. "Money is the Capitalist's tool, it is the cornerstone of his system, it is the sword of subjugation by which we are held under the heel of the tyrant. It is only by taking control of that sword that we shall slay them. To do that we need money of our own, money which will be..."

"I'm fuckin' going," announced the AY.

"An fuckin' 'enry is fuckin' coming too, i'n'e? Come on 'enry, let's go up the fuckin' Broadway – see if we can spank a fuckin' coon or two." And with that they both stood noisily, pushed their chairs back with their calf muscles, hooked their thumbs into the pockets of their jeans and swaggered to the door. "And we'll be back for our fuckin' money, don't forget that, Rudolf," the anthropoid added darkly before kicking the door open and crashing out.

Ernie faltered but picked up again and wavered on with all the conviction of an arthritic conjuror.

"...moulded to form the weapons with which we shall defeat them and then with the glorious sunrise of freedom, be melted down into ploughshares."

The rat-faced individual sitting on Deirdre's immediate right with pale, fanatical eyes and a tight, thin mouth pursed his lips and clenched his teeth so that the muscles on his lower jaw stood proud.

His name card proclaimed him to be Hugh Evans, National Organiser.

He leant across to Deirdre and whispered something in her ear, stressing his point with cutting motions of his right hand. She flushed and then laid her hand on Ernie Goad's sleeve to check his verbal flow. Before he had a chance to continue, she rose to her feet and cut in.

"Well, sisters and brothers, we have all had a very interesting and productive discussion on the furthering of our cause and we will, I am sure, leave here reinforced in our determination to smash the evil system around us and work for the glorious dawn of a true people's democracy. As Karl Marx said in his infinite wisdom, 'The dictatorship of the proletariat is our goal.' The Treasurer will now visit each of you to obtain some tangible evidence of your support for this object." There was a scraping of chairs and a movement of bodies, so she hastily gabbled the final formality, "...and I therefore formally declare this Congress closed."

The hard-faced stewards flanked the door with arms folded to discourage any further attempts to avoid contributing to the Party Funds, and after a reluctant tribute had been exacted, at a nod from Ernie, the minuscule audience was permitted to shuffle out.

The remaining four members sat in silence on the platform, with a strong suspicion that all was not sweetness and light, trying to avoid each other's eyes and, more particularly, those of Rat Face. When the doors finally closed, Rat Face got to his feet, walked round to the front of the table and turned to face the others, standing squarely in front of the self-proclaimed Chair. His eyes burned into each of them in turn. They radiated a cold, bitter anger with frightening intensity. He took a deep breath. His voice when he spoke was soft and well modulated with a faint Welsh accent, but it cut like a scalpel across taut flesh.

"What an absolute and utter bloody shambles!" Fixing his eyes on Deirdre's, he continued: "It's not a game we're playing, sister; it's not one of your upper-class debates at the fucking Oxford Union. All that dialectal claptrap you spout means nothing. Not a thing. It might sound good to you," he gestured round them, including Ernest Goad, who had slid back into his chair and was scratching a throbbing pustule on his nose, "and to the dropouts and deadbeats that you assembled here, purporting to be your supporters, but it is totally useless in our fight to bring down the apathetic monetarist system in this class-ridden country and replace it with a true socialist democracy. We need action, not advice. Results not rhetoric. But above all we need One Hundred Percent Commitment from each and every single person in this branch!"

The words fell cold and sharp as icicles. He waved his hand at the empty seats.

"Where were the shop stewards? Where were the picket organisers? Where were the union delegates? Where were the local party officials? Where were the councillors? Well? They were the audience that should have been here, not the disgusting detritus of the local doss house that you assembled. The mindless morons of modern youth like those two cretins who left. Not people like that. We want the active, the influential, the committed and the intelligent. Where were they, Chairperson? Well, where were they?" His chilling stare rifled through Deirdre's defences. "All of you are responsible, all of you, but you, Chairperson, you are especially responsible."

Deirdre flushed bright red yet again and opened her mouth to argue, but before she could utter a word, Rat Face pushed his nose to within inches of hers and crackled, "Therefore you, comrade Chairperson, will present yourself in person to the People's National Committee tomorrow night at six-thirty sharp to confess your incompetence and inefficiency. That is all." And with that, he turned and walked out of the door at the far end of the hall, flanked by the hard-faced cohorts who had been acting as stewards. The platform watched him go in embarrassed silence.

The Chairperson sat rigid in her seat, her face the colour of crushed strawberries whilst the other three, demonstrating that inborn sense of self-protection that instinctively shies away from failure as if it were contagious, congregated in a huddle in one corner and muttered amongst themselves, casting the occasional glance back to their humiliated leader. Acklem-Dite thought it was a very interesting demonstration of the Fennimore-Fawcett frightening syndrome, whereas Helga considered gloomily that a purge of Stalinist proportions would hit West Lambeth shortly.

Deirdre Plant felt humiliated, indeed was humiliated, and it was not an experience that she relished. She didn't like it one little bit and to be put in that position by a male made it infinitely less tolerable. It was unjustified, insufferable, masculine, chauvinistic arrogance; she seethed with helpless frustration. He would not get away with it, she vowed, he would bloody soon find out that he had bitten off more than he could chew with her.

The fact that he was right, and she knew he was right, made it worse; it was made even more so because she knew that however justified the reasons for the debacle might be to her, if she had dared to advance them she would have been finished. That was the trouble with democratic socialism – it didn't work if the masses chose to do something different from that which their leaders dictated. Changes would have to be made. She recalled Brecht's pithy observation that, the people having disappointed the leadership, it will be necessary to dissolve and replace the people. She felt some compatibility with Brecht at that moment but before starting on the people, she had tomorrow night's hurdle to get over.

She began to plan her onslaught on the National Committee. 'Fight fire with fire' was Deirdre's motto; the best form of defence was attack and go straight for the jugular – a philosophy she had discovered at a very early age.

Brought up in North London as the only girl in the middle of four brothers, her childhood had been competitive. Her father and mother were both career civil servants possessed by that rather British trait of left-wing political activities but right-wing personal behaviour – the peculiar inverted morality typical of the Camden Passage and Didsbury set, which turns logic on its head and completely baffles the simple yeoman of England struggling to identify a champion for his cause. As a consequence of their full-time jobs, the parents had had to leave a large part of the upbringing of their children to a nanny who happened to be inclined towards rather masculine tendencies and a corporal method of discipline.

Deirdre had thus been inculcated from the time she developed her faculties with the constantly repeated adage that any woman was worth at least four men and was treated accordingly. She herself had always been big for her age and even now the overall impression of her was of an attractive woman in which everything was slightly oversized. Her light brown hair was thick and strong, her face was wide, almost Slavic, with high cheekbones. Her eyes were large and greenish, her nose broad and her mouth generous. When she stood she was tall with solid shoulders and a strong muscular frame. Her breasts thrust forward as positive statements of domination, rather than enticing attributes of femininity.

Her background was one of constant competition with the male sex. Her alma mater had been the local comprehensive school which she attended with her brothers – her parents could not afford the fees for all five children to attend private schools and when Deirdre learned that they intended to send only the two brighter boys to private school and not her, she had kidnapped the family dog and threatened its slow torture and starvation in a hidden place unless the parents withdrew their proposals.

After six tense days of confrontation, Deirdre won her first dispute; the fact that on its release the terrified and starving animal had shot across the main road to be flattened by a juggernaut and nanny had wielded the cane to such an extent that sitting down had been difficult for three days did nothing to dim her triumph. Sacrifices had to be made for every just cause, she told herself, and the unfortunate dog, her first martyr to socialism, only steeled her resolve to beat the boys at everything.

Education had put her into increasing conflict with the establishment, particularly the male dominated one that governed The Che Guevara Camden Comprehensive, now renamed the Nelson Mandela Camden Comprehensive, liberal though it was in catering for increasing pupil power. No frugal mind hers, she absorbed socialist statistics by the ream and spat most of them back just as readily.

The 'Happiest Days' had been governed by a vendetta with the Principal because she was forbidden to play as striker in the school football team. Big for her age, she responded by kicking the shit out of each of the adolescent male incumbents of that position as she worked her way up the school. Eventually, so strong and brutal was she that no boy could be persuaded to play there and the school was forced to cancel all its matches.

She had gone on to the area sixth form college with the same fiercely aggressive attitude and won a scholarship to Oxford. Her headmistress at the college had dryly written a quotation from John Donne on her report on Deirdre to the assessors:

"O wrangling schools that search what fire
Shall burn this world, had not the wit
Unto this knowledge to aspire
That this her fever might be it?"

Once in the City of Dreaming Spires, she had found much support and fellow feeling for her strong views on the place of women in society and, as far as Deirdre was concerned, that place was in front. Not only in front, but on top, in control, leading, directing and, if necessary, driving the human race along its uncharted, unforeseeable path to the future. Women's inequality and oppression was anathema to her. The fever burnt even more strongly within.

She had affected then the kind of clothes she was still wearing. Men's shirts and faded blue jeans or flared full skirts for everyday, with short waistcoats, hand-knitted cardigans and round woollen bonnets. For special occasions she had a collection of clothing in bright peasant style or dull granny's trousseau, depending on her mood.

48

After graduating from Oxford with a First in sociology, politics and getting up everybody's nose, she then went on to do a diploma at Birmingham with similar results. Securing a job in the Social Services Department of the London Borough of Lambeth provided further nourishment for the thoughts and ideas she had formulated as an active member of the Universities Labour Parties. She flirted with the extreme left-wing militants, but with the encroachment of New Labour and its centrist ideas displacing her ideals of pure socialism, she had been persuaded that drastic action was needed to rectify matters and replace these Islington dilettante traitors with working-class politicians, and this could only be done from within the Party. Thus, as a fully fledged socialist malignant virus, she had gained legitimacy in the inner Parties within the Party, secretly attending the meetings, cadres and training sessions run by the Socialist Workers Party, the Trotskyites, The Militant Tendency and other far-left revolutionary movements.

Eventually she had settled on the extreme Socialist Organisers Soviet Revolutionary Party of Great Britain, because, apart from its political perspective, which was determinedly narrow, a large number of its members, particularly at Oxford, were Women's Liberationists. The two went well together. Subjugate the man and you subjugate the establishment and vice-versa. It seemed to dovetail nicely with her beliefs.

Ms Deirdre, as she liked to be known – surnames were detested because they were transmitted only through the male line – had been reasonably fulfilled by her job for the last four years.

Great wads of tax-payers' money had been handed out by the left-wing council on her suggestion to such worthy local groups as the Feminist Movement for the Liberation of Afghanistan, the Women's Motorcycle

Workshop, Sex Equality in Soccer, The Repeal of the Menopause Society and other worthy causes she felt should be at the forefront of the minds of Lambeth's working people. She had persuaded the Council to fund the Feminist film 'Barbara the Boilermaker' and had been instrumental in its production. She had also produced two thousand copies of 'The Cervical Cap-Fitters Handbook' on the Council's photocopier.

Within the local authority itself, she had fought several important campaigns, demanding that all calendars, posters and pin-ups showing scantily clad or naked women which were an affront to female dignity must be removed from the walls of all council offices; that sexual harassment of female staff by males in the office be stamped out and that all toilets should be free for both sexes to use. She insisted that the little silhouette figures of men in trousers and women in skirts were sexist and must be removed from lavatory doors. Her success had been modest, but as it was a one woman, or, as Deirdre thought of it, a one person, battle, she had not been too discouraged by the results to date.

Her campaign over the calendars and posters had been the most successful. By the simple process of going round the offices each evening and ripping down anything she considered offensive and sexist, she was able to destroy pictures faster than the men could replace them.

Her campaign against sexual harassment in the office had got off to a bad start when she imagined that the elderly and ailing Deputy Health Officer, on his first day back from sick leave, had deliberately brushed against her ample breasts as he squeezed past her in the canteen. She had retaliated by seizing his balls in a grip of iron. He was carrying a fully loaded luncheon tray at the time and his scream of agony, coupled with the consequent shower of tomato soup, steak and kidney pie, mashed potatoes, peas and gravy had rather over-emphasised the point she was trying to make to the other diners in the crowded canteen.

By the time she had washed all the food out of her hair, cleaned up her clothes as best she could and presented herself at the office of the Director of Social Services, the Deputy Health Officer had been delivered by ambulance to the hospital and was already having emergency treatment to repair the ruptured wounds of his recent prostate operation.

Her defence had only partly mollified the subsequent Committee of Enquiry and she had been acutely conscious that, after her opening sentence, their eyes had been rigidly glued to her oversized tits which, as exhibits A and B for the plaintiff, were pretty strong evidence.

The toilets campaign had been a failure, she had to admit, because the men had been offensively vulgar every time she had tried to use the facilities originally reserved for them. The loud straining and farting noises that accompanied each of her visits to a cubicle had eventually driven her back to the original Ladies' and, although the doors were still devoid of sexist signs, each sex stuck to its own territory now.

All her spare time, however, had been devoted to the passionate development of her prime concern, the West Lambeth Branch of the Socialist Organisers Soviet Party. She was the founder, the breather of life and being into the Branch and the motivating force behind its continuation. On the strength of her aggressive reports and persistent badgering, the National Body had finally granted West Lambeth full affiliation the previous year and as a result had sent a member of the National Committee for the first time to the Branch's annual congress – held thanks to a generous gesture by Red Fred, the Chairman of the ruling Labour Group, free of charge at the local baths.

The posters had advertised it, the handbills had been distributed, loudspeaker vans had toured the area, Deirdre herself had canvassed diligently and constantly for the past three months and a large turnout was expected. On the strength of her optimism, the National Committee had even sent what it euphemistically termed as 'stewards' down to control the crowd. The scene was set for her triumph and perhaps, who knew, elevation by popular acclaim to the highest levels borne on the shoulders of the liberated peasants of West Lambeth. Transported in triumph over the crushed corpses of the capitalist lackeys of the ruling class to the Supreme Soviet at twenty–three Inkerman Terrace, SE10.

These few weeks up to the Congress had been a heady time and now she was shattered and it was not her fault. First her committed band of women workers had the previous evening decided democratically to support the National Feminist Movement's 'On strike Against God' campaign and not her Socialist Organisers Soviet Congress and had thus spent all that day picketing the local Salvation Army Hostel. Then the area bus garage of Transport for London had staged a lightning one-day strike in support of shorter working hours and hence the majority of her supporters had been immobilised in their homes. The bulk of the audience that had found their way to the Baths Hall were local dossers who took advantage to come in out of the cold and kill time until the women picketing the Salvation Army Hostel went home and they could go down the road for a meal and a peaceful night's sleep. Rat Face had been spot on!

She dragged her thoughts back to the present. The participants in the little huddle were still mumbling to themselves and she felt a flash of anger with them. Chicken-livered bunch of crawlers, why hadn't they supported her in front of Rat Face? She was in the mood to hit out at anyone and anything and was tempted to start off by taking apart the bunch of cringing pilgrims in the corner. She rehearsed a few opening lines before some sanity returned and she realised that to lambast them would not help her cause one iota.

Taking a few deep breaths to settle her rage, she stood up and moved slowly across to join them. There was a sudden cessation of the muttering as they sensed her approach and a noticeable lack of eye contact and camaraderie when she arrived. Heads were partially averted and feet shuffled with embarrassment.

It was clear that she was going to have to make the opening move and an element of contrition was required. This would not be an easy penance for her, contrition was one of the rarest elements in Deirdre Plant's emotional chemistry and, even when detected, it had a half-life quality that could be measured in milliseconds. She screwed herself up for the effort; gritting her teeth she muttered, "Sorry about that."

There was a short pause and then she ground out, "Tomorrow will be different, however, and I shall have a few home truths to tell our National Committee. I am not prepared to take that sort of treatment from anybody when we have put so much effort into building up our branch." She was gradually beginning to stoke up the fires. Contrition had long since perished to eternity and brimstone, one of the more plentiful elements with an indefinite life, was heating up.

"How dare that man Evans..." she spat the words 'man Evans' out with venom. "How dare he speak to me like that? Just wait till tomorrow evening, the little shit will wish he'd never dared to address me in that way!" A fleck of spittle ran from the corner of her mouth. The others tried to calm her down, alarmed at the increasing pressure in her boilers and what was more important, what the effect would be on them as known associates of hers if she did explode in front of the National Committee.

Its members were not the sort of people who were kindly disposed to reactionary dissension from Party discipline, and that is certainly how they would view a Plant-like supernova fulminating in this fashion.

After a few minutes or so the head of steam began to subside and under prompting from a terrified Ernie Goad, they resumed their places at the table. Helga Gundelach and Acklem-Dite were also visibly nervous, but they, after all, were only invited speakers and not directly involved with Branch organisation; or so they told themselves.

Whilst Ernie Goad gave his impression of shortwave radio static, they were both planning as early a departure as they could, to be immediately followed by the issue of statements of disassociation from their erstwhile sister to whom they had pledged unity till death but who was now a potential deviationist. Still, as Acklem-Dite reflected, there was no conflict of probity here because a deviationist could be considered dead – certainly in political terms and, if he had been the Party chairman, in physical terms as well. He found that reasoning very satisfying – not to his conscience (he didn't have one), but to the orderly metaphysical filing system that was his mind. He didn't have a file for 'scab' in his system, at least not where the description could be applied to him and therefore, to have such a loose reference floating about unattached to a logical reason would have been irritating and untidy. Both Helga and Acklem-Dite rose to their feet simultaneously and, muttering excuses about 'catching trains – the bus strike – getting dark you know – got another meetin', folded their papers and trundled out of the hall at a brisk trot.

Deirdre watched them go with impotent frustration and then looked at Ernest. She was not quite sure why, she had to look somewhere and he was selected. She wished she hadn't. There was no inspiration to be had from that pulpit-faced cadaver. It was like surveying a three-day corpse – even his spots looked a greenish-white. He reminded her of something though.

She sighed. She would have to do it on her own as always, without assistance from anyone. Bloody men! When one came to think of it, a few bottles of frozen sperm and the world could easily do without the lot of them.

She looked at Ernie again. That was what he reminded her of – a blob of frozen sperm.

There was a tug at her sleeve. She looked around to see Suzie standing there, eyes red and puffy, tears rolling down her cheeks. Oh my God, Suzie! In her rage at Rat Face and her associates, she had forgotten all about Suzie and poor loyal Suzie had heard it all.

Chapter Three

Charlie and I left Prinknash Keep early the following morning after a hasty breakfast of rolls and coffee. We avoided the Swindon traffic by taking the back roads, and hit the motorway and the early crawl into London at the Newbury junction.

"It's your sailing trip soon, isn't it?" Charlie observed thoughtfully, chewing her lip. "I think I'll spend the weekend at Prinknash while you're away, it will give me chance to sort out the SOS committee and see if I can put some backbone into it. Bloody Gwaine Lisset is about as useful as a chocolate teapot. How we keep electing him as our Member of Parliament defeats me."

"Well maybe not for much longer," I commented, "if his majority keeps shrinking as fast as it did at the last election!"

"Oh great! But who, or what, will we get in his place? That is the question."

I couldn't answer that so I switched to thinking about my forthcoming venture across the English Channel.

For the last three years Bob Barclay, Tony Scales, Robin Fullerton and I had taken Scales' Oyster 53 from its home base on the Beaulieu River across the Channel to Honfleur in France for a weekend boys' trip.

I am not a sailor by any stretch of the imagination, so my job was to make the bacon sandwiches and open the beer, but the others were quite competent. It was always entertaining and we got a couple of good French meals out of it, plus a load of cheap booze to bring back home. Charlie was slightly suspicious of the whole thing but didn't ask any questions – fortunately.

I wondered if we would have fog again this year. Scales spent most of his income on girls and cars so the boat was not very well equipped with modern navigation aids.

The battered MG nosed through the Kings Road traffic in good time to deposit Charlie at the Royal Free Hospital before nine o'clock. I took the car on, parking at the office and just beating the senior partner through the door.

"Getting in early these days, Marcus, your love life wearing thin?" Hugo Elmes beamed at his own witticism.

I wasn't falling for that. That sort of comment must never be answered, too many hidden traps lie concealed along its length ready to distort any reply of any kind except maybe "Balls". But then, one doesn't want one's morning greeting to one's boss to be too pithy too early without any clue as to his disposition that day – not if one is hoping to enhance one's career prospects with the firm, that is.

"Good morning, Hugo, lovely day. Mrs. Elmes enjoy her trip to Harrods last Saturday?"

That didn't call for a reply either; Emily Elmes most certainly did enjoy her shopping sprees in London's retail Mecca but Hugo didn't – or wouldn't when the bill hit his doormat. Hugo's beam wavered, as he acknowledged the thin stiletto under the ribs.

"One all, I think Marcus. Glad to see you've got your wits about you so early – not like the old days when you used to arrive shagged out and hungover..."

"Thank you, Hugo, see you later," I called back sprinting up the stairs before he could launch into a more vivid description of my morning arrivals at the office in the days before I'd met Charlie. Two one to Hugo – but as I said before, he's the boss so...!

Later, I met Bob Barclay for lunch at one of the latter's favourite restaurants, The English Garden in Lincoln

Street. Barclay had devoted a large slice of his time and a substantial amount of his income to discovering the good things of life and particularly those that related to his stomach. Whenever it was suggested he should diet, he would slap his ample frame and maintain that 'it had cost twenty-five thousand quid to build it up, and he was damned if he was going to pay some snivelling little weasel in a white coat another five thousand just to remove it'.

We had a quiet table for two in the corner under the vaulted glass roof. The serious business of choosing and ordering was soon efficiently executed and with a chilled bottle of Chassagne Montrachet to tide us over until the first dish arrived, the conversation moved from generalities to the matters in hand.

"Is this Honfleur trip still on?" enquired Bob. "Scales' boat hasn't sunk, been captured by pirates or anything like that then?"

I nodded, "No, it's still on, I spoke to him on the phone last week. He was going to check out the boat at Buckler's Hard over the weekend and prepare it; said he was taking down this new device he had picked up, you screw it on a bunk and it does all the washing up. It's called Amanda."

"Jesus, doesn't he ever let up? If I buy that bugger a Christmas present I'll get him the nautical fornicator's diary," chuckled Barclay. "That's if I buy a present at all. What sort of time are we expected?"

"He's checked the tides and we should be down at the mooring no later than six o'clock, which means getting the three-thirty from Waterloo to Southampton. He also told me to tell you to be sure to bring some warm clothes."

"Great," said Barclay, rubbing his hands together, "a few days out of the rat race is just what I need at the moment, miles away from the telephone and cut off from the outside world. I expect Fullerton will be all of a nervous twitch again as soon as we cast off. A mobile phone is to that fellow what a renal unit is to a kidney patient. Do you remember the last time we were in Honfleur? He phoned the office three times in the first hour after we'd arrived and then didn't believe what they were telling him so he took the next plane back from Deauville."

I grinned and forked a whole brie favour into my mouth, crunching it between my teeth and savouring its light, juicy succulence.

"By the way, Bob, you mentioned some time ago that you were looking for a decent-sized site down in the West Country for a development. Are you still looking?"

"Yeah, can't find anything these days, not in the right place, that is. Must be a centre of population, must be near the motorway for access to Heathrow Airport, must have a main railway line and must have a decent environment."

"Have you tried Sheringford?" I floated the question easily.

He glanced up, eyes narrowing quizzically. "Our agents have looked round the place and although there are little sites here and there, there's nothing of the size I require."

I stroked my chin reflectively. "How would four acres right in the middle of Sheringford interest you?"

The eyes flashed me a sharp glance, "By God it would, but I'm not prepared to buy half the town to get it."

"You wouldn't have to." I gave him the brief details of the Joshua Grimshaw site I had discovered. "It's about four acres and I believe it's all in one ownership," I concluded.

Bob had put down his knife and fork whilst listening to this, a sure sign that his attention had been captured fully.

"We'd better have a look at it then, Marcus," he said. "When's the earliest we can do it?"

"Well, I suppose we could call in on the way back from sailing, it's down that way and we could kill two birds with one stone."

"Hmm, well yes, but in the meantime then I'll make a few enquiries and get the ordnance maps of the area, and if you can find out any more, Marcus, I would be grateful. Charlie has got some good local contacts down there, hasn't she? If we can find out unofficially the views of the local populace and politicians, it would be very helpful."

"Ah yes." I paused, the twinge of conscience felt the previous day returned abruptly. "I... er... I would prefer to keep her out of it for the time being." I shifted uneasily in my seat. "You see there could – just could, mind you – be a conflict of interests here. Charlotte, as you know, is one of the leading lights in Save Old Sheringford and to be seen to be even remotely connected with a proposal to develop a sizeable chunk smack in the middle of the area she is sworn to preserve could undermine her position, to say the least – even if she'd do it, which she most certainly wouldn't, at least in my opinion, that is, if you see what I mean."

Barclay shot me another quizzical look. "Your own situation don't seem too bright to me, squire. How are you going to explain this rank treachery of yours to the comely wench – I assume from your blathering that she knows nothing of it as yet?"

I grinned impishly at him. "We are talking about money, my fat friend; blueies, brownies and purplies in large quantities can flow from a good scheme here, the incentive therefore for a man of my enormous intellect and resourcefulness is quite sufficient to persuade me to put the whole of my talents towards finding a happy solution to this small difficulty. In the meantime, balls will have to be juggled with skill and dexterity."

"Really? Well, just make sure that they're not yours,

old son, Charlie is pretty smart so be careful," Barclay observed with a leer. "It wouldn't do my reputation any good to be seen hanging about with Britain's newest castrato!"

He added, "I'll leave it to you then, let's speak again about it in the next three or four days after I've checked the place out."

"Will you be in the Frog and Nightgown on Saturday?" I enquired, lifting an eyebrow. "If so I'll have some more information for you then."

Bob shook his head. "No, afraid not, my cousin is getting married, so I've got to go up to Oxford for the send off. I've promised to provide my motor as principal tumbril."

The meal was finished off with coffee and Cognac whilst I filled in a few more details for him about the Sheringford site. There was no doubt that Bob was keen, very keen indeed.

In high spirits I walked briskly back to the office at about three o'clock, sending a trotting dog the wrong way with a beautiful dummy sidestep, which cheered me up even more. It had been a short lunch for a Barclay lunch but I wanted to get started on research into the site immediately that afternoon, now that Barclay had confirmed his interest. There was a lot to be done to collect the background information that must be available before any value could be put on the property.

Sandra in reception gave me a nice smile. "There's a parcel for you in your office, Marcus. DHL dropped it off about an hour ago."

"Oh, thanks." I returned her smile.

No, you're wrong, there was nothing doing there. Sandra was firmly wedded to an extremely nice, and extremely large, site agent who worked for one of the bigger contractors. She was strictly off limits to all comers!

I drifted up to my hutch, wondering who had sent me what. The parcel was from Tony Scales at the National Dental Hospital. It contained two pairs of thick tights and a note that said *'Cold round the cobblers mid-channel at 3am, you'll need these!'* Well, I'd told Bob Barclay to bring warm clothes but I was thinking of sweaters; still Tony knew what he was talking about so it would be on with the tights – but only when I was on the boat. There was no way I was going to travel on the train from Waterloo to Southampton wearing tights.

I surveyed my little kingdom, the domain of Marcus Moon, Group Leader of The Consultants Company, consulting engineers to the world – if we could get the work. As I was six-foot-two and fortunately on the thin side, and my 'office' was not much more than that square, containing a desk, chair, computer terminal, filing cabinet, communication equipment and piles of drawings, reports, maps and plans spread over the floor, it did not allow for a liberal immigration policy – but it was 'home'.

I put my feet on the desk and leaned back in my chair with a notepad and pen and made a list of all the statutory undertakers who might have equipment on, under or round the Sheringford site.

Gas, electricity, telephones, water supply, drainage, TV cables, military stuff – there was a big base not far away; all needed to be contacted to provide input. The whole site could be crisscrossed with buried pipes, sewers, cables and wires. There could be underground chambers for any or all of these, all of which must be taken into consideration and either diverted, replaced or abandoned. It could be a very expensive operation, and some prospective projects have been shown to be not viable financially when the cost of the underground services and related problems has been quantified. Bob Barclay would not thank me if we suddenly discovered a ten-foot diameter old Victorian brick sewer running under the site when the excavations for the foundations were started.

I wandered through into the design office and dug out an Ordnance Survey plan of Sheringford, made a copy of it and marked the site in red. I gave my list and the plan to one of the project engineers.

"Derek, can you find out which bodies are responsible for these services in Sheringford and then ring round and ask them to send us details of their equipment on or near the old Joshua Grimshaw site. I've marked it on the OS plan. We'll have to make formal requests in writing but for the time being I just want to know if there are any major problems."

He took the list and quickly scanned it. "Yeah no problem, when do you want it for?"

"Friday lunchtime."

"Okay."

"Thanks." I nodded my appreciation, collected a cup of coffee from the machine and returned to my chair sipping it. For some unaccountable reason the machine in design office 'two' always produced better coffee than that in 'one' or the reception. The senior partners on the top floor had 'Cona' but I preferred 'two's'.

My watch told me it was twenty-to-five, which didn't leave much time to start anything new. Chewing my lip thoughtfully I resolved to drive down to Sheringford first thing the next morning, visit the Borough Engineer's office and the Rivers Board, and give the site another look, unimpeded by the hairy Mrs Hartley-Worthington, or her dogs, or a deadline with Charlie.

* * *

"Had a good day, Marcus? Anything new happened then?" Charlie was home before me and greeted my

63

entrance thus. With a sensitive conscience already twitched about a possible conflict of interests over Save Old Sheringford and Barclay's prospective development, my first thoughts on this greeting were 'what does she know and who told her?'

A moment's reflection told me that the answer was nothing and no-one, but by then the damage had been done. The flash of guilt, momentary as it was, had been detected by the sharp violet eyes.

She waited patiently for my answer, a faint smile around her lips – so I kissed them, long and hard, followed by a good hugging.

"And you?" I panted after I put her down. "How was it at the Royal?"

She smoothed down her dark hair and stretched, replying nonchalantly. "Oh, we had one five-hour op on a little girl with damaged kidneys. The Prof. did most of the tricky bits but I assisted. I think she'll be fine in a week or two. I know, why don't we eat in and then you can tell me all about your day."

I gulped. Stone me, that was a bit tricky. But she knew nothing, she couldn't. It was a fishing expedition because she suspected me of hiding something, and if I was hiding something that made it even more important for her to find out what it was.

So we ate in, and by rambling on about nothing in particular and avoiding any mention of Bob Barclay, I managed to hold out until a fortunate early bedtime, because we both had an early start the next morning.

But she knew I was hiding something, and she knew that I knew she knew, and I knew that she knew that I knew she knew!

* * *

My drive down to Sheringford was uneventful. Without

saying anything about Barclay's interest in the site, I talked to one of the engineers in the Borough Engineer's office, who knew the geology of the area quite well. It appeared that the ground was mainly alluvial deposits laid down over tens of thousands of years by the River Shering as part of its old flood plain. Beneath these were layers of sandstone and shale, so that didn't seem to create a problem for foundations for buildings. It all looked very promising and I was just heading for the door after thanking him for his help when he added, "Of course you'll have to solve the cyanide problem."

I stopped in my tracks. "What cyanide problem?" I exclaimed.

He told me that apparently cyanide was used in one of the processes for making metal drums and all the ground that had been polluted by it would have to be removed.

"And how much is that?" I enquired.

"We don't know. Nobody has ever investigated it. They've always been put off by the idea of cyanide round the place."

"I bet they have!" I exclaimed. "Are there any other little nuggets of doom buried in your archives? What about drainage?"

He gave me a quick grin and had a rapid check through his drainage plans, saying that as far as he was aware there was nothing major beneath the site but he couldn't vouch for the other services.

As I stood up to leave for the second time, an elderly man working at the other side of the room came across. "I couldn't help overhearing what you said about the old Grimshaw site. I was a junior engineer here when it closed down and I remember that at that time the Council – it was the old Rural District Council then – insisted on a report being done about the cyanide. I can't remember the conclusion but it's probably still buried somewhere in the old archives."

"And where are they? In this office?"

"No, no. I believe they were left in the Old Town Hall. This office wasn't built then."

I pondered this for a moment. Only a few days ago I had been scrambling in the roof spaces of the Old Town Hall but my interest had been more on Fleur Fullerton's knickers, not dusty old archives. I did recall seeing some piles of paper bundled up with string filling the whole of one end of one of the attics; maybe those were the archives. How was one going to get access to them without provoking unwanted interest? I wondered.

"By the way, do you happen to know who owns the site?" I asked the elderly man.

He pursed his lips. "You've got me there." He scratched his chin. "I did hear that it's in some sort of family trust, but I could be wrong."

I noted that, thanked them both and left to find out about more about the river.

The guy at the Rivers Board was much more wary when he learned that I was interested in the Joshua Grimshaw site.

"The Death Site," he said, "at least that's how the papers reported it back in the Eighties. We checked it out and as far as I can remember, thought it was okay, provided it wasn't disturbed. If you're going to dig it up we'll want to monitor the whole thing and set very strict controls. If cyanide gets into the river it could be an ecological disaster affecting the whole of the Thames Valley."

I said I appreciated his point and asked if there was anything else. It turned out that they wanted a strip of the land for a riverside walkway. Any chance of flooding was remote now, although the lower end of the site had flooded regularly in the past. They had completed a flood relief scheme five years ago which had solved that problem.

So it looked pretty good for Barclay's project. He had

something to negotiate with – the riverside walkway; the site didn't flood now, and, apart from being polluted with one of the deadliest poisons known to man, it could be all systems go!

As I drove slowly back to London, I pondered on the information I had been given. So that was why the site had remained untouched and undeveloped for so many years. It had puzzled me but now I had an explanation. No doubt the cyanide problem was well-known but this sort of thing tended to grow by exaggeration as time went by. Rumour would give the place a bad reputation and people would avoid it. I could just see it – 'The Death Site!' I chuckled at the thought, because whatever use they had for cyanide in the past, it wasn't the sort of stuff that one chucked about willy-nilly. Maybe that accounted for all the new padlocks on the buildings. The guys loading scrap outside the buildings hadn't seemed concerned though, but if they were stealing I supposed they wouldn't be.

I resolved to follow this up and get a secret look at this old report buried in the archives. But how? That was the problem. I didn't want to draw more attention than absolutely necessary to my interest in the Grimshaw site.

And then, in a flash of inspiration, I got it! Miss Prim, or whatever her name was, from The Historic Buildings Society. I still had her visiting card and I could use her name to gain access on the basis of checking out the condition of the roof timbers.

Feeling a bit chuffed with oneself, I put more pressure on the accelerator and made the office before closing time.

Chapter Four

Deirdre surveyed the clothes in her closet with concern. She was well aware that her interview that evening in front of the National Committee was going to be critical, it was vital that her case be put in the strongest possible way. All day had been spent working at her desk in the Social Services department of The London Borough of Lambeth (with the exception of the statutory tea breaks and lunch hour, of course), developing the precise wording and phraseology of the fighting speech with which she was going to hit them; nothing must distract from its sledge hammer delivery or them from being remorselessly nailed to the floor by it.

Tight blouses, missing buttons, skin-hugging jeans with straining zips or nipple-outlining jumpers were therefore out. The gear must be effective without being attractive, functional without being feminine. She bridled at that, damn them. By their sexist attitudes they were dictating to her what she could and could not wear; her feminist hackles rose in revolt. She bloody well would wear what she wanted; she would turn up looking not only capable and competent but quite unambiguously female and not swathed in thick sacking like some downtrodden Mongolian coal-heaver. No restricting, confining bra would throttle her lungs; for her there would be no simulated bondage for men's sexual gratification. Nipples must be thrust forward prominently, reinforcing her statement of assertive feminism, and hips would be clearly carved so that hands could be planted steadfastly on the bone, fists balled or fingers jutting rigidly to the fore while her argument was developed.

She paused thoughtfully for a moment. On the other hand, if she did dress like that, being acutely aware that she was a big girl, the omission of her bra might cause the finer points of the polemical arguments she intended to display to be overlooked if the pathetic men responded as the committee of enquiry into her ball-grasping exercise had responded. A difficult choice, but if it was male weakness not male arrogance that dictated her mode of dress, that could be tolerated without compromising the principles of womens' independence. Thus dialectically convinced, she selected from her cupboard a clean but crumpled grey and white striped collarless man's shirt and a brightly coloured, tight-waisted full skirt of the type worn by Slav peasant women. A drawer yielded a pair of black knickers and a substantial bra into which she lowered herself.

The effect was completed by the knotting of a bright red scarf around her throat and five minutes or so tidying up her hair. Thence bare-legged, sandalled and well supported, and without a trace of make-up, she sallied forth to put the National Committee of the Socialist Organisers Soviet in their place.

She remained quite oblivious to the fact that whilst her despised brassiere may have been riveted by the corsetieres equivalent of Harland and Wolfe, her pants were expensive Janet Reger, unashamedly designed to titillate.

This paradox was a perfect reflection of Deirdre's priorities: sex and socialism in her life were generally kept well apart, held at arm's length like two angry demanding adversaries, the burning desires of the former having to be reluctantly subjugated to the single-minded dedication required by the latter on occasions such as the one that faced her tonight. The sex lurked beneath, however, held in subconscious reserve as an ultimate card to play, always available if needed but only to be played to gain an advantage. When Deirdre went for men she demanded much redder meat than your average party worker could provide.

She leant her bicycle against the low wall outside the faded façade of twenty-three Inkerman Terrace, a shabby terraced house, a carbon copy of those along the street and in the other South London streets surrounding. The property had an empty, eyeless look with peeling paint and dusty, uncurtained blank windows. She chained the bike securely with a thick, plastic-covered metal chain so that capitalist, reactionary deviationists could not deprive her of it, and eased open the rusty gate. The building was conspicuously devoid of any form of poster or other advertisement which might identify it easily to the minions of the despotic establishment. It was deliberately low key and unpretentious.

She went up the steps and pressed the button on the answer-phone. The contraption responded with a peculiar noise which sounded as though an electrical wire had become detached and was wandering about in its interior, fusing against every other part. She interpreted this to be an enquiry as to her identity and replied, "Deirdre Plant. Chair West Lambeth Branch of the Party."

After a short pause a small panel slid open in the door and she was scrutinised by a rheumy eye. She heard the sound of bolts being drawn and the door was opened to permit her to enter.

A small, grey, wispy woman stood there. She had a washed-out, bleached face and clothes to match. She examined Deirdre with flat, watery, expressionless eyes, scanning her from her sandals to the top of her shining hair, noting with a twisted smile the sheaf of notes clutched in her right hand.

"You vill vait in here." Her voice was guttural, possibly

mid-European. She directed Deirdre to a small, uncomfortably furnished room directly off the shabby hall. There were several wooden chairs of the folding type and a kitchen table coated with brown, chipped paint on which lay dog-eared copies of left-wing publications. That was all. The floor was bare of covering; the walls, painted a pale green maybe forty years previously, were now spotted with bits of old brown sticky tape showing where posters and other propaganda had been affixed at some time in the past and then carelessly removed. There was no other decoration, no cheerful colours and no attempt to brighten the place up. It was drab, dreary, dull and depressing. Deirdre pulled herself together with a start, she mustn't think like that. Every penny and every poster, and every cent and every sinew must be expended not on inutile decoration and sterile show, but on active promotion for the cause. It was quite correct that the Socialist Organisers Soviet should subscribe to such views.

After she had sat there for two hours reading and re-reading the repetitive propaganda in the thin news sheets, the feeling of depression had been gradually replaced by a burning anger at the humiliation they were deliberately subjecting her to. Oh yes, she knew it was deliberate. The bastards were trying to wind her up, trying to throw her out of her stride. Well, they bloody wouldn't. She would stick to her plan.

Christ, it was uncomfortable in here! Even a little inutility would have been welcome – like a cushion or two. She stood up and walked round the room to loosen her cramped thigh muscles. She massaged her numb buttocks and decided to rehearse her speech to the committee yet again, but with a mobile delivery projected to the cadence of a brisk stride. It was better, much better. The speech became more of an attacking, fighting speech in which she would seize the initiative early on and systematically, methodically and clinically demolish any case the prosecution might present, reducing it to rubble before laying the foundations for her own presentation, then building it up and finally demonstrating her solid and impressive achievements. She regenerated her enthusiasm, getting the adrenaline flowing at such a pitch that she marched to the door with the intention of wrenching it open, storming into the committee room and sorting out the lot of them forthwith.

She decided at the last moment to give them exactly five more minutes, measured by the sweep of the second hand on her large watch which, under the circumstances, was probably just as well because four minutes and forty-five seconds later, the door opened and the washed-out woman beckoned her out. She was ushered up three flights of stairs into a much larger room at the top of the house. She found herself standing in front of a large heavy oak table behind which sat five men. They remained seated, unsmiling, and uttered no words of greeting but just looked at her.

Calculated contempt hung heavy in the air. She glanced round to see if there was a chair she could pull up unbidden and sit down, but this had been anticipated and there was nothing to be seen; she just had to remain standing, trying to recover her breath from the climb.

There was a long silence whilst five pairs of eyes studied her carefully and, she in turn, being determined not to speak first, returned the surveillance. She stood legs astride, shoulders back, breasts jutting forth and arms folded. She scanned each of them in turn.

The big wheel in the centre was a well-built man with broad shoulders and an upright posture. He was, Deirdre estimated, about fifty years of age with a full head of dark, slightly greying hair, clean-shaven, soft, friendly-looking face but with eyes hooded behind drooping lids so that it was difficult to determine the expression in them.

Rat Face sat to his right and beside him sat another clone from the same stagnant gene pool.

On the other side was a tiny, quick, bright-looking elderly man, his alert sparkling eyes flicking around the room ceaselessly behind heavy horn-rimmed glasses. To his left was a younger man of about thirty-five, tall, as far as she could judge, slightly receding dark hair with an intelligent face and dressed immaculately in a well-cut dark grey suit, white shirt and red and blue striped tie. All men. Her lip curled. In addition to Rat Face, she recognised three of the remaining four people because they had been on the platform and spoken at several conferences she had attended. The Chair, Arthur Winlewis, had been to Oxford several times whilst she was an undergraduate, on speaking and recruiting campaigns; the elderly, quick man was Dr Michael Pruitt, the party strategist and planner; Rat Face's clone was another heavy – Joe Klipspringer, a disgruntled South African who hated everybody and everything, but whose organising ability for protest marches, flying pickets, besieging mobs and all other public demonstrations of party strength and unanimity was without equal.

The younger man she did not know, nor was she aware of what particular function he fulfilled. Nobody enlightened her. Apart from Rat Face, she had never spoken to any of them before.

Winlewis cleared his throat, startling her slightly.

"Comrade Plant, the National Committee has discussed your case and I have to tell you that we are extremely disappointed with your performance as the organiser of our West Lambeth branch. The achievements of your branch over the past year have been totally insignificant and have not furthered in any way the cause of our comrades to bring about the downfall of the existing system and replace it initially with a True Socialist Government and ultimately with a full People's Democracy." His voice was low and nicely modulated, and his accent was, if anything, south eastern suburban.

Deirdre interrupted, anxious to secure the initiative. "If I might say a few words, Chair, I have here..." She held up her sheaf of notes, but before she could proceed further he cut in.

"That will not be necessary, Comrade Plant, we have obtained all the information we need and your case has already been discussed and decided. You are here to be told the findings of this tribunal and will be given six months to implement them – otherwise you will be replaced as Branch Organiser."

"But I..."

"The findings of this tribunal are that the activities of the West Lambeth branch of the Socialist Organisers Soviet Revolutionary Party are making no contribution towards our national effort and that these circumstances must be rectified forthwith. The Organiser, therefore, shall be instructed that unless within the next six months a major accomplishment is recorded, then the branch organisation and structure will be adjusted and the organiser's personal position and membership reviewed." He drew a breath and consulted some notes before continuing.

"The major accomplishment must be such that it will achieve national recognition and substantially enhance the progress of the Party, leading to an increase of recruitment and an expansion of its influence." He looked up. "These findings will be communicated to you in writing within the next few days. That is all. You are dismissed."

"But you haven't heard my side!" Deirdre cried, waving her bundle of papers. "You can't just pronounce judgment without hearing both sides. That's not fair! I have here a perfectly good and reasonable explanation and I demand to be heard. Common justice and decency require it..."

The sharp little man interrupted. "Comrade, if you continue to maintain these bourgeois views on equity, we shall have no option but to conclude that you are not fit to hold your present position now, and that you are probably a reactionary agent who has been planted within our organisation. You would therefore be dealt with accordingly."

Rat Face and his clone nodded agreement. Arthur Winlewis, his eyes still shielded, repeated quietly, "That is all, Comrade."

She glared at them speechless for a few seconds, giving them the full death ray treatment straight from the eyeballs but the blank, unforgiving expressions returned defeated her. As she turned to go out of the door Winlewis added, "We, of course, as the National Committee require to approve any scheme you may have for achieving the object set. You will liaise directly with Hugh Evans and keep him fully informed of all your proposals. We shall be keeping a careful eye on you, Comrade Sister."

She went down the stairs in a state of numbed shock and fury. The washed-out woman was waiting in the hall. Her moist eyes had a gleam of satisfied triumph in them as she let Deirdre out. She had obviously been listening outside the door.

Savagely wrenching the chain from her unmolested bicycle, Deirdre became conscious of a footfall behind her and, turning round, saw that it was the smartly dressed youngish member of the tribunal who had clearly followed her down the stairs. She coldly ignored him and continued fumbling with the padlock.

"Sorry about that in there." The voice was quiet, flat, expressionless; a slightly nasal monotone with a North London accent. She maintained an atmosphere of hostile antipathy as she folded the chain.

"The Comrades have to come the heavy hand every now and then it keeps the proletariat on their toes."

She stood up and pushed the chain and padlock into her saddlebag without looking round, wondering if this was some sort of test.

"Do you have any ideas for promoting the Party?"

Still seething with anger and certainly in no mood to be badgered by some male chauvinist who had obviously only pursued her to twist the knife still further, she turned to face him.

"I have been told to discuss them with Hugh Evans and it is with Hugh Evans that I will discuss them and nobody else!" she blazed at him. "So now, if you will kindly piss off out of the way..." she thrust the bicycle towards him, threatening to run over his highly polished black shoes "...I will go."

He didn't yield an inch and just smiled back. "I've got something that might interest you," he said, "in fact it could be just the thing that both you and the Party need."

"I don't need any of your patronising gestures," she snapped, "I am quite capable of sorting out something for myself, so get out of the way, and allow me to leave."

"I'm quite serious," he stated. "I'm doing it for the benefit of the Party, but I think that you could be just the person to put it into operation. Surely it can't do any harm to spend a quarter of an hour over a drink listening to what I have to say?"

She hesitated, there was some truth in what he had said, and besides, being a member of the National Committee, he might also be persuaded to give her some valuable background information that could be very useful. On the face of it he seemed both reasonable and genuine. She conceded a cautious acceptance.

"All right, but I hope you're not going to waste my time or make a pass at me, because if you are, I shall kick you in the balls."

His smile was as thin as an East wind. "Lock your bike up, we'll go to the Thames Waterman on the corner there." He pointed just across the road to a small, decaying pub. She re-chained her cycle and they went across the road into the lounge bar.

"What'll you have?"

"I'll buy my own, thank you very much." Turning to the brassy, bored barmaid, she ordered a pint of bitter. He ordered a scotch and water and they each carried their drink to a small, formica-topped table in the corner, out of earshot of the few other drinkers.

"Right," she said, "let's get on with it. What is this idea of yours?"

He took a sip of his scotch. "All in good time, first of all you'd better tell me something about yourself. Are you married?" He glanced at the third finger of her left hand, which was unadorned. "Not all married women wear wedding rings these days."

The questing look was wiped off his face instantly by the savagery of her reply. He could not have hit a more tender spot if he had been an acupuncture specialist searching out a primary nerve centre. His unconscious attempt at light conversation speared straight through the thinnest part of her skin, into a deeply felt subconscious sensitivity.

"You fucking male chauvinist reactionary shit! I assure you that it is not every woman's craving desire to get themselves attached to some obnoxious tripod and be trailed around on his coat-tails, and if you think that, you had better clear off now. I work damned hard for this organisation, probably a damned sight harder than you." She eyed his smart suit with disdain. "And I am quite capable of formulating my own views and opinions and putting them into practice without having to be guided by some politically immature, sexually prejudiced creature to which I have been attached in the

77

eyes of the law by a ritual incantation."

Taken totally aback, he looked at her blazing eyes and angry red face with astonishment but quickly recovered his composure.

"I see. Woman makes policy not tea, is that the idea?"

"You'd better believe it, sunshine," she snarled.

He thought perhaps he had better shift to safer ground and subtly changed the subject of the conversation from her to himself.

"I see you don't care much for the threads?" He flicked at his jacket collar. "Not all revolutionaries wear boiler suits or vests, you know. The revolution is far more likely to take place from within than from without in this country."

Deirdre was still severely nettled by his reference to marriage and his attempt to change the direction of the conversation was not lost upon her. She gave him a look of withering scorn.

"What the hell are you anyhow? An advertising and public relations executive?" she sneered.

"Worse." His eyes were as flat as his accent. "My name is Denis Straker and I am a civil servant with the Department for the Environment, Food and Rural Affairs."

Whatever else might be said about Deirdre Plant, she had all her chairs under the table, she appreciated his position immediately. A revolutionary and a government man – interesting, maybe he wasn't such a prat after all.

"Does this grand plan of yours for nationally promoting the Party have something to do with the Civil Service then?"

"It's much more complicated than that. What is the aim of our Party? And I don't want a load of dialectical claptrap, I want a simple specific goal."

Her hackles started to rise, she was being patronised again. Deirdre's hackles rose and fell more frequently than, but with an equal predictability as the tides around the shore. Unfortunately – or rather, fortunately for the populace of the United Kingdom and unfortunately for her – the time and energy she devoted to hackle-raising, and its consequent attendant diversionary problems, reduced her ability to concentrate as cold-bloodedly and as calculatingly on the destruction of society as a dedicated revolutionary should. Her abrupt dismissal with speech undelivered and now consigned to the saddlebag of her bike still rankled deeply.

"You conceited bloody arsehole, don't you play the superior intellect with me! If you've got something to say, spit it out, I'm quite capable of grasping whatever facts your brain can assemble, let me assure you of that!" This was immediately followed without intake of breath by a renewed vitriolic attack on his chauvinistic attitudes and thence an equally vehement defence of the role of socialist women in the workers' struggle.

It was two pints of bitter and two scotches and water later, the second one being a double, before he was able to pacify her and return her to the role of listener. By then he was beginning to have doubts about her capability to put any plan into action, let alone the one he was about to entrust her with. However, carefully selecting each word so that it was either bisexual, proletarian or unambiguous, he began to explain to her what he had in mind.

"Do you know anything about a small town in the West Country called Sheringford?"

She nodded. "Yes, I know of it, I've been through it a couple of times – so what?" She shrugged her shoulders, waiting for more to emerge. Rancour still simmered, her mind was only half switched on to what he had said as she watched for opportunities to slide in a few more phrases of self justification. One way or another, every single member of that Committee was going to be forcibly fed that speech; Straker now, the rest by written submission sent recorded delivery to each of them in person, itemising every single achievement. But then Pruitt's chilling warning surfaced. Who the hell did he think he was anyway – intellectual faggot?

"What about its politics?" Straker was asking. She shrugged again, off-hand: "Safe Tory seat, I suppose," but then memories were stirred and she began to pay more attention. "Hold on, wasn't that the place where the Tory gay had his majority cut at the last Election?" she frowned. "I also read in the papers that there's some hoo-ha about conservation around that area. But what's so special about that?"

Just in time he bit back the "Good girl", thus saving himself another fifteen minutes' vulcanism and at least eight quid for pacifying drinks.

"That is correct, you have it precisely. The sitting MP for Sheringford, a dyed-in-the-wool right-winger by the name of Sir Gwaine Lissett, had his majority slashed from six thousand to sixty-six. What's more, this was not brought about by the sudden conversion to Socialist tenets of the true blue sheep-shaggers of Sheringford or to the sterling efforts of the worthy but mediocre New Labour candidate selected from a list of equally worthy but mediocre party hacks put to the local constituency party by Labour Party HQ. It was entirely due to the influx into the Sheringford constituency of people from East London relocated through the overspill policies of the late Seventies and through the Eighties. Labour they voted then and Labour they will always vote until the day they die. Nodding donkeys, the lot of them, but we're still a few hundred votes short to be on the safe side."

A quiver of excitement passed through her; the derogatory way he had dismissed the Socialist candidate of the past must mean that they wanted – needed – somebody of much higher calibre for the future. She kept her voice level. "So at the next election, Sheringford may become a Labour seat but that will not be for at least three, possibly four more years. So where do I fit in?"

He sipped his scotch slowly, deliberately caught her eyes with his own and held them. Like flints before Jerusalem, the slate-grey irises reflected their cold, humourless mesmeric light. The semi-flippant way he had outlined the political position at Sheringford was an aberration of the past, washed away in a rising tide like flotsam from the rocks. A year of careful research and planning had gone into the proposal he was about to put and although Michael Pruitt had set up this balls-aching virago to be the frontrunner in establishing the Socialist Organisers' Soviet Revolutionary Party in Sheringford, he was not so sure. More than sulphur was required for that role; still, Pruitt was a thorough man, had checked her out and it was Pruitt's neck that was stretched over this one, not Straker's. Pruitt's job was to plan, his to implement – it didn't pay to ask too many questions and if Plant got out of line then he would just have to smack her back into it. No, it was not a matter of discipline but of ability and flexibility. They couldn't afford this one to go wrong, it was their best chance yet.

His eyes narrowed slightly. "What I am about to tell you is for your ears alone; it's your chance to correct the unfortunate impression that the Committee have formed of your abilities..." He checked her exclamation of anger. "You have been set a target by the Committee and I tell you now we meant what we said. However, it just so happens that I have something which may get you off the hook, provided you can pull it off; but I warn you – and take good heed of this warning – if you screw it up, if you make a balls of it, the comrades will be very displeased indeed and I shall have your fucking head on a plate."

Her mouth opened like a sweating goldfish, but the retort choked in her throat, held there by his expression. Straker was smiling. It was not, however, an outward expression of a hitherto carefully concealed sunny disposition; nor was it a charitable display calculated to illuminate the hearts and minds of one in distress. It was the sort of smile that Henry VIII might have worn when suggesting to Anne Boleyn that she cancel her milliner's appointments and settle outstanding bills, or Hengist the Horny on receipt of the pleadings from some Saxon wench that she had a headache. As such, it definitely discouraged further confrontation and stimulated a hasty review of past behaviour.

When he was certain that he had secured all her attention he continued, deliberately keeping his voice low so that she would have to concentrate to catch his words.

"There will be a by-election soon in Sheringford, a by-election caused by the resignation in disgrace of the present incumbent. Never mind how at the moment, just accept that it will happen. At that by-election Labour will select a new candidate against a shattered and demoralised local Tory machine. The new candidate will be none other than our Comrade Arthur Winlewis, and Winlewis will win."

He smiled again, adding after a short pause, "And the reason Arthur will be selected and win is because you will make sure that he is and that he does. Winlewis will be the first Socialist Organiser's Member of Parliament. The takeover from within will have commenced."

The earlier faint flicker of hope faded in her breast. That was all very well in theory. Disappointment entered her voice.

"And how am I supposed to bring this miracle about, pray? Stand on Lambeth Town Hall Clock and wave my magic wand like Fairy Snow?"

Straker's overtaxed patience strained a further incredible millimetre. What a bloody nettle the woman was; a contrary hope began to dawn. Maybe she would step out of line and begin to cock the whole thing up – at least in the early days. A mean man was friend Denis under his sophisticated veneer and the idea of sorting out Deirdre's hang-ups had a growing appeal at that moment. He controlled himself with difficulty.

"You, my Comrade Sister, will bring this about in two ways. First, you will take paid leave of absence from your job for a year. Make whatever excuse you like so long as it is plausible and I will square the rest with the Leader of the Council so that Lambeth accept your application; this you will do forthwith. Then you will immerse yourself in Sheringford's politics. The present Labour Party in Sheringford is soft, middle-of-the-road, amateur, run by a few enthusiasts more akin to racing whippets than driving in a Parliamentary candidate. Pruitt has lined up an SOS cadre ready to move in. You will work undercover with our help and totally re-organise the local Labour constituency party. The assistant regional organiser of the Labour Party in the South Central is one of our men; he will give you full back-up. All the important jobs will be filled with Socialist Organisers Soviet delegates, particularly the constituency management committee.

"Secondly, you will openly join with the Tories." This time there was humour in the smile, a cynical humour but nonetheless the thought obviously amused him. It did not amuse her.

"You must be joking," she spluttered, "I'd rather be dead than join that lot! For Christ's sake, do I look like a Tory?" It was a genuine cry of anguish. He surveyed her coolly, it was the first time he had procured a spontaneous response from her not pre-conditioned by assertiveness training. The large teeth that could bisect a Worcester

Permain at one bite, and the wide face were ideal for the Shires. Oxford had even rounded up her accent. Pruitt was thorough, he had to give him that. He gave a wolfish grin.

"A blouse, pleated skirt and a headscarf knotted on the point of the chin and nobody could tell the difference. There's one other thing," he added as she glared back at her tormentor, trying to think up some riposte. "It's your round, make mine a double," he murmured, sliding his glass across the table towards her. With a marked reluctance for one who so freely preached equality, she stalked to the bar and grudgingly shigged out five pounds from her purse for the drinks. She gave him his silently, he had really cracked her shell with his Tory clone observation, she didn't know what to say.

Straker sampled his double scotch appreciatively before continuing. "There is more."

"There'd bloody better be!" she muttered.

"Oh there is, have you forgotten that I'm in the Department of the Environment? I told you it had something to do with that as well, did I not?"

She scowled without replying, this guy was giving her the runaround well and truly now. The runaround was something one dished out to others, being on the receiving end was an uncomfortable and unaccustomed experience and that was most definitely not Deirdre's scene. But she could do nothing about it – yet – so she seethed quietly as he developed his theme.

"And the conservation group that you mentioned earlier happens to fall within my department's responsibility. Now like most conservation and preservation pressure groups, it has many diverse constituents: vested interests, crackpots, conservatives with a small 'c' and politicians on the make. As you have no doubt read in the papers and perhaps seen on television, this particular group is increasing both in its political influence and its publicity punch. Also, the local MP Lissett supports it. The power of its persistence has my department back on the ropes worried and defensive, and if we are in that state the New Labour politicians are even more pressed – and the interesting thing is that although this group is supposed to be non-political, the whole shooting match is bumbling along run by Tory amateurs. It needs organising."

He was watching her eyes which, until his last words, had had a hot puzzled look but now from the concentration of her expression, it was clear that she was beginning to get his drift.

"This group represents, principally, major landowners in the area whose property is likely to be affected in some way. It includes town and county councillors – all of whom are right-wing, of course – as well as considerable commercial interests. To them they have welded in common cause the misguided, idealistic enthusiasts of various preservation societies under a single vociferous and powerful lobby called Save Old Sheringford. They campaign under their initials 'SOS'. I'm surprised you haven't heard of them."

Deirdre sat for a couple of minutes with her chin propped on her hand as her mind digested, compiled, assessed and appreciated the full significance of these revelations.

"Brilliant," she muttered to herself, "quite brilliant", and then looking at him she said, "You mean we should join it, penetrate its controlling committee, take over the key positions and use it as a vehicle for promoting the Socialist Organisers Soviet? And as our price for supporting it, we shall require it to support us or at least reduce support for the Tories – bearing in mind that a by-election turnout is always less than for a general election." She paused momentarily. "But of course, on our side it won't be less and if we can swing a couple of hundred of their votes as well, we'll have stitched up all the angles."

"Good girl got it in one." It slipped out before he could stop it. He held his breath but she was so absorbed developing her thoughts that she totally overlooked the blatant, sexist implications that normally would have had her leaping to the barricades.

"We will need to know a lot more about its operations first," she said, half talking to herself. "Who controls it now, how they got into that position, what its status is and from where it draws all its support."

"I can provide you with quite a lot of that information. It comes through my department at DEFRA. We always like to keep our finger on protest groups and particularly those related to the destruction or preservation of the environment."

"Do you want to be involved?" she asked.

"Don't be stupid! As a respectable civil servant, I couldn't possibly be publically identified with a protest group, but I can feed you inside information, and if and when the time comes, maybe some more tangible support to complete the takeover. That, however, can only be considered when you have set the structure up.

No, the ball will be entirely in your court so don't make a bugger of it. It's taken me a long time to plan this, and I don't want it cocked up by..." he was just going to say "some idiot female", but he sensed that perhaps a tidal hackle of tsunami proportions would roll up, obliterating all the patient effort he had put in, and so reluctantly he changed it to "...anybody because they have not put in either the time or effort."

The hackle subsided and rolled harmlessly past.

Deirdre's brow furrowed as a couple of thoughts struck her. "But surely New Labour isn't going to let us get away with infiltrating Winlewis as a candidate?"

"Why not? Although he's known to be on the left,

Arthur has played it very low-key and is quite highly thought of at Party Headquarters. If the local committee select him there's not much objectors can do about it. It's very democratic!"

The irony was not wasted. "And what about Hugh Evans?" she continued. "What do I do about him?"

"Don't worry about Brother Evans, leave him to me. Not a word to Winlewis either, as yet he doesn't know the details and probably doesn't want to know."

He dangled a further carrot. "This is only a first step, you realise that; we have advanced plans for a much bigger push into positions of power, and those who serve us well..." The words hung in the air but the meaning was clear – or at least Deirdre thought it was.

She nodded slowly, there was much more to Denis than met the eye. Dangerous Denis the Devious Dilettante, she thought – he would bear watching carefully in the future. But this, this really was the powerful stuff, this was what it was all about. West Lambeth could get stuffed – except Suzie, of course. Suzie Kassenbaum would come with her to Sheringford.

Chapter Five

I had just worked myself into a position that was full of lovely Freudian undertones prior to the main part of the proceedings when the bedside phone went off. Cursing under my breath, I reluctantly relinquished sufficient of my all-embracing hold around the parts of Charlie bounded by the shoulders downward and the thighs upward to enable her to stretch over and pick up the handset.

"Yes, this is Charlotte speaking." She listened for a second or two then wriggled to a sitting position, removing her left tit out of range.

"Who is that? Oh, Deirdre, I didn't recognise your voice, it must be ages since we last spoke. What can I do for you?"

The wriggling had removed only a part of the temptation and I was bored already with the phone call. Presented with another interesting bit of Charlie to nuzzle, and being a nuzzler of some repute, I was not going to let an opportunity like that pass, so I pushed forward the nuzz and nuzzled away happily.

"Just a minute, Deirdre, hold on... Will you stop it?" she hissed, pushing me away, "this could be very important. Just behave yourself for a minute – no, not you Deirdre, it's the dog, keeps jumping up. Excuse me, I'll go and put him in another room." She covered the phone with her spare hand. "It's an old friend I haven't heard from for ages and I think she wants to help SOS."

I lifted my head from the concealing sheet. "I'm an old friend you haven't heard from for two minutes and I want to help SOS as well. In fact, I help SOS by keeping its secretary happy, and do you know how I do that? Well, I'll show you." I slid under the sheet again and was just beginning to advance the old nuzz once more when she leapt out of bed and swiftly put on a thick towelling bathrobe.

"Hello, Deirdre – sorry about that, I've got rid of the little beast now. Oh, a cross between a..." she looked at my crestfallen face "...a St Bernard and a Truffle Hound." She laughed her tinkly laugh. "Yes, plenty of red meat is certainly what he gets," she put her hand out to fend off my advance, "but only at meal times. Now what can I do for you, Deirdre?"

I sighed and, deciding that this conversation was going to continue for some time, with ardour held in abeyance slipped downstairs and into the kitchen. There was a chilled half-bottle of champagne in the fridge. I dug out two very large wine glasses and carefully stripped the foil and the wire from the cork. I filled one glass with the pale effervescent liquid and sipped it – it was perfect, so I filled the other glass, discarded the now empty bottle in the waste bin and carried both brimming glasses back upstairs.

Charlie was just replacing the receiver with a thoughtful look on her face and took the proffered drink with a pensive smile.

"Champagne breakfast," I grinned. "Who was that?"

"That was one Deirdre Plant who was in the same College as me. I haven't seen or heard of her for three or four years."

"What did she want?"

"Well, Deirdre was always a bit of a strange girl, very much into women's rights and sex equality. She was also left-wing and an active member of the University Socialist Party and that's what she was phoning about. She's still involved with the Labour party in some way and she wants to join SOS. She made a very good point that hadn't occurred to me before; SOS is very Tory, county and establishment at present and to be really effective, it should be either apolitical and non-party or embrace the whole political spectrum. In other words, it should involve all parties or none of them. Her point was that, as it already had right-wing Tory support, then it should also have some socialist involvement to obtain the maximum backing for its cause. She wants to discuss how she, with her contacts, can help widen our political action base. It could be very useful."

They say that there is nothing new on this earth and I reckon that's absolutely true. The same sort of thing would have happened at Troy. Old Paris would have been happily nuzzling away one morning when Helen leant over and looked out of the window. "Look petal," she would have said, "someone's left a bloody great wooden horse outside, go and bring it in, it will go nicely with our great wooden camel and give us the biggest balanced pair of bookends in the Med. And Paris, his mind more on getting back to the business in hand, would have put up only token resistance.

"Yes, my beloved," he would have replied, "if you say so", and then forgotten all about it – but she wouldn't have, and before you could say 'Agamemnon', in it would have been. Of course, I didn't know this, well not about Deirdre, it was only my basic suspicion of anybody who volunteered for anything that provoked resistance. What is in it for them? one wonders. Cynical – perhaps; hard-nosed – maybe; accurate – certainly!

I tugged at my lower lip thoughtfully before sipping my champers.

"You want to be careful with that lot; whey-faced harridans, sandals, wheatgerm and four different coloured kids under five – ideological fanatics the lot of them."

90

"Oh I don't think Deirdre's anything like that – she's a social worker."

There was a loud spluttering followed by a concentrated and prolonged coughing as some of my champagne went down the wrong tube. Charlie clapped me smartly between the shoulderblades and gradually the seizure subsided. I put out one hand grasping her shoulder and with eyes that were still watering, I scanned her face with mock rage, managing to gargle out, "Bloody hell, woman, what do you mean by using language like that in the presence of one of Britain's workers?"

"Language like what?" she looked puzzled.

I glanced round surreptitiously, beckoned with one finger and then leant towards her shielding my mouth with one hand. She automatically responded by leaning towards me to receive the whisper.

When my mouth was close to her ear I shouted, "Social worker!"

And with a great laugh, I seized her and tumbled her on the bed, demolishing the scant defence provided by her towelling robe with one hand, whilst my mouth stilled her weakening cries of protestation and my spare hand investigated areas warm, soft and sensual.

Oh Paris, you've a lot to answer for!

An hour or so later she awoke from a satisfied drowse and, after a shower, dressed and got ready for the day. I was pretending to be asleep – lying on my back with a beatific smile on my face making little bubbling sounds. She let me lie in and went out to do the Saturday shopping. I dozed off again contentedly.

When I awoke it was almost midday. I had a quick shave, cleaned my teeth, ran a comb through my hair, donned a faded blue shirt and jeans and drove down to Chelsea to the Frog and Nightgown pub. This was a ritual for Saturday lunchtime – the boys gathered here for a resumé of the week's events and the lounge bar offered friendly service without imposition.

Today, however, there was motive behind the visit. I wanted to find out the depth of Barclay's enthusiasm for Sheringford. Like most developers, Barclay was a perpetual optimist but he was shrewd enough to know that more than optimism was needed; Barclay's nose required time to sniff a site out thoroughly before he cocked a leg to mark it as his territory. I liked the simile Barclay as a St Bernard. Chuckling aloud, I hit the pub at precisely twelve-fifteen.

The Frog was tucked into a leafy corner of one of those small, quiet Chelsea squares hidden away from the bustling Kings and Fulham Roads. Squares which astonish and delight the casual stroller looking for somewhere to evacuate his dog. The sun warmed the pavements round the pub, the plane trees cast dappled shadows down the façade of the old building and the gentle breeze sent ripples through the pale-green leaves and full, fat bunches of lilac flowers suspended from the magnificent wisteria that crawled round the lower parts of the building extending over the creosoted, ship-lapped fence surrounding its minuscule garden.

Parking the car neatly on a section of vacant yellow line, I side-stepped the piles of dog crap on the pavement and made a beeline for the bar.

Strategically placed beer mats wedged under their sills held the pub doors wide open to permit some air circulation. I could hear the buzz of conversation and the rattle of glasses from within as I approached the lounge bar entrance.

There were perhaps fifteen to sixteen people in the lounge, of which seven were standing round the heavy mahogany bar. The Saturday regulars, like Tony Scales, the dentist sailor; Peter Smallwood, a Harley Street doctor; Robin Fullerton, a financial PR man; and Martin Holmes, Bob Barclay's co-director. Barclay himself was missing, being up in Oxford visiting relatives that weekend. There were also three girls, two that I recognised: Fullerton's large wife Fleur, whom I kissed chastely on the cheek whilst dropping a casual hand to her hip to check today's knicker thickness and thus Robin's current standing in the Fullerton household (Ah ha! – improving); and Smallwood's girlfriend, Anushka, whom I kissed full on the lips, sliding one hand round the small of her back and with the other squeezing the cheeks of her ample bottom. She was a super kisser and responded to the kiss in full before breaking away giggling and pink whilst Smallwood scowled ferociously.

I gave him a cheerful beam and turned to the third girl who was enfolded within the brawny arm of Tony Scales. This then was Amanda, the flavour of the month, a new experience – and experience was what Scales' girlfriends always ended up with. I beheld a well-rounded, full-lipped creature with short, neat blonde hair swept across her forehead, blue eyes and a very solemn expression.

"And you must be the gorgeous Tara that Tony is always telling us so much about – somehow I imagined you to be taller with dark hair."

Scales choked violently over his mouthful of Truman's Best Bitter, dissolving into a violent coughing fit. When he had extracted himself from all the friendly back-pounding, he pointed a shaking finger at me, struggling to force out his words before too much damage was done, and at the same time draw breath and not beer down into his lungs.

"You bugger, Moon, you absolute bugger!"

He turned his watering eyes to the Solemn Blonde, whose full lips were now compressed into a tight line.

"He always does this sort of thing, don't believe a word he says, I don't know anybody called Tara, he's just made it up. Honestly."

The tight lips remained tight and the blue eyes frosty. Scales desperately turned to the others.

"For Christ's sake, tell her, I've never mentioned any girl called Tara, have I?"

"No," I replied, "that's quite right, you haven't, I got it wrong, it was Sara – so you must be Sara. Well I must say, I'm very pleased..."

The blue eyes iced over completely and it was Smallwood who, suspecting that perhaps a sense of humour was not one of Solemn Blonde's strong points, repaired to Scales' rescue.

"Don't believe a word he says, Amanda, he has to do this sort of thing to cover up a certain – what shall we call it? A certain deficiency." He gave her a knowing look. "It's an unfortunate medical condition that occurs in the adolescent, but we don't generally talk about it."

I ignored him and changed tack suddenly.

"So you are the famous Amanda that Tony screw..."

I was silenced by a large meaty hand being clamped firmly over my mouth and Scales' voice hissing menacingly in my left ear. "Shut up, Moon – and I might buy you a drink." He turned to the barmaid without releasing his grip on my head. "A pint of best bitter, Jessie, and make it as quick as you can, Moon's in one of his talkative moods."

As Tony Scales had had an England rugby trial as a flank forward before potential damage to his hands decided him to quit rugby and concentrate on dentistry, and as he was quite able to pick up a rugby ball easily with one hand, I was somewhat relieved when the beer appeared within seconds and my head was released. Taking the glass slowly, I lined up the high spot of the day. First communion with the product of the hop. I closed my eyes and, raising the pint, took a long slow pull, feeling the fresh cool relief as the bitter beer washed the dry throat and hit the right spot.

"By God that tasted good! I've been looking forward to that all morning." I turned to Martin Holmes. "How do, Martin, long time no see."

"Yeah, how long has it been?"

You will realise that Holmes is not quite as regular at these Saturday lunchtime sessions as some people, leading with his chin like that. There was another suppressed giggle from Anushka whilst Smallwood scowled even more ferociously, vowing to interrogate his extract of émigré extremely thoroughly about her past the next time he got her into bed.

Which, he considered, brightening up and glancing at his watch, would be in one hour and forty minutes at the most, give or take five minutes.

I gave her a grin and, taking Martin by the elbow, manoeuvred him into a quiet corner.

"Has Bob mentioned Sheringford to you?"

Martin nodded, "He's had half the office checking the place out these last few days – it sounds an absolute prime pitch but who else knows about it?"

"Nobody's interested in it as far as I know now but I agree someone at sometime must have had a go at putting a scheme together on that site. Maybe that was before the bypass was completed or before the big population increase? It wouldn't have stacked up then."

Something made me hold back from mentioning 'The Death Site' reputation and its cyanide problem.

Martin continued. "But tell me, Marcus, how are you going to reconcile saving old Sheringford with your involvement in the construction of a big new shopping centre right in the middle of it?"

I seized his arm and put a finger to my lips. "Shh! For heavens sake, don't broadcast it. To be quite frank with you, I haven't the foggiest idea yet but if Charlie ever got wind that..." I shuddered – it would not be a pretty sight, the outcome would almost certainly produce a Mark One bollocking with Iron Clasp, Oak Leaves and bar. If not handled right, the consequences didn't bear thinking about. She would have to know sometime – realisation by a gentle filtering of facts throughout the next few weeks preceded by the occasional sweetener. It would be rather like hand-feeding an extremely large crocodile but the stakes were somewhat higher than the chewing off of the odd arm, depending how one looked at it.

Martin smiled sympathetically. "I hear you're going round the site next week on the way back from the sailing trip."

I nodded. So it looked as though Barclay was definitely on, subject to a site inspection. The trip would give me a few more days grace to develop – correction, think of – a feeding plan for Charlie which ensured satisfaction on the one hand and survival on the other. Maybe something along the lines that it was 'the will of the people'. Hold a public exhibition at which the worthy burgers and commons of Sheringford would unanimously acclaim a development that would provide much-needed jobs, superior shopping and the replacement of a derelict eyesore with what I hoped would be an architectural masterpiece. A somewhat far-fetched and improbable hope that was, the realist in me advised; the burgers, being mainly local shopkeepers themselves, would throw out anything which even remotely threatened their own secure, non-competitive existence and balls to the commons. I wouldn't be surprised if Thos Tugwood turned out to be the Mayor! And as for the commons, usually they didn't know what they wanted but whatever it was on offer, they didn't want it. No, I could not rely on that as a way out of my dilemma.

I brightened at a thought. Surely saving old Sheringford could not include that derelict plot covered with rusty rubbish and impregnated with one of the world's deadliest poisons? If presented skilfully and it was demonstrated how development on that site could be linked harmoniously to the rest of the old town, it should be welcomed as a benefit to the townscape, not a detriment. But life didn't work like that, I mused. The 'not in my back yard' syndrome applied, with people conveniently forgetting that everything they lived in and used had been built in somebody's 'back yard' at some time or another, otherwise we would still be living in caves.

I would mull over the tactics on our forthcoming sailing trip to Honfleur.

Behind my right shoulder, coincidentally and perhaps subconsciously stimulating such thoughts, I could hear Pete Smallwood propounding his 'Aid the Daft' theory. Basically it was that the purpose of most laws these days is to protect people from themselves. The laws are intended to try to replace common sense.

"If a fool wants to part with his money he should not be prevented by law from doing so," affirmed Pete portentously, "nor should he be prevented from drugging himself to death; smoking himself to death or eating himself to death, as long as he doesn't expect me to cure him when it's too late."

Tony Scales snorted, "Christ, this is all a bit heavy even for you, Smallwood. What's happened to the usually jolly topics from your medical diary: constipation, piles, sex and rashes? You've never been the same since you bought that damn dog of yours." He turned to us. "Do you know what he's called the thing? Phideaux. Spelt P-H-I-D-E-A-U-X. The bloody beast's got it engraved on its collar. I've seen it."

Smallwood coloured and grinned sheepishly. "Well, it's a second-hand dog and will only answer to Fido although it's very well bred. To you lot Fido doesn't sound too downmarket but for the clientele round Harley Street something much more classical is expected. A bunch that goes round noticing what the contents of your dustbin are when it gets emptied has no qualms about reading the names on dog collars. I tell you this – on Thursdays, when the London Borough of Marylebone sends its refuse squads into Harley and Wimpole Streets, you almost have to book tickets to accompany the dustcart." He mimicked an upper-class high falsetto: "'Oh my dear did you see, those Smallwoods have been drinking the Chateau Lafon Rochet for a whole week?' 'Yes dahling and '68 was such a poor year in the Medoc!' Their spiteful little eyes light up with glee at that sort of thing. The dustcart is the Marylebone sets' equivalent of the revolutionary guillotine. An aristocratic dog is a must for the aspiring professional, I tell you: that's how we meet potential clients, and the perambulating Marylebones do not want any old common dogs stuffing their noses up the rear-end of their Marmadukes of Windsor or De La Huntys of Sandringham, so Phideaux it's got to be – I tell them it's classic Carthaginian."

Whilst this had us reeling for a split second, Smallwood seized his chance to switch concentration to a less personal subject. Turning to me he asked, "How's the fight to save Sheringford going? We haven't seen much of Charlie since she decided to take on the government in her spare time."

I shrugged off-handedly, not wishing to have any more attention focused on this subject for the time being until I had got Charlie squared away with the redevelopment idea and I could discuss the matter without the nervous prickle of ill-boding twitching the nape of my neck. The simplest thing was to do a Smallwood and pass the parcel; fortunately I had the perfect recipient waiting.

"Quite well, quite well indeed; but as she's the main driving force behind it, it takes up most of her spare time." I grinned at Smallwood. "But she's very good at it, you want to be thankful it's the government she's taken on and not you." I narrowed my eyes thoughtfully and murmured as if soliloquising, "Funny creatures, women, very strange indeed..."

The observation hung in the momentary silence, a beautiful little irresistible parcel simply wrapped in green paper – and Fleur Fullerton picked it up. Keeping an absolutely straight face, I chuckled inwardly. Married women are always the most curious – I would have laid bets that she would be the first to react, there must be something in the wedding ceremony that sharpens suspicion and its external expression – intense curiosity. A bit like the Holy Ghost descending to give the gift of tongues – although in her case she'd had that sharpened as well. She didn't exactly grab it with enthusiasm, she knew me of old, and it was more of a prod with a toe, affected with an air of unconcern in case she was being set up.

"In what way, Marcus?" she asked diffidently.

I leant one elbow on the bar and considered her gravely. "Well, Mrs Fullerton, take for instance the incredible ability of the female human to sleep through shot and shell, storm and tempest, fire and flood and yet be instantly awake at the faintest creak of the first footfall of her mate on the staircase as he creeps upwards, pissed out of his tiny mind after a few drinks with friends."

It was a fact known to most present that Fullerton spent a large part of his married life in the 'dog house' because his wife nagged him about both his drinking habits and his drinking companions. We reckoned she only came down to the pub to keep an eye on him.

Fleur realised her caution had been justified and changed direction smartly but without full consideration. "My Robin does not come home 'pissed out of his tiny mind' as you so crudely put it, so I wouldn't know."

I studied the pair of them standing there looking smug, secured by the common bond that Fleur's words had just forged between them plus a pair of brief knickers for later.

"Well he certainly leaves here most evenings round seven-thirty legless. I wonder where he goes and what he does between then and home time?"

Fullerton shot upright. "Ho, bloody ho, Moon, if you think my wife's going to fall for that load of old cobblers, you've got another think coming." He looked doubtfully at Fleur. "You aren't, are you, sweetie pie?"

We all looked at Fleur she just smiled sweetly and remained silent. The common bond dissolved as rapidly as she had forged it.

Fullerton cursed under his breath, his wife fell for the same old thing every Saturday; if it wasn't me, it was one of the others. He resolved to try once more to talk her out of coming but strangely, she seemed to enjoy it – and as it looked as though he was on a promise for tonight, best leave well alone for the present. But it had shifted their attention away from me.

Scales finished up his pint and planted the glass on the bar with a flourish. "Come on, Happy, drink up," he said to Amanda. "We're off," he announced, "and don't forget, Marcus, we'll meet on the three-thirty from Waterloo, Tuesday. Robin is coming over from Cowes and I'll leave it to you to confirm with Bob. Cheers, all!" And putting his arm round an ominously silent, rather rigid companion, he manoeuvred her out of the open door.

I couldn't see that relationship lasting much longer – the extrovert Scales and the Solemn Blonde, there was no reactive chemistry there.

Perhaps he never intended that there should be; very wary of becoming too involved was our Tony.

The Fullertons pushed off on their own, presumably to try out Fleur's concessionary underwear. I wished them luck, and Pete and Anushka agreed to join Charlie and me for our usual Saturday 'Spag Bol' at the little

Italian on Grove Road. Charlie was already there sipping a glass of Frascati when we arrived, kissed us all, me last and longest, and then disappeared with Anushka to the 'Ladies'.

Chapter Six

The three-thirty Southampton train was almost empty. The rush hour, which stretched from four o'clock to six-thirty these days, had not started so Tony Scales and I had no trouble in finding a vacant compartment. Scales heaved his duffel bag onto the seat and sank down with a grunt of relief in a corner facing the direction of travel. The air in Waterloo Station was heavy and hot, other travellers milled about listlessly seeking out the odd places where a waft of breeze cooled their damp skins.

"Phew, be glad to get some of that fresh Channel air, it's stiflingly hot in here even with the air-conditioning working. It is working, isn't it?" I put my hand to the grill and confirmed a gentle waft of cooler air.

Scales rummaged in his bag for a moment and with a grunt of triumph, brandished a bottle filled with pale amber fluid.

"How about a touch of fresh Scottish Mist first just to set us up for the journey?" He produced two small stainless steel cups and poured a generous measure into each. A disturbance could be heard further down the train; banging, thumping and heaving preceding the noisy approach of a heavy body.

"Hello, hello, hello. Jumping the gun, are we?" The door from the corridor crashed open and the beefy figure of Barclay bulldozed through the opening, beaming from ear to ear.

"Do you know that the male Emperor moth can smell the secretions of a female Emperor moth six miles away?

Well, I can do the same for the products of Glen Morangie distillery." And with that he scooped up one of the cups and drained it at one gulp. I seized the other, shielding it from Barclay's grasp.

"We thought you'd be here at the last minute as usual," observed Scales as the train jerked into motion. "One of these days you'll be caught out and miss the damn thing."

Barclay held out the cup. "More," he beamed and Scales obediently refilled it before producing a third cup from his bag and pouring himself a stiff measure.

The train picked up speed as it clattered across the points and through Vauxhall station. We settled down in the soft seats, glad of the cooling draught now the train was moving.

"I hope you've both brought warm clothes and tights?" Scales grinned. "It might be hot now but I assure you that tonight when we're halfway across the Channel, you'll need the lot."

I nodded and Barclay dragged a crumpled pair of Pretty Pollys out of his trouser pocket.

"Forgot what you said till the last moment, and then had to go round all the girls in the office finding out who was wearing tights and then persuade them to peel them off." He shook out the tights so that the legs fell down and held them up to the window.

"Whose were they then?" I enquired, wondering who would wear tights when the temperature was eighty in the shade.

Barclay leered at us. "I'm having a competition. There's a crate of champagne for either of you if you can tell whose they were after you've had a good sniff."

He proffered them to Tony who shied off violently, jerking his head out of whiff range. "You are disgusting, Barclay, a revolting creature!"

"You'd be a disgusting creature too, Scales, if you were able to recognise the previous owner from one sniff. They came from Miss Millington in Accounts and I'll wager a bluey that when I put these on it'll be the first time in her life that she's had a man inside her tights. Come to think of it though, since your hair fell out, you've always had to go for the older woman. I suppose you have to when you get hard up." He patted Tony's faintly visible scalp affectionately.

"Mature is the word you're seeking, my fat friend, and my hair has not fallen out, merely thinned a little."

Barclay guffawed. "Talking of sniffing tights, have you heard the one about the duchess disappearing and the duke gave the police bloodhound a pair of her tights to get the scent?"

"No, we'll buy it, what happened?"

"Came back with the butler's balls in its mouth!" He collapsed into hysterical laughter at his joke whilst we looked first at him, then each other and shook our heads.

"Pass the scotch, Marcus," Scales said in a weary, resigned voice, "if he's going to be like this for the next four days I'll need to be smashed to stand it."

By the time the train drew into Southampton Station, the Glen Morangie bottle had long passed through Jordan's vale and lay discarded under a seat. We piled out of the carriage cheerfully and advanced on the taxi rank, three large merry men. Me, tall and thinnish, Barclay big and burly, and Scales fifteen stones of athlete with thin blond hair, drooping blonde moustache and hands like a grab dredger. The taxi driver, whose cab squatted at the front of the rank, looked up apprehensively at our approach. Barclay seized him with both hands, gripping his shoulders, looking straight into his face.

"I see before me an honest man – a hackney carriage operator of repute and integrity. Simple but loyal – hardworking and straightforward – a true yeoman of Hampshire." He turned round to address us. The man's colleagues who were now watching with some amusement suddenly found something else to do and huddled behind copies of the Southampton Evening Gazette, leaving the first unfortunate to his fate.

"This gentleman," announced Barclay, effortlessly trundling the astounded cab driver round into prominence, "is going to convey us to Buckler's Hard in his super, streamlined limousine for an extremely reasonable fare at an incredibly rapid rate. Aren't you, my friend?"

The driver, a stolid family man in his fifties, was not too sure what all this was about, but although being totally unable to move, he grasped the essence of the proposition and gathered his wits to state, with a tinge of alarm in his voice, "The fare's thirty quid."

Barclay nodded. "How long does it take, Tony?"

"About thirty minutes."

"Right, my friend, the deal is this: for each minute under thirty we will increase the fare by five quid but for each minute over thirty we reduce it by two. How does that grab you?"

It obviously didn't grab him too hard at all, but the other drivers were joining in now, urging him to take the offer.

"Go on, Stirling, show 'em what you can do."

"No cornering on two wheels now."

"Bet you wish you'd put in bettern' two star petrol?"

"Get the old toeing and heeling in action, Den."

The driver scowled but in the face of such concentrated pressure, grudgingly conceded and nodded his acceptance. We walked to his taxi, a battered Morris Oxford at least twenty-five years old.

Barclay booted the back tyre casually, nearly uprooting the body from the chassis, flakes of rust flickered onto the road.

"Ere, steady on," complained the driver.

"Tyres are a bit soft," observed Bob, "has it passed its MOT?"

"Yes it bleedin' well 'as. It's a good old bus this is, and if it's not good enough for you, then take your business elsewhere."

"I'm sorry, my friend, it's just that as you will have observed, we are a rather heavy consignment of flesh and have an abiding and continuing interest in arriving in one, or rather three pieces at our destination." He patted the driver on the shoulder consolingly, heaved his gear into the boot and climbed into the back seat.

The ancient vehicle moved through the late afternoon traffic on to the Beaulieu Road through the New Forest. It was still very warm and all the car windows were open. I watched the lush, bright green foliage on either side of the road slip by in the soft evening light and marvelled once again how beautiful England was in the summer when the sun shone.

The business traffic thinned out as the other motorists turned off to affect their daily return to the bosoms of their loved ones and the old Morris ploughed forward at a steady fifty miles an hour, crossing the heath land where the wild ponies watched, unconcerned by our progress.

"What's your name, friend?" enquired Barclay of the cab driver in a deceptively mild voice.

"Dennis – sir," the driver replied, adding the 'sir' instinctively.

"Well, Dennis, do you think that you could push the old foot down to the floorboards and get this heap out of third gear?"

"It is down to the floorboards. She won't go any faster. In fact she's never been as fast as this before." Dennis' knuckles shone white as he clutched the steering wheel, his eyes were rigidly fixed on the road ahead and it was patently obvious that he was undertaking the drive of his life. He hissed out the words between teeth clenched

106

with tension – there was no answer to that. Dennis was after the bonus. Barclay might regret his offer.

The brake shoes were forced against the drums with the bare rivets shrieking in protest as they bit into the metal, bringing the Oxford to a shuddering halt in a cloud of dust in the boatyard car park at Buckler's Hard. Barclay consulted his watch meticulously, the driver watched him with anxious eyes. Without saying a word, we got out of the car, unloaded the stuff from the boot and piled it carefully at the side. Barclay pressed the boot lid closed with a faint click and then lifted his eyes to meet those of the driver.

"Dennis, old son..." He paused. "I am pleased to inform you that you have broken the record – twenty-six minutes." He clapped him on the shoulder. "Well done – plus tip, I reckon that's a large red one." He turned to me. "Marcus, give my friend Dennis fifty quid for a first-class service and get his phone number in case we need him to pick us up when we get back." And with that he picked up his bag and strode off in the direction of the marina pontoons where the boats were berthed.

Sod me, I thought, as I fumbled in a pocket for some notes. I shall have to watch that bugger Barclay or he'll have me running every which way but straight if we're not careful.

Tony Scales was looking round with a slight frown on his face as the happy cab driver drove off with my red fifty pounds tucked away safely in his wallet. "Where has Fullerton got to?" he muttered. "He was supposed to be here with all the victuals organised and he said he'd bring a navigator to help out."

I glanced around but there was nobody else in sight. "Perhaps he's on the boat already."

"Yeah maybe, let's go see."

We carried our bags down the ramp on to the floating pontoons and Scales led the way to where his Oyster 53 racing cruiser was moored. Barclay was standing in the cockpit in splendid isolation.

"Where's the gin then? Is this a temperance cruise, Scales? It didn't mention that in the travel brochure. Is it money back if not satisfied then? Because I'm not bloody satisfied yet!"

"Fullerton was supposed to have organised everything by now," groaned Tony. "He said he would be here around two this afternoon to sort out all the stores. I spoke to him last night on the phone, he's at his place in Cowes."

I made a decision. "Come on, Bob, you and I'll go up the shop and bring back what we need for the trip across; we can stock up with the rest in Honfleur when we get there."

"And bring some ice while you're at it!" Scales shouted at our receding backs.

We were just sinking our second large gin and tonics when the puttering of an outboard engine was heard coming up the Beaulieu River through the still of the evening. A battered dory hove into sight containing two figures, one at the engine doing the steering and the other sitting huddled amidships with its back to the direction of travel.

"Yeah, that's Robin at the stern," observed Scales, "the other bloke must be his mate, the navigator."

The dory manoeuvred alongside and the fair-haired rotund figure of Robin Fullerton, cheerful now that he was no longer under Fleur's stern eye, threw a line for securing the boat, shut down the motor and climbed on to the deck.

"Hello, chaps, sorry to keep you waiting, but Peter Purvis, my navigator fellow, went down with a dose of something at lunchtime and I've had hell's own job to find a replacement. However – voila." He indicated the dory.

All this time the dark huddled figure had not moved and was sitting motionless with its back to the assembled company.

"His name is Grime," said Fullerton. "Grime, come and meet the rest of the chaps."

The figure slowly rotated its head like a barn owl on a perch and surveyed our assembled crew with surprisingly clear blue eyes, focused through round black, wire-framed granny glasses.

He was very brown and weather-beaten, face unshaven with a good two day's growth of dark beard. His dark hair was thin and matted, but he was not balding and his gaze was rock steady. His clothes were all nautical. Shabby blue, wet-grip sailing shoes worn on bare feet, faded russet brown sailing trousers, a thick, oily navy-blue crew-necked sweater sagging at the throat, exposing the top button of a dirty woollen vest. His study of his prospective shipmates must have produced a favourable conclusion because he slowly got to his feet, unwinding a wiry frame, and climbed on to the deck.

"How do all – where's the gin?" He nodded a couple of times and then disappeared below. We could hear the clink of bottle on glass, the tinkle of ice cubes and the effervescence of tonic water released from pressure, then nothing – absolute silence.

We waited for him to emerge up the companion way, looking at each other with amused bewilderment, but there was no sign of any further activity. Scales stuck his head down the hatch. Grime was propped in a corner of the saloon with a large gin and tonic in one hand, the other hand gripping the gin bottle possessively by the neck. There was a faint smile of contentment on his lips and his eyes were closed.

"Aren't you supposed to be navigating this worthy craft?" Tony enquired facetiously.

Grime opened his eyes. "Steer 168 from the Nab Tower." The effort of stating this seemed to exhaust him even further and he closed his eyes again, cutting off all further communication with the outside world.

Scales pulled his head from the opening.

"You sure he's all right?" He looked at Fullerton and raised his eyebrows. "He seems a bit odd to say the least."

"My dear fellow, he comes highly recommended – no less a person than a member of the Royal Cowes Yacht Club put me on to him."

"Is that a real name or is he called something else?" Tony asked.

"I think it's a nickname but nobody appears to call him anything else. He's known as Grime on the island, but he's supposed to be a good sailor."

Scales shrugged. "Well, if you say so." He glanced round at the early evening sky. "If we want to hit Honfleur at high tide tomorrow morning we'd better get a move on. You know that it's a tidal port with a locked harbour, they only open the lock half-an-hour either side of high water, so we don't have much of a margin.

'Nightwind' motored slowly down the beautiful winding Beaulieu River to the Solent. Once in open water we cut the motor and set the sails to take us past Cowes and down to Spithead, past Ryde and towards the weed-clad framework of the Nab Light Tower, from which marker we would set course to take us across the channel to the Seine Bay and Le Havre. From thence it was a short distance up the Seine to the old port of Honfleur.

It was hours since I had eaten and the sea air had sharpened my appetite. "Anybody hungry?" I asked, and receiving general grunts of affirmation, I went below, grilled a large pile of bacon sandwiches, brewed a huge pot of coffee and took the lot on deck with a bottle of Armagnac and four glasses. Grime was still slumped in the corner, seemingly fast asleep so I decided not to disturb him although I noticed that the level in the gin bottle was markedly lower.

The sunset was spectacular, the western sky shot pink and purple, the land a dark silhouette, the boat heeling over to a stiff breeze, creaming through the water at nine knots. Good company and mellow spirits – it was marvellous to be alive.

We stretched out on the cockpit seats, taking hourly turns at the helm until by the time the Nab Tower was abeam, the darkness had closed into that peculiar soft twilight of clear English summer nights.

A half moon hung brightly above the jib, plotting a shimmering silver road down which we sailed. The temperature dropped rapidly by thirty degrees or so. Scales stood up and stretched his arms.

"Going to be a clear night, but that means it'll be cold and maybe misty around dawn. We'll split the watches." He looked at me. "You and Bob do ten till two, Robin and I will do two till six and Grime, if he can raise himself out of his bloody lethargy, can do the conning while we're sorting out breakfast." He sank back on to the seat. "It's too nice a night to turn in, let's have another Armagnac – there are a couple more bottles in the booze cupboard."

Fullerton, who was nearest the hatchway, went down to get one. Scales continued, "Keep a sharp eye open, we cross two busy shipping lanes, the down Channel Lane in about two hours' time – and then the up Channel Lane a couple of hours after that. There are always a few rogue ships who don't stick to the fixed seaways, so watch out for them; and finally, the Southampton-Le Havre ferry is likely to come steaming up our arses sometime during the night so watch out behind as well."

Fullerton emerged clutching the Armagnac. "Did you say there were two bottles, Tony?"

"Yes, there should be. I brought three down last weekend and we've only had one so far."

"Well, this is the only one I could see, maybe the other's somewhere else."

Scales shrugged. "We'll find it tomorrow in the daylight."

We changed course at the Nab Tower and trimmed the sails. Tony Scales consulted the compass.

"Steer 168 and hold it tight to that and it will bring us into Le Havre. You don't have to worry over much about the tides because our movement down channel on the ebb will be balanced by the movement up channel on the flood later on."

I took the helm whilst the others stretched out on the cockpit seats passing round the Armagnac until they turned in, leaving Barclay and me on watch. The night stayed clear, the breeze was cold and strong, holding steady from the west, the sea choppy with a large swell and the boat lay over at a steepish angle, the portside gunwhale just taking in the tops of the waves.

I braced myself against the heel of the boat, one foot on the deck and the other on the side of the cockpit, easing the wheel off as the boat rode down the back of the wave and tightening it up as we climbed the crest of the next. The wind continued to hold steady and the boat surged through the water – the head of a phosphorescent arrow pointing straight to the French coast. It was a time for introspection, reflection and relaxation. Eye and hand automatically controlled compass and wheel, the body shifted balance instinctively to counter the pitch and roll of the boat and the mind was left free to soar with the stars.

After a minute or two of soaring, my mind returned fundamentally to earth. The softening up of Charlotte had commenced over a *spaghetti a la vongole*, lubricated with two bottles of Barollo. A gentle suggestion that perhaps saving the good parts of old Sheringford might have more power to its elbow if some of the grot that formed a big chunk of the central area was also improved had not fallen on stony ground. She had considered it thoughtfully and asked me what I meant. A bit tricky that, I hadn't expected to get into detail in the preliminaries but there was the opening – it might never occur again.

"Well, for instance there are some terribly rundown areas at the back of the High Street – maybe someone should design a scheme for something there – to blend in with the existing good buildings in that area." Not very subtle, you'll agree, but there again she had no reason to be suspicious and the Barollo had blurred the lines of my face sufficient to render it unreadable – thank God. She had hummed and hawed a bit though at that, saying she wasn't too sure so I had not pressed the point further. The important thing was that the subject had been raised without arousing suspicion and could now be referred to later.

I nodded contentedly to myself and soared again more freely this time, recalling the softness of Anushka's bottom, half envying Smallwood's basic desires that made life apparently so simple for him. Picking dense beauties had some short-term advantages but when I thought of Charlie, I felt sorry for him. You couldn't beat brains, beauty and a deep, warm nature for a totally stimulating life together.

Around one o'clock we passed through the 'up' channel seaway. A myriad of lights, white, green and red, could be seen all round but all were at a distance and the lane was safely negotiated without changing course.

The watches changed at two. I pulled myself into a sleeping bag and stretched out on one of the saloon benches. Grime was sleeping soundly on the other, making faint bubbling noises. I tucked my hands behind my head and contemplated the deck head above. My last thought before drifting into sound sleep was of Charlie. I did love her.

The noise of feet pounding on the deck above and the sound of an angry voice penetrated gradually into my subconsciousness. I pulled an arm from the sleeping bag and glanced at my watch. It said six-fifteen. It was daylight. There was also another noise that puzzled me momentarily, a deep, thumping vibration, which seemed to pulsate through the whole frame of the craft and I noted with growing alarm that it was increasing. I sat up hastily and looked through the porthole. I was stupefied to see a huge wall of black steel at the top of which were the letters in six foot high white paint 'ALESSANDROU STEPHANOPOULO'.

I shot out of the saloon and up the companionway ladder, followed closely by an equally agitated Fullerton from the fore cabin, Scales from the aft cabin and Barclay from the heads, and was horrified to behold, not a hundred yards away, the bow of the super tanker 'ALESSANDROU STEPHANOPOULO' on an obvious collision course with 'Nightwind of Beaulieu'. I also became aware of the demented figure of Grime in the bow, hanging on to the forestay with fist raised high, screaming at the top of his voice into the wind.

"Give way to sail, you fuckers! Give way to sail!"

Scales seized the untended helm and spun it hard over, turning the boat up into the wind and bringing it to a standstill, sails flapping limply. We all stood with mouths open, aghast as a quarter of a mile of black steel plate eased its two-hundred and fifty-thousand tons down our portside sixty yards away.

"Jesus H Christ!" breathed Barclay as the tanker's wake finished tossing us about and the vessel itself blurred and disappeared as it ploughed unconcernedly on through the morning mist.

Grime came back from the bow with a savage scowl on his face. "Bloody wogs, think they own the bloody sea! I'll have that Master disrated for that. I've got his bloody name and number, don't you worry, sunshine." He tapped Fullerton on the chest with a long filthy forefinger, fingernail blackened and cracked. "Don't forget this is still the English Channel, Mister." And still muttering imprecations, he vanished below without another word to our stunned quartet standing trembling in the cockpit.

Scales gulped. He said he'd stand watch whilst we had a wash and a shave.

Barclay added, "Well, if he's on watch again, he had better have some company. He's a bit of a weird bugger, is he all there?" Nobody answered. Still shaken but now wide awake, I volunteered to make breakfast.

"How about, Bucks Fizz, bacon and eggs, sausages and coffee?"

"Just the ticket." Fullerton rubbed his hands together, glad of the change of subject. "Set us up just right for a nice lunch in a little bistro, sitting in the sun knocking back the old Chassagne Montrachet '76, propped round with some fresh seafood. What time do we make a landfall?"

Scales was still shaking his head, bemused by the closeness of our escape. He glanced at his watch. "In a couple of hours, give or take an hour. We've made good time and are still on course so when the sun burns off the mist, we should see land on the portside." He scratched his chin. "The Global Positioning System went 'unserviceable' last week, otherwise we could check our position."

Breakfast was eaten on deck and a few glasses of Bucks Fizz – that ideal early morning reviver composed of champagne and fresh orange juice mixed half and half – sunk with appreciation. Even Grime emerged to wolf down his egg and bacon, interspersed with liberal gulps of neat champagne from one of the bottles that had somehow found its way permanently into his grasp.

"Bloody great!" he beamed at us all, then folded himself up in one corner of the cockpit, still clutching his bottle.

The horizon extended as the mist thinned, until what appeared to be a solid line could be seen off the starboard side. It was debated whether it was cloud or land, but as landfall was expected off the portside it was dismissed as cloud. Eventually Barclay, who had been observing the horizon for some minutes through the binoculars, said, "You know the French are extremely clever – they've managed to build a village on that cloud, and a lighthouse."

"Here, let's have a look." Scales grabbed the glasses and screwed them to his eyes. "Christ, you're right, they *are* houses!" He checked the compass and the dial indicated 168 against the luminous pin. He glanced at the sun and true to boring old form, there it was, coming up in the east.

"Where the hell are we then?"

Nobody replied.

"Have you got any charts?" I ventured tentatively.

"Yeah, down on the chart table in the saloon, they're in the top drawer."

I drew out the chart that covered both sides of the Channel coast and with a ruler drew a thin pencil line direct from the Nab Tower to the entrance to Le Havre dredged channel. With a protractor I measured the angle between the line and magnetic north and noted it. I then drew another line from the Nab Tower at an angle of 168 degrees to magnetic north and noted where the projection of the line crossed the French coast. Thus satisfied, I went back on deck.

Grime was now lying propped against the rail, his

clear, blue eyes focused on me through his round glasses as I emerged.

"Who said the course was 168 from the Nab?"

"He did," said Scales, indicating Grime.

"How did you work that out?" I looked into Grime's eyes. They gazed back steadily

"I didn't. Feller in a bar in Cowes gave it to me." The eyes drifted away into space, totally unconcerned as to whether it was right or wrong.

"That," I announced, sweeping an arm out towards the land on the starboard side, "is the Cotentin peninsular. We are about fifty miles too far west. The correct course from the Nab is 163 degrees."

"Yeah," muttered Grime, fishing a scruffy piece of paper out from somewhere inside the revolting recesses of his woollen sweater, "could be 163, didn't seem to make much odds, even the Swiss navy would have difficulty missing France from the Isle of Wight." He flashed a mouthful of yellow-stained teeth and sank back against the rail as if exhausted by the effort.

Scales went into his demented sea captain routine, cursing Grime roundly. "Blood and sand, you moron, do you realise that to get to the mouth of the Seine now we'll have to sail right up the coast and we'll miss the morning locking into the basin at Honfleur. The next one isn't until eight this evening."

Grime gazed back blandly. "Yeah." Then an idea seemed to strike him and his eyes lit up. "Then we can all get pissed."

Scales gave in and turning back to the controls, started the engine to give the boat a couple of extra knots and then changed course to the east. All morning we plodded across the Bay of the Seine with an empty horizon all round on the course I had worked out from our previous position.

"The tides could put us out here, I'm not familiar with

tides and currents in this area, so when we get nearer Le Havre, we'd better do a check on our position." Scales frowned at the horizon, which was still completely empty. "We'll ask a fishing boat – we're sure to find one around somewhere."

At two-forty Barclay spotted a Seine netter through the glasses and we changed course towards him. The wind had fallen away considerably, the sails were beginning to flap. The skipper of the Seine netter watched our approach apprehensively, standing at the stern of his ship with one foot on the low gunwale.

'Nightwind of Beaulieu' circled the Frenchman so we could get within easy hailing distance. Barclay, who claimed to speak modest French, stood in the bow.

"Bonjour."

"Bonjour, m'sieur."

"Bonjour. I say old chap, où est Le Havre?"

"Le Havre?" The Frenchman was obviously mystified by the total situation.

"Oui, Le Havre," repeated Bob.

"Mais Le Havre est en France," replied the Frenchman.

"Yes, yes, I know that you great piscatorial cretin, mais Où?... Où?... Où?... Est it là or là?"

The cent dropped and the skipper broke into a broad smile.

"Un moment." He disappeared into the wheelhouse to reappear ten seconds later and stand at the stern of his ship with one arm rigidly pointing at a fixed spot on the horizon.

"Le Havre!" he shouted.

"Hang on un moment," called Barclay whilst Scales opened the throttle to manoeuvre 'Nightwind' round behind the Frenchman's arm. Having got into the direct line, he took a reading from the compass.

"Okay, Bob, chuck the old lad a packet of fags for his assistance."

"Merci, m'sieur!" shouted Bob and as they passed alongside he threw across a full packet of King Edward VII panatelas. The skipper waved his thanks and we all waved back with the exception of Grime, who muttered loudly, "It *is* the bleeding Swiss navy."

After a couple of hours motoring, we spotted the plume of smoke from the tall power station that marked the entrance to the River Seine and two hours later had motored up the cut to Honfleur and were passing through the lock into the inner harbour basin.

The elegant, tall old buildings surrounding the basin on three-and-a-half sides looked warm and mellow in the evening sun. The ancient French port of great historical importance had remained virtually unchanged since the sixteenth century. On two sides the land originally sloped steeply down to the water's edge; the buildings, which presented a five-storey frontage to the harbour, were entered at third floor level from shopping streets behind. The whole effect was one of harmony and tradition.

The basin itself was quite full and Scales manoeuvred 'Nightwind' alongside two other yachts which lay between us and the quayside. Both appeared deserted. After securing the moorings, fore and aft, and cleaning down and tidying up the deck, we all went below for a wash and to change into fresh clothes. All except Grime, that is, who hadn't brought any fresh gear with him.

"What's the plan for tonight?" I asked.

Fullerton, who was still upset at missing his dream lunch but since he was the one who had brought Grime didn't dare say much, stood up, volunteering, "I'll go and book somewhere for the five of us, leave it to me." He set off across the other boats and up the ladder to the quay.

"Bring some fresh lemons and oranges whilst you're at it," called Barclay and Fullerton gave the thumbs-up sign.

"We're in at Le Suquet at eight-thirty," announced Fullerton a short while later, chucking a large bag of fresh citrus fruits onto the bar.

"Just the job." Barclay sliced up a lemon and handed round five large fizzing gin and tonics.

"Right lads, a toast: here's to the Entente Cordiale, Cracking Cuisine, Wonderful Wine and Screw the World!"

"Screw the World," we echoed and sank well earned drinks.

The meal was superb: *moules marinières* with a couple of bottles of Sancerre; fresh lobster grilled in salty butter eaten with newly baked, warm French bread with chilled Chassagne Montrachet, followed by a *Fraise de Bois en sirop* and a selection of French cheeses – Chèvre, Pont L'Eveque, Belle Etoile, Camembert, Brie, St Marcelin and several others of the district.

We sat back, appreciative and replete.

The proprietress was so delighted at having 'Les Anglais' who really enjoyed fine food and cooking that when Cognac was called for, she shyly produced two bottles of old Calvados from the special store in her cellar.

It had not gone without notice, I might add, that the meal had been served by a dark-haired, petite girl of about twenty summers with a perky, coquettish air and well-endowed figure. She had darted several flashing glances at Scales during the course of the evening, which also had not gone unnoticed by him, or unremarked by us.

Grime, in particular, had riveted his eyes on her, only looking away when food or drink dictated a prior call on his basic urges. On the arrival of the Calvados, one bottle was miraculously and instantaneously drawn to Grime's grasp. We invited Madame to join us in a glass and she, embracing the waitress who was now tidying up, asked if her daughter Nicole could join us too.

The daughter drew up a chair between Scales and

Grime, but considerably closer to Scales. By now, in the warmth of the restaurant, the odours emanating from Grime were beginning to overpower even the ripe Camembert.

His basic urge for food and drink, now admirably satisfied, had receded into temporary dormancy and was being slowly replaced by an increasingly randy feeling. This was considerably heightened in intensity by the expanse of bare thigh revealed when Nicole sat down and her short skirt rode up her legs.

Grime tended to respond to his basic urges in a simple, genuine and unaffected way and when his internal stimulating pressures reached a certain level, he reacted. His reactions had the subtle, sensitive and welcome beneficence of a landmine.

Leaning over, he pushed his hand up under the girl's skirt and at the same time whispered in a voice roughened by drink and hoarse with lust, which could be heard around half the town: "How about a fuck then?"

The girl slapped his hand away like lightning. She was quite used to coping with that sort of thing, serving at tables in a fishing port and although she didn't understand Grime's mutilated English, she knew exactly what the leer written across his wrinkled, unshaven brown face meant.

"Non non you notty, notty boy," she scolded in delightfully accented English, then smiling at Scales, she moved in close.

"My fren' ici, 'e will look after me. Yes?" She put her arm through his and clutched it tight to her. He could feel her soft breast pressing into his biceps and glanced across at Madame to see how she was reacting. She was beaming broadly and nodding her head. Madame had seen the large yacht sail in and quickly grasped that here could be some good business from the Anglais if they came to eat a few times – particularly as they had not yet got the bill. She would give it to the tall blond one, he was not likely to argue much, particularly after Nicole had softened him up.

I was thinking along much the same lines as I surveyed the company over the edge of my brandy glass. Perfidious Albion indeed; there was none as devious as the French when it came to true low cunning. Madame had a mind like a cash register. I wondered how far she would let Tony get with Nicole before maternal instinct overcame acumen. If he got too far, I considered, she might put it on the bill.

Food, two bottles Sancerre, three bottles Montrachet, two bottles Calvados, coffee and one screw plus TVA and local tax, that will be six hundred and fifty Euros, m'sieur. Would m'sieur like coffee in ze lounge and ze screw in ze bedroom or vice versa? Is it screws all round or just for ze one? I was just working on the development of this idea when Grime's urge overcame him again. He had slowly realised that perhaps the daughter was beyond his reach now and since then had been fixedly contemplating Madame. She had grown younger and riper as the level of the Calvados dropped in the bottle and rose within Grime; now, with two thirds of the bottle consumed, she seemed positively ravishing in her stained black blouse and skirt with her apron tied round her waist. Her dark but greying hair framing the round, homely face and shrewd bright eyes manifested a picture in Grime's mind like the Mona Lisa. He leaned across the table towards her and, seizing one of her hands between both of his dirt-ingrained, brown mitts with their blackened, cracked fingernails, he looked into her eyes and trumpeted the mating call of the Grimes again: "Well how about you, then?"

Madame tottered and blinked her eyes, obviously flattered by his attention but did not fully comprehend the deep extent of Grime's desires expressed in this call of the wild. The bellowing of the stag in the rut and the throaty howl of the lobo wolf at the moon were but polite introductions to the female compared with the primeval urges behind Grime's cry for a mate.

She patted his cheek with her other hand and chuckled again. There was no kilometrage to be got out of this strange, scruffy Englishman with the filthy vest showing under his dirty clothes. Now if it had been one of the others – the tall, thin, blue-eyed one, or the big burly powerful one or even the rotund, cheerful one, *mon dieu*, who knows, but the scruffy one was out – besides, she could smell something unpleasant and it seemed to emanate from him. She copied her daughter.

"Non, non, mon mari est là." She pointed to the kitchen. "You are naughty boy!" And she withdrew her hand laughing.

"Gordon Bennett," muttered Grime, "every bugger keeps telling me I'm a naughty boy but no bugger gives me a chance to do anything to prove it." The urge was by now overpowering. Lust must be slaked, action was called for. "Right," announced Grime, rising to his feet, "I'm off", and he made for the door with the two-thirds empty bottle of Calvados clutched in his hand.

We watched him go with amusement. However, he hadn't been outside for more than two minutes before the sounds of altercation filtered through the open door into the restaurant and Grime's voice calling, "Bob!" could be distinguished above a torrent of angry French.

Barclay got to his feet and moved to the door.

"Now what?" he demanded and was amazed to see a small, dapper elderly Frenchman smartly dressed in a lightweight grey suit with the red ribbon of the Legion d'Honneur in his buttonhole pinned into a corner outside the restaurant door, with Grime leaning over him shouting into his face from a ranger of six inches.

"Knocky, knocky, screwy, screwy, fucky, fucky..."

Under the blast, the Frenchman recoiled from the hurricane of Calvados fumes and even more noxious products of the digestive processes taking place in Grime's stomach.

"Bob," said Grime, turning his head and giving the Frenchman some relief from instant asphyxiation, "what's the French for 'knocking shop'?" He turned back to the DEF and shouted at him again.

"Où est le knocking shop? For Christ's sake, you French buggers are at it all the time, you must know where the bloody thing is. Where is IT?"

The final blast of fumes was the last straw for the DEF and with a cry of terror, he managed to break free, duck below Grime's restraining arm and bolt down the street like a scalded cat. Grime watched him out of sight without moving and then turned to Bob, a large tear slowly rolling down one cheek.

"There won't be one here, Grime," said Barclay kindly, "It's a quiet little town of conservative, straight-laced citizens. If you've got to slake your lust, you'll have to find some other way."

He re-entered the restaurant and joined us.

"Grime's got the hots," he said. "Told him to go and entertain himself and leave everyone else alone."

Fullerton sighed with relief, "Thank Christ for that, it'll give us some peace and allow the air to freshen a bit. If he gets much stronger, you can stand him on the stern and he'll push the boat back to England." He wrinkled his nose in disgust.

Madame, freed from Grime's amorous attentions and beginning to feel a little fruity herself, now sidled up alongside Fullerton so that he could sense the warmth of her ample buttocks as her bottom, spread wide by the compression of her weight, pressed against him through their thin clothing. Fullerton had mixed feelings about this. He wasn't averse to knocking off Madame, although thousands would have been; his problem was the opprobrium he would suffer from us plus our mutual friends if he did. He knew we'd never let him forget it.

I was just observing the indecision in his face and taking bets with myself over the way Robin would jump or not jump, as the case might be, when suddenly the inside of the restaurant was spectacularly illuminated by an unearthly orange glow.

After the initial moment of stunned inaction whilst the picture imprinted on the retina was analysed by the brain, we all rushed for the door in concert – the light was coming through the windows, its brilliant source was outside the café. We stopped in the doorway aghast; the whole harbour pulsated in a radiant orange light. The effect was Dantesque, totally surreal and was enhanced by the reflected glow from the clouds of white smoke billowing and thickening every second, forming a blanket thirty feet above water level.

A weird, capering figure in the bows of 'Nightwind of Beaulieu' was the centre of this inferno. It was stripping the tape from emergency flares, igniting them and, after a pause, hurling them dementedly into the air screaming "Fly you buggers, fly." The fizzing flares were spiralling through the smoke and landing anywhere at random.

Two had landed on the quayside in the middle of the road, bringing the traffic to a standstill and two more were in the harbour, hurtling round the anchorage like miniature torpedoes still spluttering and emitting both smoke and light.

Grime was about to set off a fifth when Scales, who had moved like lightning as befits an England rugby trialist, reached him and removed it from his grasp. Grime muttered darkly, "Bloody useless, these flares. Absolutely bloody useless, they don't go off properly. What's the point in having parachute flares that don't parachute? You've been done, Tony, robbed that's what you've been, I bet the bloody things are French." He glowered in the direction of the shore and then with little bubbling noises, slid slowly to the deck, completely out to the world.

We looked round in desperation at the spectacular havoc Grime had produced. There was no escaping that 'Nightwind' was the centre and source of this aggro and in due course, account would be called. Scales groaned aloud, "Stone me, there's nothing much we can do now except let the damn things burn themselves out, stupid sod!" He gave the unconscious Grime a savage kick in the ribs. The bubbling noises changed key.

We carted him below, none too gently, and heaved him on to a bunk; nobody could face the thought of undressing him, so making sure he could breathe properly, a couple of blankets were tossed over his recumbent form and he was left to sleep it off with Scales still cursing him roundly.

I picked up the discarded flare from the foredeck and examined it. From the label it was quite clearly made in England and equally clearly intended to be held in the hand. The two flares in the harbour had by now succumbed to the water and only one of those on the quayside remained spluttering sporadically. Smoke still wreathed the street lights, captured by the buildings enclosing the yacht basin but cars had begun to edge their way forward cautiously along the road. Also advancing along the road in a much more determined manner was a bulky civilian clad in a heavy top-coat slung over what were obviously pyjamas. Authority hovered heavily round the set of his shoulders; affronted indignation preceded him like a bow wave. I leant over the companion way. "Tony, dear heart, I think you'll be wanted on deck in thirty seconds."

Authority duly presented itself directly opposite the boat and stood, hands on hips, glaring down. I noted that it took the form of a large, stout, red-faced and possibly seafaring gentleman with a heavy black shingle moustache and haircut to match. He was obviously brassed off to the gunwales at being hauled out of his connubial bed where he was perhaps just putting the finishing touches to fettling up Madame Authority for a climactic conclusion to the evening. I felt for him. It was probably a long, arduous and fraught process these days, more akin to artificial respiration than erotic stimulation, but to a Frenchman, a necessary duty once a fortnight.

He was equally obviously not in a mood to be trifled with, so I decided pacification was the order of the day, or rather the night, not confrontation. 'A soft word turneth away wrath' was the saying that sprang to mind.

"Bonsoir, m'sieur," I ventured. "Comment allez vous?" He brushed aside my opening pleasantries and went straight for the jugular.

"Iz zis your bot?" The tone of voice confirmed the aggressive stance. Clearly much more spadework needed to be put in to the softening up process and equally clearly he had us sussed as Limeys. It could conceivably have been my accent but I put it down to the ensign still fluttering on the jack staff.

My second attempt at appeasement never got beyond "Mon ami lovely evening..." before it too died the death. A flushed, still angry Scales burst up into the cockpit like a bottle genie and eyeing Authority savagely, failed to draw the right conclusions.

"Look, sunshine, clear off and guillotine some garlic or something. Who the hell are you anyway?" Tony Scales was justifiably not in a placatory mood. His progress up the thighs of the promising Nicole had been rudely interrupted, the full implications of Grime's actions in hurling incandescent missiles round a mooring packed with timber, fibreglass and plastic boats had struck well and truly home and now this pompous prat was asking damn fool questions when there was work to be done – like getting the hell out of there fast.

I always wondered what happened when somebody 'drew themselves up' and that night I found out. Authority swelled visibly and, whether or not it was an illusion, I do not know, but it seemed to me that the vertical distance between his heels and his head increased by a good ten centimetres.

"I am ze 'arbour Master and I wan' to know ooze bot zis is."

"Ah!" Scales grasped the implications immediately, there was no question of getting the hell out of there then or in the foreseeable future with this cove standing at the short port in a dudgeon as high as any he had seen for a long time, for he was the Cerberus who guarded the lock gates and without his assent, the lock through which we must pass to escape would remain closed.

I now got a brilliant lesson on how to crawl – it was becoming a very educational evening.

Scales pasted a sickly grin on to his face and, injecting as much bonhomie as he could force into his voice, oiled, "Oh, are you, well how nice to see you. It's very kind of you to come and visit us, but you needn't have bothered and at this late hour as well. A commendable dedication to duty, we were coming to your office tomorrow morning to pay our dues. Still, it is most civil of you, perhaps we could settle with you now?" He dug into his pocket and brandished a sheaf of notes. "...and maybe a little drink to compensate you for your trouble? Marcus!" He motioned to me.

I picked a sick-looking bottle of Calvados out of the scuppers and tentatively held it up for inspection, concealing with my hand the fact that the liquor level was virtually zero.

The Frenchman glared angrily back at us, but by now peace and calm had reoccupied Honfleur Harbour and there was little more that could be achieved at that hour of the night.

"I ask you for ze last time, are you ze owner of zis bot?"

Scales smiled wearily: a persistent piece of Authority we have here, not one to be easily shaken off; your typical little bureaucratic bulldog who was not going to retire until he had got his answer. He acknowledged ownership. The Harbour Master straightened up in triumph.

"You stay 'ere till ze morning." He shook a warning finger. "More will be 'eard about zis. Pah, les Anglais!" And muttering imprecations to the now dark and visible sky, he strode off back along the quay to see if something could be salvaged from his earlier investment. I watched him go sadly, she would be snoring her head off by now and the whole grisly ritual would have to be repeated the following night. Merde!

The morning dawned bright, clear and sunny. I woke early feeling remarkably fit and decided to clean the boat down to remove all traces of Grime's activities and get it shipshape and Bristol fashion ready for the sail back.

Around eight o'clock the others emerged, with the exception of Grime who was both still alive and still asleep. Barclay scanned the area for threat, sniffing the air like a St Bernard, but all was serene. The bright sun set diamonds flashing in the ruffled waters of the basin yet the air was still dawn fresh.

"Just the morning for coffee, Cognac and croissant at that nice little table outside the Café Albatross I spy there." A large finger speared a cheerful-looking café on the other side of the basin where, under an awning, a rather pretty girl was setting out chairs and tables.

"What about Grime?" Fullerton enquired with a noticeable lack of enthusiasm.

"Oh, leave him to sleep it off," Barclay laughed, "he'll emerge sooner or later."

It transpired however that it was to be sooner rather than later. We had just settled down with fresh aromatic coffee, a pile of warm, feather-light croissants and glasses of Hine three-star when the tranquillity of the morning was shattered by the braying of police sirens which preceded two white Renault police cars with blue lights flashing, screaming onto the quayside from opposite sides of the harbour, each supported by a police motor cyclist in full leather gear. They screeched to a halt adjacent to 'Nightwind's' berth, two gendarmes leaped out of each and flanked the ladder down to the boat. At a more leisurely pace, another gendarme, obviously a luminary of some kind from his gold accoutrements, strolled round and stood at the top of the ladder whilst the two motor cyclists wearing helmets and gauntlets brought up the rear.

I felt a spasm of alarm. "Christ, Grime doesn't speak French, you'd better get round there, Bob, and give him some support."

Barclay took a sip of his brandy and chased it with a mouthful of coffee. "When in doubt, Marcus, do nothing. That is the motto of the morning. I reckon ten minutes of conversation with Grime will be about all they can stand." He moved his chair fractionally to obtain an uninterrupted view.

The faint echoes of shouting could be heard across the water, although the words themselves were not distinguishable. After a couple of minutes a tousled head appeared above the cockpit. The head grew shoulders then upward progress ceased. Grime stood blinking at the sunlit gendarmerie through his owlish glasses, propped halfway up the companionway. The senior policeman delivered a tirade of somewhat uncomplimentary French at Grime's head, concluding with what was obviously a series of questions. To Grime, the whole thing was a total mystery, he wasn't even sure

130

where he was, let alone what the cop was asking him. He scratched under his left armpit, his dirty cracked fingernails rasping on the sweat-stained wool of his filthy vest and opened his mouth to say something. Whatever it was going to be was lost to posterity forever because his fermenting gastric juices chose that precise moment to eject a few cubic feet of methane which erupted from his throat in a rumbling, long, deep, echoing belch. The cops recoiled even at that distance.

The luminary put his questions again but this time with a certain tentative note to his voice. Grime looked back blankly, obviously with absolute incomprehension and to reinforce his ignorance, he slowly lifted both arms sideways to shoulder level, elbows bent, palms uppermost; he raised his eyebrows and turned the corners of his mouth down. It was the old crucified look, universal throughout Europe as the bureaucrat's defence against the irate citizen – a situation Grime now neatly reversed.

The two motorcyclists at the rear of the constabulary party started to shuffle backwards in order to put sufficient distance between themselves and the rest of the party to break the connection. Having achieved this, they climbed astride their motorcycles and, without any flash or bravado, quietly puttered away until they were shielded from view by buildings. The luminary, unhinged by Grime's steady, direct and unremitting stare, made another even more half-hearted attempt to elicit the facts about the events of the night before. A note of pleading entered his voice.

Grime remained impassive, unmoving, resolute, unyielding and still totally smashed out of his mind. He was also up-wind of the French fuzz, a fact that was beginning to register with them.

The flanking gendarmes began to sidle towards their vehicles and fiddle with the door handles. The luminary, sensing the dwindling of his support, now had one object

131

only and that was to extract himself from the situation without loss of face. Accordingly he changed his tone to that of an authoritarian and, avoiding Grime's unnerving gaze, administered a massive official judicial bollocking to the airspace six feet above Grime's head. That completed, he turned on his heel and marched to one of the cars. He climbed into the front passenger seat, slammed the door and both cars roared off together along the quay.

We watched them disappear with a sigh of relief; Grime was standing unmoved, staring at the place the aurora had occupied. Fullerton burst out laughing.

"By God, what a weapon – I wonder if he comes under the classification of Biological Warfare – gas and germs division?"

"If so, we'd better keep him under wraps, he's probably banned under Chemical Warfare Treaties. Just imagine having Grime dropped into your water supply." Scales shuddered at the thought, gulping down a large snort of his Cognac.

A leisurely breakfast was completed and we wandered across to the Harbour Master's office to pay the berthing dues. Having been out of sight during the previous encounter, Barclay was nominated to face the Furious Frog.

He settled up with the clerk – the FF was not in the office. In fact, unbeknown to us, FF was still in bed, having overslept after a long, arduous and unsuccessful struggle through the night to resuscitate Madame FF. It had been like giving the kiss of life to a three-day corpse. Only when the first palings of dawn lightened the night sky and with arm aching and lips sore, did he sink into an exhausted sleep, secure in the terrible knowledge that he would have to go through the whole dreadful performance again the next night.

When he finally awoke, he was just ten minutes too

late at the lock gates, a blunder regretted for many moons.

We sprinted back to the boat, removed Grime from where he had fallen asleep on the floor of the cockpit, carried him back to his bunk and, apart from the occasional visit to the heads and a brief sojourn on deck around the happy hour for a couple of gins, that was where he stayed until 'Nightwind' arrived back in the Beaulieu River late in the evening.

Around eight o'clock the next morning he heaved himself up the companionway. Solemnly shaking hands with each of us he proclaimed, "Fuckin' wonderful to have mates like you, lads, I haven't enjoyed myself so much since Granny caught her tits in the mangle."

He climbed into his battered dory and jerked the outboard into life. He then lifted those startling, clear blue eyes and surveyed us slowly.

"Too much excitement isn't good for me, you know." And with this valediction, he twisted the throttle and moved slowly out into the mainstream.

We watched him putter out of sight with mixed feelings. There was something simple about Grime – no airs, no graces, no refinements: sod all asked for, sod all given. Man's basic framework in the raw, the skeleton of us all upon which civilization hangs its deceiving drapes and paints its garish disguises.

Scales summed it up succinctly. "Funny fellow!" He shook his head, "I wonder what he does for a living?"

We were to find out in due course.

Chapter Seven

Barclay's Rolls met us at the boat yard and drove us to Sheringford. He slotted the big car into Sheringford's public car park at two minutes past one by the Town Hall clock.

"Don't want the locals noticing a Rolls on the site – somebody might get to hear that we're interested and jack up the price."

Today the gate in the corrugated iron fence was closed and fastened with a large shiny new padlock. There was also a freshly painted notice warning that trespassers would be prosecuted; obviously, the scrap-stealers had been rumbled. We walked further along the fence until we found a small wicket gate which, with a dint of shouldering, yielded sufficiently to permit access.

"You say that on the town plan this area is zoned 'industrial', but the Council would consider any change of use if it brings employment to the town, Marcus?"

"That's what a guy in the Planning Department said. I also asked him if there had been any other enquiries or planning application made for developing the site. He said that they'd had a few enquiries for warehousing but none of those had expanded as far as a planning application. He was a bit cagey though about current interest."

"Was he now? Well, we mustn't let that worry us unduly." Barclay scanned the site slowly, a smile gradually spreading across his broad face. "I like it, I like very much." He rubbed his hands together vigorously in a familiar gesture that for him usually preceded either a three rosette dinner, a large profit or a good shag. I wondered which he had in mind today – you couldn't always tell with Barclay.

"A nice rectangular site, good location, no sitting tenant and right in the town centre. I reckon we might do something here, have you got the Ordnance map?"

I pulled the Ordnance Sheet 1:1250 for the area from my pocket and unfolded it. We spread it on top of a large rusty tank, flattening the corners down with half bricks.

Barclay took out a red felt-tipped pen. "Now these appear to be the boundaries", and he drew a red line round the area that I had originally paced out until he came to the intrusion where the old chapel stood. He hesitated, pen held over the map.

"That must be in a different ownership – probably the Methodists or Church Commissioners – still it's a wreck, they obviously don't use it and will probably be pleased to sell." He drew the line to include the chapel in the site.

I had wandered away to check on some power lines and when I returned I noticed what he'd done.

"You'll have some problems with that if you intend to demolish it," I interjected with a grin. "I didn't mention it before, because I wanted you to see the site but that crumbling pile of Cotswold crud is none other than a Grade 1 listed building."

"Christ," exclaimed Fullerton, "you can't touch those – they're bloody near sacred!"

"That isn't bloody near sacred, it *is* sacred! That church was built by Wilfrid during the reign of Aethelbald as part of a minor monastic settlement, and although altered frequently since, the rounded arches in the crypt are the finest example of Anglo-Saxon arches on 'barley sugar' twisted columns in the county. It's an architectural treasure."

Barclay frowned, tapping his teeth with his pen. "Are

you serious, Marcus, are you telling me that that pigeon crappery is enshrined in the hearts and minds of the burgesses of England as part of our national heritage? It looks as though one good push would have the lot down."

"Yes well, whoever pushes it could find himself with two years in the nick plus a hefty fine. To touch that building you'll have to get the personal sanction of the Secretary of State for the Environment himself and, being a politician, he won't do anything if he thinks it's going to lose him votes. Preservation is dear to this one's heart and a public enquiry would certainly be called if demolition was proposed." I didn't mention Charlie's reaction if she discovered such a step being contemplated, that would just complicate matters. Anyway, that was my problem.

Barclay twirled his pen in his fingers and used it to tap his teeth again. He was thinking hard and fast.

"It's still a good site with or without that church, but it's a damned sight better with. It would give us direct access on to the High Street, positive identification and a regular plan shape for the building. I think that if we were to pursue a scheme here, we would have to include the church." He folded up the plan. "Let's go and see which god is, or was, worshipped therein and see if Mammon can win one for a change."

We strolled nonchalantly round to the High Street and down the little alleyway that led to the entrance to the church. In front of us there was a faded signboard with peeling gold letters flaking from a cracked and sun-bleached background which proclaimed that the blessings and relics of one St Frideswide had once resided there for worship at Matins, Evensong and Communion, under the auspices of The Church of England. The worshipping had long since been transferred elsewhere, as presumably had the off-cuts of St Frideswide; a start could therefore be made on investigating the possibility of a sale with the said Church. The local bishop would be the man to contact.

That established, we spent the rest of the time until dinner collecting as much local information as we could. Barclay made sketches and notes of the locations and sizes of the existing shops and other traders in the High Street whilst Fullerton and I took photographs of the site and its adjacent buildings from all angles.

Later, having transferred the contents of three fine bottles of Chateau Margaux's excellent vintage claret round a passable dinner, and feeling replete, mellow and in Fullerton's case broke, Barclay made his decision.

"Not a word to anyone else about this site, Marcus. It could be a good deal for us. Your firm, of course, would be the consultant engineers and you'll get an introduction fee for finding it. Also, I think I have just the right anchor tenant in mind – but there's a hell of a lot of 'ifs'. If we can get options to buy, subject to receiving planning permission. If we can get a change of use and then planning permission for the size of scheme I want, and if we can demolish St Frideswide's ancient pile. And finally – if I can find the money for such a large scheme, in such a small place from a helpful pension fund or insurance company. Tomorrow I'll get Lapith, Son and Makern, our surveyors, to contact Joshua Grimshaw and Son or their heirs or executors, and find out if the site is for sale and if I can get an option."

I slowly rolled my brandy glass, savouring the rich, pungent aroma of the fine Cognac as it swirled and evaporated to the warmth of my hand. I watched the pale liquid until it settled down and then took a contemplative sip. I settled back into the deep leather of the lounge's 'club' armchair, drew a deep breath and quietly shat myself – metaphorically.

It would have been bad enough before, but now Barclay wanted to put the bulldozers straight through one of the few architectural gems in the county. Demolishing a derelict site that was contaminated with cyanide I could perhaps justify, but razing a Grade 1 listed building, and a church at that, would stretch Torquemada's persuasive powers to the limit, let alone mine. God knows how I was going to get over that situation! Maybe I could talk Barclay out of it before word of his intentions leaked out. It would be no good afterwards, whatever the Town Planners and Secretary of State for the Environment, or whatever he was called these days, decided. If it was thrown out on its ear, as was most likely, the fact that the idea of demolishing St Frideswide's had even been contemplated would be enough for Charlie to hit the roof. I shuddered at the thought. That brought to the fore the other major problem. What about the cyanide? Barclay was off with the bit between his teeth, full of enthusiasm, without being aware that his potential site might contain tons of deadly poison. I contemplated putting it to the test myself. A mouthful of topsoil and my troubles would be over.

What seems like a brilliant idea at the time in theory often doesn't when one is called to put it into practice.

Okay, from the business and career side, terrific, but a fat lot of good that would do me if Charlie thought that her Save Old Sheringford was being torpedoed smack in the engine room by Barclay's scheme. If she then discovered that the torpedo had been launched by her beloved Moon M...! You see the laxative. And would she? You could bet your life she would. She had already sniffed out that something was in the offing; it would not take a sharp brain like hers very long to put two and two together.

And Barclay wasn't going to be too plussed either, if he found out that his food store could be located on a site containing enough cyanide to wipe out the whole town. I was going to have to do something, and quick.

It was true that with Charlie the subject had been broached (well, maybe wafted around gently would be a more honest description) – an intangible idea which I could have slid out from under had the storm clouds gathered. Now it was not longer intangible, the word would soon get round that development was contemplated, you cannot keep that sort of thing a secret for long – there are too many people who have to be in the know. Lawyers, bankers, estate agents, architects, planners, politicians; all leaking like sieves if it suited their book to do so. And Save Old Sheringford would have its highly attuned ear well to the ground.

I had to sort out the cyanide problem first – if there was a problem, because if there was, that could be the end of any scheme. If there wasn't, then the next step would be to convince Charlie of the merits of Barclay's scheme – a delicate task akin to prodding a mother puff-adder with a short stick.

Well there was no time like the present to make a start.

I told Bob that I would not be coming back to London with them; I wanted to check out a few things and would stay overnight and catch the train back tomorrow.

I left a message for Charlie at the Royal Free saying I was helping Tony clean up the boat and would therefore not be home until the following evening. I booked a room at The Star Inn, dumped my duffle bag from the boat on the bed and next morning set out for the Borough Engineers office.

I had no trouble getting permission to look through the archives provided I didn't leave a shambles. They even had an inventory in their office which showed the location in the archives of their old files on the Joshua Grimshaw & Company's site.

I retraced my steps to the Old Town Hall and up the ladder to the dusty loft space. Fortunately whoever had packed the archives had been logical and after five minutes hunting under 'J', I found the files in a neat bundle under 'G'!

The report on the site condition had been carried out by a reputable Bristol firm of consultants. I sat down on another pile of files underneath a roof light and began to read it carefully. The geology was much as my contact in the Borough Engineer's office had said. There was a main high tension electricity cable passing across one corner but that would not present any difficulties. The rest of the site was pretty clear apart from the old factory drains and sewers, which were now moribund.

I came to the heading 'Pollution', and continued to read slowly. Apparently there was ground that was badly polluted by cyanide but this was only in one area, under a building referred to as the 'Fettling Shed'. I looked on the site plan at the back of the report but no such building was identified. No other mention of it or clue as to its size or location could be found. I read the section again. It stressed that the area was heavily contaminated and words like 'deadly poison', 'fatal to all life' and 'tight security' were heavily underlined. On first sight this would deter anybody from going near the place. I wondered about that.

Replacing all the documents where I had found them, I descended the ladder puzzling over this. The thing to do was to visit the site again and see if there were any clues there. Thinking about it as I went down the narrow lane, I realised that if cyanide was being used, then logically they would put it as far from the river as possible. Squeezing through the wicket gate, I headed for a large portal-framed structure clad in rusty corrugated iron sheets at the side of the site furthest from the River Shering. It was one of the bigger buildings on the site and my heart sank. The rusting rails of a gantry crane protruded from the far end and extended over a small lean-to shed built of brick. The slate roof of the brick building was still intact and there was a stout wire fence topped with barbed wire round the area, which prevented any close inspection.

The big building had nothing on it which gave an indication of its previous use so I wandered along the fence to where the door of the brick building was visible and there, in faded lettering painted in red, above the door, were the words 'Fettling Shed'. I could just make out the word 'Poison' and a crude skull and crossed bones painted on the door.

With a surge of excitement I checked the other buildings in the vicinity but they were not fenced off, nor did they have any indication that lethal substances had lurked within them. Returning to the 'Fettling Shed', I paced out the dimensions of the building and fencing and jotted them down in my notebook. It was a small building and, judging by the extent of the fencing round it – which presumably protected the extent of the cyanide polluted ground – the amount of earth to be removed would be minimal. It was a reasonable assumption that the rest of the site was unaffected because it was accessible to all. I made a note to get some soil tests done just to make sure, but it looked as though the second potentially major problem could be sorted out. There only remained Charlie. Only! It was a very big 'only'.

Her first meeting with the loony left had been this week. I wondered how she had fared – there had been no answer when I rang earlier. I suspected that the meeting had been arranged deliberately to take place whilst I was away sailing, but that was no great deal. I couldn't have cared less about Deirdre Plant; she sounded a real pain, not my type at all. Charlie could handle it, of that I was quite certain and in any case it wouldn't affect me in any way. Would it?

Well, before you answer that, just reflect on this. At any time there is always somebody somewhere over whom you have no control, doing something that is seriously going to interfere with your life, whether you like it or not.

I forgot that!

I was feeling quite chuffed with myself as I returned to the wicket gate but as I rounded a corner I nearly collided with a small boy. He reacted quicker than I did and took off like a bat out of hell, disappearing behind a building before I could say anything.

I heard a crash and then a yelp of pain. Running after him, I discovered him lying on a pile of rusty corrugated iron sheeting, clutching his leg and crying.

"It's me leg," he gasped, "it's been cut!"

Sure enough, I could see blood seeping through his jeans.

"Let's have a look," I said with a reassuring smile. "It can't be too bad."

I rolled up the leg of his jeans and it didn't look too good either. He had suffered a nasty deep cut across the side of the leg and it was bleeding profusely. There were traces of rust round the tear in his trousers and I thought about blood poisoning. The boy was looking at me wide-eyed and fearful, a pleading look in his eye.

I said, "The best thing is to let it bleed for a minute or two to wash out any dirt and then I'll bandage it with my hanky."

If he'd known what state my hankies were normally in this would not have been as reassuring as it sounded; however, the one I was now dragging out of my pocket was reasonably clean. I tied it tightly round his leg and it pressed the two sides of the cut together, staunching the bleeding. The question was: what to do now? The boy obviously should have hospital treatment but I had no means of getting him there.

"Where do you live?" I asked him.

He pointed across the site to a row of terraced houses. "Over there."

He had stopped crying now but clearly he was shocked and the leg was starting to hurt. There was no question of him walking home; it would start the bleeding again. I would have to carry him.

As I bent down to pick him up, a close-up of his acne-speckled forehead jogged my memory. This was the kid I had crossed swords with outside Thos Tugwood's sweet shop a few weeks ago. I think he recognised me at the same time.

I hoisted him on to my back piggy-back style, and set off towards the wicket gate. Just as we passed through the gate, we met the vicar coming the other way.

"Playing hopscotch, are we?" he beamed benignly at us and drifted past. I didn't know what hopscotch was so just gave a weak grin.

We arrived at the kid's house after a five-minute walk, and I rang the bell. The door was opened by a burly man in a none-too-clean collarless shirt who glared at me and said, "Yes!"

He then realised that I was carrying the fruit of his loins on my back and snapped, "What the fucking hell are you doing with our Kevin?"

I lowered the kid to the ground, but before I could explain the kid cried, "It's his fault. He chased me and made me cut my leg! Look!" He dangled the bandaged, blood-soaked, jean-covered limb in front of the man.

"Get inside you!" the man snapped, giving him a cuff round the ear. "I'll deal with you later." He returned to me.

"What are you, a fucking peedi... thingy?" he snarled savagely.

"Paedophile," I said helpfully, and then wished I hadn't.

"Hey, Barry," he called, "come here. We've got a fuckin' perv on our doorstep. He's been chasing our Kev. He admits he's a peedi... thingy!"

Another burly man, in a sleeveless vest containing a large stomach hanging over belted trousers, heaved into sight and glowered at me. "Cut his balls off!" he growled.

This was not going entirely as I had anticipated; in fact it was taking a definite turn for the worse.

"No, you don't understand," I said desperately, and I launched into a description of events.

They looked sceptical. "What were you doing on the site then?" the man called Barry asked.

This was tricky. I couldn't reveal what exactly I was doing because any idea of development was supposed to be confidential at that time.

"I work for the Council," I lied, "I was doing a survey."

Their piggy little eyes narrowed. "The Council, eh? So it's the fuckin' Council's fault our Kev has been hurt then?"

They looked at each other.

"Sue the bastards," said Barry. "And him," he added, pointing a finger the size of a Cumberland sausage at me. "Compensation. That's what we want. Compensation for mental whatsit: assault by a peedi and damages for being hurt." Greed shone in their eyes.

"I am not a paedophile, I was just helping young Kevin home after he had hurt himself," I repeated.

Just then Kevin made a reappearance to add, "And Dad, he was the one who tried to touch me up outside the sweet shop."

I had had enough. "The vicar saw the whole thing," I bluffed, "and he'll back me up, so don't waste your time suing anybody. And if I were you I would get the little bugger down to Accident & Emergency at the hospital sharpish, before he develops gangrene and lockjaw."

144

Whilst they were digesting that hammer blow to their hopes of instant riches, I turned back into the street and tried to be nonchalant as I walked away.

'Yeah, clear off, you perv and keep away from our Kevin or we'll 'ave yer!" was shouted, half-heartedly, at my retreating back.

I thought that there was very little chance of my hanky being returned washed and ironed so I didn't bother to leave my address.

* * *

Five days later, I was seated at the desk in my office facing the most difficult decision of the day. I went to the bookcase and consulted one or two reference books and made a few notes.

The telephone rang as I was weighing up alternatives. I pressed the button on the intercom and picked up the handset.

"Marcus Moon."

"Oh, Marcus, I have a Mr Barclay for you..." The telephonist paused, waiting for me to decide whether or not I was 'in'.

"Put him through, Sandra." I could hear the clicks as the connection was made and then the line cleared.

"Now then you old far..."

"I'll put you through to Mr Barclay," came the very stiff reply from the obviously ruffled Sloane Ranger on the receiving end. I waited, stifling a grin until I heard the booming tones of Bob Barclay.

"Good news and bad news, Moon – which do you want first?"

"Good morning, Bob. Is the good news very good and the bad news only relatively bad or is it the other way round? Before you reply, your lunch could depend on it; I've just decided to take you to lunch at..." I glanced at the notes I had been making "...T'ang for an excellent Chinese."

There was an audible groan. "Alas, Marcus, I cannot. That's part of my news. I'm going down to Sheringford in five minutes with Jane Treadwell to meet the solicitors of The White Horse Property Company who have been revealed as the proud owners of your site."

My heart jumped a little. Jane Treadwell was the lawyer that Barclay always used to negotiate his property deals and draw up contracts. She had risen to partnership in Moresby Treadwell Hart and Pearson of the Temple by sheer ability and at thirty-fiveish, give or take five years, was the best real estate lawyer I had come across. If she was active in the situation, then things were on the move.

"Tell me more. Is that the good news or the bad news?"

Jane Treadwell was not the most scintillating company for any long car journey; she talked non-stop about the law, interspersing the monologue with lawyers' in-house anecdotes of the 'non sequitur habemus in corpore mensam' kind. She also smelt strongly of cats. I often wondered if the secret of her success lay in this. After a while on a hot day in a centrally heated, old-fashioned office, the acrid feline musky odour became oppressive with evolutionary undertones of the jungly kind. This perhaps put the respective parties in the relative situations of lioness and prey – for the prey not the best negotiating position. In the close confines of Barclay's Roller, it would not be a pleasant experience.

He laughed – he knew what I meant.

"You chauvinist sex maniac – women do have uses other than for slaking your lust! We're all equal now in this emancipated, free-living, free-thinking society of ours. No, my lad, that's the good news. Soundings have been made and apparently my overtures to purchase would not be rejected out of hand. The bad news, and

146

this may not be a problem, is that The White Horse Property Company had engaged a professional design team a couple of years ago on a 'no duck, no dinner' fee basis to prepare schemes and plans for the redevelopment of that land. So far, there has not been any duck for those people and likewise no dinner. White Horse do not want to pay fees for schemes that they will no longer be involved with and have, therefore, proposed that we take over their design team, lock, stock and obligations and either pay them off or re-engage them to do our new design on some offset basis."

My heart sank, but before I could comment Barclay continued: "I have insisted, however, that I shall want my own consulting engineer to look after my company's interests and I think that will be accepted."

I slowly let my breath escape through pursed lips. "Thanks, Robert. Who are the others?"

It transpired that the architect was one Fitzallan Percival, with a practice somewhere near Great Portland Street tube station and the quantity surveyor was a Norman Crabbe. Barclay had neither heard of nor met either of them; Crabbe was not known to me but the name Fitzallan Percival rang a bell somewhere in the recesses of my mind. I couldn't immediately recall the circumstances, but I had a feeling that the bell was an alarm bell. However, there was no point in being alarmist without positive reason and the thought was dismissed – it was vague anyway, and probably of no importance.

"...and what are you going to do? Pay them off or take them on?"

"You know me, old son, don't like to waste money, but I'll obviously have to meet them first. Anyhow, I'll let you know how we get on. I'm taking Martin with me and will probably spend two or three days, three if necessary, checking things out."

I replaced the receiver and sat back with a growing

feeling of satisfaction. The plans were working out and once Barclay got his teeth into something, he worried it and chewed it until he got it into the shape he wanted. Barclay never let go of his own volition once his mind was made up. He might be forcibly separated from his objective by external powers, but that was no easy task and those powers knew they had been in a fight at the end. It was a question of placing a succulent enough morsel between Barclay's jaws to trigger the muscular reaction that clenched them and then leaving him to it.

I flicked at the piece of paper on which I had written the names of a couple of restaurants, turning my mind back towards lunch. It would be a shame to waste a lunch after so much careful research and if business was not available, the pleasure must prevail.

I contemplated the rest of the day that lay before me; the evening was going to be a bit of a drag. I had to drive Charlie to an important, for her, meeting of the SOS Committee at Sheringford Town Hall and then attend a reception afterwards given by the mayor to generate more support for the bandwagon. For me that did not hold any promise of lively entertainment. In fact, Mrs Hartley-Worthington was sure to attend and the incident with her dogs was still uncomfortably fresh in my mind.

The afternoon I had free, my diary showed no meetings or appointments and as a celebration of the Sheringford plan, a little truancy would not impinge over heavily on the conscience. The policy being decided, it only remained to fill in the details.

Fact one: I had lined up a good restaurant specialising in Chinese dishes. Fact two: Charlie had the afternoon off as she had taken half a day's holiday to prepare for her SOS meeting that evening. Fact three: I could continue softening her up over the proposed development. Fact four: Chinese food always made me feel randy. Fact five: Chinese food always made her feel randy. What was it Archimedes shouted when he had finished doing whatever it was he was doing in the bath? 'Eureka!' I reached for the telephone and dialled Charlie's number.

Chapter Eight

"Nice to have another pretty girl in the ranks, my dear," whispered Colonel Corrigan-Croot in a boom that set the pigeons fluttering outside the window, attracted a savage glare from Mrs Hartley-Worthington and lip-biting, gritted acceptance from Deirdre as she carefully calculated the range to Corrigan-Croot's private parts. Fortunately for the Colonel, he removed the hand with which he was paternally patting her thigh before his chances of future fatherhood faded from his horoscope for ever.

She forced a weak laugh. "Thank you, sir, nice to join."

God, this was not going to be easy, she reflected angrily, but sacrifices must be made and in truth this committee had been an absolute pushover. Anyone who could afford the time was welcomed by the overloaded members who quite clearly hadn't the slightest idea how to control or direct the juggernaut they had created and seemed purely to respond to the demands of the media. Well, that was going to change for a start, the media were there to be manipulated, not to dictate policy and her first task would be to get a firm grip of the publicity machine.

Her introduction as assistant secretary, franked by Charlotte Prinknash, had resulted in unquestioned acceptance. Straker had been right: dressed for the part she fitted the image. Although she wouldn't accept that, he had insisted that she toned down her dress militancy and appeared as more or less normal – at least until she gained control. So for the meeting, the reception in the Town Hall to follow and dinner after that at Prinknash Keep, she confined herself to a mid-length, brightly coloured Romanian skirt, a hand-knitted waistcoat worn over an open-necked man's white shirt and black, calf-length leather boots. A broad black belt in the same material held in her shirt tightly at the waist, allowing the upper part to billow out, thus permitting Corrigan-Croot a few grunt-provoking glimpses down her cleavage that ensured his support for her nomination.

What a bunch of amateurs! Even the dimmest graduate of the Socialist Organisers Soviet's school could have infiltrated that bunch of chinless wallets with no trouble at all. They were ripe for manipulation. Amongst the lot of them only Charlie had any grasp of organisation and she had admitted that she couldn't spare time from her hospital duties to control this rabble and tackle the increasing workload demanded by the on-rolling bandwagon. It was astonishing that they had got so far. Deirdre ground her teeth bitterly at the thought of all the dedication and effort she had put in to get the West Lambeth Branch of SOS onto the political map without so far causing the merest cartographic flutter, and yet this bunch of wallies who didn't have the slightest idea of political organisation, wholehearted dedication or ability, was making the government tremble. It made you sick when you thought about it. She did, however, grudgingly admit to herself that the one strength they did boast was unity of purpose in a popular cause. And that was what Charlie had cleverly harnessed to advance their case. It was precisely that aspect that Straker had lit upon to promote the Socialist Organisers in the guise of the local Labour Party and parade them as fellow conservationists marching hand-in-hand against the indifferent government of the day. It was clever, thought Deirdre, very clever; but with randy old buggers like

Croot around trying to stick his hand up her skirt, it was going to be very taxing on the patience indeed.

The local Labour Party too had not been significantly different with its soft centrist views and its cosy working men's club atmosphere before she had started on it. Contented to go along with the undemanding New Labour philosophy of 'just follow our lead'; they were unaware that backbone was being inserted, resolutions drafted and candidates for local office filtered out.

Never in its long history had Sheringford returned a Socialist MP or anything approaching it until recently. The local constituency Labour Party had behaved as more of a secret society than an active political force – a small, tightly knit group of amateurs with a siege mentality. The influx of working-class people from the city overspill programmes had been observed but, like the rest of Sheringford, this intrusion had been resented and its political implication not fully appreciated. Wrapped tightly in their homemade red flag, they congratulated themselves in astonished exultation on the Party's election performance but made absolutely no further efforts to expand the potential of their political base. If anything, the election result convinced them that what little they had been doing was totally responsible for the improvement in the Party's affairs and thus they became even more determined to continue as before. The tiny little republic contained within the four walls of Sheringford Labour Club was more conservative than the Tory Party. True, all the standard socialist clichés were expounded, class grudges were nurtured; unequal division of wealth was savaged; injustice, unfairness and discrimination were condemned; but the New Towner's were different – grockles from the east, not 'local' people – so they were not encouraged to join the inner sanctums or to take part in such policy formation as there was.

Deirdre despised their guts, she despised the whole of their setup – bourgeois crap of the worst kind. She despised the individuals who promulgated this sort of thing more than she despised the hated Tories. At least the Tories fought for their class with the kind of ruthless dedication she admired, whatever she thought of their policy. But these people, Socialists wets and whiners with no ambition themselves and a dedicated determination to prevent anybody else from having any, were vile traitors – traitors to their class and traitors to the great proletarian cause. Trotsky would have strung every single one up from the nearest lamppost. Straker had been absolutely accurate in his briefings: the Sheringford Labour Party was soft-centred, complacent and just ripe for takeover. The protective shell that the present incumbents had erected round themselves was too brittle, too inflexible too vulnerable and when the time was right to crack it, it would split asunder and the whole lot drop like a broken egg into a well-placed receptacle beneath.

Deirdre had had no difficulty getting herself accepted as unpaid assistant to the local constituency party secretary; he was an idle sod quite happy to let somebody else do all the work while he attended boozy committee meetings with his mates. But this had given her what she wanted – access to the Branch records and finances, it was now simply a question of methodically gathering up all the reins to become the only one who could drive the coach. Already canvassing amongst the New Towners had indicated that the branch's card carrying membership could easily be doubled with 'brothers' and 'sisters' recruited only from the younger militant end of the spectrum. Shop stewards and union convenors had been encouraged to form works cadres and hold union political committees and meetings with the assistant regional organiser of the Labour Party in the South central – one of Straker's men had guaranteed support at regional level. It was all going quietly and smoothly; even Straker had been moved to acknowledge her efforts with grudging acceptance.

But this reception and dinner were a nuisance; no, more than a nuisance, even a fraction of the cost of this reception alone would have set up the West Lambeth Wimmin's Motorcycle Workshop for five years. Still, if she was forced to attend then she was fully entitled to grab her share. Consequently, the Chairperson of the Local Residents Association found himself smartly shunted sideways by a beefy shoulder to confront a mound of sad-looking cheese rolls the moment the limited supply of smoked salmon sandwiches appeared, whilst Deirdre piled her plate high.

Victualled up, she eased into the group containing, amongst others, Sir Gwaine Lisset, Conservative Member of Parliament for the Sheringford constituency. It was the first time she had seen Lisset in the flesh, although she had seen and studied countless photographs of him in the press and Tory Party propaganda leaflets. She surveyed him as she would a biological specimen; he represented the epitome of all she despised in politics: wealthy landowning family, public school and guards regiment, non-executive directorships of minor City companies, back bencher in the House with a minor role in 'defence', unmarried – a man who had never wanted for anything and never achieved anything. A Tory parasite!

He looked much older than the touched up dodger on his press handouts. The skin on his face was translucent and tinged with yellow, dark lines radiated from the corners of eye and mouth. He carried a patrician nose, from each side of which pale, expressionless, watery eyes focused on infinity. Six inches taller than Deirdre, he gazed loftily past her right ear as Charlie made the introductions, giving a brief resumé of Deirdre's new role in Save Old Sheringford. He couldn't give a toss.

"Really," he drawled, "that sounds frightfully important. Keep up the good work, what", and turning to the man at his side asked off-handily, "What time is this dinner, James?"

James Hartley-Worthington, the brother of the villous vicaress, glanced at his watch. "Eight-thirty – about three hours – leave here at six."

"God!" exclaimed Lissett, refocusing his eyes on the horizon as he girded himself to wait out the time.

Put down, patronised and dismissed in two short sentences. Deirdre seethed. Fucking reactionary ponce! Revenge had now become a personal matter and it would be all the sweeter for that when it came – and she was, if anything, even more determined that it would. The Tory Party machine, very much in evidence today, was prosaic and pathetically stereotyped – just too bloody complacent. That humiliation would be repaid in kind – the pompous prat. Just wait.

She turned away to find some other target on which to vent her engorged spleen and spotted one immediately. Skulking at the back of the room hovered the perfect butt for her venom-tipped arrows. Tall, thin, blue-eyed, light brown hair, handsome in a lugubrious sort of way and wandering about like a little boy lost, there was your stupid, city-suited, chauvinist male. These were the sort of people that she could chew up, swallow and spit out the pips – no problem. Deirdre's fibre diet. She shouldered her way through the throng, unsheathing her claws as she went. Her eyes flashed as, typically at her approach, she saw that his gaze had fixed itself firmly on her tits.

I was also a reluctant attendant at this shindig – this kind of thing with local bigwigs, Chambers of Trade and various other protest and protectionist groups, all with axes to grind and interests to vest was definitely not my scene. Charlie had roped me in to make up the numbers at the dinner up at Prinknash later, otherwise they would have had thirteen at the table. This part of the festivities I could have done without, principally because I was having to devote most of my time to avoiding Minerva Hartley-Worthington who had taken up pole position in the centre of the room and was holding court there. This reduced me to sliding around the walls behind everyone else's back. The number of hands that were clapped on wallets and back pockets – at least I hoped it was back pockets and not backsides – and the wary eyes that followed my passing weren't calculated to add to my confidence or reputation. There was no spiritual compensation either. The watery muck that the local authority's budget had run to wouldn't have stimulated a sick goldfish and the two glasses that I had seized from a passing waitress had been sunk in two gulps during my mural reconnaissance.

My way was blocked by a brown corduroy jacket wrapped round an elderly, pink-faced man with thin grey hair who was scanning the assembled company with shrewd brown eyes. I noted that everything about him seemed brown apart from his face and his socks, which were red above suede shoes. He looked bored stiff so I raised my glass and said, "Not very exciting, is it?"

"Gnat's piss," he sniffed, surveying his own glass with disgust.

"No, I meant the 'do' but I suppose you're right about the booze."

"Bloody Council – tight as a duck's arse!" He turned to face me. "You're nothing to do with it, are you, by any chance?"

"No, are you?"

"Local Planning Officer for my sins – overworked and underpaid, that's me!" he snorted irritably.

I digested this piece of information with sudden interest. This was the guy that would make the vital recommendation to the Planning Committee whether to pass or reject Barclay's scheme. I didn't want to prejudice that by putting a direct question but thought that a little probing might be useful.

"Really?" I murmured. "But there doesn't seem to be much development taking place in Sheringford at the moment. Is there a lot in the pipeline?"

He snorted again. Was there something in the air in the Town Hall? I wondered. An overabundance of grass pollen perhaps? I couldn't see anyone else with streaming eyes and runny noses so maybe it was just him who had the allergy.

"Are you feeling all right?" he enquired solicitously. "You seemed to go glazed over for a minute."

I refocused my attention on him with a start; this could be quite important for my future, I should concentrate on what he had to say.

"Sorry: you were saying?"

"No there bloody isn't a lot of development in the pipeline. Part of my job is to make sure that no damned developer rips off a fortune out of my town and they know this and keep away."

This was not exactly what I had been hoping to hear, it didn't accord with the general view of town planning, but I supposed it explained the red socks and the Hush Puppies.

"Is that what planning is all about then?" I asked curiously.

He gave me a sharp look. "You're not a developer, are you?" he enquired, a look of caution spreading across his face.

"Do I look like one?" I replied with a laugh. "No, I'm a friend of Charlotte Prinknash. Just here for the gnat's piss."

"Oh!" he said, suddenly losing interest, and turned away to talk to an adjacent group.

I reflected thoughtfully about what had been said. That was not going to be particularly good news for Bob Barclay, but there was something else lurking behind that brief conversation. The Planner seemed disappointed that I was not a developer, in spite of his avowed antipathy to that breed.

I shrugged it off and continued my meander round the perimeter of the hall, ending up at the rear of a duo in earnest conversation. The Vice Chairman of the SOS committee, a venerable crust named Lady Bridger, doyenne of the local aristocracy, had her back towards me and was addressing a tall angular fruit propped in a baggy dark blue suit and sporting a huge maroon handkerchief spilling out of his breast pocket. This alone would have been sufficient to identify him as establishment! Apart from rabid homos and retired actors, nobody else would have the effrontery to dress like that, but there were other clues as well: the red-veined, bucolic nose; the blue and white Turnbull and Asser shirt with a soft collar; and the biggest giveaway of all, the tightly knotted regimental tie pinned up so high on his thorax that it bulged a good three inches in front of his waistcoat. I had noted this phenomenon before. With the flowing handkerchief, it was one of the principal establishment badges affected by those such as stockbrokers, merchant bankers, Tory politicians, Guards' officers – in civilian clothes, of course – and, strangely, budding estate agents. Probably a product of the teachings of public schools, I considered, to conceal one's view of one's willy and thus put temptation out of the way. I couldn't for the life of me imagine why embryo estate agents dressed like that, knowing their disgusting predilections, but I supposed anything could have its imitators amongst lower forms of life.

I was just putting this theory to the test and trying to see if one's neck could be extended sufficiently far forward so as to see over an imaginary bulging necktie when my progress was brought to an abrupt and violent halt. A backward moving Lady Bridger had strayed into my path undetected. She had apparently been about to pronounce on something fundamental and had unstabled her equilibrium to create room for suitable emphasising gestures. Her diet of suet pudding and ground glass proved no match for the momentum of my twelve-and-a-half stone and on impact, she was propelled sharply forward and precipitated nose first into the angular cove's chest.

"Whoops, terribly sorry your ladyship!" And I reached out, putting my hands on her shoulders to rock her back on to her heels nearer the vertical. "Entirely my fault, I do apologise."

There was a lot of 'What-ing' and 'Ah-ing' as she fingered her injured proboscis whilst the aristocratic cove brushed ineffectually at the large powdery nebula that now fogged the crest of the Blues and Royals. Both of them fixed me with hooded peevish eyes and for a couple of minutes I was subjected to a display of hand flapping and harrumphing reminiscent of two blackbirds having a bath, which I could only conclude was the way recalcitrant servants were upbraided in the shires. However, notwithstanding that, the result of this forced encounter had left me tentatively established as a third member of the little group and, quite strategically, with my back firmly to Mrs Hartley-Worthington, I decided to stay there in comparative safety and surveyed my new conversational companions with a welcoming warmth. It was not returned.

Lady Bridger was a formidable, formerly handsome woman. Her dark hair shot with silver was immaculately coiffured. Beneath her maquillage, the skin of her cheeks, suspended from the pendulous bags under her eyes like ruched curtains, framed the prominent prow of a classical nose. It was the sort of nose that must have led British cavalry into the charge throughout the ages, from Henry V at Agincourt to James Thomas Brudenell, pointing the Light Brigade into the muzzles of the Russian guns at Balaclava. I examined it with interest. To receive a blow in the chest from that beak must have felt as if the recipient had been rammed by a Saracen galley. Under the circumstances, perhaps the strange noises that the AC was emitting were an attempt to draw air into his compressed chest and not, as I had first concluded, the sort of bollocking normally reserved for boot boys and ostlers who over-ostle. I decided to reserve judgement on this for the moment and returned to my examination of Her Ladyship's map.

Beneath the overhanging cliff of her nose, she had a tight, pursed mouth so that the lower part of her face resembled the rear end of an old, ready-trussed chicken. Behind heavy horn-rimmed glasses, which rested halfway down her nose, two watering eyes like chips of wet flint returned my examination. Supporting her wattles was her badge of office – a double string of pearls pulsating on a heaving bosom of magnificent proportions. Her bare arms were blotchy and mottled and the translucent skin of her blue-veined hands was embellished with several heavy diamond and gold rings.

The 'parson's nose' moved imperceptibly.

"D'y'know how much we raised larst wik, Thompson?" Her eyes had a peculiar glassy glare. She's absolutely smashed, I thought. I'd always believed these country types could take much more than two or three glasses of dry sherry, particularly this weak muck punted about by the Town Council. Normally they can hit the sauce to the tune of three or four stirrup cups, a few gins, a magnum of decent claret and at least a couple of decanters of vintage port without missing a fence.

"Ay arsed you a kestion." Her eyes bored into me and it was with a start that I realised that she wasn't plastered at all, she was addressing me in 'Ryndabite'. I grinned inwardly. 'Ryndabite' was the language of the Counties. It derived its name from 'Roundabout', as in motoring and crossroads. The problem with 'Ryndabite' was that every second word is unintelligible to the uninitiated and therefore, to get the gist of the conversation, one had to listen carefully and construct comprehensible sentences from the one word in every two which was understood. Unfortunately, having cracked the code, the message was still incomprehensible – at least to me. Thompson, whoever he was, may certainly have understood but Thompson was not standing there in the frame. I had to play this on my own.

"No?"

"Two thighs and pines..." There was a minor explosion like gas bursting from volcanic mud. "An' maest of the produce was hame grane." The fumarole fell silent – expectantly. I quit. It was like putting third form French against a Parisian taxi driver.

"My name is Marcus Moon. I'm a friend of the founder. Charlotte Prinknash is my er... um... we're... er... um... she's a friend of mine."

The chips of flint watered further at the impact of this news but did not soften.

"How fraightfully interesting. I say, Rupert, Mr... er... er whatsit is a frien' of Charlotte's, he's not the gardener chappie at all." More splutters.

Rupert's face still wore an expression of distaste as though a portion of distinctly overhung grouse was suspended within each flared nostril and he still scratched ineffectually at his tie.

"Really? Could have sworn – spittin' image an' all that."

Rupert also had an accent that was so far back he had to fetch it from Eaton Square. His brains, I decided, did not constitute over-provision.

"Trying to give her a bit of moral support," I pronounced, slowly articulating each word carefully. It was like addressing two foreigners and unconsciously, I had raised my voice as if confronted with a brace of mentally deficient French peasants.

"Yerse," said Lady Bridger, "quate."

Rupert nodded his head vigorously, his long straight hair flopped over his eyes and he had to flick it back with an affected toss of his head. Somehow or other these remarks seemed to be a communication between the two of them that I was not really of any account, socially, politically or economically and therefore, without another glance in my direction, they resumed their conversation. I stood there silently for a minute or two then, realising I had been frozen out, muttered, "Well, I must circulate now", nodded to both of them and moved on. My passing was unacknowledged.

Resuming my cautious easing round the room, I suddenly beheld cruising purposefully through the crowd towards me, parting the way like a Russian ice-breaker in full sail, a hefty, brightly-coloured woman.

Plan B dictated that at cocktail parties, receptions and frolics of that ilk, if one did not know anybody to talk to then one looked round and selected the woman with the biggest boobs on the basis that whether or not she was an interesting conversationalist, at least you had something to look at. And bra-less as the approaching vessel clearly was made it even more interesting. I preferred the jigglers shading towards the swingers category, whereas looking even larger were a couple of 'heavers' – but beggars can't be choosers.

I smiled. "Hello," I said, "my name's Marcus Moon", and I held out my hand.

"Is it! So what part are you playing in these proceedings?"

I gently massaged my crushed knuckles whilst the brain did a bit of rapid reclassification. This was all a little forthright and assertive for openers. There were some hidden factors here which I could not immediately grasp. I decided therefore to be defensive.

"Are you involved in Save Old Sheringford Society then?"

"I asked you first."

"Well," I replied cautiously, "I suppose the answer is no and yes."

"Don't you know?"

"Er, well, I personally am not but the friend I'm with is."

"I trust you're not one of those people that don't have any convictions at all?"

"Well, the answer to that is really yes and no."

"You don't seem to know very much about yourself."

I tried a weak grin and an even weaker joke. "Yes, I often wonder what became of me." It bounced off without as much as a blink.

"Don't change the subject, I asked you quite clearly what convictions you had, if any – don't you have any opinions or are you totally wet?"

"I suppose it depends on the subject under discussion whether I have strong, medium, weak or any convictions at all about it," I replied evenly.

"You suppose? Don't you know that either?"

I suspected that I was not getting the better of these exchanges acting as a verbal punch ball; every time I swung back into the upright position, before I could respond, another blow knocked me backwards. It was like being bludgeoned steadily with a blunt instrument. A shifting of the initiative was called for and at the same time the penny dropped as to her identity. A tough cookie, as the Americans would say – or trying to give that impression – and the Iron Curtain gear clinched it.

"You must be the Deirdre Plant that's representing views to the left of centre on Charlie's committee," I observed. "What on earth do you lot want to get involved in this for?"

She inclined her head. "It's Ms Deirdre and the people of this country are just as concerned about the preservation of their environment as the privileged classes. More concerned if anything, as they're going to inherit it all before long—"

"If the red revolution comes," I interrupted.

"It's not 'if', Marcus, it's when."

"What, in this country?" I laughed. "The people in this country are too well off and far too sensible to get themselves involved in left-wing revolutionary nonsense," I said, 'it's only those who are too bloody idle to work for their own who preach the sharing of everybody else's. You don't find those left-wingers who do own something distributing their property around, but they're still all in favour of getting their bloodstained, covetous little hands on other people's – what's yours is mine and what's mine's my own – that's the slogan you march under."

Deirdre folded her arms; dealing with this level of argument was Lesson One at the Socialist Workers Party training seminars. It would neither be prudent nor tactically advantageous to reveal the true extent of her commitment and activities at this time just because of the provocation of a simple, politically immature male. She recorded with some satisfaction, however, that her initial judgement had been satisfactorily confirmed. I noticed the tightening of her jaw muscles and the slight narrowing of her eyes, but her reply when it came was relatively disarming.

"You don't want to believe too much about what you

164

read in the papers, Marcus. True socialism is a vibrant, caring political system. We had people like you at Oxford that came from public schools, holding the views you hold, but after learning what satisfaction the true democratic processes gave, they converted to the People's cause of common ownership of property, common labour and all sharing the common product."

"You were up at Oxford were you, what did you read?"

"Sociology and politics," she replied.

"Hmm," I observed, "at least you've received an education that enables you to despise the wealth it precludes you from earning."

She looked at me sharply but the well trained Marcus face remained expressionless. I, on the other hand, read the expressions that flitted across her face perfectly and was entirely satisfied with the outcome. All that guff about socialism being a vibrant, caring political system and all sharing the common product! There was something phoney about this overstuffed aggressive woman – her reason for joining Save Old Sheringford didn't ring true. People like that just didn't do something for nothing. There was always an angle somewhere. And this aggression, the pushy interrogation and over-assertive manner; by the necessity of its adoption, it almost certainly concealed some weakness either conscious or subconscious. It was worth a little probe or two. I studied her carefully. She didn't appear to be butch, but from the gear could conceivably be a woman's libber. I decided to pursue that line.

"It's nice to see so many women on the committee," I ventured. "Gives it a better balance and broadens its horizons."

"Like hell it does!"

I waited with faint astonishment for her to elaborate.

"Ninety percent of people on that committee are there because of who they are and who they know – not for what they can do and that includes all women, bar one perhaps."

"You?"

"No, not me, I wasn't talking about me. Charlotte Prinknash. She's the only one there that has got any idea of conjoint action and getting things done rather than waffling on about what they can do through their connections and influence. The rest of them..." her voice changed to a passable imitation of Lady Bridger "...must have a chat with old Bertie – Lord Fistulas Withers, y'know, his nephew is the Minister for Frigging Affairs. He'll soon put them right about this damn thing, knock some sense into them don'tcher know what – etcetera, etcetera. They don't believe in the hard graft and efficient staff work that is necessary to change this rotten traitorous government."

I raised an eyebrow. "Oh, is that the purpose of Save Old Sheringford? I was obviously under the mistaken impression that its objective was to preserve the old town, not bring down the government."

She realised too late that she had made a slip and hastily covered up with an instant smokescreen of naivety.

"Well, how else should we make an impact?" She intended it to be a purely rhetorical question. She didn't expect any reply of consequence but I was tired of her abrasiveness and decided to do a bit of provoking myself.

"If you believe that the government is wrong and that a particular policy it is pursuing will endanger our national heritage just to obtain some political short-term gain, then you have to show that there is at least one viable alternative. I don't see that bringing down the government provides an alternative to the preservation of fine old buildings – or perhaps that's not what you seek?" I smiled at her in a disarming way.

166

A slight prickle of unease touched Deirdre's confidence. "There's no point going into a confrontation with an intransigent opponent like the Prime Minister if one does not go all out to win and none of us should forget that, whatever the consequences. To have the workers of this country supporting the preservation of the relics of the feudal class system will be a major historical development."

"The end justifies the means, is that what you're saying?"

"Well, yes and no," replied Deirdre, somewhat disconcerted at being forced onto the defensive.

I followed through. "To paraphrase an earlier speaker, you don't seem to know very much about your convictions either", and then, seizing the chance to end with a psychological advantage, I continued: "Well, it's been interesting talking to you, you seem quite bright, au revoir." I gave her a little pat on the bottom before strolling off. Hmm – thin knickers.

Her mouth stayed open, jaw slack, erudite riposte undelivered, ricocheting round her teeth. She momentarily debated whether to release it at my retreating figure or hurl the remains of her Council sherry after me, but that would entail double the humiliation if it was ignored.

"Shit!" she ground out, forcing her teeth together. "Shit! Shit! Shit!"

A few heads turned in her direction as, fists clenched, she glared after me. "Patronising male bastard, ignorant, politically naïve, chauvinist pig!" she muttered savagely. She turned away to leave the room but was stayed by a touch on her shoulder. She turned angrily to find me beside her again.

"Don't forget that all historical developments are basically due to economic phenomena," I said, pointing a finger at her nose. "Isn't that what Marx proclaimed?"

167

And I patted her again and walked away quickly before she could gather herself.

Spitting blood, she started after me, intent on exacting instant retribution but before she had taken two steps, her progress was checked by the groping hand of Corrigan-Croot at her waist. The bulbous Colonel came closer to a posthumous decoration at that moment than at any time during his forty years in the Artillery.

It was not, however, a quick squeeze of firm flesh that he was after for once (not primarily, that is), although the opportunity was taken; he wanted her to meet his companion of the moment, a blue-rinsed veteran of the local council.

The temporary distraction reprieved me from one female fate only to land me right in another. My escape route from the dreadful Deirdre had taken me away from the sheltering walls and put me squarely into the track of the powerful figure of Mrs Hartley-Worthington trundling along with the Reverend Percy tucked in her slipstream. Coincidentally, Charlie also hove into sight at the same time, having spotted our possible encounter from afar.

Ultimately, this worked to my disadvantage; I was just about to slide past the female juggernaut unremarked when Charlie's arrival halted both of us. The Rev. Percy was brought to a standstill a micro-second later by collision with his wife's hindquarters.

"Have you met Marcus, Mrs Hartley-Worthington, he was at the dinner at Prinknash last month?" Charlie eased me round to confront Mrs H-W's broadside, which allowed her to inspect me before replying.

I composed my face into what I hoped was an intelligent professional look. Thank God I was in my best suit. The blue shirt and plain tie contrasted with my sweatshirt and jeans on our last encounter in Sheringford, so although my face was vaguely familiar to her, she assumed it was from the dinner. Her judgement of me was not unfavourable, a bit too 'city' for her taste and therefore soft with a poor seat, but apart from that, my rather lugubrious face reminded her of a spirited hunter she once owned and so she warmed towards me a little.

"How do y'do, young man?" She brushed her moustache with the back of her hand. "Sportin' evenin', what? Damn civil of the Mayor to invite us here." A thought struck her. "Have you met my husband?"

She turned and, fumbling within the folds of her heavy tweed skirt for a moment, suddenly whipped out the Reverend P in front of my eyes. I was quite impressed with this feat of prestidigitation and looked benignly on the slightly bewildered features of the little rector, blinking at his instant transportation into the limelight from the quiet obscurity of the mothball-scented recesses of his wife's clothing.

"Percy, this is Mr Mouton, Charlotte's friend."

"Moon – the name is Marcus Moon," I murmured as I shook hands with the vicar. "Yes, we have met, we sat opposite each other at the Prinknash dinner."

The little man smiled as recognition dawned. "Oh yes, you were the gentleman who was so interested in my theory that the purpose of Stonehenge was to act as a control tower for extra-terrestrial landing craft. I remember you were able to give me some useful mathematical data regarding the statistical probability of the astronomically related alignments being coincidental." He turned to his wife. "Do you know, Minerva, that the time required for a complete oscillation of the angle of swing is 18.61 years – which is of enormous significance, Mr Mouton tells me."

Mrs H-W snorted with irritation and forthwith put a stop to that sort of nonsense with a swift verbal cut across the flanks.

169

"Not now, Percy." She addressed me. "Sherry makes him talkative and I haven't been able to break him of the habit – yet," she added ominously.

I was a bit nonplussed by the vicar's revelation of our conversation in front of Charlie and gave a nervous smile. Charlie shot me a quick frown of suspicion in return, causing me to shift uneasily from one foot to the other, not sure whether to bask modestly in the warm light of the Rev. P's eulogy or prepare a case for the defence on a charge of 'taking the piss'.

I was saved from the responsibility of making a decision by the explosive arrival of a florid-faced, elderly gent with white hair cut short into a bristle crop, neatly clipped white moustache, bulging blue eyes and a veined nose like a large red gooseberry. The knotted brow and fist-shaped head immediately categorized him in my view.

We all have a system of classifying people on first acquaintance. With some folk it is just a gut feeling, with others there is some sort of instant magnetism which either attracts or repels. I tended to go on facial appearance and demeanour, not, I acknowledge, the most reliable parameters. Based on those, I slot people into one of four categories: Hostiles, Fellow Feelings, Nothing-in-Commons (known as NICs), and Wankers, referred to as Merchant Bankers. It wasn't an infallible system but it had the flexibility to allow changes as the acquaintanceship grew, and generally it worked for me.

Bullocking into our midst we had a classic 'Hostile', an 'aggrohonky' in current parlance. In fact he could have a double blue in hostility and merchant banking, as evinced by the booming voice accompanied by the shower of spittle that enveloped the whole group as he addressed Mrs H-W directly, ignoring us completely and slashing straight through the conversation.

"I've been meanin' to have a word with you, Minerva – about your damn dogs!"

Nice opening, I thought, all the sensitivity of an armoured column.

"Menace to the neighbourhood," he continued, "blasted bad-tempered beasts should be put down!"

Get to the point, man, I thought, don't beat about the bush, say what you mean. I glanced at Mrs Hartley-Worthington interestedly, wondering how she would respond to this unexpected attack, and anticipating a blistering reply. Mrs H-W, however, knew her position in the county pecking order, and when challenged by the Master of Foxhounds, one responded respectfully. With no more than a tightening of the jaw muscles she enquired, "What is the problem now, Major?"

"Chasing my servants on their bicycles – that's the confounded problem – put the jolly old wind right up my housekeeper, I can tell you – left her in a right tizz wazz – blasted animals!"

He gave a snort of irritation and brushed one hand across his moustache whilst Mrs H-W groped for a reply.

I interrupted, addressing Mrs H-W.

"Do you know how to prevent that, Mrs Hartley-Worthington?" I waited for the straight line; it came.

"No, Mr Mouton. How?"

"Lock their bikes up!" I guffawed loudly – and solitarily.

Two pairs of glassy eyes fixed themselves on my face, united against a common idiot. Charlie moved in close and hacked my ankle sharply. The Major's complexion crimsoned even further and his eyes protruded from this florid field like twin blisters on a sore heel.

Mrs H-W frowned thoughtfully. "Haven't we met somewhere else?" she asked. "I'm sure that I've come across you recently."

Charlie seized me by the arm and pulled me away, making some excuse to leave the group.

"You twit," she hissed, "another minute and she'd have connected you with her dogs!"

"She thinks I was connected with them before, that's the problem," I muttered, a little abashed at the close shave.

Charlie ushered me into a quiet corner, seizing the chance, now that I was on the defensive, of laying down the rules of conduct for future behaviour at the forthcoming dinner that evening. With an admonitory finger emphasising her points, she set out the parameters within which my conduct was to remain, otherwise I would find a high treble well within my future musical range.

I listened impassively, knowing from experience that that was the thing to do both for expediency and for future relationships. It was not easy to keep one's face immobile when one was dying to laugh, but it was the only way. If I let a trace of a quiver into my rigidly set jaw and eye muscles, I would be lost and definitely in for a Mark Two bollocking.

"For heaven's sake, say something, Marcus, it's like talking to a damned wooden Indian when you adopt your 'trying to be good' pose!" She scowled at me ferociously. "I hope you've taken note of what I've said." Her face relaxed into a grin. "Anyway, I've seated you next to Deirdre Plant and she'll keep you in order one way or the other – or break your arm in the process."

"Oh, thanks a bunch, so she's coming to the dinner, is she?" Now that could be interesting; I didn't mention that we had met already, otherwise another lecture would have followed.

Charlie continued, "We're giving her a lift to the Keep, she's staying the night." And, misinterpreting my heightened look of interest, she added, "In the west wing, well away from you so behave yourself or...' She ran her hand across her throat significantly.

More people were drifting away by now and Charlie judged that it would be acceptable if she also departed, so after making farewells with me in tow, we left to find Deirdre and pick up Charlie's car.

She was standing outside the Ladies', angry at having to queue.

"You!" she burst out, hackles flaring up again at the sight of me with Charlie. Her look flashed between us as she made the connection and the consequent conclusion that the public flaying alive of Charlie's boyfriend outside the Ladies' lavatory would not be to her advantage. Besides, she wanted to 'go' badly and the sound of an emptying water cistern denoted that it was to be her turn next.

I nodded. "Hiya, Deirdre – is it a big job or a little job, we don't want to be hanging about here all night?"

The queue chuckled as Deirdre flushed crimson, but she was saved from further embarrassment by the opening of the door and the exiting of the previous occupant, sheepishly surprised by the audience outside.

I added for Charlie's benefit, "We met earlier when Mizz Plant, or whatever she calls herself, was explaining to me how you were now the vanguard for the forthcoming red revolution to overthrow the democratically elected government of this country."

Charlie gave me a quizzical look, she wasn't sure whether I was teasing her or not. Neither was I, for that matter.

There was a jangling and clanking from inside the loo, it told us two things. The first was that Deirdre's had been a little job, the second that the cistern was a slow filler. Now there is one fact everybody knows about slow-filling cisterns – you just have to wait until they've filled. No amount of jerking and swearing will make them eject their contents until they are ready – in fact, if you try earlier the small spillage of water lost each time just means you have to wait even longer. You know it, I know it, we all know it – all, that is, except Ms Deirdre. She believed that determination and aggression would overcome reactionary lavatories so it was some time later before she eventually emerged, red-faced and furious to a few sarcastic cheers.

"I should give it a couple of minutes if I were you," I commented to the next one in the queue as Deirdre stalked past, before taking Charlie's arm and heading for the car. "C'mon, let's hit the road and get outside one of your father's decent drinks, I need one after that Council gnat's piss in there."

I was relatively quiet on the drive to the Keep, sitting chivalrously in the back of the car and allowing Deirdre to occupy the front passenger seat. Charlie, however, became conscious of unexpected tensions emanating from her committee colleague. Deirdre remained tight-lipped and monosyllabic for the whole journey, making little or no attempt to contribute to the conversation that Charlie tried to engender about the committee activities and the recent reception.

On arrival at Prinknash, Deirdre went straight to her room after acknowledging David and Angela Prinknash's welcome in the most cursory manner.

"Commissar Plant seems a bit put out," I observed cheerily after kissing Angela Prinknash heartily on the cheek. "Perhaps, it's the surroundings – she doesn't like slumming it in accommodation inferior to that occupied by area offices of the Trades Union Congress."

Whilst the women chatted, David took me by the elbow and eased me skilfully into the library.

"Scotch do for you, Marcus? All that cheap pale sherry goes straight through you – comes out as it goes in, pure acid in the gourmet's guts. I think they only serve it to disguise the taste of the disgusting food that usually follows it. But take your fine malt whisky, now that is a gentle drink for gentlemen; caresses the oesophagus and soothes the stomach, preparing it to receive the most delicate flavours that the culinary arts can prepare. Tonight, my boy, it is to be breast of wild duck *en croûte* with spiced red currant sauce and minced pine kernel stuffing." He kissed the tips of the fingers of his right hand and flicked them outwards, French-style. "Supreme, fine food for a fine family."

The smooth spirit, a product of the finest malted barley, heated over the peat coals, matured in the oak, inhaled in the glass, drawn in by the lips and exercised round the tongue – now stuck right in the throat!

To the casual observer here was merely a distinguished, amiable gentleman stimulating the gastric juices of both himself and his younger companion. A true *bon viveur* expressing anticipation at the outcome of careful planning and staff work to produce a quality product to the right people at the right time. To me, after the last observation, it was now a veritable minefield, a softening up and hemming in process calculated to lower my defences and cut off retreat when the inevitable follow-up topic of conversation was broached as it was surely going to be. The decanter was proffered again.

"Er... um... well just a small one sir please, it's getting near dinner time and I'm sure you'll want time to dress and receive the other guests."

"Nonsense, my boy, if we members of the family can't have a little chat together, what's the world coming to? Oh I forget, I'm sorry, Marcus, I always look upon you as a member of the family..."

He propped a foot on the fender and leant one elbow comfortably on the mantle shelf expansively. Here we go again... continue the line, produce an heir, do the honourable thing, two hearts beating as one, united souls intertwined striding down the long pathway of life, etcetera and etcetera. This was an increasingly familiar theme, the pressure was put on with great delicacy and with no hint of offence. The problem was that although my intentions were, I supposed, ultimately honourable, I, and Charlie for that matter, preferred to come to our own conclusions when we decided that the time was right. I felt very embarrassed when fed little fatherly fireside chats like the one coming over the horizon any minute now.

I was reprieved by a discreet cough at the door. Simmons, the butler, materialised soundlessly to announce that Lord Firrs had arrived.

"Blast," muttered David Prinknash, "he's early. I'm sorry, Marcus, I'll have to leave you and see to old Firrs, please excuse me." And with that he followed Simmons back into the hall, leaving a somewhat relieved me thanking heaven for my escape.

I gulped down the Scotch neat, choking over the reaction, replaced the glass on the table and legged it smartly out the other door. Avoiding the hall, I sprinted up the back stairs to my room to get bathed and changed. That was a close call, a bit too close, I was going to have to concede sooner or later but thank God I had escaped to live another day.

As I lay up to my neck in steaming hot water, I reflected on this. It's working, all this pressure is gradually having an effect. I'm now feeling guilty each time I meet the Prinknash family, I'm beginning to feel that it would be a relief to concede and settle for married life. I heaved a heavy sigh. My mother was on to me about it; she just wanted to brag to her cronies in the Townswoman's Guild that her son had married a baronet's daughter – it wasn't the same just living 'in sin' with one to the straight-laced ladies of the City of York.

My old man did keep muttering about 'gilt-edged investment for the future, my boy' but being a bank manager, he would.

The only one who wasn't putting pressure on me was Charlie; she was a great girl she was, and understood these things. She appreciated that a man likes his independence, doesn't want to be tied down at this stage of his life, needs air to breathe and space to grow. The body and soul must be unfettered so they could expand to meet any challenge and soar into the stratosphere, developing their maximum potential without restraint. True, trundling down to The Frog every Saturday was not exactly in the stratospheric bracket, but then one must also have relaxation and recreation to allow the cerebral information transfers to take place. I was beginning to enjoy developing this theme and had almost succeeded in convincing myself when the earlier message of thanks arrived on God's desk. It was a mistake, wasn't it? Of course it was, marriage is one of His institutions, isn't it? So what did he do – he returned the thanks with pins sticking out all over.

I suddenly sat upright, causing a wave of warm water to roll down the bath and slop over the end onto the carpet. Why the hell wasn't she putting pressure on? What was she up to? Perhaps she didn't want to marry me? I sat there momentarily paralysed, appalled by my own hypothesis. My mind began to search through past conversations, looking for clues. There was nothing I could pick out specifically, but I was still left with an awful nagging doubt. Our lovemaking had been as ecstatic and affectionate as ever I imagined it could be between two people; we touched each other and smiled in everyday life, and I certainly felt that inner sense of unity and concord that must be love. I ached for her when we were apart and blossomed in her company. I feared for her in her absences and relaxed protectively around her when she was with me – and I had always assumed she felt the same way, so why hadn't she pressured me? Why? Why? Why? Maybe she didn't want that. Maybe I was just a convenient interlude – a bit of amusement to fill in the spare time of a career girl.

I'll strangle that cunning old bugger David Prinknash, I'll bloody swing for him for putting these doubts into my mind. The pins by now had found their way well into my conscience as well, and gentle jabs were being administered.

Maybe it was my fault; perhaps I could be more thoughtful in my treatment of her. Maybe I did spend too much time with the boys at the pub on Saturdays and should not leave discarded pants pulsating on the bathroom radiator. I knew she disliked my spoon beating the brains out of boiled eggs, preferring her own quick surgical slice, and we argued frequently over the Pepsodent – I was a methodical roller-upper and she an undisciplined squeezer. But these hardly seemed fundamental to the fracturing asunder of two hearts intertwined, it had to be something much deeper and more basic than that.

Sod it, it had left me all of aflutter – and I bet that business with Lord Firrs was a fix, a put-up job sorted out with Simmons beforehand. The confounded aristocracy had never arrived early for anything after the first handout of land but they were there at the front of the queue for that all right. I got dried and dressed and, still agitated but composing my face to the Marcus impassive look, drifted with a nonchalance I didn't feel down to the pre-dinner drinks.

At the pre-dinner cocktails, I was once again left to my own devices whilst Charlie and the Prinknashs introduced the guests and established them within the gathering. Standing strategically close to the Glen Morangie, I was able to study the arrivals at leisure. Charlie had given me a copy of the guest list to commit to memory so I tried to work out who was who from amongst the faces that I didn't recognise.

Apart from the Prinknash family and the redoubtable Mizz Deirdre, dressed in the same outfit she had worn at the reception that afternoon with the exception of a different, and I trusted clean, blue man's shirt, the other people I recognised were the Hartley-Worthingtons, cruising about like swan and cygnet; Lady Bridger; the Lord Firrs and the Member of Parliament for Sheringford, Sir Gwaine Lissett. The latter looked haggard and drawn, he looked old, but clearly this didn't prevent him exhibiting the normal politician's tendency to enjoy the sound of his own voice. He was at that moment holding forth to a group of three well-dressed, sharp-eyed, tough-jawed men, none of whom I recognised. From a glance at the list and a process of elimination, I identified them as another MP, Harold Baldry; a local industrialist from Bristol, Adam Driver; and the Chairman of the County Council, Geoffrey Marsh. Who was which was difficult to ascertain but I took the two politicians to be the ones who were desperately trying to get a word in edgeways through Lissett's monologue and Driver to be the one listening and watching.

The purpose of the dinner, as Charlie had outlined, was to persuade the three heavies having their ears bent by Lissett to give both financial and political backing to the Society. Although, of course, this would not be specifically mentioned, that was the intention. Lissett was laying some groundwork but it seemed to me that having talked himself in, if he didn't wrap up for a moment, he would talk himself right out again.

I poured myself another stiff malt whilst I decided which bunch to join. I didn't really fancy any of them so in the end, after topping up my glass again, I wandered over to Angela Prinknash, a very well preserved, fine-looking woman in her early fifties. If the 'look at the mother to see how the daughter will turn out' theory was right, Charlie had a good prognosis.

"Oh hello, Marcus, have you met everyone?" She glanced around, like the good hostess she was, to see if there was anyone wandering like a lost soul in purgatory. Her eyes lit on Ms D Plant, who happened to be looking somewhat spare at the moment. "Why don't you go and talk to Deirdre, I think she feels a little out of place here. See if you can help her relax a little."

It wasn't exactly what I had in mind, nor did I think that I would be the solution to Deirdre's problem, but I supposed I had better help out. I took another gulp of Scotch to brace myself for another three rounds of all-in verbals; the best of three falls or a submission, and eased into first gear to move off.

Deirdre was feeling violently anti-social, savagely tense and in some discomfort; her period had (apparently) now started unexpectedly and she had just learned from Charlie that she was to be seated between those she held responsible for this condition – me and Corrigan-Croot. Her boilers were being worked up to a full head of steam, preparatory to sorting both of us out. In the meantime, she desperately needed a bone to gnaw on. Any helpless morsel would do.

At that moment, a quirk of the ventilation wafted Mrs Hartley-Worthington's skirt aside just as she sailed off in a direction away from Deirdre. The Reverend Percy, caught unawares by this sudden upping of the spousal anchor, hesitated momentarily but that split second was enough to separate him from the protective field circumscribing his wife.

Deirdre spotted him instantly. His clerical collar and receding chin identified him immediately as a part of the establishment and vulnerable. She had him like a peregrine taking its prey, picking him out of space with a lightning movement and pinning him into a corner before he could utter a squawk. He fluttered and flapped

180

helplessly, covered in confusion and conscious of his defencelessness out of range of covering fire from his escorting battle cruiser.

"Good evening, vicar." Deirdre's voice was deep, powerful and authoritative. His eyes widened with apprehension, he knew all about large dominant women and the fact that this one was young and clean-shaven diminished his qualms not one whit. She sensed his trepidation as a cat senses fear in the mouse and to heighten her pleasure, gave him a nice friendly smile.

"The Reverend Hartley-Worthington, isn't it?" she asked.

"Yes, yes indeed," he stammered and, emboldened by the smile, tried an ecclesiastical funny. "Yes, I know who I am young lady, but who are you?"

Her smile broadened, perhaps this was going to be fun after all, the little twerp had spirit.

"Ms Deirdre, I'm a friend of Charlie's – Charlotte's," she amended, seeing his brow begin to furrow.

"Oh Charlotte's friend, yes indeed, most interesting." He pressed the tips of his fingers together. "Mirzz Deirdre?" he questioned. "Are you a foreign lady? Hungarian perhaps?" That might account for her peculiar method of dress, he told himself. Foreign, yes, that must be it. His head nodded up and down unsuspectingly.

Deirdre winced as a sharp stabbing period pain shot through her lower abdomen, driving the last shreds of compassion from her soul. The time had come to put the boot in before the doddery old sod nodded off. She glared into his filmy eyes as she picked her words with deliberate care to expose his utter inadequacy, strip him of his pretensions and leave him naked and without dignity – yet another defeated male chauvinist.

"It's Mizz, and I am not foreign. I am a committed socialist, pledged to change the traditional notions of a deity based on illogical patriarchal assumptions. Pledged to sweep away the superstitious nonsense with which charlatans like you enslave the minds and bodies of men – people," she corrected quickly, "and replace it with a thinking, caring society in which mystical mumbo jumbo has no place."

His watery eyes blinked as her attack sank in. The words themselves didn't have quite the shocking effect on the Rev. Percy that she anticipated. Mystical mumbo jumbo, as she put it, didn't play much part in his ecclesiastical practices. Religion as dispensed at St Stephen 'neath the Willows, bore more of a resemblance to a travel agency than a spiritual experience. Baptism – welcome to a new customer; confirmation – sign the banking form and pay deposit; marriage – Club Mediterranean for life; death – emigrated to Denmark. Having once spent a holiday in Denmark, he viewed heaven as a sort of permanent extension of Danish domesticity – cows with friendly faces and no hills to climb. Only counselling and confession gave him problems. Sexual matters, of which there seemed to be an ever increasing abundance in his parish, he referred to his eager curate at the first hint of bodily functions. The lank, deep young man, always fumbling under his cassock, gladly took all that Percy passed on. For the rest it was Percy's sadness that although genuine compassion swelled within his breast, he was totally unable to communicate it. Over the years, the parishioners of St Stephen's had learned to solve their own problems and these days his only extra canonical contacts seemed to consist of directing tearful, bulging girls in the direction of the curate. His operation was, in ecclesiastical terms, way down the candle.

It was the manner of Deirdre's delivery that got through to him; it was far too close to home to be comfortable. His life was directed by women and all of them authoritarian. Minerva H-W ruled the rectory with a rod of iron; finance, furniture and food she dictated.

The Mothers' Union ran the parish with an equally totalitarian direction which brooked no argument or deviation, required a great deal of full-bosomed singing and a ponderous talent for arranging chrysanthemums, which he hated. Praying was not encouraged, being regarded as Catholic and subversive. No bells or smells were permitted in Percy's services. There only remained for him the private comfort of personal prayer all by himself in the empty, echoing church. It was only in those moments that he felt he established a warm communion with the Almighty. For it, he suffered all the terrors of discovery of an adolescent masturbator. The thought that Minerva or some other dragon of the Mothers' Union might catch him on his knees in front of the altar made him sweat.

He was beginning to sweat now under the relentless scrutiny of this assertive creature. Aggression exuded from her like garlic. He looked round wildly in the hope of finding some relief. Deirdre drew back her metaphorical boot again, shifting her aim from the ribs to the balls.

"Do you realise, Rector..." She paused. "You are Church of England, I take it?"

He jumped visibly, her words had got through there. He was shocked that she should even consider he would represent anybody other than an English god.

"Oh yes. Indeed I am, my word, yes."

Deirdre nodded. "I thought so, you can always tell." She bared her large teeth in a humourless grin.

"Do you realise that because the Judeo-Christian view of history is linear, the mythological theme of the four ages of the world has influenced concepts towards a superior state of existence? And are you also aware that these views are reflected by Karl Marx?"

She got right through there as well; at the mention of Karl Marx Percy twitched violently as though Lucifer himself had suddenly materialised in all his ghastly form. Percy pressed himself against the wall and desperately looked for an escape route whereby his ears could be relieved of such assaults from this terrifying Amazon which he foresaw as growing even more blasphemous and shocking.

"Well, are you?" She tightened the screw.

Percy shook his head, "No, but thank you, young lady I... er... I really must be..."

She caught and held his gaze with her own like a stoat with a rabbit and ignoring his feeble protestations, continued almost conversationally.

"Marx taught a theory of history in which there is a staged progression, a final battle and a final classless society in which the 'evils' of private property will be eliminated and man will live in peace. Marx stressed the relationship of religion to social conflict rather than to integration. Religion, he maintained, is administered by those in high places purely to preserve and maintain their own power." A harsher tone entered her voice. "When he said religion is the opiate of the people he meant, in addition to the deadening, crushing, crippling effect it had on the masses, that its priests and practitioners – parasites like you – were no more than the drug peddlers of capitalist cabals, pushers of poison to numb the will and paralyse the spirit of the poor and the oppressed."

Percy listened, mesmerised; it came as a complete surprise to him. He had never even contemplated the idea that Karl Marx and people of that ilk had given even a passing thought to the Church of England in general and Percy Hartley-Worthington in particular. Even the suggestion that such events had taken place and that, therefore, he might be on the Soviet Socialist Republic's hit list was equivalent to three bottles of castor oil. Oh

God, why didn't this awful woman leave him alone? She was far worse than all the Mothers' Union put together and heaven knew they were bad enough. He desperately wanted to go to the lavatory now, perspiration was trickling down his back and his face wore a glassy sheen.

Deirdre was really enjoying herself, there was not likely to be any comeback for roughing up this pathetic weed. She tightened the screw.

"Your basic concept of a male deity is totally without foundation and based purely on hearsay and speculation developed by the ruling classes to maintain their grip on the proletariat. The artists and poets of their ages were ruthlessly used to promulgate chauvinist propaganda to promote that fictitious belief. Michaelangelo was just a lackey, he has a lot to answer for with his portrayal of the alleged Almighty as a venerable patriarch with a long white beard."

She stuck a powerful finger half-an-inch under Percy's nose, and he nearly went cross-eyed trying to keep his eyes on both it and her whilst she hammered home her final words with the dreadful relentlessness of a Tyneside riveter.

"It is my belief that God is a black female person and I defy you and your comparative mythology to produce one shred of evidence that can contradict this."

Percy groaned in shock. This was the ultimate horror, his Room 101 in Orwellian terror. His face grew pale; his breathing became rapid; his pulse shallow, he began to gabble to himself.

"Oh God, who livest in heaven showeth thine divine mercy upon thy faithful servant and in thine infinite wisdom let light shine down and illumine the hearts and minds of those who seek but do not find, who hearken but do not hear. Doth not thine humble servant – no perhaps 'doth' was not quite right in that context, being the third person singular of the present indicative, and maybe now would be the moment to throw in a quick 'beseecheth'." As he was somewhat pushed for time, he decided that to do so would not be too inappropriate and, having put in the basic spadework, he didn't want to have to go through 'divine mercy' and 'light shining down' again – he thought that God would understand if he just picked it up at the punchline. "Dost not thine humble servant not beseech thee..." No, Percy. NO! NO! A double negative there could be very confusing. He began to panic over his prayer, anticipating the celestial pips as his three minutes became exhausted, and more investment in the form of 'Bringer of all understanding' and 'Knoweth all things' would have to be inserted into the God slot, delaying deliverance that much longer.

God, however, had a softer spot for Percy that evening than he had had for other people I could mention and, being all comprehending, sussed out the problem and despatched an immediate solution. Not the Archangel Gabriel with shining sword and the massed bands of the heavenly host – although no doubt that would have put the shits up La Plant – but none other than me.

Of course, I didn't realise that I was the celestial sphincter tightener. I thought I was just doing my duty under Angela Prinknash's watchful eye. I had been about to accost Ms Deirdre before but her lightning swoop on poor Percy had pre-empted me so I had just hovered in earshot but with my back towards them.

At Sheringford Town Hall Deirdre had been entertaining, somebody who was easy to wind up, but now I began to see that she was damned dangerous. Anybody who was ruthless enough to savage gentle little Percy just for the sake of humiliating him, seeing him cringe and cave in, was nasty, extremely nasty. And anybody that nasty infiltrating your organisation meant big trouble. I was just wondering what it was she was really after when God pushed me sharply between the shoulderblades and I found myself at her elbow.

"Evening, vicar." I smiled at the priest and, turning to Deirdre, nodded. "Evening to you, Deirdre, see you've dressed for the occasion."

Without waiting for a reply, I returned to Percy and continued: "Been having a little chat? You want to watch Deirdre or she'll have you converted to the left-hand path in no time. Very aggressive she is. What is it they say around her, 'A whistling maid and a crowing hen is fit for neither God nor men'?" I smiled again, this time at her.

"Why don't you piss off, we're having a private conversation," she snarled, flushing scarlet.

Percy, however, seized my arm like a drowning man seizes a log. "No, no, please join us. Please don't go."

I tutted at Deirdre gently. "Tut, tut, Ms Deirdre, tut, tut, tut, that's not very nice coming from a lady now, is it?"

We eyed each other for a few seconds and I think she realised that I had overheard her savaging Percy because she looked away without response.

Percy, in the meantime, had launched into a prayer of thanksgiving for the arrival of the sixth cavalry. Eyes screwed shut in his sweating face, he was muttering almost inaudibly.

"Almighty Redeemer, Saviour of heaven and earth by thy just and merciful hand, thou who hast suffered much and shed thy blood..."

He was interrupted by a grip on his elbow and, opening his eyes, beheld my concerned face examining him from close range. I thought the poor chap was about to conk out.

"Are you all right? Would you like me to fetch you a glass of water or something – perhaps if you sat down for a minute?"

"No. No, thank you, Mr... er... er... Yes, I shall be fine in a second."

With my arrival Deirdre had retreated a pace or two and spotting, the gap she had left, Percy muttered, "I er... er... I must just make an important visit – will be back in a moment or two – er... yes." Then he neatly slipped between us and headed for Prinknash Keep's plumbing with his knees tightly pressed together.

We both watched him go. Deirdre spoke first in an attempt to recover some initiative.

"Why do priests always hobble?"

I considered this observation for a moment and realised that there was truth in it. I shrugged, not really wishing to support her attack on the clergy.

"I suppose it's a combination of clothes and economy; the wearing of a cassock and the necessity to have thin rubber re-soles on well-worn shoes."

Thankfully for both of us, the necessity for further conversation was avoided when the butler eased into the room at that moment and announced that dinner was served.

Much to my intense relief, the preponderance of men had required an adjustment to the seating arrangements. Deirdre found herself promoted up the table between Lissett and Marsh, whilst I was at the end presided over by Angela Prinknash, seated on the corner with Corrigan-Croot on my left.

I chatted to Angela for a few minutes, but when she turned her attentions to other guests and Corrigan-Croot seemed more interested in wolfing down his food than talking, I lapsed into quiet contemplation of my food, content with my own thoughts.

Even being generous, I could not say that I had taken to Deirdre Plant; the woman spelt trouble. The bullying of Percy had been a sadistic and unnecessary act. What, I wondered for the third time today, was an aggressive bitch like that doing here? Sheringford's crumbling stonework and La Plant's vitriol made strange bedfellows.

No, it didn't gel, something somewhere was wrong. Still, it really wasn't any of my business. It wasn't for me to rock the boat when there were other people much closer to the situation and who were quite capable of working it out, whatever it was – Charlie for one. As long as La Plant didn't interfere in my life, then what the hell. Unfortunately – for me that is, although I don't suppose it made much difference in the end – I couldn't keep my big mouth shut just for once.

"Mr Mouton. Mr Mouton, if you please?"

I was suddenly jerked out of my reverie by an awareness that silence had fallen over the gathering and, returning to active membership of the company, I discovered to my disquiet that all eyes were fixed on me.

Mrs Hartley-Worthington was leaning around Corrigan-Croot like a pop-eyed walrus, frown on her face, moustache bristling and large eyes glaring at me, jabbing a finger in my direction. "Game stuffing, Mr Mouton.?"

I responded instinctively. "Well, I am if you..." The voice tailed away as twin warning lasers from Charlie bored through my skull. Deirdre, however, gave a muffled chuckle and Colonel Corrigan-Groot's complexion demonstrated a marked shift towards the red end of the spectrum.

'...if you would like me to pass it," I finished lamely, casting round to see where the offending dish lay. It was at my elbow, placed there by Angela Prinknash. I hastily seized it and passed it up the table. In an attempt to recover the situation and noticing that the carrot tureen was in front of me, I proffered it also with a helpful smile.

"Would you like carrots up your end as well, Mrs Hartley-Worthington?"

La Plant now guffawed loudly, putting me right on the spot. However, explanations would only make matters worse and to bluff it out and say with a confident grin something along the lines of 'Perhaps I'd better re-phrase that. Ha! Ha! Ha!' would have just drawn attention to the double meaning. Mrs H-W narrowed her eyes, indicating that somewhere inside that hairy coconut brains were being cudgelled in an effort to recall past events.

A quick transfer of focus was called for so I asked loudly, "May I enquire what you find so amusing about that, Miss Plant?"

That wiped the grin from her face instantly. Corrigan-Croot's bulbous eyes swivelled on to her like blister turrets on a flying fortress. The smirks that had appeared on two or three other faces also disappeared in a flash, to be replaced by bland, enquiring expressions.

Deidre looked round frantically but by now she had no one to pass the parcel to and very little time to compose a suitable reply. She floundered.

"Just a thought – something private."

But the object was achieved. The attention had been switched away from me and whatever Deirdre said now, the assembled company knew she had demonstrated publicly that she had as dirty a mind as they had in private. I had a little chuckle to myself as I dipped a forkful of succulent wild duck into the redcurrant sauce before transferring it to my mouth. The general level of conversation was resumed, leaving Deirdre to extract herself from the chill of genteel ostracism.

The score was now me three points, Deirdre nil. I knew it, but didn't really care. She knew it now with vengeful determination – and the match had barely begun.

Chapter Nine

Researching the engineering aspects of the Sheringford Scheme occupied my waking hours for the next ten days but the delicate matter of acquainting Charlie with my involvement in the concept of its re-development occupied my mind. Since the Prinknash dinner she had, if anything, been even busier with Save Old Sheringford. Voluminous correspondence, numerous telephone calls and long evening meetings, the latter two mostly with the Plant woman.

"You seem to have upset Deirdre," I was informed with a frown. "I know she can be a bit aggressive but try to get on with her for my sake, Marcus."

Well I suppose I should, but it seemed to me that Ms Deirdre was one of those bullies who liked dishing it out but did not appreciate it when she got some back. I resolved to make an effort, but I couldn't rid myself of the feeling that something about Deirdre was phoney.

On the development front I had had to bide my time to raise the issue for there was no doubt it was going to be controversial. It was tempting to come right out and put all my cards on the table and tell Charlie the truth, but I was scared she would go bananas without some gradual introduction – particularly as wheels had been set in motion which could not now be reversed.

My plan was to ease the possibility of some re-development into her mind slowly, and then convert it gradually into a probability before it became a finality.

Some hope, you might think – and you would be right

to think so. Those of you who are closely aligned with the female sex will know that they tend to see straight through that sort of thing and rip out your jugular.

Notwithstanding that, keeping my chin well tucked over the vulnerable vein, I drip-fed information and suggestions steadily to her.

A hint here: "Don't you think Sheringford has lost a lot of the zest it used to have when it was a market town? Needs a little more – what is it the Yanks called it – pzazz. Ha! Ha! Ha!"

A suggestion there: "Now here's an idea for you. Why doesn't SOS prepare an overall master plan for the whole town centre, including all the derelict land? I'm sure I could find a property development company who might be interested in having a look at it."

And even a positive proposal. "Sheringford should have more shops you know. It's no good saving Britain's heritage just for the sake of it. It has to have some positive benefit. If you want future generations to appreciate what you've preserved they have to have other reasons to visit the town as well as to see old buildings. To get people there to enjoy it you need some more modern commercial attractions."

But she said not a word, nodded rather absentmindedly now and then, but the door I was seeking to ease open remained obstinately closed – until our pre-lunch drinks party on Sunday.

It was my idea really to have friends round that day. Nothing pretentious in our little terraced house in Fulham – just a few close friends; 'twelve till two;' beer, some decent wine, and a selection of Marks and Sparks canapés.

Bob Barclay was invited with wife Jennifer: a plump, jolly lady who livened up any function. As were Pete Smallwood and Anushka. Tony Scales turned up with some magical mystery girl with luminous eyes who clung to his arm like a limpet the whole time and hardly said a word. I never did learn her name. Clearly the solemn Amanda had not come up to scratch and been dropped from the card. The Fullertons couldn't come, they had to attend lunch at Fleur's mother's. Charlie's younger brother Simon brought his current girlfriend, a pale wispy creature, dreamy-eyed and heavily into ecology – and other things from the smell of her cigarettes.

I had warned Barclay by telephone, urging total discretion, about his development ideas for Sheringford. "Not that it's likely to come up, you understand, and even if it does Charlie will have been told by me quite firmly what we have in mind. But there could be other ears around – Save Old Sheringford you know – it could cause a few ripples if things leaked out prematurely, so best not to mention it, okay?"

"Okay, sport, if you say so, pas de problem, you know me, see you Sunday."

Not entirely reassured by this pyrites-edged, four-pound-note auto-testimonial, but pride dictating that a fuller explanation could provoke snide comments regarding the mastership of this household, I had replaced the receiver and decided that hope, not having been called upon to act on my behalf for some time, was due for a responsible innings.

Thus Sunday was allowed to dawn without any other preparation and initially all went well. The Moon-Prinknash hospitality being what it was, proceedings extended well past the two o'clock deadline, plunging deep into a hazy afternoon and even deeper into my booze cupboard. Spanish brandy, Ouzo purchased as a still unpresented last minute gift for Aunt Joanna at Heraklion Airport three years ago, and a label-less bottle of what looked like congealed Advocaat were all brought forth and consumed. Tongues grew looser, conversations louder and minds relaxed – except Charlie's.

From afar, or as afar as you could get in our small

sitting-room, I heard the quiet question slash through the hubbub of conversation as though it had been shouted in my ear.

"I hear you're looking at a scheme in Sheringford, Bob," she enquired innocently.

I sobered up ten points in a split second but it was a lost cause, I had been fixed. Vladimir Karpov couldn't have manoeuvred me into a more ineffectual position to influence his reply. I was pinned in the far corner of the room, squeezing the last few drops of Osborne from the Spanish brandy bottle. Barclay had his back to me and was thus out of frantic signal shot and by the time I had zipped over there, hoping against hope that he would remember my warning, it was too late.

"Good old Marcus," boomed a flushed and ebullient Barclay, "a real little treasure. Do y'know he was the chap who first spotted the potential of that site, set the whole thing up he did." He clapped me roundly on the shoulders, beaming with enthusiasm. "Brilliant he is – and very discreet too."

I stood aghast, brain shocked, plans shattered and eyes fixed afar, watching hope high-tailing it over the horizon with its arse aflame.

"Did he now," murmured Charlie, "and is he?" She riveted a cold ultra-violet look on to my face, lifting one eyebrow questioningly.

"Didn't I tell you? I'm sure I must have mentioned it." The tone was very unconvincing. I knew it and she knew it.

"Well, you can tell me all about it again later, my beloved," she said and, giving the others a tight smile, drifted off to join another group, leaving a puzzled Barclay and me cursing the unreliability of cherished expectations. Bloody Pandora should have slammed the lid on that still small treacherous voice skulking at the bottom of her blasted box.

"Have I said something I shouldn't?"

"No, no," I said. "No, don't worry about it, she's probably forgotten but never mind, you know what women are. Ha! Ha! Ha!"

Barclay nodded slowly, he did indeed know what women were and if he was any judge of the situation I was about to find out for myself in full force. Under the circumstances, therefore, he decided to do what any loyal male comrade-in-arms would do, having dropped his mate in it up to the eyeballs. Gathering Scales, Smallwood and company in his train, he bellowed his thanks, kissed Charlie soundly on both cheeks, grabbed his coat and departed off at high speed.

"Have a nice day," I called sarcastically after him.

He had the grace to look sheepish. "You too, old son, you too!"

Tidying up the house and the washing and drying of the plates and glasses we carried out in frosty silence. Old Damocles was a relaxed man compared to me – just one word would be sufficient and the whole lot would descend upon my head – so I held my peace, pretending that all was well and leaving it to Charlie to open up the subject. The atmosphere bore all the portents of a Mark One bollocking, and from the ominous temperature and pressure readings, one with brass knobs on. I swallowed anxiously and, replacing the last dried glass on its shelf, sidled towards the door.

"How could you, Marcus, just how could you do such a thing to me when you know how hard I've worked for SOS?"

There was a catch in her voice and I thought I could see a film of tears misting her violet eyes. The awaited opening barrage was even more devastating than expected. A row I could have handled, but this thrust which went straight into an already overly sensitive conscience was deadly. I felt a real shit. Well, I was going to have to say something, and there are only two alternatives when caught red-handed – deny everything or come clean. Injecting as much sweet reason into my voice as I could, I denied everything.

"Do what, scrumkin? I'm not sure that I know what you're talking about?"

"You know bloody well what I'm talking about; I'm talking about Sheringford, I'm talking about your plan to devastate the place while I am trying to preserve it; I'm talking about going behind my back in front of my face to keep things from me that any two reasonable people with trust between them would not have concealed; I'm talking about..."

I interrupted here, "Only owls can do that," I said.

"Do what?"

"Go behind their backs in front of their faces."

It was not a wise observation in retrospect; I should have let her get it all off her chest and kept quiet.

"Oh yes, everything's just a joke to you, isn't it? Silly old Charlotte with her SOS, let her play with preservation if it amuses her, if it keeps her happy. Well it doesn't amuse me, I don't do it for fun, I care about it; it's my hometown where my family have lived for centuries and I love it. I love all of it, its silly old walls and its silly old people, its silly old stone and its silly old inefficiency and I don't want to see it all crumbling and falling apart or knocked down and replaced with some hideous chrome and glass monstrosity. Deirdre warned me you were trouble and she was right!"

Tears streamed down her face as she glared defiance at the whole world in general and me in particular. I felt an even bigger shit now for upsetting her. Christ, that was the last thing I wanted. Slightly devious I might have been – perhaps if you were generous you would say over cautious rather than deceitful and I did have a strong point, although whether it could be put over now was in doubt. Still, apart from a complete acknowledgement of all she had said, which would in the long run be totally disastrous for our relationship, I had nothing else to try.

"Look," I said with some trepidation, "I've tried to tell you on several occasions, not in so many words exactly but enough for you to have got the message. I didn't want to hide anything from you, you must believe that, it's just that it all got out of hand a bit too quickly before I had got round to giving you the full picture. And besides, there's no question of Barclay knocking down old Sheringford and replacing it with some ghastly modern crap. He wants to build on that grotty old derelict factory site at the back of the High Street." I skated over St Frideswide's chapel for the present; that could be introduced at a later date – if there was going to be a later date. Anyhow, she was listening at least.

Emboldened, I continued, "Don't forget that whereas SOS is important to you, it's not your livelihood, I still have to earn a living and I do this by finding work for my firm in the places I visit and with people I know."

"But you could have told me!" she cried.

I winced. I knew I could have, I knew I should have, I wished desperately that I had and even more desperately that she wouldn't keep putting her finger precisely on this, the tenderest spot on my conscience, because this was the nub of it, this was the point at issue. It wasn't really about Barclay's redevelopment scheme, it was the fact that I hadn't taken her into my confidence in the first place – and the fever had not climaxed yet. My numerous shortcomings still awaited a comprehensive listing.

With beseeching hands, I pleaded with her. "I tried to, I really did but I didn't think you'd understand if it was put to you bluntly, just shoved in front of you as a *fait accompli*. I would have loved to have told you and shown you the drawings at the same time so you could

197

see for yourself that Barclay's scheme was sympathetic to Old Sheringford, not conflicting with it. So you could see the advantages as well as the disadvantages – not that there are any of those, of course."

"Of course!" she said savagely. "So then why didn't you?"

"Why didn't I what?"

"Show me the drawings!" she snapped.

I sighed. There were times when I felt it might be an advantage to love somebody thick and stupid rather than the incisive mind opposite. Even D'Artagnan couldn't have kept thrusting more accurately at my weak points.

"Well Barclay hasn't got an architect yet so we haven't got any drawings."

The floodgates opened on my head – I got the lot.

No trust between us; let me down; what can I say to the SOS committee; how can I hold my head up in Sheringford again; cannot rely on you to behave decently for one minute; thoroughly unscrupulous underneath that sleazy charm; so-called friends exercising a bad influence; easily led; all you can think about is yourself, what about me; and finally, totally and utterly irresponsible. She paused for breath, she needed a few lungsful after that so I took the opportunity to play a speculative sexual card – I put my arm around her. She shook it off furiously.

"Don't you touch me, don't you dare touch me ever again, you – you Judas, you!" And with that she fled from the kitchen. I heard her feet on the stairs and the slam of the bedroom door, little flakes of plaster floated down from the ceiling. I waited a couple of minutes, listening with anticipation; this was the crucial moment. Sure enough the bedroom door opened and slammed once again, increasing the snowfall. That would be my duvet plus whatever random selection of my clothes and other effects she had managed to gather together to make her point, being hurled out on to the landing – and maybe down the stairs. Christ no, not down the stairs that would be with gold knobs on.

I peered round the kitchen door anxiously The staircase was pristine, I suspected that would be the case, nonetheless I couldn't help releasing a small sigh of relief. It was just gong to be a couple of weeks in the doghouse by the look of it, maybe my argument had had some effect after all or maybe she was just making a point. Blood and sand, but life was difficult at times!

I slumped into the nearest chair like a plumber's bag, moodily contemplating the brief shadow of enforced celibacy on the lumpy mattress that passed for a bed in the spare room. No wonder the parents and 'in-laws' were reluctant to stay with us.

I also contemplated three other matters, one good and two not so good. On the good side it was nice to know that I had 'charm', sleazy or not. Until then I would not have put 'charm' as one of my attributes but there you are, you never know these things until somebody tells you. On the 'not so good' side I wondered how Charlie had known about Bob Barclay doing a scheme for Sheringford – because there was no doubt in my mind that she did know. I had never mentioned Barclay and Sheringford in the same context to her. And, finally, where did Deirdre Plant fit into all this? Because she did. Clearly she and Charlie had been talking – and about me. But why?

Chapter Ten

For the next few days the atmosphere at home remained arctic, warming to frosty, conversation concentrated on the bare essentials and physical contact non-existent. We both worked at home in the evenings – Charlie dealing with the increasing mound of correspondence that Save Old Sheringford was generating whilst I found myself doing washing up, carting clothes to and from Cassius Butterbuckets Lightning Launderette and even doing the ironing.

Barclay was pushing Sheringford on apace with the bit between his teeth. All the professionals, the architects and quantity surveyors as well as my firm, had been formally appointed and I had spent my time collecting and collating as much background information about the site as I could find. The first big project meeting had been scheduled for June 12th.

On the morning of the 12th I checked the files I needed; there was a set of aerial photographs that I had persuaded an accommodating aerial survey firm to provide, the 1:1250 Ordnance Survey maps of the area, some old drawings of the existing buildings copied from the local authority records and some details of the ground strata and flooding levels obtained from the Borough engineer's office. There were one or two other items of possible interest in addition. I considered that for starters I had done quite well with this collection. Pushing the folder into a battered briefcase, I nodded to my secretary as I passed her on the way out.

"Just going to Mr Barclay's office for a meeting on Sheringford, Jane – be back about twelve-thirty," I grinned sheepishly.

"Like hell you will!" She wagged a finger in mock anger. "More like four-thirty, wellied up to the eyeballs. I'll put the black coffee on and get the Fernet Branca ready."

"Honi soit qui mal y pense," I retorted.

"In which case, Marcus, you must be a very evil thinking man – the things that happen to you!" she riposted with a laugh.

There was no immediate answer to that and I was too pushed for time to pause at that moment to bandy further repartee. However, just as I was leaving the front door of the office I met Hugo Elmes, the senior partner, coming in.

"Leaving early, Marcus? I would have thought that ten o'clock on a Thursday morning was a bit premature even for your weekend."

What was so special about today, I asked myself, that made it 'Taking the Piss out of Moon Day'? Were they trying to tell me something? If so, it defeated me what it was.

Ignoring Hugo's heavy wit, I floated, "I'm just off to the first project meeting on Sheringford. That architect friend of yours, Fitzwhatsit, will be there, a bit of a brown-noser I'm told – know him well, do you, Hugo?" And with that I made to slip past, giving the older man a knowing wink. It was Hugo's turn to do the ignoring, but he caught me by the arm.

"Here, hang on a minute. If you're meeting Fitzallan Percival, watch him – and warn Bob Barclay to do the same." He held up a warning finger. "I'm serious. There are too many rumours about him and some of his nefarious practices for there to be no truth buried in them somewhere."

I paused. I had researched Percival's background to

some degree but I was interested to hear what Hugo knew. "What sort of rumours?"

"Well, for a start he's one of the most arrogant, conceited and inefficient buggers I've ever come across in my career. He did some work for my old practice – well, I say did some work but the point was he didn't. He laid it off on to everybody else, took the fees, tried to take all the credit and if there was a problem, passed off the blame. The only thing he did do was try to bribe the local planning officer and the chairman of the planning committee. Fortunately for him it was done in such a way that nothing could be proved, but nobody wanted to work with him again and the client was livid. Percival was lucky to avoid jail. Other people claim to have had similar experiences. If you're not careful he could try to pull the same stunts again."

I thoughtfully chewed a lip as I considered what Hugo had said. Bob Barclay had appointed Percival to be his architect having taken him over from White Horse Properties, but I didn't think he knew anything of his history other than that White Horse's lawyer had recommended him.

The problem was whether or not to say anything. I decided not to for the time being, but to keep a close eye on what went on.

"I'll watch him, Hugo," I said, "but our instructions come from the client, not Percival. He's not going to have us running in all directions while he takes the credit, I assure you."

Hugo grinned triumphantly. "Now don't let your temper get the better of you, Marcus. I know you well and you don't suffer fools gladly. Try to exercise a little tact and discretion and not upset the team – there's a good chap. Remember a drop of oil helps the works go round far better than a belt with a hammer."

He patted me on the shoulder and then continued

through the reception towards his office, leaving me speechless on the doorstep.

Two-one to Hugo again – I grinned with affectionate bewilderment. Perhaps one day if I actually got a result, they might make me a partner.

* * *

The battered MG threaded its way through the traffic, fortunately thin at that time of the fine June morning, towards the West End and I arrived at Bob Barclay's office in Chesterfield Street with a couple of minutes to spare. I parked the car in a slot under Barclay's office, just managing to squeeze it between a delivery van and a badly parked shiny white Mercedes sports model with green tinted windows and bristling with an array of aerials. Its number plate bore the letters and number PER5E and the five had been rounded to make it look like an S – a cut-price attempt at a personalised number plate. Sprinting up the stairs to the first floor office, I greeted the red-haired piece of comeliness who masterminded Barclay's reception.

"Morning, Lucy – like the new hairstyle – Mr Barclay free? I've come for the Sheringford meeting."

The girl responded with a warm smile. "If you go through to the conference room, Mr Moon, I'll let Mr Barclay know. I think everyone is here now. Would you like a coffee?"

I nodded, "Please" and, glancing round to check that no one was within earshot, leaned towards her and asked quietly, "Who's here Lucy, anybody I know?"

She looked at her visitors' list.

"Apart from Martin there's a Fitzallan Percival who claims he's an architect," she wrinkled her nose, "and with him was a Mr Crabbe. The only other person is Mr Fullerton."

I smiled my thanks, slightly relieved. Martin Holmes and Robin Fullerton were friends of a like mind so with a relatively light heart I wandered down to the conference room and pushed open the door.

"Morning, fellow workers." I shook hands with Holmes and Fullerton who were standing talking by the door and then turned to the other two occupants, both of whom were seated at the large, baize-covered table. The nearest person was a blocky, ugly, pock-marked individual, squarely built and of medium height. His short dark hair was fixed with hair cream and the parting, incised arrow-straight up the centre of his head, showed brilliant white against the slicked mat of black hair either side. Two small black eyes gazed unwaveringly at me from each side of a nose like a blind cobbler's thumb. He was probably fifty years old. Martin introduced him as Norman Crabbe, the Quantity Surveyor. He nodded but didn't stand or extend his hand. The mouth moved imperceptibly.

"Pleased to meetcher." The eyes remained fixed and glassy.

If he was, I thought, he was doing a great job of concealing his ecstasy on this deeply moving occasion.

Circumnavigating Crabbe, I moved alongside to the fourth individual who was seated in the slightly larger armchair at the end of the table, the chair normally occupied by the chairman and in Barclay's office that was Barclay. I examined the contents of the chair with interest. This must be Fitzallan Percival. He was a small, dark, podgy man with a bald, brown dome like the top of a British Standard egg projecting through a surrounding fringe of black hair – too black to be wholly natural at his age, which I put at forty-fiveish. Humpty-Dumpty's face was not visible because he had his head down and was writing feverishly with a green felt-tipped pen on a purple notepad. He was dressed in a plain dark blue suit devoid entirely of pattern or stripe and cut with a very high narrow collar; underneath was a frilly-fronted purple shirt and a billowing purple handkerchief gushed from his left sleeve. When he eventually condescended to raise his head, I could see around his neck a large, floppy, bright-red bow tie. The eyes that slowly fixed themselves on me at Martin's introduction were dark brown, flat and expressionless. Highly magnified behind heavy, dark-framed spectacles, they looked like bulls-eye glass in a sweete shoppe window. The clean-shaven, puffy face had the smooth all-over tan of the sunlamp devotee.

A soft, limp hand was extended and momentarily squeezed just the ends of my fingers as though it was flushing a not too hygienic lavatory. Percival's expression confirmed that impression.

"I hope we are going to get full co-operation from your practice, Mr Moon, this is a large, complicated job and I trust you can handle it." The voice was clipped and slightly forced like an actor's with a faint nasal twang. The elocution lessons hadn't totally eradicated his underlying East End origins.

"Don't worry, Mr Percival, we can cope. We've handled projects of this magnitude on previous occasions." And, if the truth be told, ten times the size, I thought, which is more than you have, Percy, my little aubergine.

I had done my homework well, gleaning as much as I could about this man in the two weeks available to me before this meeting. Fitzallan Percival was an adopted name changed in the distant past from something Balkan ending in -ov or -ic. He had become an architect, not by study at university or art school but by serving an apprenticeship to a small practice in Whitechapel that specialised in brewery and public house work, elbowing his way upwards over the declining health of the elderly owner to eventual senior partnership. From thence he had achieved some reasonable success through connections, trickery, bribery and other means devious and doubtful. His main claim to fame lay in a reputation as a skilful negotiator and as an appellant for maximising planning permissions. His practice was still quite small compared to my firm, perhaps only a twentieth of the size or less, and to him Sheringford would be one of his largest, if not *the* largest job he had handled. There was no way, however, that he was going to admit that to anybody, let alone me.

"I must remind you, Mr Moon, that we've not had the pleasure of having you work for us before and therefore I have no knowledge of your firm's ability. I much prefer to have people work for me that I know but as Mr Barclay seems to insist on your practice being involved then I suppose we shall have to make the best of it. However, I shall want one or two things established quite clearly from the start so that there are no misunderstandings between us."

There crept over me that tingling feeling that assails all collectors of *objets d'art* when they spot what could be a priceless example of their particular pursuit hidden in some unremarked, unexpected place. I kept a straight face and asked, "What sort of things?"

Percival sniffed. "I prefer to wait until Mr Barclay condescends to honour us with his presence." He shot his wrist forward violently to expose from a frilled, purple cuff, a hairy, evenly-tanned forearm around which was strapped a wafer-thin gold watch on a lizard-skin bracelet.

"He's already five minutes late. I'm not used to being kept waiting. I'm a very busy man and my time is valuable."

The excitement increased. Things were definitely looking up. Here, I thought, we have the makings of not just a plated specimen, but a fully assayed, London hallmarked, twenty-four carat, solid gold 'merchant banker'. He fitted the classification perfectly and would, I reckoned, have certainly won this year's 'Best of Breed' rosette in the little brown turds category at any international competition. The effect that Percival was going to have on Bob Barclay – and vice versa – could be spectacular. It could be a very interesting project to work on – for Barclay!

I was just savouring the angles when the door burst open and Barclay breezed in.

"Morning all! Morning, Marcus – managed to get here on time then? Where have you parked that old banger of yours? Right across my bloody garage exit, I'll be bound."

I grinned. "No, for once I managed to find a parking place in your yard, and slid the old MG neatly between a Fortnum's van and some ponced-up white Mercedes with a faked number plate that must be illegally parked there."

Percival's thin lips tightened perceptibly and he flushed. Barclay caught the expression and grinned at him.

"Aren't those your wheels, Mr Percival?"

Percival didn't reply but glanced pointedly at his watch.

"Right," said Barclay, "let's get down to business." He looked round. "Will you sit there, Marcus, you're okay, Mr Crabbe, and will you sit in that chair, Mr Percival?" He indicated a chair on the right of the chairman's place.

Percival sat tight. "I prefer to chair all design meetings, Mr Barclay. Architects are trained to lead the team and it will be far better, you'll find, if I run the meetings for you. We are skilled in these matters."

I folded my arms and leaned back in my chair, catching Martin Holmes' eye. Martin smiled. Norman Crabbe just sat stolidly picking his teeth with a dirty-looking plastic toothpick he had unearthed from his breast pocket. Fullerton slid into a chair at the far end of the table.

Barclay gave a thin smile. "Yes, well we can sort out later who will run design meetings, but this is a client's briefing."

Percival cleared his throat defiantly. "I would much prefer that the principles be quite clearly established now. You can have full confidence in me as your architect to handle all matters relating to sub-consultants," he glanced at me, "to design and, through Mr Crabbe, to control the cost. I shall deal with the planning and local authority officers and also advise you regarding possible tenderers for the construction and who to employ as the letting agent. The bond of trust between client and architect is still a precious thing in these days of hard commercialism, and as far as my practice is concerned, it is there for you to use to full advantage."

Unction oozed from every pore as he rested his soft, lamp-browned hands on the table in front of him and leant back in the large chair.

Blood and sand, I thought anxiously, I hope to hell Robert doesn't fall for that ripe load of old cobblers – it virtually gives an inefficient architect a blank cheque and that's obviously exactly what this smooth, ultra-violet irradiated arse-bandit is angling for.

The smile stayed on Barclay's face but his eyes hardened.

"Excellent, Mr Percival, I'm all in favour of establishing a clear pyramid of responsibility and I'm delighted that you have accepted the burden of undertaking these duties – but you will do so under my direction as the client, so if you will kindly get your backside out of my chair and sit where I have asked you to sit, we can commence."

He stood towering over Percival, waiting, and still smiling. Crabbe found a piece of gristly bacon somewhere in one of his dental cavities, forked it out on the end of the toothpick and scrutinised it carefully. Holmes and I both sat with our arms folded. Fullerton suppressed a chuckle. After a pause of a few seconds which seemed like minutes in the silence, Percival shuffled his notes together and, with a flushed, angry face, slowly got up and relocated himself in the designated chair.

"Thank you," said Barclay, and sat down. "Now, I believe you've all met each other, but just to make things one hundred percent clear, I'll run through everything briefly once more for everybody concerned."

"Mr Percival here is the architect, he's been with this site a long time and knows all the problems and, I trust, the solutions to them. As he rightly says, he will run the design team and he has kindly undertaken to accept full responsibility for the successful operation of that side of the project including all programming, cost control and design – an undertaking which I accept. Likewise, of course, should it go wrong, it's his arse that I shall kick and his balls that will be torn off, minced and fed to piranha fish."

Barclay beamed benevolently at Percival, and Martin Holmes duly noted the essence of the statement in the minutes of the meeting.

Fitzallan Percival looked distinctly uncomfortable. This was not quite what he'd had in mind, he was being pinned into a position he was not at all happy about. He tried a little back-pedalling.

"It is not my responsibility to check that the other professionals in the consultant's team do their duties correctly, particularly," he added, his eyes flicking to me, "people who haven't worked under my system before."

Barclay considered him gravely.

"Naturally, each firm takes full responsibility for their own performances but, Mr Percival, it *is* your job," Barclay stressed the 'is', "to ensure that budgets are adhered to and programmes met. Do I make myself quite clear or are there any questions?"

Percival grew more agitated; managing the project on his terms was fine, it meant he could get away with what he wanted; he could get the other consultants to do most of the work and thus increase his profit substantially for a start. Any mistakes or omissions on his firm's part would be glossed over or concealed, whereas the others under his direction could, if he chose, have their problems and troubles exposed to the full light of day – particularly to the client. That was heady power indeed. But Barclay was intending to make him, a sensitive aesthete, he complained to himself, fully responsible for Barclay's budgets and Barclay's programmes and that meant fully responsible for all parties' performances.

A shiver of apprehension went through him, he didn't know how to control a job by planned management – bluster and bullying was his forte and the awful realisation that this would not suffice in this case was beginning to dawn upon him. He increased his rate of back-pedalling to that of a trick cyclist in a three-ring circus.

"I beg to differ slightly with you there, Mr Barclay, a question of semantics rather but I see myself in more of a co-ordinating role. It is a position I assure you that I have successfully undertaken on many previous projects to my clients' entire satisfaction." He felt quite pleased with this neat little positional sidestep, so pleased that he allowed his primary motivation, greed, to overcome his ill-advised relief at so adroitly shifting his ground – or so he assumed. "We usually obtain a small additional fee for performing this service; perhaps we can discuss this after the meeting?"

His elation was shortlived; his sidestep had taken him smack into the most solid brick wall of all – one of Bob Barclay's principle prejudices, that against a person who styled himself a 'co-ordinator'. Barclay crushed him flat with thumping rhetoric.

"Jesus Christ, that's the last thing I need! As soon as I hear the word co-ordination mentioned, I clap one hand on my wallet, the other on my arse and go and lock up the family silver. It has the same effect on me as a politician pronouncing that he has 'a mandate from the people' or a lawyer that 'has nothing to hide'. You know damn well you're going to be bored, reamered and screwed if you believe it. It signifies that the self-proclaimed co-ordinator is too shit scared to get out in front doing some leading but to justify his fat salary or fees, he thinks that by calling himself 'project co-ordinator' everyone will believe he's the key man." Barclay snorted with scorn and continued remorselessly as Percival paled under the onslaught.

"Co-ordinator is one of those nebulous, new sociologically acceptable words that's designed and delivered to create the impression on the impressionable that all parties are equal but, with the exception of the co-ordinator, are disorganised and deficient, requiring the steadying influence of direction from the person of the project co-ordinator himself. Balderdash and poppycock, Mr Percival – what we need in this country and what I need on this project is a team leader and director, out in front leading and directing in the real sense of these words, not a bloody co-ordinator! Now you've just told us you're trained and skilled in these matters and well experienced. The team will, I presume, be delighted to have the benefit of your leadership and experience so I repeat; is it quite clear that as from now you are up at the sharp end of this job, leading it?"

Norman Crabbe removed his toothpick. "Clear as a bell, guvnor, finger out and feel the difference, eh."

I nodded my agreement just to seal off any slight loophole that Percival might probe should I show reluctance to accept his leadership. Percival bit his lip and ran his hand over his shining brown pate a couple of times whilst he considered all the angles. There was no way out that he could see at present and all eyes were on him. He grudgingly conceded his agreement.

"Well, if you insist, but I shall require the fullest co-operation from all parties."

Barclay beamed again. "Fine, now let's get on with the planning."

Martin carefully wrote down Percival's acceptance whilst the drawings were being spread on the table.

For the next hour or so we discussed the layouts and the planning of the project. Because Percival had been involved with the site for such a long time he had sets of drawings covering pretty well most of the possible alternatives and gave a comprehensive and knowledgeable exposition of the background, history and current feeling about development there. He also advised on local opinion regarding the retention or otherwise of St Frideswide's – the views of the local authority's planning committee and in particular those of the Chairman and the Planning Officer were also presented through the medium of Percival.

The drawings he produced were little more than pen line sketches with lots of overlaying, thick coloured lines and arrows from the felt-tipped marker pens so beloved of the flamboyant architect. Martin Holmes produced population and economic statistics for the Sheringford area, including detailed information about the existing business and commercial enterprises that were operating and also those which were proposed.

I outlined the subsoil conditions, the availability of water, power and drainage, suffering frequent interruptions from Percival requesting clarification of minor points, who, when I had concluded, said huffily, "I'm surprised you've done this without my knowledge.

I wasn't aware that you were making these enquiries. A lot of this information was and still is available at my office." He turned to Barclay. "I would much prefer it if all future investigations done by other consultants are channelled through me or my approval is obtained, then I can ensure that it is done thoroughly and correctly and not in some unilateral, half-hearted manner. Otherwise how can I be expected to exercise the control that's so obviously needed on this project?"

Barclay nodded partial agreement. "All parties should send copies of correspondence to Mr Percival but I don't think it's practical for them to seek your approval to undertake their professional duties – just keep you informed." He turned to Norman Crabbe. "Are building costs in Sheringford significantly different to anywhere else or much the same?"

Crabbe glanced across at Percival, who gave a slight nod. I, feeling slightly ruffled from Percival's previous comments, picked this up immediately. These two charmers were in cahoots; either that, or Crabbe was terrified of Percival. Maybe Percival provided him with most of his work, but considering them, they were a most unlikely pair. Crabbe's strong East End accent and the faint echo in Percival's modulated tones were perhaps a clue to mutual origins but that seemed to be the only thing they had even remotely in common. An eye would have to be kept on the relationship between these two, particularly if it affected Barclay's development.

Crabbe's nasal drawl interrupted my deliberations.

"Wot I say is all fings to all men, as you rightly say Sheringford isn't so different from the rest of God's little acre – this sceptered isle. There might be a bob or two here or a quid or two there, but takin' all in all and fings bein' equal, should have no problems."

Barclay made a note on the pad in front of him then sat back, clearly having made some decision.

"Thank you all for your contributions – they've been invaluable and to a large extent support what I've felt all along. Development, as you all know, is a risky business, whatever the popular press may condition the great unwashed to believe. One must have a feel for a site and I have a feel for this one. The present situation is that I have agreed Heads of Terms with the freeholder's advisers, the freeholder being a trust for the benefit of the sole surviving member of the Grimshaw family – the descendents of the old Joshua Grimshaw Company. Mr Grimshaw is apparently a difficult man to meet, being rather eccentric, but subject to his final agreement, then we'll have either a purchase contract subject to receipt of planning permission, or an option to purchase for a period of three years. The financial differences between the two reflect the risks involved and the financial commitments necessary to obtain consent to develop this site." He turned to Fitzallan Percival. "So, Mr Percival, it all depends on you."

"Don't worry about that," Percival smirked, "I know the Chairman of the Planning Committee personally. He's a friend of mine and I've got the Planning Officer like that." He gestured downwards with his thumb. "Right under there, he is – no problem. Just leave it to me."

A burst of adrenaline shot through me as Percival's comment registered – I recalled Hugo's warning and my brief conversation with the Planning Officer in Sheringford Town Hall. What was it he had said? 'Overworked and underpaid', and then lost interest when he discovered I was not a developer. And the Chairman as well – unless he was so undiscerning and frivolous with his friendships as to include Percival within that circle?

Barclay too looked sceptical, but did not pass further comment and returned to the drawings littering the table.

"What we need, therefore, is a well thought out,

214

worked up scheme with nice crisp elevations and some strong expressions of positive interest from prospective tenants. Now this is what I have in mind..."

Percival interrupted him. "Mr Barclay," he gestured in an agitated way to the sketches, "I was under the impression that you were merely going to take over my conception and put some finance into it. Are you now proposing some amendments to these layouts and if so, I must inform you that an enormous amount of work has gone into the most careful consideration of this scheme and changes would not be at all advisable. No, sir, I would not recommend any changes. I must counsel most strongly against any alterations."

He caught Barclay's gaze fixed on him and was slightly disconcerted by the unwavering stare. He shifted uneasily in his chair – was the initiative slipping from him? He sensed that too rigid a stance might harm his position; a small compromise could be offered without doing much damage.

"Perhaps one or two minor adjustments could be made, but we would have to be extremely careful not to make them significant enough to affect the planning, otherwise we could be in trouble."

"Why is that?" Barclay enquired in a deceptively quiet, almost docile voice.

Percival relaxed a little and with his uncanny instinct for misjudging situations, tried to haul himself back to regain pole position.

"Because, my dear Barclay, I have agreed these plans with the Planning Officer – unofficially, of course, but I can assure you that both the planners and the committee fell over themselves with delight at my proposals. Indeed, one member went as far as to comment that they combine simplicity and economy with flair and brilliance." He sat back with an air of finality.

Barclay stretched his arms out and then stood up and

removed his jacket, draping it over the back of the chair. I realised that he was creating a distraction to buy a little time whilst he organised his thoughts. This obviously meant that Bob's thoughts were somewhat disturbed and that did not bode well for someone. Barclay sat down again and leaned forward, speaking to the table at large.

"At the expense of repeating myself, I thank you all again for providing me with the detailed background pictures that you gave. From this information and from my own knowledge of the site's potential, I will establish the design brief and that is what I intend to do." He turned to the architect. "Whilst I'm sure that your previous scheme for the trustees is everything you claim for it, Mr Percival, it is not what I want to build. That scheme is a proposal to construct streets of shops open to the elements, which is the sort of thing that was built just after the Second World War. That's outdated now, people want something better than that these days. They want to shop in comfort, sheltered from our British weather, with fun things for their children."

Percival spluttered. "Now just a minute...!"

But Barclay held up his hand to silence him. "What I want to construct here is a covered country shopping centre, everything under one roof. I want it superbly designed as a logical extension to the present High Street, and it must incorporate two four-storey office blocks, for which I already have potential tenants."

Percival's features turned a dark red, his face suffused with anger.

"You can't do this to me!" he shouted. "I've told the planners that my scheme will be built. I'm not prepared to stand for this sort of treatment. My professional integrity is at stake and I'll resign rather than be treated in this manner and have my considered advice ignored in such a cavalier fashion!"

I brightened perceptibly and wondered if there was

216

some way in which I could accelerate the resigning process. I needn't have worried.

Barclay had also cheered up momentarily, but was trying hard not to show it, because he felt with a sinking feeling that it was just a bluff. However, it was worth a call.

"Well, Mr Percival, if you feel you must resign, then you must." He quickly ran through the polite formalities and uttered the usual platitudes about 'thank you for all your efforts' and 'respect a man who sticks by his principles', hoping that this would firmly bolt, lock and bar the door now that Percival had opened it and exited himself. He even threw in a final kick in the butt: "Of course, we'll pay you for the work you've done on my scheme to date."

Percival was made of sterner stuff, however, when it actually came to detaching his grasp from something as potentially lucrative in fees and prestige as the Sheringford project. His skin was far thicker than his principles were resolute. No Victorian unmarried mother he, to be cast out into the driving snow, never to darken Barclay's door again. As soon as he saw the old bolts being oiled ready for shooting home, he was back beating on the barrier, demanding to be readmitted. Prising open the portal before it could be finally sealed against him, he thrust a foot into the gap.

"You can't do without me on this job, Barclay, I'm indispensable!" he blustered.

Bob hit the intrusive appendage with a sledge hammer. "On your way home tonight, Percival, you just pay a visit to the cemetery and you'll see a lot of fellers there that the world has managed to do without." There was no point in making it easy for him. Percival flinched but kept his foot firmly wedged there and powered in with his shoulder, hurling moral obligations, ethics and decorum.

"No," said Percival, "I've decided that my professional ethics will not permit me to resign and leave you in a position of helplessness so, although it's distasteful to me to have my advice rejected, I'm still obligated to do my best for you and at least try to turn into well planned, workable architectural solutions whatever it is you insist on. I cannot let you down." He would hear no more of it and, although Barclay pressed him to the limit, it was no use. Percival had widened a gap enough to enable him to squeeze back inside the fold.

For the rest of the meeting I watched with interest as Barclay outlined his ideas on shopping with sizes and locations for the various kinds of trader that he wished to attract and Percival sulkily and grudgingly, but with some skill, sketched and re-sketched layouts, movement diagrams, pedestrian flows, servicing arrangements and all the other planning considerations necessary for a successful shopping development to be schemed out. It dawned on me slowly that the reason, and possibly the only reason why Fitzallan Percival had resisted Bob's idea so strongly initially was to avoid having to redesign the project from scratch. It had nothing to do with losing face with the local authority, it was entirely to escape having to do some extra work. So much for professional ethics, this fruitcake was just idle. I decided it was time to take him down a peg.

The discussion eventually centred on the location of a main access from Sheringford High Street through to the proposed new shopping mall on the site. Barclay stabbed his finger on the forecourt of St. Frideswide's.

"That is the ideal location – directly opposite a pedestrian crossing near the bus station and flanked closely by some of the big name traders already in the town. It's the only place for a link to the High Street."

"But what about the chapel?" I enquired innocently. "You'll have to demolish it." I looked at the Ordnance

Survey map. "Or alternately go around it on both sides."
I smiled disarmingly.

Barclay sat forward. "Say that again, Marcus."

Percival cut in with a heavy sigh. "What Mr Moon
was trying to say, Mr Barclay, was..." He shot me a 'mind-
your-own-business-and-stick-to-engineering' look
"...that one could demolish the chapel which, as we all
know, would cause problems, or use the small path along
the side here to gain access to the site." He pointed to a
narrow path that led down the side of the chapel and
originally must have served as an entrance to and exit
from the small vestry.

"In my view, of course, it's far too narrow and utterly
useless as an access." He smiled across at me as if to say,
'So please don't waste our valuable time with your
ridiculous, unconsidered interruptions in the future, you
artisan oaf'.

I smiled back blandly and paused a moment, just for
effect. I quite enjoyed a little theatrical gesture now and
then, particularly when the puncturing of a pompous prig
was to follow.

"As a matter of fact..." I began, but Percival
interrupted again crossly, glancing with a flamboyant
gesture at his thin gold watch.

"Really, Mr Barclay, can't we get on, I have another
appointment shortly and I would like to bring this
meeting to an early conclusion."

Barclay raised his eyebrows questioningly towards
me. I kept smiling gently and replied, "Well if Mr Percival
is in a hurry, perhaps we could discuss it after he's
gone...?"

Percival spluttered furiously but, realising that he had
no option but to remain if he was to retain some sort of
authority, muttered something about 'another few
minutes wasted can't do much harm". Barclay,
suspecting something afoot, motioned me to continue.

With eyes fixed on Percival, I began again. "Whilst I appreciate Mr Percival's interpretation of what he thought I meant, it was not quite accurate." Still watching Percival's face, I continued: "This Ordnance Map is an old plan and now out of date. The two properties on either side of the chapel forecourt have been redeveloped since this survey was drawn and as part of the deal, both original owners retained the rear parts of their properties after demolition. So, although this plan shows buildings extending down either side of the forecourt as far as the chapel, they don't extend that far now and the spare land, which isn't visible because it's behind those high walls, is in separate ownerships and could be purchased. You could thus have a five metre wide walkway down each side of the chapel, which I believe would be more than adequate."

Barclay seized the plan, asking excitedly, "Is that right, Marcus? Are you sure? How come Mr Percival wasn't aware of that?"

I nodded and looked at my notes.

"The pieces of land are owned by a Mr Arthur Jackson on the left and the Misses Threadle on the right and I understand from my contacts in the area that both are willing to sell for a price."

Everybody looked at Fitzallan Percival – the 'expert' on the area. Barclay frowned.

"Were you aware of this, Mr Percival? I did ask you to check ownerships and you assured me that you'd done so."

Percival inwardly fumed and squirmed with embarrassment. He had visited that part of the forecourt but, having scuffed the toe of one of his patent leather, gold-buckled shoes on a projecting stone cornice, he had been deterred from climbing up the walls to see what lay on the other side in case, in the process, he did further

220

damage to his Guccis and his nine-ounce merino wool handmade suit.

His mind raked rapidly through possible replies. 'I didn't think you'd be interested' would undoubtedly bring Barclay's wrath down on his head and Percival was beginning to get the message that Barclay was not going to be exactly the kind of pliant client he had hoped for when this meeting commenced. The true explanation about his suit he seriously considered offering because maybe Barclay would understand – he himself dressed well – but a glance across the table at me, who in return was considering him in the sort of way a stoat eyes up a baby bunny, dissuaded him rapidly from that reply. So he plunged wildly into a desperate gamble.

"Oh I did, I assure you, but I considered that you would not want to pay the sort of price they would be likely to ask." And when he saw the expression on Barclay's face at this presumption, he ploughed on ever deeper and made his final throw. "I consider that, with my expertise in public enquiries, you would have very little difficulty in obtaining consent to demolish the chapel, and thus the acquisition of this land would be unnecessary."

Barclay checked the thunderbolt he was about to launch. "Let me get this clear, Mr Percival, you're saying that if we buy the church, which we can for a reasonable figure, then you can virtually guarantee that we'll get permission to demolish it and thus save ourselves the cost of acquiring these two adjacent sites which will undoubtedly be expensive. Is that what you're saying?"

Percival gulped and passed his hand across the top of his head a couple of times as if to make sure it was still there. "Yes," he said in a low voice.

"Marvellous!" exclaimed Barclay, nodding at Martin Holmes to make sure he recorded word for word what had just been said. "Well, as you're so confident and as you know my philosophy of 'No duck, no dinner', then I presume that you'll present our case to the planners and to the public enquiry at no cost to us, and when we receive planning permission as you've guaranteed we will, then we shall pay you a full fee with pleasure."

Fitzallan Percival went sickly under his tan. Money was as dear to him almost as his life. He wasn't married and therefore possessions had taken the place of family and to him were objects of devotion. At home he touched his leather upholstered chairs with a sensual caress, he fondled the curves of his stainless steel tables as though they were the breast of his nearest and dearest; the feel of his fine linen and the smoothness of his silk carpets gave him an erotic sensation – and all this sprang from money. Here now he was being asked – no, told really – to risk ten, twenty thousand pounds on something he knew he hadn't a snowflake in hell's chance of winning and he had talked himself into it – or rather 'that bastard Moon' had pushed him. We were all awaiting his reply. He nodded miserably and Martin Holmes recorded his assent diligently.

Barclay beamed again at the table in general.

"There are just two more things to settle then before we fix the date of the next meeting. The first relates to the details of the plans you'll prepare, Fitzallan. You don't mind it if I call you Fitzallan do you, it makes it so much less formal?" And taking this for granted he continued, "I think we will have two sets of plans; one with the layout assuming the chapel is removed as guaranteed by Fitzallan and the other, just in case the impossible occurs and we have to preserve it, for a scheme showing two nice malls down either side. In that event also, of course, we would have to restore the chapel fabric and find an alternative suitable use for it. Marcus here would propose a knocking shop, but then that's all he thinks of, but you, Fitzallan, should be able to come up with something better – a craft museum perhaps?"

All except Percival, who still looked as though he had been force-fed a ripe lemon, chuckled dutifully at this heavy humour. We were checked by Barclay's exclamation.

"One other thing – my God, I nearly forgot this!" He clapped his hand to his head. "The bloody badminton court! Christ Almighty, yes! As part of the deal, the church want us to build – at our own expense, naturally – a hall for badminton at the rear of the chapel. That's vital. The whole agreement rests upon this. You must realise that these days the Church of England revolves around badminton. It has virtually superseded the crucifixion in the liturgy of worship through which both clergy and laity communicate with The Almighty.

"In future centuries archaeologists will uncover these strange flat surfaces marked out with rectangles and no doubt conclude that our generation worshipped white magic through rectangles just as they worshipped black magic through pentacles. So for Christ's sake, literally, don't forget the badminton court.

"Finally, there's the programme. Can you have your preliminary drawings ready two weeks from today, Fitzallan? A firm of your size and reputation should have no trouble with that." Percival nodded assent glumly. "And the final presentation drawings four weeks after we've approved the preliminaries."

Percival baulked strongly at that, and even I thought Barclay was putting the screw on too tightly – he could end up with a crap scheme if it was too rushed. I chipped in here, "I think six weeks is more realistic – don't forget we have to provide Percival and Partners with structural sizes that will take a fortnight and Mr Crabbe has to check that the cost plan lies within the budget."

Barclay agreed. "Okay, six weeks then, but that's fixed and no slippage will be accepted – understood?"

We agreed to circulate information and drawings and

I handed out my visiting card to Crabbe and Percival. Percival looked at it sourly, said he would be in touch and, with Crabbe in attendance, exited smartly without further acknowledgement.

Barclay stood for a moment then looked questioningly at me.

"You free now or have you to rush back?"

"No, quite free."

"Okay, let's break out the gin. I need a large one after that and then we'll get some lunch, first things first."

He called his secretary on the intercom. "Janet, book the four of us; Martin, Marcus, Robin and me, at Chez Lecluse today, we'll try Pierre's cooking for a change – and then bring in four large G and Ts as fast as you can."

We all waited till the drinks arrived, tidying up notes and folding drawings. When the four large, frosted glasses of clear effervescent liquid were placed before us, with thin slices of fresh lime, each paused in momentary reverence. Then with a quick 'Cheers', we lifted the cool glasses and sank half at one pull. I closed my eyes to get the full pleasure from the first swig of the first gin and tonic of the day. That initial drink of the chilled, sharp biting fluid was ecstasy; it cleared the mind and the mouth, washing away the gunge and glob that had accumulated in one fresh draught. After that, the drink was relatively ordinary, but the initial pull – *fantastic*!

Now came the crucial time – crucial for my future wellbeing, that is. I looked at Bob Barclay pensively, wondering how to put it.

"What about this for an idea?" I floated. "I didn't want to bring it up in the meeting and let Percival off the hook, but instead of trying to demolish the chapel, which will only alienate the local people whether you get permission to flatten it or not, have you considered offering to totally restore it to its former glory? That would swing local

224

opinion your way. You could extend the centre roof over the chapel covering the two access paths either side as far as the High Street and make the restored chapel a feature in your scheme – say an exhibition centre for local artists and craftsmen."

There was a long pause; the others were looking everywhere but at me. Bob was studying the ceiling, Martin and Robin each other.

"Well I just thought it was an idea," I offered lamely.

"Bloody brilliant!" shouted Barclay. "Brilliant, it could be just the catalyst we need to win local support – particularly that mob that Marcus's crumpet is running, Save Old Sheringford, isn't it? Well, we'd be saving its most priceless architectural jewel, that must stand us in good stead. I'll tell Percival to scrap the demolition proposal and work that idea up." He clapped me on the back, spilling half of what was left of my drink. "Percival won't like that either!" he chuckled.

That brought thoughts of Percival back into the frame. We all paused momentarily.

"By the way," I began, "I met the Borough Planning Officer at one of Charlie's 'do's in Sheringford. He's your typical 'not in my backyard' and 'over my dead body', left-wing, 'nobody's going to make money out of my area' official."

"It figures," growled Barclay, "we've seen 'em before and we'll see 'em again."

"Yes, but I think this may be different." And I repeated what the Planner had said to me, emphasising the 'underpaid' element of the conversation.

"D'you think he's looking for a bung then?" enquired Fullerton.

I then told them what Hugo had told me about his past experiences with Percival and the rumours that were floating about him trying to bribe council officials and members in the past.

"He hinted at a close relationship with both the Planning Officer and the Chairman of the Planning Committee in Sheringford. Do you think he's at it again?" I pondered.

"He'd bloody well better not be," growled Bob savagely, "any suggestion of that and he'll be out on his ear *tout suite*! Anyhow, if he is, he's mistaken if he thinks I'm going to put up the money for that. I don't want to spend the next ten years of my life banged-up on bread and water. No, and he's too mean to do it with his own money." He pulled at an ear. "It's worth watching though!"

I looked quizzically at Barclay, not making any comment. Barclay looked back, and Fullerton and Holmes looked at both of us. It wasn't for me to say any more, I hadn't brought him in.

Barclay spoke first. "What a fucking banana! Jesus H Christ, where do they produce people like that?" He groaned. "For one blessed moment, I thought he actually was going to resign, but the bastard's too crafty for that. He knows he's written into the sale agreement and I can't fire him unless he's totally incompetent, but if he resigned then that would be a different matter altogether. Oh blessed day, but not today unhappily."

He turned to me with a plea of anguish. "For Christ's sake, keep an eye on him, Marcus, watch him like a bleeding hawk, otherwise he could cost us tens if not hundreds of thousands."

I nodded. "You won't get the best out of him or very much at all out of him, Bob, unless you set him a precise brief and a clear and unequivocal detailed programme. If you don't he'll give you the runaround. Hugo Elmes knows him of old, with scars to prove it."

Barclay raised a finger towards Martin. "Write the minutes of that meeting as though they were the principal defence at your trial for murder." He grinned wolfishly.

"Because your life could well depend on them if Percival finds a loophole to slip through. I think we've stitched him up tight for the present, but we'll do as Marcus suggests and fix a detailed programme at the next meeting. In the meantime, Martin, I want you to go down to Sheringford and stay there until you've tied up Option Agreements from both..." He glanced at his own notes "...one Arthur Jackson and the Misses Treadle."

"Threadle," I corrected.

"Yeah, well whoever it is owns those two sites. They're bound to be pricey but it will be easier now than when the publicity hits the fan and despite what that bullshitter Percival claims, I want a backstop. I just have a feeling about those two sites, they could be crucial."

"There is one other thing," I ventured. "I wonder why neither Percival nor Crabbe mentioned the cyanide problem. They both must be aware of it yet neither of them brought it up!"

Barclay had been briefed by me about the whole issue and didn't consider it of any great significance.

He grinned. "They're probably going to drop it on you as a bombshell, to demonstrate to me that you're not on top of your job and I should have taken Percival's advice and put in the firm he recommended as consultants."

"Drop it on both of us," I said. "If it was serious then it would cost you a fortune to neutralize the land."

That took the grin off his face. "The bastards! Just to spite us. I do not like that, I can tell you. I do not like that!"

"Just leave it for the moment, there's no harm done and it may be a useful card to play in the future." I smiled mischievously. "You could use it to negotiate their fees down a bit!"

He did like that idea and laughed.

"Right, is that it? Okay, let's put festering Fitzallan

behind us for the moment. Have another gin and retire to Pierre Lecluse's hostelry for a sumptuous repast."

* * *

I was getting too predictable. It's a terrible thing when you find that happening; if people know what you're going to do before you do it, it can seriously damage your self-confidence. I was mulling over that fact as I sat in my office around four-thirty with the Fernet Branca in one hand and the black coffee in the other, both put there by Jane the moment I floated through the door on a cloud of gin and tonic and good claret. Fortunately all the other senior staff were out, or busy somewhere else so the usual pointed comments were avoided.

But I was a happy Marcus. Not even the thought of working with Messrs Percival and Crabbe could take away the satisfaction I felt from persuading Bob Barclay to save St Frideswide's. That was going to be my peace offering to Charlie and could well help restore conjugal relations. It had only been four days since the fourth ice age had descended on our little house, but already I was feeling massive withdrawal symptoms. And my back was killing me from that lumpy mattress in the spare room.

"What are you looking so pleased with yourself about?" she snapped, as I strolled through the front door and into the kitchen with a metaphorical song in my heart. "I haven't forgotten what you've done, you know, so don't think for one moment that you're out of the doghouse, Marcus Moon!"

"I come as the bearer of great news, my little angel!" I exclaimed, wondering whether I should put my arms round her in a fond embrace. However as I hadn't actually told her what the 'great news' was yet, I resisted the temptation and avoided the possibility of ending up with a panful of Bolognaise sauce over my head. I contented myself with taking her by the shoulders and turning her to face me, thus moving her out of reach of the cooker.

"You know that Grade One listed architectural gem of Sheringford now crumbled to an unsightly ruin, the St Frideswide Chapel?"

"What about it? I suppose you're going to knock it down, thus protecting the inhabitants of Sheringford from suffering terrible damage to their eyesight!" she said bitterly.

"On the contrary! On the contrary! Bob was proposing to do just that but I've persuaded him to do exactly the opposite. He is now going to completely restore it, turn it into an arts and crafts centre dedicated to the local community and incorporate it within his scheme."

I saw the hostility begin to fade from her eyes and she turned back to her cooking.

She muttered something about "Well it's time you did something useful. Why don't you go and open the wine?"

I wasn't sure if she meant that opening the wine would be useful, or it was an acknowledgement about St Frideswide's. Nothing more was said on the subject during the hasty meal, and she had to go out to a meeting straight after we had eaten. But at bedtime, I found that my duvet and clothes had been moved back into the main bedroom – and there was a packet of Panadol at my side of the bed for my bad back!

Chapter Eleven

By the time August blew itself out into a sunny September, it had been a pretty miserable summer all round. Save Old Sheringford had been totally reorganised under Deirdre Plant's direction. The Main Committee was still chaired by Lord Firrs with Lady Bridger as Vice Chairman. Garden parties and summer balls proliferated, with other jolly fund- and support-raising activities. Ministers were still being button-holed in their clubs, letters written to The Times, Telegraph and Guardian and speeches made at political dinners. The general groundswell of middle and upper-class indignation fuelled by the publicity was putting increasingly embarrassing pressure on Her Majesty's Government. Its attempt to swing over a clutch of New Town voters with the Nippon Kansun bribe was looking decidedly sick when compared with the prospect of a vociferous Tory backlash. The Prime Minister knew it, the Secretary of State for Industry knew it and the Secretary of State for the Environment knew it.

So did Deirdre Plant – and she had barely started putting the boot in yet except into my ribs. Nothing direct to me, you understand; but every now and then – and frequently enough to be wearing – Charlie would drop a comment of the 'Deirdre's right about you being politically immature', and 'even Deirdre says that you only think of yourself' sort. I wondered how much of this Charlie was being fed and just how chummy with Charlie dear Deirdre was these days. Frictions had arisen between Charlie and me over SOS and the amount of time she was spending on it, frictions that were not between us before; and these had, uncharacteristically, spilled over into our other activities. Oh I still showed up at dinners and shindigs of that ilk, but there was a faint chill in the air.

Little huddles formed without me, which fell silent as I approached; glances were cast over shoulders to see if I was in earshot before things were said and I always seemed to end up talking to or seated between 'randy' Nisbett the Borough Surveyor and the Reverend Percy Hartley-Worthington – tucked out of harm's way with the ineffectuals. The old poison was being slipped in very dangerously and I was getting a bit brassed off with Sister Deirdre and her influence all round on our lives.

The newly formed Finance and General Purposes Committee of Save Old Sheringford, the brainchild of none other than Ms Plant, chaired by her with Charlie acting as both secretary and treasurer, was rapidly increasing its powerbase and controlling influence. Deirdre, a practitioner of left-wing semantics who could match any civil servant in the art of drafting English syntax so that it meant two entirely different things to the originator and the recipient, had carefully prepared a series of resolutions for the Main Committee. By shrewd lobbying from both Charlie and herself, they had steered these through virtually without comment. Deirdre's scathing observation to me some time ago on the afternoon of the Sheringford reception to the effect that none of the committee, with the exception of Charlie, wanted to do any work or were prepared to graft proved to be the key which unlocked the Pandora's Box of the F and GP Committee.

Thus the resolution by which the F and GP took over full responsibility for organising all fundraising from the members of the Main Committee delegated what, to the aristocracy, was nothing but a rather unpleasant chore but effectively gave full control over the Society's finances to the F and GP. Likewise a directive that the F and GP would prepare an Action Programme for all future activities ensured that the F and GP controlled policy and again removed the responsibility for doing anything from the aristocracy. The resolution did not specifically state that the F and GP could go ahead with its Action Programme, but neither did it require the programme to be referred back to the Main Committee for comment and ratification. Deirdre and Charlie intended to go ahead; the Main Committee assumed they would be consulted

In a very short time under Deirdre's direction, the F and GP set up and organised such a complicated arrangement of activities that it became quite clear to me that the Main Committee had lost all control and were 'riding on the back of the tiger'. After a few protests, which Deirdre apparently dealt with by the simple expedient of saying, "Well, if you want to run the F and GP and think you can do better, you are quite free to do so", the Main Committee clearly decided that they really had no option but to let the tiger run and just cling on. Accordingly, to give her activities legitimacy, another carefully worded resolution, drafted by the ubiquitous Deirdre to the effect that 'it has been resolved that this committee authorises the Finance and General Purposes Committee to devise, develop and put into action such measures as it may decide are necessary to further the cause of SOS and bring its aims and objects to the attention of the politicians and the public', enabled the Main Committee to save face and Deirdre to breathe life into an Action Sub-Committee. Armed with these authorities, she lost no time in packing it with hard-faced young activists provided by Straker.

Charlie was losing out, she knew in her heart of hearts that control was on the move. At first when it moved away from the Main Committee to the F and GP, she was delighted. The extra effort injected by Deirdre, coupled with the wider political base, was undoubtedly bringing more power to their protest. But the time and drive that Deirdre seemed able to devote solely to SOS meant that more and more decisions had to be left for her to make unilaterally if progress was to be maintained.

A feeling of unease had begun to steal into Charlie's elation. Some of Deirdre's decisions and activities seemed to be directed more at stirring up political mayhem just for the sake of it than saving Old Sheringford from the ravages of acid rain. But she was damned if she was going to admit it – particularly to me, the 'Taker-of-the-Piss-in-Chief' about Sister Deirdre and her pushy cohorts. No way, so it was either let go or keep up. She redoubled her efforts to stay in there and regain a measure of control over SOS policy, but it was devilishly hard and time-consuming and very taxing on the self-control.

Ever since our row over Barclay's development scheme, I had noticed a gradual change taking place in Charlie. Not towards me specifically, although it obviously affected me considerably, but towards everything she did. There was an increasing despondency in her manner, a sort of desperate urgency which crept into her work both at the hospital and for SOS. It was as if she was being forced to compete with the clever new kid who had just been put up from 4B – and it was quite obvious who the 'new kid' was. To start with Charlie had been waxing eloquent about Deirdre Plant and wouldn't hear a thing against her. She was 'really getting a grip on things', sorting out the numerous problems, spending 'eons of time' tying up loose ends; had great new ideas for 'promoting our cause'; brought in lots of 'new blood'; dealt with all the paperwork, canvassing, fundraising, posters and whatever. In short, she was being a real help – 'unlike somebody I could mention', etcetera, etcetera.

Charlie had gone wholeheartedly along with all this from day one, backing Deirdre to the hilt – even when it started to become clear that the output of Save Old Sheringford was developing a pronounced left-wing slant. Her argument was that as the whole point of her getting Deirdre involved had been to provide political balance and thus obtain wider support, one shouldn't complain if there was a shift from the right-wing leanings SOS had previously exhibited to a more upright position.

Also, she added, I shouldn't forget that as the primary purpose of SOS was to pressure the government of the day – whatever its political persuasion – into activating powerful legislation to ensure clean air and abandoning the Nippon Kansun project, then whatever activities did pressure and embarrass them must be for the good of the cause.

All very logical if one believed in the purity of political motives, but I was of the 'What's in it for them?' school and I couldn't for the life of me see what dark motive lurked behind Deirdre Plant's muscular forehead. I also refrained from pointing out that it was Deirdre who had inserted herself into SOS in the first place and that posters, handbills, pamphlets and placards proclaiming in screaming colours and capitals 'Whitehall Out, SOS in!', 'SOS says Save Our Jobs', 'SOS says Spend On Social Services' and 'No Nukes in Sheringford' had nothing to do with preserving old buildings – except maybe the last, I did concede a point there. But of course Charlie knew this as well as anybody – what was worrying me was that she was actively supporting it and going along with it. When we did discuss SOS, which was less and less frequently as she got more and more prickly about it, it was always 'Deirdre's doing this, Deirdre thinks that, Deirdre says the other', and although Deirdre was now apparently shacked up for at least part of the week in Sheringford, Deirdre's Action Committee meetings –

which Charlie insisted on attending – seemed always to be held in London. I was growing cheesed off to the eyeballs, both with Deirdre Plant and with having to drive Charlie twice a week to the more dismal areas of the capital – Lambeth, Islington, Newham and Southwark. To dark, soot-grimed, terraced houses or dingy rooms above tiny nondescript shops where the Lady Bridgers of this world wouldn't be seen dead. These meetings were never held consecutively in the same place and after a while, as I told the boys down in The Frog, Charlie dispensed with my services as her driver (because I grumbled too much about all the waiting around) and drove herself. "...I know not where," I complained.

Pete Smallwood tried to cheer me up.

"She's having you on, Marcus, it's nothing to get worried about – women behave like that at times, want to get away on their own and 'Go walkabout' – perfectly normal. I see it regularly in my profession as physician and confidant to the hoi polloi."

"Is that so?" I brightened.

"Indeed it is, we Harley Street specialists have a clinical name for it – Smallwood's Syndrome, it's called. Named, I might add," he glanced down modestly at his beautifully manicured fingernails, "after me. It's called, in the vernacular, my dear Moon, 'Not getting enough'. That's the trouble with your good Charlotte – Night Starvation. You are failing in your duty as a man and she, to compensate, is shoving off up the East End and, not to put too fine a point on it, having a touch of legover with some hairy, sweaty docker until fulfilment as a woman is restored." He looked triumphantly at me and paused. The others, broad grins on their faces, waited too, but I wasn't to be fooled into indiscreet confidences by Smallwood's feeble trap.

"Smallwood, I don't know in what coin your blue rinse, sex-starved Mayfair dowagers pay you for your so-called advice but whatever it is they should, under the Trade Descriptions Act, demand a refund if that is a sample." But I couldn't resist adding, "And anyhow, my relations with Charlotte, I assure you, do not need any supplemental benefits provided by the Dock Labour Board."

I waited whilst ironic cheers died down and then lied with a forced grin, "That's the least likely source of our problems. No, my concern is that she appears to be getting further and further embroiled with this left-wing lot who seem to have somehow infiltrated themselves into the Save Old Sheringford campaign. It was all going so well in the early days and things were great but now she's hardly ever in the house. Committees here, rallies there, speeches everywhere, she's absolutely knackered when she gets home."

I stared gloomily into my beer as I contemplated an increasingly celibate Marxist existence and wondered briefly if Smallwood's Syndrome might be the root cause. After a suitable nervous penance on the corrugated mattress of the spare room, the Mark One Bollocking had abated but in its wake had come an increasingly wearied, exhausted Charlotte which did even less for my sex life. Opportunity without enthusiasm is no turn-on, believe you me.

I had had two months of teeth-gritting aggro at work, with Fitzallan Percival changing his mind every second day. God knows how he had managed to get himself together sufficiently to prepare a planning application for Sheringford Council for Barclay's scheme, we must have redesigned it six times in as many weeks. And just when I was looking forward to our summer holiday in Ibiza, Charlie had had to cry off. Pressure of work she said, but I knew it was trying to keep up with that damned Plant woman, I was sure of it. So I spent my two weeks up in York with the parents, digging my mother's asparagus bed in the pouring rain and drinking Sam Smiths in the Conservative Club with my father. Good beer that – it was the high spot of the fortnight. Then back to the grind again – more Plant and Percival. The little brown job, fortunately, pushed off somewhere – I didn't ask where – for his vacation shortly after I returned but Plant had now started coming round to the house. The first night I was back she rabitted on the whole way through England versus Russia. I missed all three goals and went to bed in a towering rage – a poor homecoming to the arms of my loved one.

Something was going to have to be done about Sister Deirdre – but what? Quite frankly, I hadn't a clue.

"Life's like a stick of Brighton rock, Marcus, one minute it's sweet and in your grasp and the next somebody has stuffed it up your arse."

I looked miserably at the speaker – a friend of Tony Scales.

"Thanks a bunch, Rollo, that's very illuminating that is – a great deal of help. What I need is a proper plan of campaign. Fight fire with fire, provide a strong counter-attraction, devise some means of separating Charlie from this fiendish feminist friend of hers who's got sod all else to do but make trouble, and who seems to be the prime mover in this situation. Not..." and I shot a glare at the previous speaker "...some feeble philosophical witticism thought up during the long hours of boredom draining the National Health Service of its millions under the pretext of stimulating oral hygiene."

"Talking about oral hygiene," said Rollo Prenderville, quite unabashed by my sarcasm, "have you heard the one about the young lady from Westphalia?"

"Yes I have and no, I do not want to hear it again and finally it was bloody disgusting, particularly the way you tell it with all the revolting actions!" I snarled.

Movement behind the bar ceased. Big Jessie, who had

not heard the one about the young lady from Westphalia and had moved closer in order to do so, put down the glass she was polishing and gave a disappointed smile. "My, we are in the dumps today, aren't we? You'd better have another on the house." She took my glass to refill at the same time as she fended off all the other proffered glasses from the suddenly weeping, wailing crowd.

As she drew the half, she philosophised out loud. "What she needs is a good man, innit? That's what she needs – that's what we all need," she added wistfully.

I saw it in a flash, by the centre – that was it, that was the solution!

"By God, you're right, you gorgeous piece of pulchritude!" I cried, I put a hand to my forehead. "I must think, I must think – but I do believe you've hit the nail smack on the head."

I looked round for a bit of privacy and the others watched with mild astonishment as I took my glass and my person off to a quiet corner and ensconced myself on a lonely stool isolated from the world. They shrugged their shoulders and grinned to each other at this instant conversion from savage celibate to hostelry hermit, but after a few pointed asides directed at my unresponsive back, gave up and concentrated on the usual Saturday lunchtime topics: sex, sport, easy ways to make a living and food.

Big Jessie's wistful observation had set a train of thought in motion. When I had first met Deirdre Plant I had felt that there was something not quite true about her. I couldn't put a finger on why, maybe it was just the fleeting shadows deep in her eyes or a feeling that an aggressive manner concealed a vulnerability – either a conscious or subconscious vulnerability. It was more probable in her case that it was a subconscious one, and she either didn't realise she was vulnerable or she was, again at a subconscious level, suppressing it. This tough, assertive image of independence and self-sufficiency was projected to repel any suggestion of an offer of emotional or sympathetic support from any person – particularly and emphatically any *man*. Her independence was not that of quiet self-containment and confidence. It was thrust forward like a bayonet, saying, in effect, 'Don't you dare try to venture into my territory without an invitation', and thus demonstrating a fear that her guard was vulnerable and her defence, once penetrated, would collapse.

Now I must add here that on the few occasions when I go off into deep Freudian analysis, my success rate has not been high. Being honest about it, and taking all things into consideration, I can, with hand on heart, say that so far I would estimate I have been in the region of ... well, actually... a hundred percent wrong. Not that that has ever been allowed to inhibit my optimism in any way as to my abilities to undertake fruitcake philosophy, and I lived in expectant hope that one day I would be right. But it was a failing I was aware of. On first impressions, my average was pretty good, based on the Moon classification table; however, today was to be a smart ass day, and based on that a plan was gestating. Just a little more analysis was needed to flesh it out.

The mind began to tick faster. If, as I believed, Deirdre's aggression was in fact defensive and had the Freudian undertones I attributed to it, then she must be harbouring a secret desire for some virile 'stallion' to take her on face to face, smash through her carefully constructed defences and not only venture into her territory but take absolute possession of it, making himself well and truly at home. In other words, to paraphrase Freud in Moonian terms, she needed somebody to screw the arse off her with such accomplishment and so frequently that she would not only become a desperate and hopeless addict to it, but she would fall for this provider of pecker with a commitment so intense that it would concentrate her entire existence on a single, divine fulcrum. Her ability to dedicate her efforts to other activities would vanish and thus her command over Charlie's time would disappear. Deirdre would fade into the rosy sunset, shagged senseless; and Charlie, released from the tiger, would be free to resume with me our erotic evenings and halcyon nights together without falling asleep halfway through.

Of such stuff was born Moon's Plan A!

Perfect, I decided, but just to double check I ran through the scenario once more. The re-run confirmed the plan but threw up, not exactly a flaw, more of an administrative difficulty. The scheme was sound. It was the casting that needed some work doing on it – such as, for instance. who was to be the principal stud in this 'dramatis personae' of lust and debauchery?

Me? I contemplated the idea of playing this role for a moment, but whilst I was all for a bit of nooky under certain circumstances, poking Plant in cold blood was definitely not one of them. I just did not have that Germanic dedication to duty that driving a Panzer column through Poland required. On the other hand, neither did I possess the total indifference of the real sex maniac. One who could carry through any dreadful lechery without batting an eyelid? Besides, if I was principal boy, Charlie would be certain to find out and I didn't think she would appreciate the sacrifice for an instant. A defence that screwing the eyeballs out of Plant was entirely for Charlie's benefit was not one I felt I could put forward in the sure confidence of complete understanding. So that idea was thankfully scrapped but the problem remained. It had to be somebody who could actually do it, and almost certainly somebody I knew well.

An inward glow followed by the spreading of a slow smile warmed my breast. What were friends for? I asked myself. After all, it wasn't his life I would be asking him to lay down – just his person, and I knew just the man for the moment.

I swigged the remains of the gratuitous half pint, descended from my perch and strolled back to the mob with a spring in my step and resolution in my heart to put Plan A into operation forthwith.

Chapter Twelve

Ten days later, Charlie and I threw a small diner party at the house in Fulham. It had to be limited in numbers because of the size of our dining-room and I insisted that eight was sufficient, although in the past we had squeezed in as many as twelve for dinner. However, I didn't want too many bodies round the place so that the target's attention could be diverted elsewhere and I didn't want too few so that Charlie would get suspicious when she saw happening what I hoped would happen. Luck had also smiled upon me the previous Monday evening when I eventually got hold of Tony Scales on the telephone. It transpired that Scales had given the quiet, luminous girl the shove – 'couldn't stand her rapier-like wit' – and was therefore footloose and fancy free. Which meant he was hunting.

"I'll see what I can do for you, old son," I said, trying to keep the glee out of my voice. "You like 'em well built and a bit of a challenge, don't you? Or that's what you're always telling us."

I sensed Scales's apprehension at my offer – he had had a taste of my blind date organisation once before and ended up with a tall, skinny buck-toothed girl who looked more like a garden rake than a fulfiller of man's lust and desires. On top of that she had picked her teeth all evening, not spoken more than ten syllables and finally, just as he got her into bed, been sick all over his sheets. He had not been pleased, but as I pointed out to him later, "Well, you said you'd take what was left and she was the one that was left." He had retorted that he didn't mean left over from a sale of garden hardware. Hence on this occasion he was perhaps understandably cautious.

"Now hang on, Marcus, don't rush me. She's not the one who's left this time, is she?" He shivered at the recollection. I laughed.

"Not in the way you mean, my dear cavity filler, but she does incline politically towards that side. Thinks all public school Tories are affected pansies and the only men worth their salt in this world of patronage and nepotism are those duffle-coated, scruffy, megaphone-bellowers on picket lines. I have noticed of late in visits to your surgery that you could qualify for this so you should get on. She is, however, not a bad looker at all, I promise you, and very bright." I paused as if in speculation. "In fact, I just wonder if it would be more appropriate to seat her between two of the intellectual guests – not to worry though, I'll think about it."

I put the phone down, leaving Scales spluttering indignantly, and then pranced about on tiptoe like Sylvester the Cat, chortling with glee and capering round the room until I became aware of Charlie's scrutiny from the open doorway.

"What on earth are you doing?"

"Nothing, beloved," I grinned sheepishly. "I've just been trying to interest Tony in Deirdre Plant." I added hastily, "If they're going to be the only unaccompanied people on Tuesday, I didn't want him ignoring her all evening, as he tends to if he doesn't like someone, and I didn't want her putting a verbal half-nelson on him in round one and winning by a submission before we're through the pre-dinner drinks."

Charlie nodded and turned away, saying over her shoulder, "I don't think he's Deirdre's type. She goes for the small, helpless kind of male, rather than the he-man. It arouses the maternal instinct in her."

As this innocent observation sank in I felt as if I had been socked plumb in the solar plexus.

"You what?" I gasped at the realisation that all my planning could be wasted as well as the cost of this dinner and the expensive wines I had bought.

"She prefers little, insignificant men that she can dominate," Charlie confirmed, "like Jeremy Leach-Edgington – he's more her type. They have surprising stamina some of these little chaps," she added wickedly. "Anyway, she already has a companion."

My heart, already sinking with the news about her taste in men, sank even further.

"I didn't know! Nobody's ever mentioned Deirdre's bloke before."

"It's not a bloke, it's a girl. That thin wispy creature who hangs about her in Sheringford, Suzie her name is. She lives with Deirdre, they share a flat in the New Town."

"But you said she goes for insignificant men!"

"She does. Deirdre swings both ways."

That was a bit more encouraging, but Scales could hardly be called insignificant at six foot four and fifteen stones.

"Bugger," I muttered, "bugger, bugger!"

"I shouldn't worry too much, Marcus, they should both fit in with the rest of the company."

"I suppose so," I muttered gloomily, as I contemplated Plan A falling apart at the first hurdle. I wanted them fitting in with each other, in more ways than one, and I couldn't give a monkey's toss if the rest of the company loathed the sight and sound of them.

* * *

Despite my fears, the dinner proved to be a great success, I had decided not to abandon Plan A on hearsay evidence alone and arranged the table seating accordingly. Scales

I put well away from Charlie, between Deirdre on the one hand and Pete Smallwood's Anushka on the other. Smallwood always went in for the thick but ravishingly beautiful type of girl. If I want intelligent conversation, he would say, I can talk to myself, but for the rest, give me the best. Anushka's conversation was therefore limited and it was a surefire certainty that after half a minute trying to make conversation with her, Scales would give up and concentrate on Deirdre on his other side, who would, no doubt, have plenty to say. The other two guests were a married couple, friends of Charlie's from the Royal Free, good mixers and bright and cheerful. To assist matters even more, I placed myself next to Deirdre, with Julie, the Royal Free wife, on my other side. I intended to devote most of my time to her so that Deirdre would be left with no option but to talk to Tony, or shout across the table. She didn't want to talk much to me in any case, so it wouldn't be a problem.

At the preliminary drinks it had started to go in the right direction. Deirdre looked quite ravishing in the subdued lighting. All her heavy features were softened and the tiny craters of teenage acne were invisible at a lighting intensity of less than ten lumens. Scales, after general greetings including a rather too enthusiastic kiss on Charlie, had, of his own volition, made a beeline for Deirdre and as they moved to sit at the table, he gave me a thumbs up and a leer of approval.

Charlie is a super cook, and I had invested some hard-earned money in a few bottles of decent wine. I also laid on a case of Trubshaw's Finest Ale in case Deirdre decided to follow her proletarian path. Not so, but she drank the wine like beer, great gulps at a time that made me fear for my stock, and I had to hold back myself to avoid running out.

Fortunately Julie was a good conversationalist, so with one ear on her and the other eavesdropping on Tony and

Deirdre, I got through the meal with a few smiles, nods, grunts, and the odd 'oh really?'

My apprehension faded – perhaps all would turn out well in spite of my earlier misgivings. One thing was for sure – Scales was certainly not interested in Deirdre for the qualities of her mind. Judging by the expression on his face, I could see the cerebral undressing taking place in front of my eyes. The randy big ferret had had her clothes off and on at five minute intervals throughout the meal and even now as we stood drinking our coffee and sipping brandy, he was either rubbing against her or sinking his eyeballs down the front of her low-buttoned shirt.

I examined Deirdre to see how she was taking this and to my amazement her face wore the same sort of expression. Lips slightly parted, cheeks with faint flush, nipples hardening and bright sparkling eyes firmly focused on the power bulge in the front of Scales's trousers. Off duty Scales tended to wear what his tailor euphemistically called 'snug-fitting' trousers. "If you've got it, baby – flash it," was his motto, "let them have a tantalising glimpse of what paradise could hold for them if they play their cards right."

Well, it seemed that the Scales sexual magnet was doing its share of pulling that night, a delighted me concluded. If the Plant woman was going to he held captive by the old magnetic field after she had rotated on its exquisite north pole, then the outcome could be the answer I was seeking.

Humming away happily to myself as I cleared the table and stacked the dishes for Charlie to wash after they'd gone, I wondered when the great coupling would take place. It wouldn't be tonight, Deirdre had to travel back to Sheringford and Tony Scales started in his surgery early at eight the next morning. But they had surreptitiously exchanged bits of paper which I assumed contained phone numbers, so it could be fairly soon. That would be a clash of titans. I started to chuckle at the idea of two great hippos charging together in the rut, it would be some bed that could withstand that event. I became aware of a pair of violet eyes boring into my skull.

"What's so funny then?" Charlie enquired.

I grinned at her. "I was just thinking of the outcome of the Tony-Deirdre scenario. They seemed to hit it off rather well, I thought."

She frowned and put down the plate she was holding. "What are you up to? You seem very concerned about Deidre's wellbeing these days. That's not like you, unless..." She paused. "Unless you're up to something?"

"I'm just happy to see two souls entwined as one, walking hand in hand down the path of life." My grin grew broader.

"Well as long as it doesn't mess up my SOS work you can entwine who you like." She raised a warning finger. "But don't forget, I know you, Marcus Moon." And she wagged her finger before turning back to the sink.

Chapter Thirteen

The sun continued to shine, the birds sang, the fruit ripened and our discussions with the Sheringford Town Planning Department were going astonishingly well. I say 'astonishingly' because, following the Chief Planning Officer's observations to me at the Town Hall SOS reception about developers ripping off and defiling his town, all appeared to be sweetness and light. Mind you, the Chief Planner didn't actually attend these meetings; he left them to his deputy – a young, more enthusiastic woman, fresh from qualifying as a Member of the Royal Town Planning Institute, who looked at things refreshingly constructively. She hadn't had time yet to transmogrify into the cynical world of the career-blighted, small town Planning Officer; a critic of garden sheds and dormer windows; of bathroom extensions and outside lavatories. No, this was her big chance in Sheringford and she wanted it to be a success.

As long as the proposed development didn't conflict with existing buildings in scale or materials, she was supportive. I had to admit that Percival's scheme did look impressive, and after she had 'suggested' a few changes it fitted in well with the local environment. So he wasn't a complete architectural 'dog'. Beneath that flash, sun-lamped, microwaved exterior there lurked a flicker of aesthetic appreciation and she managed to squeeze it out of him – although he took all the credit, of course.

Only Percival attended meetings with the Chief

Planner, and with members of the Planning Committee, but he waxed eloquent about the reception his designs were receiving and kept coming back with glowing reports abut these. "It is just what the town needs," and "It could be an architectural gem," he quoted.

I persuaded Charlie to get the Save Old Sheringford Committee to invite Bob Barclay to give them a presentation about his scheme, emphasising the restoration of St Frideswide's and its conversion into an arts centre. In spite of some strong objections from Ms Plant, this had gone down well, and, after some discussion, the committee decided that saving the wreckage of the rusting sheds on the old Grimshaw site was not a part of their remit, whereas saving Grade One listed St Frideswide's was. Accordingly they agreed not to lodge an objection to Barclay's scheme. Ever the opportunist, Barclay suggested that it would be more helpful if they could write a letter of support to the local council rather than just stay silent. Again Deidre objected but was overruled and, as secretary, was instructed to submit an appropriate letter.

Charlie gave me the gist of what had transpired and I passed the information on to Bob.

"That bloody woman," he grumbled, "can't you do something about her?"

"I take it you're not referring to the apple of my eye, Barclay; otherwise I shall have to call you out. Custard pies at dawn!" I grinned.

"No, you idiot, that Plant person. What have I done to offend her?" He frowned pensively.

I could think of a very long list of things starting with his whole lifestyle, but decided that in the interest of harmony silence was the answer to what I hoped was a rhetorical question.

The final design team meeting to confirm that all the information necessary was available prior to submitting the application for planning permission was held in Barclay's offices, attended by all the principals: Barclay, Fullerton, Holmes, Percival, Crabbe, Ronnie Delf the letting agent, and myself. At the end of the meeting Bob had laid on some decent wine and canapés to toast the success of the application. Whilst we were tucking in to this Percival, with a glance at me, took Bob to one side and said, *sotto voce*, "Can we speak privately?"

"Sure," replied Bob, apprehensively eyeing up the emptying bottles of Premier Cru Chablis. "I hope it's important and won't take long, otherwise there'll be nothing left after this lot have been let loose for five minutes."

Percival frowned irritably at the lack of importance Bob appeared to attribute to his request but followed him along the corridor to his office.

I wondered what that was about – a punt for extra fees? an invitation to dinner at the Waterside Inn? No, I jest, spending a couple of hundred quid on a meal for a knife and fork artist like Barclay would not be one of Percival's foremost thoughts. It was much more likely the former!

The "You *what*?" echoed down the corridor and through the building, followed by the sound of a door slamming and further raised voices rendered unintelligible by the closed door.

We canapé-munchers and wine-drinkers paused in our munching and drinking and looked at each other with eyebrows raised and glasses stilled.

"Bob don't sound too pleased," offered Norman Crabbe.

A door crashed open and a very red-faced, tight-lipped Percival hove in sight at a brisk trot, followed by an even redder, heavily-breathing Barclay. Without so much as a glance at the rest of us, Percival hurriedly gathered up his drawings and notes and legged it out of the door.

A clearly shaken Barclay seized the nearest bottle of wine, poured himself a large glass and took a long draught.

"Fucking unbelievable!" he exclaimed, shaking his head. "Where do people like that come from?"

"Problem?" enquired Crabbe tactlessly. There was no fooling Norman. Barclay took a deep breath and steadied himself.

"Nothing I can't handle." He brushed off Crabbe's question and finished the rest of his wine. "Come on you lot, drink up, we've got work to do. Marcus, a word with you please."

Wondering what this was all about I finished my wine and followed Barclay back down the corridor to his office whilst the others drifted curiously away.

"Take a seat," he said, pointing to one of the armchairs and he sank into the other. "Do you know what that prat just told me?" Again a rhetorical question because I had no idea, and it didn't feel like the occasion for speculative humour like 'He's been sleeping with your wife?', so I waited. "He proudly announced that he had done a deal with the Chief Planning Officer that in return for supporting his scheme – note '*his* scheme', by the way – I would make a contribution to what he referred to euphemistically as the guy's pension fund! Fifty grand into a Swiss bank account!"

He stood up and strode round the office. Fortunately it had a thick pile carpet and could take the wear.

"So what did you tell him?" I ventured.

There was not necessarily an obvious answer to my question. It was not unknown in the developer's world for some form of sweetener to be paid to Planning Officers, and indeed to councillors, to assist in obtaining a planning approval, so I awaited Bob's answer with interest.

"Tell him! Tell him! I told him many things, mainly about his ancestry and his future, but principally to make it quite clear to the Chief Planner, and anybody else who may be in cahoots with him, that there is no deal. Also to make it equally clear that I knew nothing of this, and if word gets out I'll call in the cops and shaft the pair of them!" He looked at me. "You're not saying much?"

I responded thoughtfully, feeling slightly guilty about my earlier doubts. "I was just thinking, what effect, if any, this will have on your planning application?"

Bob sat down again and rubbed his chin.

"Well I suppose having supported us so far – presumably on the basis that he thought he was going to get a 'bung', he can hardly switch round at this late stage. His whole department would know. I don't know; we'll just have to play it by ear. I'm ninety percent certain it will go through, particularly as we've got the backing of Save Old Sheringford. I've told Percival to get the application in now whilst the sun is shining and before anybody has time to change their mind."

* * *

The Indian summer was short lived. On the eighteenth of September the politicians of the Sheringford Planning Committee considered Barclay's planning application for his development scheme briefly and, without any serious discussion, threw it out.

Percival had assured Barclay that it had gone to the Planning Committee with the full support of the officials. It had – and wallop straight out on its ear. Sixteen against, nil for.

The grounds for rejection Barclay got over the phone from the Deputy Planning Officer the morning following the Planning Committee meeting. The Chief Planner had shrewdly taken 'diplomatic leave' that day.

"I shall deny that I ever said this, Mr Barclay, if you ever repeat it publicly, but it was purely political!"

"Purely political? How do you mean purely political?"

The Deputy Planner dropped her voice confidentially. "Apparently the members got together with the Chief Planning Officer beforehand at a private meeting and decided that, with Save Old Sheringford piling on the pressure about preservation, and the local elections coming up in March, it was too hot a political potato to handle, so they copped out. Their view is: let the Secretary of State decide, and whatever criticisms are then levelled, it wouldn't be as a result of their doing."

Barclay was aghast at this news.

"But Save Old Sheringford were supporting the scheme!" he cried. "Once they knew we were going to restore St Frideswide's and get rid of all the pollution and rusty buildings on the site, they agreed to back us. My architect was specifically instructed to obtain a supporting letter from their secretary."

There was a puzzled pause. "The Committee received no such letter," said the DPO, "and none was included with the documents that the architect submitted."

There was another pause, but before Barclay could respond the planner continued: "And that was another thing, Mr Barclay, I know I shouldn't criticize a fellow professional, and we had no problems with Mr Percival because we get all types in here and are used to dealing with... shall we say..." She couldn't think of the right word but Barclay was thinking of plenty.

"Go on," Barclay growled.

The DPO continued, quite relieved to have got off that hook. "It's just that the local politicians down here aren't city types and didn't appreciate being constantly badgered by Mr Percival. To put it bluntly, he got right up their noses!"

Barclay digested that, but returned to principal point. "But what are the actual planning reasons for chucking it out? I mean, they can't just reject it for 'political reasons', or because 'Percival got up the Committee's noses'! Those aren't sound basic reasons under planning law, surely?"

"Oh, we'll cobble something up – doesn't conform to the new draft plan, increased traffic will overload the existing road system, excessive retail space detrimental to existing traders – you know the sort of thing. The tragedy is that really everybody wants this scheme."

Barclay did indeed know the sort of bullshit that could be given as reasons for rejection and was highly annoyed off about it.

"I'm going to appeal this, you know – it's a load of bloody nonsense, all our studies and reports demonstrated that there wouldn't be any problems in those areas."

"Well we expected you would – it will mean a full Public Inquiry, you realise that. The irony of it is, much as we'd like to see your scheme built, we shall have to oppose you."

"And if I lose, Sheringford is left with a pile of rusting crap on a cyanide contaminated site, with a Grade One listed building crumbling to dust that your Authority will have to pay to maintain, and in view of that, have a much weakened case for its preservation. How will that benefit anybody?"

The DPO gave a cynical chuckle. "The local politicians will benefit, they'll get re-elected!"

"I'm in for the whole confounded legal rigmarole, Marcus," Barclay complained when he phoned me with the bad news. "Solicitor's, planning experts, junior counsel, senior counsel, all the King's horses and all the King's men, they'll all be in on it with their inflated daily rates and five hundred quid 'refreshers'. It's going to cost a bomb!" He sighed resignedly. "We shall need you to give evidence about the site and the traffic. Can you re-check the figures to make sure they're rock solid?"

"Will do, I'll have to run them through the computer

again but the County Highways Department have checked them and come out in writing to support us."

Barclay groaned. "Yeah, it's not really that anyhow, it's those bloody chicken-livered local councillors, and that devious bastard the Chief Planning Officer. They fight like rats to get themselves elected to represent the local people and then haven't got the guts to make any positive decision which they think might be the slightest bit controversial, even though they know it will ultimately benefit all those who elected them."

He paused thoughtfully. "I wonder how many of them were on the take for a slice of Percival's largesse. Be very difficult to prove."

He continued switching subjects. "And there's one other thing. What happened to that fucking letter that was supposed to be sent from Save Old Sheringford? The Planning committee never received it, and Percival told me this morning that he didn't pursue it because he thought his scheme was so wonderful that it wasn't necessary. I bet that beefy butch bird that's running your life never produced it."

I tried to conceal my disappointment, ignoring his last comment.

"So what happens now, Bob?"

"So we appeal to the Department for the Environment, Food and Rural Affairs; they appoint an inspector and fix a date for a Public Inquiry to be held in Sheringford. On the appointed day we trundle up with half the legal profession in our train; Sheringford Borough Council do likewise with the other half; the great unwashed throng outside to put in their pennyworth; the inspector buggers off on his holidays to Florence or Pisa and after six months, if we're lucky, a decision filters down somewhere in the inner recesses of Whitehall where the sun don't shine. Probably some junior clerk tosses a coin.

"Anyhow, enough of my problems for the present –

to change the subject, what's happening with Tony Scales? I hear he's 'entertaining' a new girlfriend. Do you know anything about it?"

That was typical Barclay. *His* problems indeed! His problems were also my problems. Hugo Elmes was not going to be overjoyed when he learned that planning permission for Sheringford had been refused. He, like the other consultants, wouldn't get much of a fee if the job didn't go ahead – and neither would we get the very profitable site introduction fee. My esteem in the eyes of the partners hung in the balance here.

However, there was one chink of light on the personal horizon and Barclay's remark had illuminated it.

"Yes I do," I told him. "The 'beefy butch bird' that you claim 'is running my life' happens to be the subject of Tony Scales 'entertaining'!"

"No! Really?"

"Yes! Really! Tonight's the night. She's to be subjected to the ultimate test. Scales is taking her out and, according to Charlie, giving her the full treatment: show, dinner, the lot."

I hoped it was the lot! A show, dinner, a peck on the cheek and thanks for the memory was no good to me. But I knew my Tony, and Deirdre Plant didn't look the type to be hanging on to her virginity till Mister Right smiled across a crowded room. No, I could be on a winner here.

Barclay sounded sceptical.

"But is she Scales's type? I didn't think he went in for the feminist intellectual heavyweight."

I didn't want to hear doubts.

"She's a woman, isn't she?" I snapped. "Thus she's certainly got the bits that Scales is interested in. I'm not looking for a meeting of minds here; a discussion on the dictatorship of the proletariat. I want them at it like frenzied ferrets – overcome with lust and longing. Any fusing of intellect can come later just so long as he gets her off my back and on to hers! Anyway, I've given him a full briefing about her and the benefit of my advice... so nothing can go wrong."

Barclay finished off with what sounded like a cynical snort. "Oh yeah?" and put the phone down.

Of course nothing could go wrong, could it? Could it...?

Chapter Fourteen

Scales had been peculiarly reticent about his evening with the Plant woman – unusually so for a notorious *bon fourrer* like him. There was a noticeably evasive forced heartiness whenever I brought up the subject of his excursion into left-wing bliss, as I did at every possible opportunity. I naturally wanted to know if my plan had succeeded, but Scales's deliberate obtuseness was not helping.

"For God's sake, Scales, will you give me a straight answer once and for all? Has the delectable Deirdre fallen under your spell as Trilby to her Svengali? Yet another notch on your metaphorical gun, another ring around your totem pole? Or has she not? A lot depends on your answer – so for heaven's sake, tell me!"

The Frog and Nightgown was quiet this Saturday lunchtime, a lot of the regulars were away for one reason or another: late holidays, weekends off, watching the football or just felt it was too swelteringly hot to make the effort. It was one of those very rare September days when London buses shimmered and hovered in the air and the tar melted on the roads; a day when dowagers too stately to move fanned themselves with a flick of the wrist and the proletariat found odd corners where they could catch any gentle waft of passing breeze.

Over Scales's shoulder I could see Football Focus flickering on the pub television, diminutive figures darting about to an excited broad Scots commentary. I sighed deeply, suspecting the worst, and switched my eyes back to a twitching Tony.

"Well, has she?" I demanded again.

He just grinned and clapped me on the shoulder, extending his long arm right round to give me an affectionate hug. He winced as he did so and drew back slightly as if experiencing a sudden cramp.

"Needing to get all your kicks second-hand now, Marcus?" He shook his head in mock disapproval. "It's the start of the long slide down the ladder of depravity that is, having to rely on other people's sex lives for your stimulation – the next step is acquiring a dirty raincoat and doing a bit of flashing on Wimbledon Common."

He looked into my frustrated eyes for a moment. "Yes, I can see there quite clearly signs of unfulfilled sexual desire. You're obviously off your oats – your eyes give you away, my lad, hence I suppose the need for third party passion." He dropped his voice confidentially. "Now there is a very good little porno cinema I've heard of in Charing Cross Road – dirty raincoats, half price; an afternoon there should put you right... or send you blind," he added as an afterthought.

"Stop trying to change the subject, there's nothing wrong with my eyes," I snapped back defensively. "They are clear and sharp, sparkling and penetrative and what is more, they can see right through your facade of bluster and bonhomie. You failed, didn't you? You bloody well failed to score. She turned down the great..."

He cut in. "That's what I mean, old son: the eyes." He tapped the side of his head just behind eye level. "Your eyes are normally all bloodshot and watering, puffy and sunken, with deep dark lines round them from all that shagging and other perverted activities with which you fulfil your lustful desires, but all that has cleared up, gone, not a trace of depravity. You look human – well, almost, for you."

I controlled myself and smiled gently, but the jibe about my eyes worried me a little. That was the second

259

time in the past few months that people I knew well had commented that my vices were reflected in my eyes. It may have been in jest perhaps, but nevertheless, two independent observations seemed more than coincidence. First Charlie about drinking and now Scales about sex. I made a mental note to examine myself carefully in the mirror, the eyes in particular, the next time I over indulged in either of those, but for the present it must be back to the issue in hand. I was right, I could sense it, Scales was worried now – he always resorted to abuse when worried, it was a sure sign. I tightened my grip on his embarrassment; he wasn't going to get away with this if I could help it.

"Well, well, well, the great lover himself has failed to pull it off. Is that it?" My voice was raised deliberately and the other three members of today's drinking group – namely Smallwood, Keith Cocker, an interior designer and Fullerton, who had been talking amongst themselves – paused as this observation penetrated their airspace.

Scales's discomfort was obvious, a silly sodding smile was pasted on his face and his eyes were rolling about like two glass marbles in a mixing bowl. Cocker picked up the thread instantly.

"What's all this then? Did I hear that our cavity filler has failed at long last to fill the cavity of his choice? Is that true? Who is the unlucky lady – or rather lucky lady? Can it be that she's so well catered for that she can afford to turn down Scales's offer, an offer that no known female has been known to refuse?"

Scales gave a short laugh and shifted his feet uncomfortably, fiddling with his beer glass.

"It's just Marcus exaggerating again as usual – it's really of no consequence." He took a long draught to finish off his remaining beer and, plonking his glass down heavily on the bar top, affected to shoot a glance at his watch, exclaiming, "Good Lord is that the time? I really must go. Well, cheers, chaps, see you next Saturday." He headed for the door; you could sense the relief rising in direct proportion to the closeness of his proximity to the exit.

"Wednesday," I corrected, and seeing a frown of puzzlement flicker across his forehead, added, "You've invited Charlie and me to dinner."

"...and us," added Fullerton.

So relief was only to be temporary – I knew it and he knew it.

"Ah yes, Wednesday then, eight o'clock. See you." And with a nonchalant wave of bravado he bustled out, giving an unconvincing impersonation of a man in a hurry.

It was with a sinking feeling that I watched his departure, abstractedly I noticed that he was holding himself with an unnatural rigidity and his gait was peculiarly stiff, but I thought no more of it at that time.

"What was that all about?" enquired Fullerton, anxious as always that he might be missing something.

I gave them a brief history of the Deirdre Plant saga and the little plot to intoxicate her with Tony's libido, concluding, "...but it looks as though it's failed miserably and for what reason I know not." I paused reflectively. "But I'd love to find out." I couldn't suppress a grin at the thought. "There's more to this than meets the eye, fellers. I've never seen Scales so cagey about his women before. We're usually into full gynaecological details before Big Jessie has finished pulling the first pint, but this time nothing. No air of conquest or knowing winks and leers."

Fullerton scratched his chin.

"Do you think it's serious? He could have fallen in love with her."

I hadn't thought of that. I considered the idea briefly, eyes wandering to the flickering images on the bar television.

A pimply giant with thighs like tree trunks stepped between two white-shirted defenders and slotted the ball wide of the advancing goalkeeper. As the crowd rose baying triumph, he was felled to the grass by his team mates where they all rolled about on top of each other like a bunch of Bloomsbury faggots. Maybe I should put the whole of the Chelsea football team to Deirdre Plant; that ought to keep her quiet, or them out of the Premier Division.

I turned back to Fullerton. "No, it's definitely not that, because he's not taking her out again or so I understood. So in that respect it's not serious, but it jolly well is in other ways."

Fullerton scowled. "We'll get it out of him on Wednesday, one way or another, but I reckon you're right, Marcus, he's missed out."

We contemplated our beer in reverent silence, each trying to imagine the circumstances in which Tony Scales had found himself on the downside of Venus's mound. And each wondered with increasing morbidity how and when it could happen to him, growing more maudlin with every successive pint thereafter.

* * *

By Wednesday the weather had returned to late September mists and the autumn tints were spreading over the plane trees that lined our road. Chelsea had been stuffed 3 -1 by Tottenham, and I had come to terms with the collapse of the original Plan A for distracting Ms Deirdre from interfering in my life and produced a modified Plan A. The principle was exactly the same, it was just one character who was to be changed.

This revision followed a lengthy but subtle Sunday interrogation of Charlie over La Plant's preferences in men. From what Charlie said I could not understand why Deirdre had gone out with Scales in the first place. Charlie was adamant that Ms Plant preferred small weak men that she could dominate, and recalling how she had treated poor old Percy Hartley-Worthington at the Prinknash dinner seemed to confirm that. Perhaps she thought that Scales, with all his masculine bonhomie and muscles, was shielding a soft defenceless interior that she could command. If so she was definitely wrong there, and this might account for the failure of the relationship to flourish along the lines I had hoped.

However, that was past history now; and Scales, of the 'macho' school of acting, was to be given the 'don't call us, we'll call you' routine, and substituted by a more suitable follower of the 'Tiggywinkle' school. Charlie had unwittingly nominated the contender for the part it was now a question of getting them together.

Jeremy Leach-Edgington was a pest, a major irritant in Charlie's life. Only a very small cog in the Save Old Sheringford machine, he badgered her persistently about his particular forte – the Red-Shanked Speckled Reed Warbler.

"Who will rid me of this turbulent twitcher?" misquoted Charlie one day in a fit of despair after yet another hour-long phone call.

Now there was an opportunity to kill two birds with one stone – a very apt cliché under the circumstances. Fortunately for him, Jeremy was currently blissfully ignorant that his experience of the power of nature was about to expand – well, if not exactly beneficially, certainly in a direction that I was positive would be different!

Thin, weedy, languid wet. He was serious, self-centred and dogmatic: heavily into nature and bird life. He flitted about behind things, always in the shadows, keeping well clear of the limelight.

263

My conscience pricked at the thought of subjecting him to the full glare of Deirdre's aggressive mesmerism, but surely a little verbal domination couldn't do him much harm, could it? In fact he might very well enjoy the experience. You never knew, I might be bringing together two souls who would intertwine, like bindweed and honeysuckle. Souls who would mutually benefit from the introduction – and then I remembered that one twisted one way and the other the other!

Well, whatever! Meet they were now going to, no harm would be done and both Charlie and I could be rid of our 'turbulence'.

Scales was going to be told that his services as a stud could not longer be relied upon; he was to be pensioned off like a knackered donkey and put out to grass. I had no sympathy. He of the allegedly well notched bedpost had not come up to scratch when the trumpet sounded. He had failed me.

It transpired, however, that such a devastating let-down to his ego was not to be necessary. There were eight at the Scales' dinner party; me of course, with Charlie – absolutely stunning in a violet dress that perfectly matched the colour of her eyes. The deep plunging neckline that went down almost to her navel was set off with some fine, delicate gold jewellery that I had brought back for her from the Middle East. Her eyes sparkled and her face bore that beautiful smooth colouring that those fortunate ones of dark-haired Celtic ancestry possess. If anything there was more than a faint flush in her cheeks which, coupled with our delayed arrival, demonstrated the effect her dress had had on me when she put it on for the first time. Half an hour later she put it on for the second time. Well, we still had our moments – it was just that currently they were not as frequent as I thought they should be.

Fullerton was under the armed escort of Fleur. The

remaining two guests were a colleague of Scales' from the National Dental Hospital, Rollo Penderville, the oral hygienist with the dirty jokes, and his wife. Scales, being temporarily 'without' as they say, had roped in an old girlfriend, Linda, to act as hostess for the evening. Typically of those who fancy themselves as cooks, he was all fretting and shirty before we arrived, moaning that his *soufflé stilton avec chanterelles* was ruined.

He had the door open in a flash at the first ding of the bell, paused momentarily whilst his eyeballs, in a conditioned reflex, ran themselves over Charlie's equipment, hovering twixt navel and throat before good manners prevailed, and then kissed her on the mouth, holding the kiss rather longer than I considered necessary; and then, without taking his eyes from her face, shook me by the hand.

"What do you see in this tardy, mournful streak of pump water?" was his greeting. "A woman like you has the world at her feet, you could choose anybody at all, even me," he added modestly, before continuing with a catch in his voice: "...and yet your love for God's poor creatures, your compassion for the crippled, the ugly, the deranged, your pity for the bird with the broken wing, the beast with the thorn in its paw, leads you to devote your life's service to this imbecile, the flotsam of our society, the jetsam of our cities. It's tragic." And he leaned against the door post, burying his head in his arm whilst his shoulders heaved with mock anguish.

I sighed heavily. "Christ, we must be late if you're smashed already, Scales, or are you still a broken reed after your experience with Ms Plant?"

That brought him upright instantly. He reached for Charlie's stole and shot me a warning glance; simultaneously he ushered us smartly into the flat and closed the door. Making sure that Charlie was well ahead, he laid his hand on my arm and hissed quietly, "Not a word about Plant here, Marcus, and I promise to tell you everything later when we're clearing up. Promise mind." And before I could respond he had turned to the others and, embracing the company, made the introductions.

"Right, does everyone know everyone? No, Charlotte you don't know Jill and Rollo Prenderville here, Charlotte Prinknash with her father Marcus Moon, whom I believe you already know."

Linda served the drinks whilst he dashed off into the kitchen to minister to his savoury *soufflé* and *gigot d'agneau roti avec menthe,* as he described his roast lamb with mint sauce – a pretension which later led Rollo Prenderville to refer to the *soufflé,* which was delicious but came out slightly misshapen, looking vaguely like a crouching yellow and brown frog, as Scales' *'soufflé au crapaud'.*

After the meal I was looking forward to settling down and surrounding a large brandy when I noticed Scales jerking his head towards the kitchen.

"Marcus, will you give me a hand with the port and liquors?"

I struggled back to my feet and followed him towards the door; as I left I heard Fullerton ask, "Should you hang a toilet roll so that the paper comes off the front or the back?" Clearly I was not going to miss much.

As soon as we got into the large kitchen, Scales closed the door and stood with his back to it. I made the sign of the cross in front of him chanting, "In Nomine Patris et Filiis et Spiritu Sanctu – Amen."

"What the fuck are you doing?"

"Well, if I'm about to hear a confession I thought that sort of thing was necessary for starters. I trust you've reflected and repented since your evasive behaviour last Saturday and decided to come clean and tell all to Father Marcus." I tried to look pious. I would hear the confession first and then tell him to collect his 'cards' and 'down the road' afterwards.

I could see the struggle taking place within the Scales' bosom. He was still weighing up whether the truth, even just a part of it, would be more or less harmful to his reputation than the rumours.

"Well, yes, okay, but it's not what you think." He shook his head slowly as if emerging from a thousand year trance. "That bloody woman is a man-eater, a great white shafting shark, an insatiable ingrate, a carnivorous copulator. There is no subtlety about her whatsoever – it's 'wham bang and thank you man' before you can draw breath."

"Isn't it bam?"

"Isn't what bam?"

"Isn't it wham bam and thank you ma'am?"

He gave me a withering look and snorted, "Stop frigging about, Marcus, for Christ's sake and listen. In her case it's quite definitely bang. Bang with a capital B. And not just Bang – it's Bang Bang Bang Bang like the 1812 Overture, except that she goes on for the whole symphony. I was lucky to escape alive, I'll tell you." He shuddered at the recollection and his eyes took on a faraway look.

"I still haven't fully recovered from the experience. I lost a lot of skin that night I did." He seized me by the arm as if to prevent my escape. "Do you know what her idea of foreplay was? No, of course you don't. Well I'll tell you. Having got me back to her place under the pretext of cosy convenience, she took off my jacket and tie and under the guise of slipping into something comfortable, disappeared into the bedroom. I was just browsing through her bookshelves, contemplating an evening perhaps more of enthusiasm than finesse, when the next second I'm hurled to the floor with a rolling cross-buttock throw and she's kneeling on my chest, tearing away like a frenzied badger at the old Turnbull and Asser. Having ripped off my clothes, buttons, zips and all, she then proceeds to whale the living daylights out of me with a damn great riding crop she produces from somewhere."

"Oh very sexy," I couldn't help but grin, "you must have enjoyed that or you'd've soon put a stop to it, a big strong chap like you."

"Stopped it, for Christ's sake?" he bawled. "What do you think I tried to do? But when you're having your private parts belaboured by some beefy devotee of the Marquis de Sade you jolly well keep your hands round them, that's what you do, and that makes it damn difficult to get up." He paused. "Particularly..."

"Particularly?"

"Particularly when at the same time she has one foot rammed into your chest with a spiked heel and she's a powerful woman is Plant, I can tell you."

So that was why he was all stiff the previous Saturday – it all came back to me now. I began to picture the fragile frame of Jeremy Leach-Edginton in the hands of this muscular madam. Lord, she'd kill him. I began to laugh out loud. Scales stared at me indignantly, face reddening.

"It's no laughing matter, Marcus, and what's more, if you breathe one single bloody word of this to a living soul, I'll mutilate you beyond the limits of your imagination. Just you remember, the next time I get you in the chair at the National Dental I'll drill every single nerve out of your teeth without anaesthetic."

His face was flushed and he brandished a large meaty finger under my nose. I wiped my eyes and straightened my face.

"I'm sorry, Tony, I wasn't laughing at you but at a thought."

He wasn't mollified by this at all and so in the interests of friendship I decided that it would do no harm to come clean. Extending a long arm, I drew a chair out from under the breakfast bar and motioned Tony to do the same. When we were both seated, I told him of my concern for Charlie, the plan to divert Ms Plant's attention to matters more erotic and finally my selection of him to top the bill in that production.

"...so you see it could have been for a good cause and fun as well."

"Oh really! Thanks a bleeding bunch! I'm deeply moved to think that in your hour of need you feel I'm the one to call upon for assistance, even though you appear to believe that my considerable talents rotate only around my goolies." He drew himself up to muster some dignity. "If you'd told me the full story of your plight beforehand, I might have played my hand differently, but there's no way I'm going in to bat with her again, even to prevent nuclear war – and God help Jeremy thingy-whatsit if she gets her hands on him, poor little bugger."

Relieved that he had taken it so well, I nodded and was just going to stand up when a thought struck me.

"What happened after your little romp on the floor then?"

Scales groaned and held his head between his hands.

"That was even worse, at least the foreplay was only an attack on my person physically. When she got me on to the bed it was a complete assault on my manhood. She went at it with gritted teeth and the dedicated intensity of a Born Again Evangelist, as if to tear the very root of masculinity out of my body."

He paused for a moment, recollecting the occasion, and then flashed a quick smile.

"I reckon though I got an honourable draw out of that eventually. She had me underneath to start with and I was still smarting from the previous stimulation to care much one way or the other but when she started to bounce up and down, my shoulders began hitting some kind of metal or wooden strut across the bed under the mattress. When the pain faded a bit, I was bloody angry and the old procreative instincts began to reassert themselves."

His smile grew broader. "You know, apart from that strut cracking my spine, it was a bit of a turn-on. So I said to myself, 'Tony,' I said, 'you're in familiar territory here, old son, a slight readjustment of the initiative and honour could be restored.' So with a quick heave and a roll I up-ended her so that she was underneath and then I hammered into her well and truly. Christ did she grunt! Our combined weight of twenty-seven stone or so ramming down onto that bar every second damn near broke her back. I could hear her teeth rattle at each thump and by heaven did I thump her. She's got some stamina though, it was touch and go who cried 'quit' first. In the end we just fell apart, totally exhausted. I put on my shreds of clothes, got into the car and thankfully made it back here without being intercepted by the fuzz." He shuddered. "That sort of experience can put you off rogering for life; it had all the subtle interplay and emotional stimulation of a runaway tank."

We both sat silently for a few moments, contemplating the awful emptiness in our lives in the event of such a psychological shock. I had a slight pang of guilt now about my deception and subsequent lack of faith in my friend's expertise as a poker of note and was toying with the idea of a semi-apology, when we were interrupted by Linda calling from the sitting-room.

"Are you two going to be in there all night, we're waiting for our drinks."

Scales shook his head to rid himself of such grim thoughts and, seizing the tray of port and liquors, called, "Okay, on their way." Then he hissed at me with a scowl, "Remember, not a word," and ran the side of his finger across his throat in a gesture of significance.

For the rest of the evening I pondered Scales's experience and in my mind weighed the question of submitting Jeremy Leach-Edgington to human sacrifice. I did not think of myself as an unkind man; ruthlessness was not in my nature. As a fascist dictator or president of some proletarian state I would not have lasted five minutes; even as a general I would not have been able to commit men to certain death. But pose a threat to my domestic bliss – and a threat was how I regarded Deirdre Plant – and then there was roused within me the pitiless determination of a double glazing salesman. Horns and tail appeared and the milk of human kindness curdled. Thus by the end of the evening, painful though the decision was, I had decided to continue with Marcus's Plan A and JL-E was to be fed to the shark.

* * *

I had become so focused on the effect Deirdre was having on Charlie and thus, by proxy, on me, that I had never given much further thought to what might be behind her huge enthusiasm for saving Old Sheringford. I couldn't believe that all that effort was entirely on behalf of a couple of streets of weathered Bath stone. The public relations slant seemed to have been tilted away from badgering the government and other national bodies and more towards local politics. The poster and advertising campaign concentrated only on the Sheringford area. The local papers carried advertisements for people to support SOS and, mystifyingly, to vote for SOS when the time came.

From things Charlie mentioned from time to time, I knew that Deirdre was getting involved with local politics but all Charlie knew about that was that she spent a lot of her time in Sheringford New Town – a virtual 'no go' area for the county types who supported SOS.

"She rents a small flat there somewhere, but I've never been."

I suppose it was selfish of me but I took the view that Charlie knew full well what both of them were doing, and although she was clearly not over enamoured with it, she was prepared to go along with it, so I went along – except where it affected me.

I had my job to do just as Charlie had her full time job at the hospital, so Deirdre had a virtual free hand. She had come to dinner once and to supper a couple of times but apart from that I saw very little of her. I can't say it left a hole in my life because it didn't, but for Charlie's sake when we did meet I tried to be civil. However, it didn't stop me from questioning her motives and the stonewall answers she gave worried me even more.

"Are you sure she's not up to something nefarious and just using SOS for whatever purpose she has in mind?" I asked Charlie.

But she just passed it off with, "You know Deirdre, she's always been involved in the Women's Movement and left-wing fringe politics. It's what she lives for, but as long as she and her crowd support SOS, that's fine by me. It can't do us any harm to be represented right across the political spectrum, can it?"

"I suppose not," I replied thoughtfully, but there was a fishy smell about Ms Plant and I remained unconvinced.

Chapter Fifteen

"So how much longer do you need before you can guarantee Winlewis's selection? You've had six months now and it's costing an arm and a leg. When we put you into this assignment we expected results." Straker's eyes narrowed. "You haven't been frigging about founding Wimmin's Movement Units, Anti-Capitalist Committees and Lesbian Working Parties or crap like that, have you? Taking your eye off our ball? I trust you haven't because I can't move on Lissett until you can guarantee me Winlewis – so how long?"

Deirdre glared angrily back at Straker, face reddening with indignation and a touch of guilt. She was firmly under the self-generated impression that she had done extremely well to get as far as she had in such a relatively short time, but to forcefully put over the Wimmins Movement case and at the same time ram that impression well and truly up Straker's nose would not be productive for either. With incredible self-control for her and biting her lip hard, she ground out, "You can't rush these things, I should have thought that's clear even to you, they'll smell a rat immediately. They're already getting a bit twitchy over the changes I've introduced."

I'll bet, thought Straker grimly. He shook his head with growing impatience. "Look," he said determinedly, "let's go through the whole thing again, see where the gaps are and decide what can be done about them."

She bridled at this. "I've gone through it all once, that's not fair, you've..."

He cut her off in mid-protest. "Fair, fair, what the hell has fairness got to do with it? We're not taking about judging the Women's Institute flower show, this is important! A lot of our time, money and planning has gone into the Sheringford project and I don't care how it's done or who does it – I want results!" His eyes bored into her. "And one other thing; you've been told before about these unfortunate lapses of yours into reactionary bourgeois thinking..."

But Deirdre was not having any of that. Deirdre had a cause, and a grip of it; she had decided she was in the pound seats. "Don't give me that shit, Straker!" she snapped. "I've done bloody well to sort out Sheringford for Socialist Organisers. I know it and you know it. I'm indispensable to you and before we go any further, I want some answers from you about this so-called planning you're always on about."

Straker's eyes narrowed. So Sister Plant was feeling her oats, was she? It looked as though a sharp slapping down was due – but all in good time. She was continuing now.

"I want to know about Lissett. I want to know how you propose to get rid of a sitting Member of Parliament in mid-term, and in particular a person who's held the seat for twenty years."

"That's none of your business."

But Deirdre was in full flight now, eyes agleam, chin thrust forward, she knew the strength of her position and was not going to side-tracked by some feeble put-down like that.

"It is very much my business! As you have said yourself, the timing of this operation is all-important. We can't afford to show our hand too early in case the Party National Executive get word of our activities and decide to step in and impose their own candidate; but if we're too late we could lose the reselection process.

Deposing a sitting MP must be a lengthy business, and then there's the time before the government moves a writ for the by-election and after that the time to the election itself. By my calculations, we need to have our organisation in place no earlier or later than two months before Lissett actually goes, so that date is crucial. So is he going slowly or fast? Is it to be a road accident or what?"

She had a point. He looked at her carefully, she really didn't give a stuff what happened to Lissett in the slightest. He was disposable and his future irrelevant. It was only the timing that concerned her. A real hard case; a pity she was so emotional and crude in her thinking. He chewed his lip thoughtfully, weighing up the pros and cons and made a decision.

"Okay, I'll tell you all you need to know – but no questions. There'll be no more information. And if this should ever leak out..." There was a pause as he held her eyes with his chilling gaze. The threat was unmistakable.

"Lissett is a practising faggot – most people suspect this, we know it for certain. He's also a member of the Joint Defence Committee. Generally he has confined his buggery to a plentiful supply of old school chums but of late he's switched to hunting around for a different kind of partner. We know what he likes and we're going to lay what he wants out on a plate for him. We'll provide a very sympathetic companion." Straker gave a thin smile. "There's one thing you can rely upon with benders: they don't waste time before getting stuck in. Photographs will be taken and tapes made of their encounters without Lissett's knowledge and then we'll spring the trap. The companion will ask Lissett to look after a valuable miniature for him. He'll say he is frightened because he thinks he might be robbed. The companion will propose that to avoid any chance of him being followed and thus lead the thief to Lissett's flat, they should meet in a public place to transfer the painting. When they do, as they will, the media will be there with cameras, tape recorders and all the paraphernalia of exposure. The companion will be revealed as a diplomat from an Arab country passing a parcel containing a large sum of money. He will claim diplomatic immunity and disappear, the media will get our photos and tapes and the day the story breaks Lissett will resign. It will result in the biggest blaze of scandal to envelop this parliament and the Tory Party for years."

Straker paused for a moment, letting it all sink in.

"You see that we can't risk putting Lissett and the Arab shirt-lifter together until you have your end sewn up tightly. To do so would set the time bomb ticking and the longer it ticks the more unpredictable the outcome and the greater the chance of accidental discovery; the consequential publicity of which would screw us up well and truly if you're not ready."

Deirdre listened with begrudging admiration. It was brilliant; a master plan calculated to have maximum impact in the media and do maximum damage to the Tories as well as clear the way for her at Sheringford. And the clever part about it was that Lissett's downfall under the shadow of treachery for sex, and homosexual sex at that, would swing the floating Tory vote right away from them in disgusted reaction.

But there was a catch to all this, a nasty dilemma. Brilliant it might be but the simple fact remained that it was not her plan. Sheringford was hers, she had put in all the effort, done all the hard work whilst the fat cats back on the central committee had been swanning about the metropolis. She did not want any outsider, Straker or anybody else, siphoning off credit in any way – credit which was rightfully hers. Resentment bourgeoned in the ample swelling of her bosom and she went on to slow simmer. Clever dick with his cocky assurance that his plan was foolproof! She even began to hope that maybe there was a flaw, that somehow it would be his plan that would get screwed up, just to wipe the conceit from his male chauvinistic arrogance.

She became aware of a silence. He was staring at her with a puzzled frown, trying to read the myriad expressions flitting across her face.

"Say something, for Christ's sake, even if it's only 'sex is punishment'." An off-the-cuff jibe but it hit Deirdre dead centre. What did Straker know? She gritted her teeth, there was no way now she was going to acknowledge his plan and give him any satisfaction whatsoever; the only way out therefore was to do as he had demanded and plunge once more into a résumé of the current situation prevailing in the Sheringford Labour Party.

"Right," she said savagely, "as I've told you before, there are sixteen members on the constituency management committee, of which eight are the old soft centrist guard and the other eight are mostly trade union delegates appointed by the various unions. The latter eight are all SOS members. I always meet them privately before any meeting, to decide our policy, and then they vote as a block.

"Tony McPhail, the regional organiser of the Labour Party's South Central area, has told the constituency management committee that in accordance with national policy, a reselection process must be implemented to select and agree the Party's candidate at the next election. The old guard, believing this to be three years away, weren't that interested and were easily persuaded to vote with our block to institute a mandatory selection process at which all candidates must be considered afresh. Davies, the beaten candidate at the last election objected strongly but was pacified when I pointed out to him that it was the required democratic process approved by Party

Conference but behind the scenes, nod nod wink wink, he would walk it – stupid sod! So we're now ready for a list of candidates to be prepared and I've agreed to do this for submission to the secretary for consideration. The good point about this is that the more unknown the names, the better chance the secretary believes Ken Davies will have of an easy ride. There'll be no problem at all in putting Winlewis forward in the middle of a few other no-hopers."

Straker tapped his teeth with his pencil frowning in thought. "You say you have a block of eight SOS who'll support the selection of Winlewis; what happens if the other eight pick Davies? The Chairman has the casting vote and is he a Davies man?"

Deirdre smiled confidently. "No chance. Three of the prospective names, all New Labour, have been put forward by so-called moderate committee members. I've made sure that there's so much internal conflict between these people that none of them will back another's candidate. Winlewis will ride home on a split vote."

Straker shot her sharp look. "A bit risky that, what if the old mob do get their act together? It could happen, I don't like it! I don't like it at all! It's a loose end. Can't you get another couple of delegates on to the committee?"

She shook her head slowly a tinge of scorn creeping into her voice. "No, no way, all the local unions have delegate representation already, I've told you that, and unless somebody dies on the other side, I can't shift the others – unless you have some clever ideas."

Straker, further nettled by her arrogance, seized his chance. "Well why don't you invent a couple of unions? I should've thought it was perfectly obvious! You pick two genuine sounding names or better still, two genuine unions who don't happen to be in the area but who could be and you appoint delegates to the committee from these 'ghost' unions. Nobody will check, the SOS guys will support you and the other delegates are so dim that they couldn't find out what was going on if they tried for a month of Sundays. Do some thinking, Sister Plant, that's what you are supposed to be there for. Get off your fat arse and get this thing tied up rock solid. I don't want anything left to chance and the changeable whims of a few old die-hards. They could rotate like weather cocks in a whirlwind if they so much as sniffed the smell of a plot – and you tell me they don't yet? Bollocks! With half the committee packed with hefty, scruffy megaphone bellowers hurling abuse, anger and malevolence at everything they say? Christ, even they must realise that something is going on!"

Deirdre was in two minds, both furious; she was torn between defending her position viz a viz the constituency management committee or denying the fatness of her behind. By the time she had sorted out her priorities, Straker had tossed back the last of his lunchtime Scotch and was standing over her.

"So just go and get it arranged properly like I said and if you so much as breathe one word to anyone about Lissett, you're out! Not even Winlewis knows about that. I'll give you another three months, that's all, so do try to use a little initiative, Sister Plant."

And with that he turned on his heel and strode out of the bar, leaving Deirdre with mouth wide open, backside un-championed, Wimmin's Movement undefended and a Saharan thirst for male blood.

* * *

Jeremy Leach-Edgington was a thin, some would say wistful young man who was to be seen gambolling in the meadows with butterfly net and scout shirt in the summer and lurking in the reeds with binoculars and Cagoule in the winter. He was a devoted naturalist, at one with the hedgerows and the fluffy white clouds. He communed with the trees as they bent their branches to acknowledge his passing, he swayed with the grasses at the water's edge when the first breath of winter came out of the east. He flitted through the dingle dells and tripped across the ponds crystallized by Jack Frost's icy caress.

He was, in a nutshell, a pillock.

His knowledge of affairs sexual was severely limited by his strongly held belief that every time a fairy sneezed, a baby was born. He was interested in women, but as companions to waft with him down the summer breezes trailing yards of tulle and chiffon across the meadow-sweet and cow-parsley. What he was actually going to do with them after that never entered his mind; perhaps if a fruity feeling did creep up on him, he ran around the glades and clearings at night, sprinkling sneezing powder over mushrooms.

Of late he had become a bigger pain in the neck, and was now threatening Charlie if she didn't arrange for him to appear on television to plead his cause, so the quicker his lesson about the true facts of life commenced, the better. The transition from the birds and the bees and the sycamore trees to the savage suction of Deirdre Plant's muscular thighs was likely to blow his mind.

Jeremy's involvement with SOS had come about when he learnt that the Nippon Kansun project would irretrievably damage the only nesting site in Sheringford of the Greater Red-Shanked Speckled Reed Warbler, and he had henceforth thrown the weight of his 'Protect the Greater Red-Shanked Speckled Reed Warbler Action Group' behind the expanding Save Old Sheringford Society, appreciating that it might have more political clout than his lone voice protesting in the wilderness.

He was only partly right: it was amazing how the Great British Public, threatened with inundation, disfiguration of their homeland or perpetual disturbance to their lives and loved ones, will shrug their shoulder, hunch their heads into their chests and challenge the world to prevail against them – which it invariably did. But let the earth movers threaten the Greater Red-Shanked Speckled Reed Warbler, then by George, fairness came into it! Caterpillar tractor's bulldozers versus Sheringford's bird life could not in any circumstances be considered a match of adversaries at equal weights, and it was this that stimulated in the GBP that greatest and most moving of British attributes – the sense of fair play. Outrage welled slowly up from the mantle and the GBP reacted with all the violent explosiveness of an awakened tortoise. Its head emerged from its chest, it sensed and sniffed the air: the driving forces began to propel it forward and slowly and inexorably it began to increase in momentum and size. As the hare discovered to its cost, you treat the tortoise with contempt at your peril. Thus Jeremy's little effort had helped SOS to some degree by pulling in support from 'twitchers' round the country – support that otherwise would have remained passively dormant.

As a result, Jeremy thought himself much more important than this modest addition to SOS's armoury warranted. To his chagrin he was not put on the main committee but on a small sub-committee that dealt with the preservation of the countryside around Sheringford. However, even on that his personal contribution was not significant, in fact he did nothing apart from flap a limp wrist now and then and occasionally burst into tears when the thought of the little pale eggs being crushed under the grinding steel tracks of some muck shifting monster became too much.

He did, however, persistently badger Charlie to get him on television so, as he put it, he could put the case for 'our dumb feathered friends to the people of this country'. He had stamped his foot, gone red in the face and become threatening when she turned him down.

As far as I could ascertain from Charlie without provoking undue suspicion, he had not as yet come into contact with the dreaded Deirdre. She moved at a different level to him, in the stratosphere of SOS to his tree branches. It was thus fairly simple to persuade Charlie to invite him to a Prinknash dinner, ostensibly as compensation for his absence from our TV screens, and Ms Deirdre always showed up at all important SOS functions, so securing her presence presented no problem.

At seven-thirty that evening the cast for Moon's revised Plan A began to assemble in the drawing-room. Hovering near the door, I collared Jeremy L-E the instant he parked his anorak and shoved a large fresh orange juice into his hand well spiked with a double vodka.

Deirdre hadn't showed yet so executing a sharp 'coitus interruptus' on the mating habits of the Meadow Pipit, I began to direct his mind towards television in general and what Deirdre Plant might do for him in particular – if he played his cards right. All right, I admit I was economical with the truth about this but after ten minutes and another stiff orange juice, he was quite convinced that she was his answer to the plight of the Greater Red-Shanked Speckled Reed Warbler and the key to his television debut. Remembering what happened to the Reverend Hartley-Worthington in this same room, I knew I could rely on her predatory instincts for the rest.

She couldn't have timed her entrance better. Face flushed and tits trembling, she dominated the doorway like Juno before Latium. Jeremy stood rigid, gazing at her in awe. "My word," he whispered, "is that her?"

I reached behind me for the vodka bottle but it wasn't necessary. Jeremy was transfixed.

"She's beautiful," he murmured. "Beautiful."

In all fairness I must admit she did look attractive – if

you like them built like a Challenger tank. I wasn't to know that the colour in her cheeks was conjured there by the thoughts of the roughing up Straker had given her earlier and, anger unabated, she was still slavering for male meat. I only felt guilty later when I learned that it was three weeks before Jeremy was allowed out of the discreet private clinic, tight-lipped and with a few welts still showing purple and yellow across his thin frame.

I braced up the remnants of his orange with the Smirnoff and he drank it abstractedly. The vodka helped to transform her shirt and ankle length skirt into chiffon and tulle and by the time she moved off with her feet out of focus to his myopic eyes, she was to him as gossamer drifting down the breeze. Instinctively he began to stretch out his arms and lean forward. I thought for a moment he was going to honk and hastily shifted my shoes out of the way, but his urge subsided temporarily and she passed by to join another group.

Suggesting that a little flattery and admiration of her organisational abilities might be a good opening lead, I was just lining him up for the 'shafting shark's' gun sight when we were summoned through to eat. It didn't matter, I had slipped into the dining-room earlier and switched a few name cards round; Deirdre would find herself adjacent to but upwind from Jeremy, thus concealing him from Charlie who would be seated close to her father at the head of the table. Forsaking my usual place at the other end next to Angela Prinknash where I could get quietly smashed on the port, I put myself opposite Jeremy to help cement the union with a kindly word if necessary.

I needn't have bothered. It wasn't thirty seconds before Deirdre locked on to the adoring attention of the spindly bindweed beside her, doe-like eyes blinking through an alcoholic haze. After giving me a brusque nod she scanned him with a passing interest, then more intently. Before long he was blurting out his story about the imminent demise of the Greater Red-Shanked Speckled Reed Warbler and within five minutes he was sobbing quietly into his *consomme au Xerxes*. She slipped an enfolding arm like a York ham round his heaving shoulders and gripped him firmly until he stopped. They sat there, the pair of them, like a Mothercare logo.

I watched all this with the unblinking fascination of an entomologist observing a preying mantis envelope its victim. Charlie had been spot on in her assessment of Deirdre's preferences in the male sex.

Throughout the remainder of the meal, she talked to Jeremy with hardly a word for the rest of us. When I ventured an interruption or two just to test the strength of the bond, I got snappy answers and she refocused back on him immediately.

She was not going to let this one slip away if she could help it. A slave, she had always wanted a slave, male of course, and he could service Susie and her on demand. And here he was on a plate, a male creature that could be made totally subservient, a body and intellect that she could dominate absolutely – she the sexual master, and he the servant; her own tame semen pump. Traditional chauvinistic roles would be reversed without a flicker of the flame of rebellion. Perhaps he could be kept on a lead, confined and conditioned like one of Pavlov's dogs, stimulated by her eroticism but restrained from responses until a flash of white thigh sent him wild. A flick of the fingers and there he would be, E-shaped and ready to do her bidding. She shifted excitedly in her chair, the juices flowing. That really would be a blow for the feminist movement – and if he slacked then a little fettle-up with the riding crop would add spice to the whole event. The scent of sex hung heavy in the air, even Jeremy felt reciprocation of his immature adoration but without any inkling of the full import.

Watching like a hawk, I detected the change in Deirdre's demeanour, the flush that crept into her cheeks and the increasing outline of hardening nipples through her shirt. Blow me, she's turned on already, I realised with astonishment, and little Jeremy was obviously infatuated. He was staring at her with the concentrated intensity of a mesmerised rabbit. Bloody good I concluded; that my old Machiavelli, is a plan well plotted or a plot well planned; and with a quiet sigh of relief I settled down to enjoy the navarin of lamb with cauliflower *au gratin* and duchess potatoes so carefully prepared by David Prinknash's cook.

I was able to glean very little about what happened subsequently, other than to learn that JL-E had been found four nights later wandering in the streets of Sheringford moaning and mumbling incoherently. He was possessed of lacerations to the region between waist and knee and had been taken into hospital and thence transferred to a more discreet nursing home, which privately treated those sufficiently influential or rich, for ailments of mind and body which they preferred not to publicise.

Jeremy steadfastly refused to say a single word to anybody about the origins of his experiences and continued to maintain his Trappist attitude long after his release. He did, however, subsequently announce to Charlie that he no longer had any desire to appear on television and that his faith in fairies was no more. He was resigning from SOS and the Greater Red-Shanked Speckled Reed Warbler could stuff itself up its own orifice. He then tried to push his hand up Charlie's skirt, burst into tears and fled, never to be heard or seen round Sheringford again.

La Plant, in the meantime, continued to grow even bigger in the frame of Charlie's life, and I returned dejectedly to the proverbial drawing board.

Chapter Sixteen

A few days after Jeremy Leach-Edgington was found wandering in the streets of Sheringford bewildered but beautifully marked, I was propped in my cubbyhole, euphemistically referred to by the partners as an office when it came to salary review time, desperately trying to persuade myself that Plan A still had life somewhere in it. That amongst the ashes of a burnt-out butterfly chaser there still lurked one ember that could be fanned into a blaze of success.

A sudden footstep in the corridor had me scrabbling hurriedly for my draft report on foundations in the alluvial deposits of the River Shering.

"Oh, it's only you." I tossed the draft back into the shambles of paper that served as a desk top and replaced my heels on the radiator.

"Well you needn't sound so gracious about it," snapped Jane McBride, the secretary I shared with another engineer in the firm. "I come bearing a message."

Beware, they said, of Greeks bearing gifts, and secretaries who normally leave notes, bearing messages. I studied her expectantly.

This morning she had her black hair swept back and tied with an elastic band into a ponytail. It made her look severe, an effect enhanced by the big eyes and a very solemn expression. My heart began to sink. I could sense another loser floating to the surface here. What was it now? Another unpaid parking fine – 'Skin' Flint in the accounts had regular foaming fits over those – or was it my monthly expense sheet? Couldn't be – apart from the usual inflated mileage claim, the rest had been very modest: a couple of lunches, a few taxi fares and £8.50 for a round of drinks with Barclay. Peanuts! Was it work? I shook my head slowly; apart from Sheringford my other jobs were small and nowhere near a stage where trouble could lurk unknown. Maybe it was just me – a touch of the paranoids. I eased down little.

It wasn't.

Wallop – straight between the eyes.

"Mr Barclay's secretary has just phoned to ask if you can attend an urgent meeting on Sheringford this afternoon." Jane paused hesitantly as if fearing the fate that bearers of bad news suffered in feudal times. "Also, she told me to tell you that Mr Barclay had said to stop all work on that project. He'll explain all at the meeting."

I shot upright at this bolt from the blue. "Stop all work?" She nodded confirmation. "Christ," I muttered.

"What the hell has gone wrong now? It's that prat Percival, I'll lay a pound to fifty that he's at the bottom of this somewhere." I turned back to the girl. "Did she say if everyone has to stop work or just us?"

She shook her head. "Didn't say – just to tell you not to do any more work."

I thought for a minute, drumming my fingers on the desk, thinking things like 'no duck, no dinner' and 'no dinner, no job'. You know, little thoughts like that, the kind of things that spring to mind when your big deal suddenly evaporates like scotch mist and a bony finger beckons from the door of the local Job Centre. It couldn't be as bad as that – could it?

"What time is this meeting? As far as I know I've got nothing else on today."

"Four-thirty at their place."

I shrugged a nonchalance I did not feel. "Okay, well I suppose I'd better go and find out what's happened. Will you ring back and confirm that I'll be there."

She smiled acknowledgement and I thought for the umpteenth time that when she smiled it lit her whole face. There must be a much warmer nature hidden behind the austere façade she normally presented in her daily duties.

"I've already confirmed it; I checked in your diary and the afternoon was clear."

Capable and efficient too; what would she be like buried deep in the soft mattress of a big four-poster bed on a cold night? Dreamy, dreamy; apart from her husband, I'd forgotten about him! Dennis or Desmond was his name. I had met him on a couple of occasions. A shagged-out, pasty looking cove, I had assumed consequent upon late nights working as manager of Tescos in Purley, but perhaps there were other deeper reasons.

I was just letting the mind range over what they might be when I suddenly realised she was still there, watching me with an amused smile her face. I came back to earth with a start, now aware that I must have been staring fixedly at her. I hoped to Christ I hadn't spoken any thoughts out loud.

"Oh, well, arr, yes, thanks Jane, fine, fine."

She went out, still smiling enigmatically, leaving me somewhat disconcerted and vowing to be careful in future. Shagged out her old man might appear but the fellow was a big nasty looking sod and stopping a case of Heinz Beans dropped from a great height with my head one dark night, was not a fate I relished.

I debated whether or not to telephone Fitzallan Percival and eventually compromised with a phone call to Norman Crabbe. The switchboard put the call through immediately.

"Nathenmeoldfruitwazzamatta?"

I looked at the handset, the strange sound rasped through the earpiece like gravel trapped under a door. Something wrong in the works somewhere. I gave the handset a couple of hard bangs on the desk to see if it cleared the line, and then held it back against my ear. There was silence, the line sounded clear now. I congratulated myself.

"Hello, may I speak to Mr Crabbe please?" There was a strangled squawk, and then a shaken voice, still semi-intelligible, crackled and grated down the line.

"Stone the bleedin' crows, what the fuck was that? Is that you, Moon?" It suddenly dawned that the gravely crackling I had heard was Crabbe's normal voice electronically mutilated by British Telecommunications.

"Oh hello, Norman, I'm sorry about that, I thought we had some static on the line or a loose connection..."

"You bloody madman!" Crabbe howled, interrupting me. "It's you that's got the friggin' loose connection. You bleedin' well shattered my eardrum. I've got very sensitive ears I 'ave. I bet you did that on purpose?"

I suppressed a chuckle and repeated pacifically, "I'm sorry, Norman, it's just that your voice sounds crackly over the phone."

Crabbe savagely muttered something under his breath, but I continued unabashed.

"Have you heard any news on Sheringford? I've just had a phone call to ask if I can attend a meeting later today and I understand that we're to stop all work."

There was a long pause, I could almost hear the cogs going round in Crabbe's mind as he shifted his concentration on to this new development.

"Yea, but that's just bleedin' Barclay, innit?"

"I'm sorry, I don't understand. What do you mean?"

"Well it's obvious, innit? Barclay's putting the arm on a bit."

"I'm sorry Norman I still don't understand what you're talking about. Putting what arm on whom?"

"Leave it out, John, you know what I'm talking about, they're all at it aren't they? Get you all excited and enthusiastic, get you committed to a lot of work until you're well and truly on the 'ook, and then whammo, the old bite goes on."

I was amazed. "Are you suggesting that Barclay's doing this because he wants something out of it?"

"You want to get out a bit more, John. They're all at it, bung 'em a few quid and the wheels start rollin' again. And if you don't, well it's a one way trip to croak city. These buggers don't take no prisoners, y'know."

"Really," I murmured, trying to fathom out what the hell he was taking about. However, I realised I was not going to get much further with Crabbe, he knew as little as I did.

"Well thank you, Norman, at least you take an elementary view of life." Or was it me? I wondered, after Percival's performance with the Chief Planner. "Will you be at the meeting?"

"Nah, just Fitzy, I always leave 'im to take care of the passing of notes on account of his ancestry."

There was a sucking sound like the sudden clearing of a blocked drain – Crabbe was laughing.

I'll bet you do, I thought, as I put the receiver down. I should think that that sort of design technique is right up the Little Brown Turd's street – it probably comes as chapter one of elementary architecture in his book under the heading 'Professional Probity – Never Dish Out Counterfeit Slush, You Could Be Struck Off'.

So Crabbe hadn't a clue why the job was halted. I was just beginning to chew a finger to the bone when the phone rang again. This time it was Martin Holmes.

"Hello, Marcus, you got the message about this afternoon?"

"Yes,"

"Well I was just ringing to cancel it. Bob, Jane and I are going down to Sheringford this minute to see if we can get over the problem, can you come?"

"What problem?"

"Christ, haven't you heard? You know Bob had everything agreed with the White Horse Property people and the executors of the Joshua Grimshaw estate? The lawyers had done all their searches and drawn up the contracts, et cetera? Well, everything had to be ratified by old man Grimshaw, and we've just heard this morning that the barmy old fart has put the mockers on the lot by refusing to agree to the sale, so we're going down there to see what we can do. Their lawyer said he was totally eccentric and an impossible bloke to do business with, so it doesn't look too good."

"Jesus O'Reilly," I groaned, "it's nothing to do with the Little Brown Turd then – or anything else for that matter?" I added.

"No, why?"

In spite of myself I couldn't help but laugh as I related Crabbe's diagnosis, homespun philosophy and conclusions.

"...so the LBT is probably on his way over hot-foot to your place with a bundle of brownie bribe sheets clutched in his pudgy fist to ward off the evil eye and bring continued blessings down upon his speckled head."

Holmes chuckled. "If he does we'll take them, nothing like a little bread to lay up in heaven and subsidise some good future eating. Isn't he a prize prune? It just shows what most of his clients must be like. But the question remains, can you come? Your local connections may just be of use."

"Oh yes I can come if you think it'll be a help."

"Okay, pick you up outside your office in fifteen minutes. Ciao!" And he was gone.

I put the phone down with a depressing feeling of emptiness.

I thought of Jane: nice figure, good boobs, firm and rounded with nice up-tilted points – it would be very

291

comforting to rest the old nuzzler on those for a few minutes whilst the troubles of the world passed by. But I couldn't be absolutely sure that the partners would wear that sort of therapy in the office at this hour of a Tuesday morning I could just picture Hugo Elme's face should he find me writhing intertwined on the office carpet. Being the sort of Englishman who would pretend that everything was normal, he would probably clear his throat and say something like, "Marcus do you think you could spare five minutes to cast your eye over this report – there's no hurry, when you've finished whatever it is you're doing will be fine."

Well, maybe another day... I reached for my jacket, flashed Jane a 'keep it warm' smile and hit the stairs.

Barclay, Holmes, Jane Treadwell and I arrived in Sheringford just in time for a late lunch. We had an appointment at the solicitors acting for Joshua Grimshaw's trustees at three o'clock so we decided to settle for the fixed menu at the Copper Kettle. The interior of the restaurant was 'olde tea shoppe' traditional: heavy dark wooden beams festooned with horse brasses, ochre walls hung with the other equestrian tack and little round black tables with wagon wheel chairs for the customers to test their arthritis on. The place was almost full but we managed to find a table for four half way along the wall near the gentlemen's lavatory. The tired looking waitress in lace cap and small apron drifted over.

"Ready to order, dear?" She flicked a grey looking cloth at an old gravy stain disfiguring the tablecloth

Replacing the crumpled serviette over her arm, she extracted a small notepad and pencil from her apron pocket, licked the pencil point and raised her eyebrows to signify that she was awaiting our attention. Barclay nodded acknowledgement.

She closed her eyes and went into her ritual litany: "Soup of the Day's tomato, Dish of the Day's roast lamb,

Veg of the Day's cabbage and Sweet of the Day's spotted dick – and there's chips." She opened her eyes and waited, pencil poised for the spell to take effect. Barclay beamed and, receiving nods all round, began.

"Right, my good lady, we'll have four of those and speaking for myself, you can omit the spotted dick."

She frowned at this deviation. "It's all in."

"Yes, that's as maybe, but I don't want to have it."

"You'll have to pay for it."

"Well if I must, I must, but nevertheless, I still don't want it."

"Well what shall I do with it?"

Barclay controlled himself admirably. From the tight expression on her face it appeared as if many customers had disposed of their spotted dick in the way he might suggest; but instead he smiled kindly.

"Just leave it in the kitchen, dear – I've got to watch the calories." He patted his ample stomach.

"Is there any chance of a bottle of wine or something like that?" I enquired.

"Sorry, dear, we don't have no licence. I can give you fruit juice or squash."

Barclay grimaced with distaste so I concluded, "No I think we'll leave it then and have water."

I was just turning back to ask Jane Treadwell a question when I heard my name spoken tentatively from close behind. Turning round I found myself gazing at close range into the clear round blue eyes of a large brown owl apparently in an advanced stage of moult. I recognised it instantly.

"Grime! What on earth are you doing here?"

Grime rotated his body further round to coincide with the direction in which his head was pointing, thus reducing the owl-like effect. He was wrapped in an old brown duffle jacket with a hood, his face was still heavily tanned and his blue eyes still had that clear intensity through the big round spectacles he wore. He was sitting alone at a table for two. His face cracked into a beaming smile of open pleasure.

"Bloody great to see you, Marcus, and you, Bob. Bloody marvellous! Eh, those were the days weren't they? Best four days of the summer those we spent in Honfleur with the lads. Great bunch of fellas. I really enjoyed myself then." His smile faded. "Not like the bunch of wankers in this place."

I glanced round at the stolid burghers of Sheringford chomping away through plates of spotted dick – NICS possibly but 'merchant bankers' seemed a bit extreme. Still, you never knew in these country towns.

"Yes, well it's great to see you again, Grime, and glad to see you looking so well, but this is a bit off your pitch, isn't it? What are you doing here?"

Grime glowered. "Business," he said, spitting the word out as though the very sound of it caused him offence. "Some greasy little Yiddish jerk is trying to screw me out of my family inheritance, and I'm here to see that he doesn't." He lapsed momentarily into a short bout of incoherent muttering which seemed to relieve him a little. His open smile returned and he rejoined the conversation.

"Anyhow, what are you doing here?"

Barclay shrugged. "We're negotiating to buy a piece of land but we've run into trouble."

He was just about to elaborate when the waitress came carrying Grime's bill and a disapproving expression. She confronted Grime with both.

He looked at his watch. "Oh Christ," he said, "Got to shove." His eyes brightened. "Are you around for a bit?"

Barclay nodded. "Yeah, we'll be tied up for a couple of hours and then we're free."

It was like watching a human pinball machine as the thought bounced around before dropping into a slot.

"Pub, six o'clock for a drink? Star on the Bath Road is best."

Barclay considered that by six o'clock he would probably be in need of some restorative and, having a soft spot for Grime, we agreed. Grime tossed some money on the table, and giving the waitress's thin tits a passing squeeze thereby raising a squawk of protest, shuffled out with a leer.

"Who on earth's that?" asked Jane Treadwell. "A tramp?"

Barclay grinned. "A bloke we met sailing." He shook his head. "Totally impossible to tell whether he's pissed or sober, only his behaviour gives it away, and by then it's usually too late. I'll tell you more about him later."

Picking fibrous lamb from our teeth and glutinous spotted dick from our palates, we arrived at the offices of Spottiswode, Trenchard and Spottiswode promptly at three o'clock and were shown into the waiting room.

After a couple of minutes a door bearing the legend A G Spottiswode Senior opened and what I assumed correctly to be the earthly remains of Spottiswode Senior creaked into the room. A tall, stooped elderly figure well past its sell-by date surveyed us gloomily through small gold pince nez, pince nezzing a long sharp nose. After shaking hands all round Mr Spottiswode shook his head, his wrinkled wattles jerking rhythmically and his rheumy eyes blinking back moist tears. It could not be said that happiness was evident in his emanations.

"It doesn't look too good, Mr Barclay, not too good at all. My client is totally inflexible in his opposition to the sale of the site. He didn't even want to meet you, but I persuaded him that he should do so as to give you one last chance to explain your proposition. I have done all I can, I assure you, Mr Barclay, all I can; it has put me in a very embarrassing position. A very embarrassing position indeed." He blew his pointed nose on a large spotted handkerchief which he pulled from his breast pocket, and wiped it several times before tucking the cloth away. He seemed about to burst into a flood of tears, but pulling himself together with a loud sniff, he motioned us to follow him and rustled back towards the door. Barclay rolled his eyes as we all trooped after the ancient through to his office.

The office was dark with that peculiar smell of mustiness that originates from piles of decaying paper. It was heated by a brightly glowing gas fire and furnished with old but well maintained heavy mahogany furniture. A colourful but faded Axminster carpet covered most of the floor and where the boards showed they were well waxed and shone with a soft lustre. It was warm and comfortable. This I took in at a glance but the object on which all our eyes focused was the huddled figure of Mr Grimshaw slumped in a heavily stuffed, buttoned leather armchair, gazing fixedly at the floor.

"Grime!"

The man's head rotated and the bright blue eyes focused on Barclay. "Bob!"

Barclay was the first to recover.

"Jesus, are you the Grimshaw of Joshua Grimshaw?"

Grime nodded, looking at Bob with a puzzled expression on his face. "But you're not the chap who wants to buy my land, are you?"

Barclay nodded. 'Yes. Of course, Grime – Grimshaw. Well bugger that for a game of soldiers!"

Old Mr Spottiswode was standing there with his head jerking from one to the other, wattles swinging like a turkey one step ahead of the Christmas axe.

"Do you two gentlemen know each other then?"

"My word yes," said Grime, "this is one of me best mates, you don't go sailing with a bloke for four days without getting to know him well you know. By God,

Bob, if I'd known it was you wanted to buy the land, you could have had it for a song!"

"Now steady on, Mr Grimshaw," interjected Mr Spottiswode fluttering nervously. "We mustn't let personal feelings become involved in business, must we? Mr Barclay has made a very good offer, as I've told you before, and if now you can see your way to accepting it as we recommend, then I'm sure that both parties will be extremely satisfied."

He began to rub his hands together with a dry whisper of relief. Grime stared at Mr Spottiswode enquiringly.

"Hold hard a moment, squire, then who was the greasy, bald-headed little brown shit with the big nose you pointed out to me?"

Spottiswode looked slightly flustered but the description was blindingly accurate. Definitely a 'fellow feeling' was Grime.

'Ah, yes, well I think you must have misunderstood me, Mr Grimshaw, that was Mr Barclay's architect, Fitzallan Percival, a professional man like myself."

Barclay's antennae detected an inconsistency here – a sort of evasive shiftiness had crept into old Spottiswode's demeanour. A forced offhandedness and a touch of smokescreen.

The old man continued. "Ah, well if we can perhaps run through these documents then, Mr Grimshaw, I am... er... sure that... er... without a lot of... er... difficulty... ah... we shall... ah... be able to bring the matter to, ah, an amicable conclusion?"

"Just a moment," said Barclay, looking at Grime, "do you mean to say that you don't know this chap Fitzallan Percival?"

Spottiswode shuffled papers noisily and started to lay them out in front of the two main participants. Grime shook his head.

"No way. Saw him once, couldn't stand the sight of

him, never want to see him again. A real shyster."

'But I thought he was your architect?" Barclay expostulated. "I understood it was you who wanted him kept on the scheme and insisted on him being written into the documents." Grime shook his head again.

We all slowly looked at Mr Spottiswode, standing there caught with his finger up his bum and his mind in neutral. He allowed a brief glimpse of pink, ill-fitting dentures as he eased out a nervous smile towards Grime.

"Ah! Yes! Well, Mr Grimshaw, I may have inadvertently omitted to mention it but he did give us a little advice when we were considering doing some development ourselves. We, I that is Messrs Spottiswode, Trenchard and Spottiswode, on your behalf as... er... advisors to the executors of the estate and to the White Horse Property Company, felt it desirable to have a well known, prominent London architect to give our... er... your... I mean these proposals a little more stature. You do understand of course?" We got another nervous flash of his dentures.

We all understood perfectly. In fact only too well as far as venerable old Mr Spottiswode was concerned. It was quite clear that venerable old Mr Spottiswode was a venerable old bent Mr Spottiswode and that did not describe his posture.

He had obviously been trying to see if he could get a development going behind Grime's back. If it looked promising he would have used a third party to buy the site from White Horse at a knock-down value; told Grime it was a good offer, and turned in a fortune. Fitzallan Percival had persuaded Spottiswode to use his services as architect; presumably, from what Norman Crabbe had told me this morning, by bunging a wad of notes into his Swiss bank account, but the scheme had foundered for some unknown reason. It could have been the cyanide problem.

On the 'no duck, no dinner' principle, this would have left Percival without payment. Hence to salvage the situation Percival had persuaded Spottiswode to dump him on to Barclay so that Barclay would stand his fees. There was not much that could be done about that now, contracts had been signed, but a careful eye needed to be kept in future on the flexible integrity of Spottiswode, Trenchard et al.

All these thoughts went through our minds in a flash. I looked at Bob and then at Martin. They were both looking at Spottiswode with cynical smiles and raised eyebrows. He got the message.

Grime was puzzled by these exchanges but as they didn't seem particularly relevant to the current proceedings he growled, "Let's get on with it; I've a throat like a Turkish wrestler's jock strap."

Bob clapped his hands together, and turning to Spottiswode said, "Miss Treadwell's got our side of the purchase agreement signed and sealed, so all that we need now is your client's signature with you as the other officer of White Horse Properties as witness, and the company seal affixed. The price is agreed, is it not?" He gave Spottiswode a penetrating stare, but Spottiswode had got the message and nodded agreement without further argument. He ferreted in a file and pulled out their copy of the sale agreement, pushing it towards Grime and indicating with his pen where Grime should put his cross. Grime signed with a flourish; to my astonishment his signature was beautifully written in an immaculate hand. Spottiswode signed up as witness in a cramped style that looked as though somebody had squashed a crane fly on the paper. The seal was applied, the documents exchanged and Bob handed over a large cheque as a twenty per cent down payment.

Spottiswode beamed at everybody and, turning to

Grime, said unctuously, "Very satisfactory all round, Mr Grimshaw."

"Yeah, yeah," said Grime, "that's okay by me, if there's any other problem let the lawyers sort it out. Now, Bob, what can we do for the rest of the afternoon?" He frowned. "The pubs are shut until five-thirty." Then his eyes flickered over Jane Treadwell like paint stripper. He had all her clothes off in an instant and then hastily put them back on again. He looked at Mr Spottiswode with the same expression, causing him to bridle with alarm.

"Come on, Spottiswode, you must have something we can celebrate this deal with? Crack open the old booze cabinet."

Spottiswode's pale blue-lined hands fluttered nervously.

"Well... ah... I think I might be able to lay my hands on a spot of dry sherry."

Grime looked him straight in the eye. "Champagne," he demanded, "Champagne or there's no deal and no fees."

Spottiswode wooffled and chuffled a bit, but he knew his Grime well. "If you really insist, Mr Grimshaw, ah... then I'll see what I can do, but there are some papers you'll... ah... have to sign before you leave. I'll arrange from my secretary to bring them in."

"A case, Mr Spottiswode, a case! None of your stingy half bottles."

The lawyer staggered a bit. "A case, Mr Grimshaw, a whole case?"

"A case, Mr Spottiswode – of Dom Perignon!" He leered at the lawyer. "You can choose the year."

By the time we arrived back in London that evening, having been driven by Jane Treadwell all the way, we had king-sized hangovers to go with the signed contract. She dropped Barclay off first at his flat before taking his car on with her. He stumbled out of the car with a big grin on his face and gave her a kiss on the cheek.

"It's a bloody hard life," he said, "the things one has to do to get business." And still grinning all over his face, he let himself into his flat.

Chapter Seventeen

One thing about good vintage champers, it doesn't lay one on you next morning. I was just ruminating on the previous day's events as I wrapped myself round a large helping of bacon, egg, sausages and tomato when I flicked over a page of the Daily Mail lying on the kitchen table. A small headline caught my eye.

"Hey, Charlie, have you seen this? Old Gwaine Lissett is packing in his seat. Applying for the Chiltern Hundreds on grounds of ill health it says here." I read on. "Hmm, reading between the lines they're speculating that he could have got AIDS. Says he's lost a lot of weight and hasn't been seen around for a month or two."

She grabbed the paper out of my hands and rapidly read the brief paragraph.

"Oh my God, if this is true, Marcus, do you realise what it means?"

"Yeah, it means the nasty little shirt-lifter has been enlarging the circle of some rather unpleasant friends and vice versa."

"No, not that, his packing his seat in, I mean. It means a by-election in Sheringford. God knows what effect that will have on SOS but it's for sure that SOS is going to have an effect on the by-election. I must ring Daddy later and see if he knows anything."

David Prinknash did not, however, know any more than he had read in the morning's Times – again, just a brief paragraph – and he knew nothing about the reasons for Lissett's resignation but said darkly that he'd always had his suspicions. "Never trusted the chap, handshake like fondling a sick cow's udder and one of those fellows that always kept his handkerchief in his sleeve."

"Surprised he didn't keep it up the leg of his knickers," was my observation when Charlie reported the result of her conversation to me when I returned home from work. Given a whole day to do some ferreting, the media had wormed out much more information by the time the nine o'clock news was transmitted on television that night. There was video film with zoom shots of the curtained window of a private clinic in west London in which it was rumoured Lissett was confined in isolation. A spokeswoman for his constituency party reluctantly admitted that he was having tests for a blood disorder but did confirm that he had requested appointment to the Chiltern Hundreds – effectively resigning his seat in Parliament. And finally there was a long item on AIDS in general, making particular references to a couple of earlier departures from the benches of the House of Commons for, allegedly, that reason, which invited viewers to draw their own conclusions.

"They'll have to move the writ for the by-election fairly soon, I suppose. I wonder who the Tories will put forward," mused Charlie. "It was a close run thing last time, Lissett had something less than a hundred vote majority and he was well thought of locally for all the rumours about his sexual inclinations. At least he gave active support to SOS against the government, whereas if we get some bright young flower foisted on us by Tory Central Office, he or she's going to do what they're told by the Party and that doesn't necessarily mean they'll support us. That's going to have to be worked on and some convincing done. Mind you, he or she is going to need every vote they can muster if the Tories are to hold on to the seat, so that gives us some leverage."

I pondered on this for a minute whilst I poured us

both a glass of wine. The sheep shaggers of Sheringford may have narrowly voted him in, but Lissett had seemed to me to be nothing but a first class pain in the arse – if you'll excuse the pun. I suppose he must have had his uses if Charlie said so.

"But what about New Labour then? Now they're in with a definite fighting chance, what position will they adopt on Save Old Sheringford? They'll be against it, I suppose. Its very objective is to stop acid rain eating away the old stone buildings; it's set up to directly oppose their policy of locating more industry in the area. The fact is SOS is campaigning for less industry and, with Nippon Kansun, New Labour obviously want more. More means more working-class people in Sheringford, and thus more Labour votes."

Charlie screwed up her eyes and wrinkled her nose thoughtfully. I checked the wine hurriedly to see if it was 'off', but it seemed fine to me, so that was not the cause of her concern.

She went on, "That is a bit of a puzzle. Deirdre claims to support SOS, and, if you recall the reason she gave for getting involved, she wanted to give it more of an 'across the political spectrum' appearance. But that was before there was any thought of a by-election. It'll be interesting to see what stance she adopts now she has to support New Labour policy. Will they drop us like a hot brick, pull out of SOS and swing round and support the location of the Nippon Kansun factory in Sheringford, or what?"

She was right, there was a conundrum here. Deirdre, a loudly proclaimed socialist, had done her best to undermine the government by actively supporting the preservation movement, and yet all the publicity that had been produced since her involvement had a strong left-wing slant. Why? I wondered.

At the by-election she certainly would not be supporting the Tories or the Liberal Democrats. Support for any of the loony parties was also out of the question for such a political zealot. So it had to be the socialists – and in Sheringford that meant New Labour. So was she intending to try to swing SOS behind the New Labour candidate? That seemed the obvious tactic, but I could not reconcile this with her strongly expressed hostility to that movement.

Still, who was what in the by-election was not my principal concern; at the moment that remained getting Barclay's scheme through its forthcoming Public Inquiry. There remained a mass of useless evidence to collect to demonstrate vital statistics such as proving that the number of people entering the new shopping centre would exactly equal the number leaving, and that the more shops there were the more people would be employed and the whole neighbourhood would be improved.

Then it hit me. I looked at Charlie and she turned those violet eyes on me, full of sadness. There was a long silence as each of us waited for the other to speak. The same thought had crossed both our minds simultaneously and each knew what the other was thinking. I waited and finally Charlie said apologetically, "I suppose this is going to increase the amount of time I shall have to spend on SOS."

I grasped the implications immediately. "Does that mean that our week in Tenerife is in danger?"

I knew full well what she was driving at. It wasn't that the week was endangered; it was likely to be totally extinct. Yet I lived in hope as usual.

She flushed guiltily. We had planned a spur of the moment trip for a touch of winter sun to compensate for missing out on our summer trip to Ibiza. What with SOS, other calls on Charlie's time and Barclay's Public Inquiry, the 'window' available before the end of the year had narrowed down to some time within the next fortnight.

It now looked as if Lissett's sudden resignation had heaved a half brick through it. I had already laid out a tenner on a couple of bottles of Piz Buin Sun Factor 4, in an off season sale at the chemist.

She hesitated; we could both do with a break so she was as reluctant as me to abandon the idea.

"I don't know, I'm not sure, it depends on what immediate effect Lissett's resignation has on SOS – and Deirdre, of course."

"Of course," I said sarcastically, "if Deirdre says do this, or if Deirdre says do that... O'Grady says stand up, O'Grady says sit down, O'Grady says stand on your head..." I chanted childishly before being withered by a steady violet stare.

"Look, I'm sorry, Marcus, but you know the situation, it's not of my making, and the next few weeks could be crucial for SOS after all the hard work that's been put in."

That was true and it was stupid of me to have realised that. I put my arm round her.

"I'm sorry, Charlie, you're right. You must be even more disappointed than me if we have to cancel the holiday. With Ms Deirdre lurking centre stage, to go away and hand over total control of SOS to Wimmin's Socialism at its most virulent would be irresponsible."

I made a mental note. That was another point to be clocked up against La Plant in my little black book – a reckoning that would be settled at some time in the future.

* * *

If Lissett's scratching from the parliamentary stakes had concerned Charlie, it had thrown Deirdre into total, frantic panic. She didn't read any of the capitalist press, a bracket that embraced everything from The Times to The Beano. She limited her periodical reading to Militant and Spare Rib. As neither was available at 8am in

Sheringford newsagents, the first she knew about Lissett was from a chilling phone call from Straker.

"I don't give a monkey's whether you're ready or not, you get your total act together now! Your first priority is to make certain Winlewis is selected as the Labour candidate. We can deal with the votes, and anything else, later. Now, what's the current situation with the constituency selection committee? Have you got sufficient of our people in there to guarantee Winlewis's selection? Who are the other candidates likely to be?"

These would be three laxative questions for Deirdre at the best of times – even if she had done her St John the Baptist act and prepared the way for Winlewis's coming, following her last meeting with Straker. But at eight o'clock in the morning after a heavy night, with Suzie getting all emotional because the dildo was floppy, and a good three months before she could reasonably be expected to have the answers, they were positively dysenteric. Try as she might she could not stop her stomach churning over and it angered her.

Who the fuck did he think he was to put her under pressure like this? It was Straker's plan that Lissett had cocked up by resigning unexpectedly, not hers. So it should be up to him to come up with a solution. She was arranging for two 'ghost' delegates from 'out of the area' unions to be appointed but that took time, he must realise that. Three months he had said and three months it would have been.

Now just two weeks later he was coming the heavy hand. It just wasn't fair.

She had another part of her life to live as well as carrying out his requirements, couldn't he appreciate that? No, perhaps not; even full of anger she realized the inadvisability of pointing out such a thing at this time.

And Suzie was no sodding help these days. These close, caring interpersonal relationships were not as simple as they should have been between two committed... She hesitated over finding the right word and couldn't find it.

Ever since Suzie had given up her job as a trans-personal counsellor and psycho-dramatist at the South Lambeth Anti- Nuclear Cuban Dancing and Fibre Centre, and moved into Deirdre's Sheringford nest, she had done nothing but moan and be difficult. At first Deirdre had put it down to a heavy dose of PMT, and to pacify Suzie, because she 'couldn't stand anything male' near her, she'd had poor Trotsky the tomcat's balls cut off. A protest, Suzie claimed triumphantly, 'against the cockocratic state on a planet dominated by gonadicy'.

This didn't work; well it did for Trotsky the cat, but not for Suzie.

Deirdre was even unhappy when Suzie wanted to get to work on Jeremy Leach-Edgington with her Swiss Army knife, and was only persuaded otherwise by the argument that to reverse the sex role of a fully equipped male would be much more satisfying than doing it to a helpless eunuch. Leach-Edgington's escape through the lavatory window had ended that debate, and Suzie had sulked ever since because she'd never even got the chance of a whack at him.

This morning she had stormed off raging about her dildo, to emasculate her car engine by stripping out its pistons and thus work off her frustration of the night. Deirdre had been left alone to cope with the world and Straker.

Well, if she was going to persist with that attitude, Suzie could make her own bloody way to the Silbury Hill Womyn's Wigwam on Saturday. And with her car engine strewn all around the Sheringford Single Parent Centre and Brownie hut she would very likely not be able to make the pilgrimage at all to that bulging womb of mother earth. A thought struck Deirdre: she must remember not to bang in tent pegs this time and use stones to secure the guy ropes or, better still, site the tent on the flat bit at the foot of the hill just inside the fence. The 'Sisters' had been a bit pissed off over that unfortunate activity last year – particularly as Deirdre had been swinging a fourteen pound hammer to drive the stakes home into the 'earth's pregnant belly' as if nailing a vampire to the floor of his coffin. She didn't want more trouble on top of Straker.

Oh shit, back to that! He was waiting for her answers. Well it was Straker's responsibility to sort out Winlewis and Lissett, not hers and Straker should have foreseen AIDS as a contingency in dealing with any gay. She had strong misgivings in any case about using 'gay' behaviour to entrap a person; it was morally wrong, although Lissett was such a right-wing fascist, in his case it was easy to swallow her objections. That did not, however, absolve Straker from inadequate intelligence; he should have found out earlier, much earlier, that Lissett had AIDS.

"Well...." she began with some hesitation.

"Well, you'd better get your frigging finger out, Sister Plant, starting as of now. You'll phone this number," and he quoted a series of figures, "every day at six o'clock in the evening precisely with your report on progress – and there'd better be some. That's all." There was a click as the call was terminated and Deirdre was left juggling pent-up resentment with a London telephone number.

"Shit!" she spat. "Shit, shit, shit!" She hurriedly scribbled the number Straker had given her on the wall beside the phone before she forgot it, then she began savagely punching her pillow. The arrogance of the bastard when she knew she was doing a good job! She had the constituency committee virtually in her pocket; eight out of the sixteen members were Socialist Organisers and she herself was the committee secretary. The records of the meetings and the agenda, arrangements, timings and locations were under her direct control. Of her seven supporters, two were registered unemployed and two more either held jobs in the Sheringford offices of the Department of Health and Social Security or in the Town Hall. She had lied a little to Straker about that; apart from the National Association of Local Government Officers delegate, only three others were from accredited unions, and these were from the small leftie unions on the fringes of industry: draughtsman, caterers and cleaners. The big boys wanted nothing to do either with her or her philosophy but they moved so slowly and ponderously that as yet they hadn't bothered to get their act together to attempt to counter her plans. She arranged where possible that committee meetings were therefore held at lunchtime in an office in the DHSS, which made it difficult for the eight moderate party members who worked in different industries on the outskirts of town to attend.

She had still not drawn up the final list of prospective parliamentary candidates but the draft list for interview which she had prepared included some ten names. Ken Davies, the narrow loser at the last election topped the list followed by a party hack put forward by Labour Party National Executive to reward some hardworking donkey. Then there were eight other names proposed by different committee members, both the moderates and SOS supporters, with that of Arthur Winlewis slipped in amongst them. Soothing noises had been made and any ripples caused by the long list stilled, it was assumed, by the old sweats that Ken Davies would walk it. It was also assumed by Davies himself that he would walk it and he was still highly cheesed off at the idea of having to attend for interview.

"Waste of bloody time and money," he whined, "why have interviews, why can't the committee just announce that I've been re-selected?"

When the Chairman put this to Deirdre, she pointed out that, like justice, democracy had to be seen to be done whether it was done or not; Davies would have to attend an interview just for show. And what a show it was going to be! If Davies thought he was being hard done by now he would have gone positively berserk if he'd had an inkling of what Deirdre was going to do to him at that interview. Somebody was going to suffer for Straker's chauvinism, she didn't care who as long as it was a man.

Suzie was taking it out on her car engine, Deirdre was after the real thing. Mollified somewhat by this promise to herself, she bestrode her crossbar and pushed off to Sheringford Labour Party Headquarters.

It was whilst she was pedalling vigorously along the High Street that the real problem and consequences hit her – they obviously hadn't occurred to Straker either. No Lissett, no meeting with a Middle Eastern gay, no passage of money, no exposure, no disgrace – a dose of AIDS was hardly in the same bracket as high treason – and hence no Tory backlash. The crucial few votes would not swing over easily now, they were going to have to be worked for. Straker's brilliant plan had fallen apart at the seams and through no fault of hers. She had him, she had them all now, and she was the key player, the only player now in the game for high stakes. The whole thing depended upon her, at last she was indispensable. If she got Winlewis selected and if she then swung the voters to get him elected, all the kudos and credit would be hers – and the power that went with it. If...! But it would not be through lack of effort if she failed, about that she was determined. What was needed now was some high profile publicity to replace that which a disgraced Lissett would have provided. And who was going to be the vehicle for this, trundling his trolley in blissful ignorance just below the horizon? None other than Bob Barclay.

The Womyn's Wigwam weekend at Silbury Hill had been a disaster. Suzie had managed to reassemble her car engine at the cost of three crushed fingers and hands and arms ingrained with engine oil. As a consequence Deirdre had to drive and Suzie had back-seat driven all the way there and all the way back. If she hadn't been such a caring person, Deidre would have smacked her face, but every time the urge came over her, Suzie's watering eyes and quivering lip stayed her hand.

The Sisters at Silbury hadn't been over-welcoming either. Memories of last year's enthusiastic brutalising of Mother Nature's womb with a fourteen pound sledgehammer still hung heavy, and although Deirdre pitched the tent on the flat ground using stones to hold the guy ropes this time, the spot she chose happened to block the first rays of the rising sun from striking a cavity in the hill the Sisters called 'nature's vagina'. This resulted in another row when Deidre refused to budge.

Round the campfire she had hoped to recruit a few of the Sisters to Socialist Organisers Soviet, at least those who lived within striking distance of Sheringford and could add weight to her supporters. But the sour bitches refused to get involved, concentrating their efforts trying to blockade RAF Lyneham, the transport airfield for the Middle East

Suzie and she arrived back in Sheringford on Sunday night cold, miserable and irritable. Suzie spent the rest of the evening sharpening her Swiss Army knife whilst Deidre ran through the composition of the Labour Party selection committee for its parliamentary candidate. Lissett's resignation had caught her on the hop, although there was no way she would admit this to anybody except herself.

There were still eight members, plus the Chair, whose votes that she could not guarantee would support Winlewis. The selection meeting was ten days away, insufficient time to suborn all eight to her cause. The answer was to split them. The candidates would be selected by a majority, and with eight votes for Winlewis, if the others were split, he would get through. She looked at the draft list of candidates again. There was only Ken Davies as a potential challenger.

She reached for the phone, calling each of the eight members in turn and asking each one to nominate a candidate for the list. Five named Ken Davies but the other three named different local socialists. She tore up the old draft and wrote a new one with Ken Davies at the top, and Winlewis's name slipped between the other three nominees.

Chapter Eighteen

On January 30th the Public Inquiry into the planning application submitted by Barclay Developments to alter St. Frideswide's Chapel and construct shops and offices on the Joshua Grimshaw site commenced precisely at 'ten o'clock in the forenoon', in the Council Chamber of Sheringford Town Hall. The Inspector appointed by the Secretary of State for the Environment to hear the inquiry was a Mr R R Donaldson, Fellow of the Institution of Civil Engineers, Fellow of the Royal Town Planning Institute. Barclay Developments were represented by Mr James Mather QC and the Sheringford Borough Council was represented by John Henry Fletcher QC. The various other societies, organisations and members of the public who wished to give evidence were also present and introduced themselves to the Inspector. Ms Deirdre Plant, representing Save Old Sheringford and the Sheringford Labour Party – very clever that, to tie them together – requested that she be permitted to give her evidence early in the inquiry because her "many and varied commitments would make it difficult for her to be available throughout the whole of the proceedings".

The Inspector was still a man with a drop of the milk of human kindness lying within his breast. New to the department, he had been given Sheringford as a fairly straightforward, no-trouble assignment. No scars yet disfigured his psyche, no excrement through his letterbox, no paint stripper across his Volvo; none of the customary expressions of dissent which enabled the more experienced to identify the nutcases unerringly at the first hearing had accumulated to total his experience. He had not learnt to separate the potentially vitriolic contributions from the serious argument. Accordingly, he noted Deirdre's request and said he would arrange it.

In all fairness to him, Deirdre did appear reasonably close to normal, dressed as she was in purple t-shirt under turquoise bib-fronted overalls. The chrome-plated shoulder buckles strained lopsidedly, emphasising the swell of her magnificent breasts. Her thick hair shone in the subdued winter sunlight filtering through the old leaded light windows round the stately chamber. All in all she did look a bit of a turn-on with colour in her cheeks and a sparkle in her eye. Deirdre was geared up for her big moment.

It had all gone brilliantly so far; the factional fighting amongst the old guard had split their votes at the selection meeting and the SOS block had secured Winlewis as Labour's parliamentary candidate. Arthur's pseudo bluff manner and staunch socialist background had gone over reasonably well at his interview. "A decent, likeable sort of chap," said the Chairman, swallowing his disappointment.

"Christ, not even Arthur would claim that!" chortled Straker when the result was reported to him by a jubilant Ms Plant. Ken Davies had been crucified. He didn't know what hit him. He had been dealt questions on black sections in the Labour Party, aid to Nicaragua, increases in public spending for ethnic minorities, state ownership of everything and finally women's rights. The first few had rocked him, the last slayed him – he was a male chauvinist when he entered and an incoherent shattered shell when he got the bullet.

That being settled, Deirdre had then concentrated on building the case she intended Save Old Sheringford to present at the Public Inquiry. The Main Committee had wanted to engage a prominent planning counsel to represent them but Deirdre was having none of that. She knew there would be massive press and TV coverage if this was handled right, and no stuffed shirt QC was going to get a look in and steal her thunder. She would represent them herself. The timing was perfect, the government had moved a writ for the Sheringford by-election to take place on March 12th and the Public Inquiry began in the middle of the run-up period. Already the media were zooming in on the town, carrying out their own opinion polls, and interviewing the prospective MPs, digging up the dirt, spreading rumours and finding angles. Save Old Sheringford was really getting its message across hard and the government gritted its teeth as the pressure piled on.

The prospective Tory candidate, one Augustus Withers, was your typical Tory Party Central Office selected prat. Public School, Oxford, called to the bar and fucking useless. He was picked because he toed the party line and was consistently non-committal about everything. This had alienated the right-wing section of SOS, which was hoping for at least some public indication of support for their cause.

"Thick as pig shit," observed one of the farmers on the Committee, when it was clear that the man was so self-centred that he failed to grasp that at least a nod in SOS's direction could secure him a block of votes at the forthcoming by-election.

Withers had turned up at a Save Old Sheringford Committee meeting, brought along by Colonel Corrigan-Croot. A medium height thin type with an indignant nose sporting a large dewdrop which he regularly removed using a flowery handkerchief that he whipped out of his breast pocket. He had a tight mouth and no chin; his throat flowed in an unbroken curve from his lips to his neck, giving him the appearance of a chicken reaching for the last grain of corn. Mrs Hartley-Worthington had rocked him by asking the chair, *sotto voce*, who the 'weasel' was.

His only contribution had been to ask SOS to write a testimonial supporting his candidacy, and then to lose all interest when he was told that SOS was non-political.

After the meeting Deirdre had pinned him in a corner like a specimen butterfly, grilled him about his views – which didn't take long – and harangued him for half an hour about hers. That was enough for both of them. He had emerged stupefied and trembling, and she was full of glee as she stirred up dissention in SOS with a large spoon.

She was beside herself with excitement and anticipation. She felt that her big moment had come and she was ready for it. The town was buzzing with media folk. The 'nationals' were short of news so, in desperation, they had focused their attention on the Sheringford by-election. It was a dangerous time and needed to be handled with skill. Anything that was happening within the town became a story, and even things that weren't. The opinion polls had the main parties neck and neck, with the Liberal democrats running a poor third. The various journals and TV were doing their best to stir up controversy wherever they could.

Deirdre couldn't believe her luck!

Charlie had told me that the SOS objections to Barclay's scheme were more a matter of principle than specifically targeted at his proposed development. In fact they rather liked the design, and certainly supported the restoration of St Frideswide's. However, to maintain their credibility as a preservation pressure group they felt they must lodge some objection to any new development in the town of whatever kind but, in this case, not make a big issue out of it. The committee had also agreed that Deirdre would put their case at the Inquiry.

That was what Charlie told me. She was quite specific that that was the brief the committee had given to Deirdre Plant when they submitted to her argument that it would be a waste of money to employ a full legal team.

I explained all this to Barclay and Percival. Barclay nodded. "Well that's only to be expected – the Local Authority has said much the same thing in their Rule Six statement."

Percival muttered something about hoping we didn't have a spy in our camp. I assumed he meant me but I let it pass. Deirdre, however, had different ideas; she wasn't interested in the outcome – that would not be known for six months at least – she was only interested in the immediate effect. The message was to be simple: caring socialism linking Save Old Sheringford, with Socialist Organisers Soviet being the only voice speaking out for the people against the reactionary forces of the establishment. Something along the lines of 'Greedy developers lining their pockets by pillaging this ancient town lovingly built by the working people down the ages – just the sort of scheme this traitorous, non-caring, reactionary Government would support – Inspector just a lackey at this sham, a tool of the system – whole concept immoral and against the people who could not be there themselves because they risked dismissal from their jobs – she was representing them in their thousands... et cetera, et cetera!' You know the sort of thing, it's been heard from Liverpool to Lambeth and the voting fodder laps it up.

Deirdre reckoned half an hour of that would drive the Inspector to insisting that she must keep to the point or shut up. She, of course, had no intention of doing either and her Socialist Organiser cohorts distributed round the chamber would bellow their support, babies at the breast would scream and the proceedings would grind to a halt with sit-downs, occupation of the podium and microphone and a constant barrage of heckling.

After she had finished her impassioned speech the mob had been primed to swing into action. She calculated that, with a bit of luck, the protest could be kept going for the whole day.

Eventually the police would be called and the whole thing would turn into a spectacular punch-up in defence of free speech, workers' rights and non-violent protest against the reactionary forces of the government.

The Town Hall would be occupied: huge red banners would be unfurled with the motto 'Socialist Organisers Soviet Says Save Old Sheringford'. Placards waved 'Vote for SOS, Vote for Winlewis' and 'Winlewis Says Save Old Sheringford'. Speeches shouted over the microphone; the platform seized, and her supporters chained to the chairs, radiators, street lamps and anything else obstructive.

Suzie was intending to disembowel the Inspector but, after consideration, Deirdre decided that this might be counterproductive and took her Swiss Army knife away. The police would eventually be provoked into turning out the full riot squad; helmets, batons, shields, padded clothing, the lot. Winlewis had been driven down especially so that he could be seen to be acting as a calming influence on the mob.

The press and television had been primed in advance that something controversial was to happen, and would be there in force to record everything. To relay to the working people of Sheringford, and the world in general, that the peace-loving Socialist Organisers Soviet Revolutionary Party were the party to represent their interests.

It would be a spectacular coup; Socialist Organisers would get more publicity from this one event than they had ever had with all their previous efforts put together. Those arseholes in Inkerman Terrace – Winlewis, Pruitt,

Straker, Rat Face and his clone – would have to eat their words and she would enjoy ramming them down their throats. She nearly had an orgasm at the thought.

* * *

The Inspector outlined his programme. Barclay's architect was going to be opening proceedings, and he would take up the first day. Following her request to the Inspector to be 'on' early, Deirdre was to be the first witness at the commencement of day two. That suited her perfectly.

* * *

Barclay, Percival and I were drawn up in conventional battle order ready to bat first. The principal evidence for Barclay Developments was to be given by Fitzallan Percival and after preliminary, introductory speeches by respective counsel, the Inspector called Percival to take the stand and commence his evidence. I and the remainder of the Barclay team listened with interest as Percival, after a hesitant start whilst he assessed the tolerance level of his audience, gradually opened up into full harangue. To give him credit, he had taken a lot of trouble in preparing display stands with coloured up drawings, elevations and artists' impressions. He had plotted pedestrian flows and traffic flows. He had got maps of old Sheringford, Sheringford as it was now and Sheringford as it might be. He had obtained enlarged photographs illustrating the decrepit state of the old chapel taken on a wet, gloomy day; they showed water pouring through the roof, gushing from the broken drainpipes and seeping down the wall. For two hours he effused grandiloquently on the disadvantages of leaving it in its present decrepit state. I was impressed, but then you expect the best quality bullshit from a professional bullshitter who is an acknowledged master of his craft. Counsel for Barclay Developments deftly drew out of Percival the few points he had missed and then they both sat down whilst the Inspector clarified one or two items. All in all it was a masterly performance: commanding, arrogant, confident and delivered with just the right amount of panache and vanity that was calculated to get right up the nose of every single person present. Or so I was concluding as I looked around at the assembled forty or so people scattered around the benches of the old Chamber.

But not so. I suddenly realised my analyis that everybody present was irked up to the eyeballs and bored out of their nettled minds by the insufferable conceit of a puffed-up Percival at his most pretentious was not accurate. Whilst the rest of the congregation were picking their noses, reading The Sun or doodling on their notepads, pretending they were recording an event of great importance, one member was leaning forward in her seat, cheeks flushed and eyes riveted on Fitzallan Percival. I did a double take – there was no mistake, Deirdre Plant was sitting there as if entranced. Even when Percival was back in his seat receiving the polite plaudits of the Barclay team, she was still gazing at him transfixed. I had a strange feeling, there was that faint surge of adrenaline that comes when you sense a twitch on your fishing line, await the pulling of a Christmas cracker or the draw in the rugby club raffle – not much, but it could be, just could be, my lucky day.

Percival hadn't noticed her, he was still smirking all over his podgy brown face and doing his reincarnation of Sir Christopher Wren bit – lots of sweeping gestures and waffle with eyes focused on far horizons. I glanced back at Deirdre, she hadn't moved her gaze one inch and her bosom was beginning to heave. I did a little staring myself; Deirdre's unfettered breasts heaving were a noble sight indeed.

Well stone me, this was a turn up, but what exactly did it all mean? This would take a little evaluation. Could it be that Lady Luck, at her most coquettish, was about to put a little something my way?

The Inspector looked at his watch and checked it against the large clock with faded roman numerals, black curly hands and a face cracked and yellowed with age fixed on the wall opposite him. The minute hand of the clock oscillated gently over the twenty-nine minute mark before, with what seemed to be a laborious effort, it finally heaved itself the last remaining few millimetres to bottom dead centre indicating twelve-thirty. So apparently did Mr Donaldson's watch because, carefully folding his notebook, he pronounced the morning session adjourned for one hour.

Proceedings would recommence at one-thirty precisely with the cross-examination of Mr Percival.

"Thank you, ladies and gentlemen."

I stood up from the hard oak seat with its worn padded cushion and stretched my legs.

"These seats must ensure a very rapid transaction of Council business. Christ, my bum's numb after a couple of hours of that. If I were the leader of the council, I'd take all the opposition's cushions away or failing that, give them the thin ones. That would limit dissention." I massaged the deadened part of my anatomy to restore some circulation.

"Let's go across to The Star, they do a good pub lunch."

"Lead the way, old son, this is your patch, you pick the trough." Barclay shuffled his papers into a neat pile.

"Do you mind if I join you?"

Barclay turned in mild astonishment to stare quizzically at the turquoise-suited apparition that had suddenly appeared. His astonishment increased when, without waiting for an answer, it did join us and marched with our group through the large double doors into the foyer.

Barclay had only briefly come into contact with Deirdre before, so he knew who she was and something about her from the many and lurid stories he had heard from me. I could see he was both intrigued and irritated by her self-imposed presence. He glanced at me enquiringly for some guidance but I could sense a developing position coming up here and there was no way I was going to cock up Lady Luck's arrangements – it was about time she gave me a break. Therefore Barclay received a blank look in return, then I quickly made introductions all round, leaving Lady Luck to make the running for a little longer whilst I tried to assess the angles.

Fitzallan Percival happened by coincidence of local geography to be at the end of the greeting line, still basking in his own glory when I presented Deirdre. She had given each of the others a curt nod, moving rapidly on with a noticeable lack of interest, but arriving at the Little Brown Turd she stopped, a red glow suffusing her cheeks. Percival glanced down. The effect was stunning. It was as if two powerful magnets of similar polarity had been put within their respective fields of mutual attraction. They hurled themselves together with a gravitational intensity, their hands remained clasped in an unbreakable union and their eyes locked together, searching each other's faces with intertwining eyeballs. With her gaze riveted on his face, she breathed, "I thought you were magnificent in there, a commanding performance by a man at the peak of his profession. You slayed them, you stitched that inquiry up. I doubt if anyone'll dare challenge you now because they'll look such fools. It must be marvellous being an architect, to combine art and imagination with respect and dignity –

and you had such dignity. I admire a man with dignity."

Barclay goggled, Martin Holmes grinned all over his face, Fullerton burst out laughing and I felt my heart give a leap of excitement. Steady boy, I thought, steady. At this stage in the conception of a budding union, matters are mighty fragile. It was essential to let the coupling cells get a firm hold round each other before encouraging them to multiply, so I hovered in protective amazement at this *coup de foudre*, as the French – who know about these things – would have put it. At least I think that's what they would have said – or is that a blast of wind, not a lightning strike? Never mind, either was appropriate – maybe a blast of wind more so!

Percival, however, noticed none of us, he found himself totally immersed in the warm glow of self-adulation that such confirmation of his own opinions brought. Corroboration not by just anyone but by this stunning, intelligent, understanding woman who obviously was possessed of both discernment and taste. And in front of these people too, that was really the climax to his morning. To be publicly eulogised in front of these doubting Thomases! His cup was full to overflowing. His imagination expanded; what a team they would make, he on the pedestal of the muses and she in perpetual adoration. An Echo to his Narcissus.

I quickly recovered from my astonishment and, sensing the transfer of reins from Lady Luck to me at last, moved in rapidly to cement this flash friendship into an indissoluble bond. The idea of Fizallan Percival having the living daylight beaten out of him by a concupiscent Plant stimulated by the sort of primeval sexual urges that had patently smitten the pair of them nearly overshadowed my principal purpose of diverting La Plant from Prinknash politics. Shangle me, what an opportunity to kill two birds with one stone! It was like having a priceless piece of Dresden thrust suddenly into your hands; you didn't want to put it down, but you were terrified of dropping it.

"Perhaps you would escort Deirdre to The Star, Fitzallan?" I tentatively proposed, but I was wasting my time. They were already in motion, wandering along, still holding hands, looking into each other's eyes, oblivious to the world around them.

He was saying, "Architecture is so basic. The need to create a perfect environment for personkind dominates and stimulates one's inherent abilities to the limits of their capacity. The perfect house is a product of complete sexual harmony, it should be an extension of the womb. This must be fundamental. Biology is irrelevant. It is not the root of masculinity and femininity, it is outside influences which fashion our psychology to fit what is thought to be masculine and feminine. Children should not be subject to these prejudices and the environment of their development should not seek to impose preconditioned notions of what boys should do and what girls should do."

Deirdre could hardly believe her ears, she decided there and then that this was the man she wanted to assist in the creation of her children.

"I believe that a house should be uterine," continued Percival. "It should be generous, colourful and ethnic. It should be rounded not rectangular, representing the full fecund shapes of the female principle. Pod, egg and bean shapes..."

I left them to it. I couldn't stand much more of that verbiage anyway. But there are times to take action and times to leave well alone; instinct told me that this was most certainly one of the latter.

The Star was busy but Barclay shouldered his way through the crowds round the bar and found a vacant table for six. Following the British tradition of service, we cleared all traces of the previous occupants ourselves, piling the dirty plates and used glasses at one end; sweeping the breadcrumbs and blobs of Thousand Island dressing on to the floor, and settled into occupation whilst Barclay and I ordered the drinks.

As soon as we were out of the earshot Bob looked at me questioningly.

"What's between The Aubergine and Shirley Temple back there?"

"I'm not too sure, but I think that we've just experienced what would be termed in a bodice ripper as 'love at first sight'. I'm keeping my fingers crossed that that's exactly what it is."

"But isn't that overstuffed bird the one you've been having all the trouble with?"

"The very same, hence my enthusiasm for seeing her enraptured by Percival. They could be perfect for each other – and me."

"But isn't she also the one that beat the bejesus out of Tony some time ago?" By now the Scales escapade had become common knowledge amongst the Saturday lunchtime drinkers at The Frog.

I grinned wolfishly. "The very same, the very same. Exciting isn't it? You get my drift."

"Bugger me. Yes, I do indeed."

"Watch this space for further developments eh?"

Barclay scratched his chin pensively. "Yeah, that's all very well but she, my dear Marcus, is opposition. She is an objector – a major objector – to our application and we can't have her lodged in our camp suborning our principle witness, arsehole though he may be."

"But I don't believe that's what's happening. You heard what she said to Fitzy, she thought he was marvellous, for Christ's sake. The question now is; is she going to lay into you, the evil developer, and therefore, by implication, Percival, or is she going to hold back a bit?"

Barclay's brow was furrowed as he ordered the drinks, including a pint for Deirdre. We returned to the table with five pints and a Campari and soda for Percival, and then joined the queue for the cold buffet.

When I arrived back with a heavily loaded plate – as much as you can eat for eight quid – Percival was still prattling on.

"...architecture and the female body are analogous, there is a parallelism in which both are degraded and deified by the common person. The ethos of each is so powerful that men will dissipate themselves and even die for them and yet each is subject to violent inner tensions and torturing self criticism..."

This was rich. Of all Percival's least obvious attributes, self-criticism was the one he concealed most effectively. Barclay, on the other hand, had had enough of his intended post-mortem of the morning's events being superseded by Deirdre's intrusion and Percival's monologue and decided to regain the initiative.

"Why don't you then, Fitzallan?" he enquired innocently.

"Why don't I what?" Percival frowned at the interruption.

"Well, if you subscribe so devotedly to self-criticism you know what the most sincere form of self-criticism is, don't you?"

"No?"

"Suicide. It would at least persuade the Inspector of the strength of your convictions."

Percival flushed angrily, but before he could reply, Deirdre flashed to the defence of her new-found cub. Her eyes gave Bob Barclay a visual enema as she interposed herself between the two men, her breasts jutting forward like twin eighteen-inch naval guns on the forward turret of a Dreadnought.

"How dare you! How dare you speak like that to a

man who has just given his all on your behalf. Sacrificed himself on the altar of your rapacity. All people like you care about is money, money and more money, you have no soul, no sensitivity. You're just biased against Mr Percival. Well I'll tell you something..."

She was cut off in mid-flow by a now very angry Barclay.

"No, *I'll* tell *you* something. The purpose of this meeting is not for the benefit of either you or Fitzallan here, it is to discuss my project and as that is what Mr Percival gets his corn for, that is what he is going to do if he wishes to remain as my architect. We have a lot of ground to cover and very little time to cover it in; this is a working lunch and those attending it are expected to work. You, Miss, are here only under sufferance – so you have two choices, sit down and shut up, or go."

Barclay towered over her and there was no doubting he meant what he said. Deirdre turned pink and opened her mouth to launch a savage reply, but Percival, who by now had had some experience of Barclay, put his hand on her arm to restrain her. I noticed that she covered his hand with her own and remarkably she kept quiet, although the two of them glared at Barclay like sparring tomcats.

Martin Holmes, thinking he would take some of the heat out of the situation, suggested that, as Percival was going to be cross-examined on his evidence in the afternoon, we might run through any areas where we considered there might be a weakness.

Percival flushed again and retorted. "There are no weaknesses in my evidence. I've covered everything thoroughly so it would just be a waste of time." Then he leaned back, a smug expression spreading over his face. "If you're looking for weaknesses," he smirked, pointing a finger at me, "you should look at his evidence."

To say I was taken aback would be to understate the

situation by about a thousand percent. They all looked at me questioningly.

"What do you mean? I think you'd better explain that remark – and be quick!" snapped Bob Barclay.

Fitzallan Percival was still smirking and I hadn't a clue what he was on about. As far as I was concerned my evidence was perfectly straightforward. The ground was strong enough to bear the foundations. They would have to be piled, because of the proximity of the river and the consequent alluvial deposits, but that was not significant. The traffic studies agreed with the County Councils figures, there was ample capacity in the existing drainage to accommodate the proposed development. There was plenty of water and electricity. I was bemused by his comment.

"Cyanide!" he said triumphantly.

There was a chilly silence as the implications of this remark began to dawn. "Go on," said Bob quietly, "What about cyanide?"

"The whole site is polluted with it, that's what! Why do you think nobody has bothered to try to develop it in the past? And he should have found out about it if he'd done his job properly." He jabbed his finger at me again then turned to Barclay. "I warned you of the dangers of not allowing me to appoint my own team. You should have allowed me to appoint the structural engineer and then we wouldn't be in this mess!"

I opened my mouth to speak but Barclay held up his hand to forestall me. "Just a minute, Fitzallan, let me get something clear here. You've known about this cyanide problem all the time and apparently you've not thought to mention it to Marcus – or me? Is that so?"

Barclay's calmness caused the smirk to fade from Percival's irradiated features and he shifted uneasily in his chair. Deirdre squeezed his hand encouragingly.

"Well it's his job to find out about that sort of thing.

He gets his fees for that. I don't," he mumbled defensively.

Bob smiled benevolently at him and Percival swallowed heavily. This was not the response to his bombshell he'd anticipated.

"I'm glad you brought that up," Bob said, "because you'll be pleased to know that Marcus did find out all about the cyanide and put in a huge amount of time and expense in solving the problem. He's identified whereabouts on the site and researched the methods for treating it. We can deal with it economically, thanks to Marcus, but it has cost me a lot of money in extra fees to his firm for all the work he's had to do from scratch."

I blinked. This was news to me, but I held my council.

Bob continued. "Now if you'd told him what you knew about this cyanide it would have saved him an awful lot of time, and consequently me an awful lot of money. Do you follow me?"

I did, but I didn't think Percival had got there yet.

Bob continued. "So all the extra money that I've had to pay out in fees to Marcus's firm I'm going to deduct from your account! We're supposed to be working as a team and what you have tried to pull is as reprehensible a stunt as I've ever come across from a so-called professional man. The Royal Institute of British Architects wouldn't be pleased to learn that one of their number had behaved in such a manner."

Fizallan Percival got there then, gulping and blanching under his tan. The deal was clear: pay up or be reported to the professional practices committee.

"How much?" was all he could say.

"I'll let you know in due course." And Bob flashed me a quick grin. "It depends how extortionate Marcus is with his fee demand to me!"

I suppressed a smile; that should keep Percival off my back for a bit, but I was still shocked at the malevolence

330

he had exhibited. It was way over the top to prejudice Barclay's project just to get back at me for some slight – real or imagined.

We finished our meal as two groups: Percival and Deirdre in a huddle muttering to each other; and Bob, Martin, Robin Fullerton and me in the other, going through Percival's evidence to see if we could anticipate what questions he could be asked.

It turned out that Percival was wrong when he claimed there were no weaknesses in his evidence. In the afternoon session he came under some heavy hammer from John Henry Fletcher QC, representing Sheringford Borough Council. The thrusts of John Henry's questions were directed at the proposed alternative future uses of St Frideswide's chapel. Percival avoided the obvious trap when asked if he had considered what alternative uses the chapel could be put to after it was restored, but replied "of course". But he was then made to expand in detail on each and every use he floated out airily with waves of his hand – and it was not convincing. It was clear that he had not given much serious consideration to the possibilities, and when he floated "Bingo Hall" and "Fast Food Outlet", he was torn to shreds. The quietly-spoken QC poured withering scorn of the idea of a Grade One listed piece of Britain's Heritage pushing out Kentucky Fried Chicken and French fries from the choir stalls.

"And do you see the thousand-year-old rafters ringing to the call of 'Two Fat Ladies', Mr Percival?"

Barclay shifted irritably when a relieved Percival was eventually released to resume his seat under the reverent gaze of a flushed Plant. He made a note to rectify the situation when it was his turn to speak.

There being three-quarters of an hour left before four o'clock – the official finishing time – the Inspector called me to give my evidence. It was all straightforward. I confirmed that the cyanide problem had been sorted out and the River Authority was delighted that the cyanide would be removed and disposed of on a government hazardous chemicals dump several miles away. I couldn't help but glance at Fitzallan Percival then, who looked as though somebody had just fed him a bad oyster. Apart from St Frideswide's the rest was just routine. I explained that we had done a full structural report on the fabric of the chapel, which I had previously submitted as written evidence, and summarised the report's findings. "Although the building had suffered terribly from neglect and exposure to the elements it was basically structurally sound and could be restored. The Borough Engineer had been a party to this report and was in agreement."

After a couple of mild questions, more to clarify than to disagree, the Inspector and counsel for Sheringford completed the afternoon session and my stint as a witness. The time being four o'clock, the Inspector adjourned the Inquiry for the day, announcing that the next session would commence tomorrow morning at ten o'clock and he would be asking Mrs Plant to present her case first. I liked the 'Mrs'; it boded well for an entertaining morning tomorrow.

We repaired back to The Star, this time without Deirdre. Percival was prattling nervously: "Well that didn't go down too badly... I think we scored a few more Brownie points with the Inspector... Their QC seemed a bit weak... Did you notice how he tried to trick me with his question about alternative uses...? Ha, ha,.ha! It's an old one that is; everybody knows that for a listed building one must look at alternative uses."

Barclay had been ominously silent during the walk to The Star but once inside and wedged against the bar with a pint in his hand, he centred Percival in front of him and began.

"You told us at the first design meeting that if I bought

332

the chapel you would have no difficulty in getting permission for it to be demolished."

Percival gave a weak smile. "Well, I don't think I put it quite like that. After all, nothing is certain in planning when you're in the hands of politicians and lawyers."

"No," said Barclay, "you didn't put it quite like that. What you actually said was..." he reached over and took sheet of paper from Martin Holmes "...and I quote the minutes: 'Mr Percival guaranteed that he would secure permission to develop St Frideswide's chapel, thus saving Barclay developments the cost of site acquisitions for adjacent land'."

Fitzallan Percival's eyes flickered round, seeking an escape, but there was none. He licked his lips and took a nervous sip of his Campari.

"Yes, well, I still think we're in with a good chance, a very good chance indeed. The engineering evidence was a trifle weak. I thought more stress should have been laid on the poor quality of the foundations in my view."

"Really," murmured Barclay, "and what do you say about that, Marcus?"

You had to hand it to him; he was a trier, not a very good trier but he tried. "I think I once mentioned that the crypt on which the chapel stands had the finest example of barley sugar twisted columns in Wiltshire. Eight hundred years they've stood there supporting that building and probably good for another eight hundred. I don't seriously think that one could claim they were 'poor quality'."

"No," said Barclay, "I don't either. Still, we can all remain optimistic in view of Fitzallan's guarantee, can't we?" And with that he changed the subject. Personally I would think a chocolate fireguard more reliable than Percival's guarantee but I had other things on my mind.

Fitzallan Percival turned down Barclay's invitation to dinner in the evening; Barclay proposed to take us all to a country house restaurant he knew near Warminster but Percival announced he had to get back to London – 'couldn't possibly spare any more time, very busy you know, important clients, etc', the usual load of flannel we got from him but this time there was a suppressed eagerness that contrasted markedly with his normal pseudo haste. He was clearly dying to get away. I kept my fingers crossed – and sure enough, when Barclay released him, he scurried off to the carpark where his Mercedes lurked between the Astras, Metros and Cavaliers.

There, waiting patiently, was a large turquoise-clad frame. They both got in the car and drove off together. Deirdre – patient! It did look good!

* * *

But Deirdre had a problem, she had been thinking about it all afternoon as Percival stumbled from ineptitude to blunder and back – not in her eyes, of course – and that was how to deliver her attack without seeming to criticise his architecture, even by implication. She wasn't sure whether to discuss it with him over the dinner he had invited her to share. They hadn't had time to touch on, let alone explore, each other's politics yet.

* * *

"Mrs Plant, if you would like to come to the rostrum please, we will begin with your contribution. Er... I don't seem to have a transcript of it, do you have a typewritten proof available for distribution?" The Inspector was feeling benevolent after his bacon and egg, toast, marmalade and coffee at The Star that morning. Mrs Donaldson only permitted him All Bran to keep him regular. The problem with that was that it also kept him frequent, whereas some good old bacon and egg could be relied upon to hold the fort at least till lunchtime.

It was thus with sunny confidence he began to tackle the day's work. Deirdre strode tight-lipped to the indicated rostrum, a sheaf of notes grasped in a meaty fist, bosom surging beneath a collarless red shirt, long black skirt swinging round her strong calves.

There was an expectant hush from the unusually large public gallery, the press benches were also packed whereas yesterday only the Sheringford Comet and the Wilts, and Gloucs Informer had been present. On my way in I had noticed TV outside broadcast vans in the courtyard; I had assumed to cover the by-election campaign, but now I was not so sure. Astonishingly, Percival also showed up looking very smug murmuring something about "seeing this thing through to the end for my client's sake".

"Right, young lady, er... as... er... there doesn't appear to be a transcript perhaps you would care to proceed and lay your offering before us." The Inspector sat back with a self-satisfied smile. I sat forward, determined not to miss a word.

The 'offering', when it came, was not exactly laid before him, it was rammed into one end at maxi decibels so hard that it nearly came out the other. Mrs Donaldson's All Bran would certainly have yielded but The Star's bacon and egg just held firm.

Deirdre wiped the smile off his face with her first two sentences. After basking all yesterday under the deferential address of 'Sir', it came as a bit of a shock to be referred to as a 'slimy puppet of the capitalist establishment'. This was followed up with a brisk dressing down for calling her Mrs. She, she stated very forcefully, was Ms Deirdre, representing the Sheringford Labour Party and Save Old Sheringford – I noticed the switch in emphasis – and had he got that quite clear, because if he hadn't she would have it spelt out in large capitals and presented to him somewhere aft of his bacon and egg. And what is more, if he patronised her again she would put his desk, chair and microphone after it.

The press licked their pencils and cleared the fluff from their ballpoints. The Inspector attempted a rebuke but Deirdre was off, well underway now, and in ringing tones drowned out his protest as she set her socialist scene in which she illustrated that in a true people's democracy lackeys like the Inspector, the Secretary of State, both counsel, all the Judges and Barclay would have been strung up from the lampposts of Sheringford by the surging masses fighting to throw off the shackles imposed for centuries by The State, The Law and The Church.

"We shall not be silenced!" she bellowed, and indeed at that volume she had a point. "We shall be heard here and we shall be heard throughout the length and breadth of this country." I agreed with that as well, she probably could be already, but such an output requires at some stage some input; so, seizing his chance as she filled her lungs, Mr Donaldson stepped in, enquiring impudently what that had to do with St Frideswide's.

Deirdre gave him the full, double-barrelled presentation. Both eyes at full glare, both breasts at full point.

"The Church has had a major hand in the subjugation of the masses, any symbol of that hated oppressor will be torn brick from brick, stone from stone. To the people of Sheringford, the real people, the farm workers, the artisans, the peasants, the oppressed labouring classes, the typification of their bondage is that pile of blood-soaked stone. It is Sheringford's Bastille and as such must and will be destroyed without trace. About that there is no argument; all we are debating is when and by whom. It is not the rapacious developer who should decide, nor this bloodthirsty government, and it is not you, the appointed lackey of the Capitalist State. It is the people guided by their leaders who, of their own time and choosing, will decide what to do with their town under caring socialism. We true socialists of SOS are the only people to represent the masses, the poor, the out of work and I say to you..." The old finger was lifted high in the air and the decibel production began to rise again. The Inspector, being not yet a man experienced in the handling of the vast collection of fruitcakes that infested most Public Inquiries, was somewhat at a loss but sufficiently attuned to the situation to realise that trouble could be afoot here if not handled very carefully. The silencing of Ms Deirdre in full flow was a task for which he was not well equipped. However, he was both kindly and resourceful and decided that if he could get her to make her point he could then cut her off with thanks and rapidly adjourn for lunch. He interrupted.

"I take it, therefore, Miss Deirdre – it is Miss I presume?" He tapped the third finger on his left hand which was encircled by the broad gold band of his own wedding ring. There was a momentary silence, then his reservoir of experience received more rainfall in the next few minutes than it had over the last five years.

She went for the jugular.

Thirty minutes later, as Deirdre came to the end of her harangue on male chauvinism, the Female Dimension, the role of women in a patriarchal society in which the rules have been written by men biased against women and finally, a ten-minute dissertation on sexual symbolism in civil engineering, the Inspector had had his mind filled with other matters than Deirdre's marital state. She had pounded him from all angles; he had tried to stem her flow but it was like pissing at a waterfall. He was bellowed over each time he opened his mouth by her demands that she had a right to be heard. She pulverised his attempts at reason, ignored his directions to get to the point and refused to be silent. The hostility emanating from sections of the public was almost tangible, feral in its scent, the big cats closing in on their quarry, and the Inspector was wary. He decided that, discretion being the better part of valour, he would let this harridan run her course.

It was a brilliantly shrewd move, had he known it. He completely ruined her plan to cause as much public disruption as possible by lying down and meekly rolling over. And the irony was that she had contributed to the ruining by banging on continuously so he couldn't get a word in, and thus rent-a-mob wasn't given the chance to accuse him of depriving her of her right to speak.

Eventually she cottoned on to the problem and paused, waiting for him to explode; waiting for him to lose his temper and castigate her, or call security and have her silenced, or even physically ejected from the chamber. But nothing happened. The opportunity had passed.

Having decided to let her expend her powder and shot harmlessly, he had drifted off into another realm whilst she did so.

Her sexual symbolism observations had been particularly penetrative for a man whose career had been spent in restoring the crumbling spires and cracking domes of Britain's heritage. For until his appointment as a Department of the Environment Inspector, Mr R R Donaldson, Fellow of the Institution of Civil Engineers and Fellow of the Royal Town Planning Institute, had been Surveyor to the fabric of the Roman Catholic diocese of Arundel, and a 'tit' man. He had never connected the two until Deirdre's homily, during which she laid great stress on man's frustrated sexuality resulting in the design and construction of such things as towers, spires and chimneys to compensate for an inadequate erection, and the love for domes substituting for frustrated contact with mammary glands in a breast fetishist.

He realised now his great affection for Westminster Cathedral and Brighton Pavilion had been motivated by forces more primeval than architecture or engineering. Maybe the old monks and even the young monks who designed the great gothic masterpieces of Ulm and Koln, of Salisbury and Chartres, had constructed the towering spires as a cry to God for help, a symbolic request for a relief massage. He was just developing this theme when he realised the chamber was silent; they were all looking at him waiting.

I was wondering if he had fallen asleep, although such an event would have been truly remarkable under Plant's tongue. But the man was just sitting there immobile, as if in a trance. Deirdre had said and done all she could think of to provoke him but the man had gone into a coma. Apart from physically assaulting him, she couldn't think of anything else she could do. The Inspector raised his eyes to look at her. Mrs, Miss or whatever the damn woman was, was standing there, flanks heaving, eyes glaring and apparently awaiting some response from him.

"Er... would you mind repeating the last sentence, I couldn't make a note fast enough." He waved his ballpoint pen in the air vaguely. She gave an exasperated snort.

"I said, in conclusion, cloth-ears, that the Socialist Party of Sheringford fully supports the superbly designed scheme presented by Mr Percival, it will create jobs for the people of this town; but we despise the capitalist lackey who is going to batten on the blood of working people and make huge profits out of this development. It should be done by the people, for the people, and with the people's money. Save Old Sheringford fully supports this view and is in favour of transforming that bloodstained opiate of the people, St Frideswide's, into a

Bingo Hall. Personally I would tear it down stone from stone and fasten each stone round the neck of people like you and hurl them into the Shering."

"I see," he made a note, "so Miss, Merss Plant... on behalf of the... er... Socialist Party and save Old Sheringford Society you are... er... in favour of the scheme as a whole but not the demolition of St Frideswide's. Is that your position?"

She had one last try.

"Fuck me, are you thick or something? I thought I had made it perfectly clear to everybody what our position was." But the spark fell on wet tinder. He knew he was nearly out of this and there was no way he was going to get embroiled in an argument with her at that stage.

"Well... er... thank you Merss, Miz Plant, thank you."

She was beaten. She glared at him angrily – you can't fight with somebody who won't be provoked. Disappointment enveloped her like a shawl but somehow it didn't seem to matter as much as it should. There were a few supporting heckles from rent-a-mob but they too didn't have a cause on which to hang their protest. Reluctantly she yielded the rostrum, muttering 'spineless fucking chicken' as she passed Donaldson. She came and sat next to Fitzallan, exchanging intimate smiles with him, and the Inspector, after a bit of head-scratching and paper-shuffling, adjourned the enquiry until two o'clock to give himself time to recover and regain control. He decided not to telephone Mrs Donaldson that evening; he was definitely 'off' women for the time being. A half bottle of scotch, the Gideon Bible in his hotel room and a sleeping pill had much more appeal.

The press and TV folk were totally brassed-off, however. After being promised fireworks, all they had got was some butch-looking woman slagging off a Planning Inspector who had played it very cool. He had cleverly let her get on with it and then ignored her. So where was the news, where were the headline grabbing incidents they had been promised that would hit the front pages of the tabloids and prime time television? Nowhere! What had taken place that morning was run-of-the mill stuff, it happened at just about every Public Inquiry. Some fruitcake shot off their mouth, leapt about indignantly, made a song and dance for an hour or so and was then consigned to history.

Grumbling at the waste of time, they packed their gear and trudged out into the street bearing their cameras and tape recorders. They shouldered through the scattered crowd, ignoring the limp banners of the Socialist Organisers Soviet and the placards of the disgruntled mob that were milling aimlessly about, their cause having failed to materialize, and headed for the nearest pub to get in a few before finding something better to focus on that covered the by-election.

"What do you make of that?" a bemused Robin Fullerton murmured to no one in particular, as we wandered to The Star for lunch. There was so much going on to make something of, that I wasn't sure if I could answer his question in less than a couple of hours.

We were all thinking different things.

* * *

Barclay was thinking that, taken on balance, Deirdre's attack on the Inspector hadn't done his cause any harm. She was not one of his team and had been thought of as an objector. In fact the Inspector's brief summary of her ranting and raving had been to record that the groups she claimed to represent were in favour of the development.

However, the thing that was puzzling him the most was: why was the thrust of the Inquiry directed at St

Frideswide's? There had been no criticism of the shopping development in Percival's cross-examination. It appeared that the council were happy with the scheme, but concerned about the future of the chapel.

Percival was thinking: 'What a woman!' She had really rammed it into the Inspector what a brilliant scheme he had designed. He had always hoped that one day he would find somebody who would appreciate him for what he thought he was, and here she was, in his eyes big, beautiful and sexy with it.

Deirdre was thinking that the stupid cowardly sod of an Inspector had ruined all her carefully laid plans to get maximum publicity for the Socialist Organisers Soviet, Arthur Winlewis, and last, but by no means least, herself. The bastard couldn't even put up half a fight, the chicken-livered swine, but that was typical. But on the plus side, no harm had been done to Winlewis's election chances, and – her heart beat faster at the thought – she had found a soulmate. A man who was not all chauvinistic, arrogant, hairy and stupid, and what bit of that there was in him she could soon beat out. No, it had been a disappointing morning but not disastrous.

Fullerton, whose observation triggered off this frantic brain activity, was thinking how lucky he was to be married to Fleur, because, before her attack on the Inspector, he had rather fancied Deirdre.

And I was thinking that the bond formed the previous day between Fitzallan Percival and La Plant seemed to have survived the night, and that boded well for the future. It might not be just a short-term supernova.

Chapter Nineteen

The whiff of treachery that floated across the flared nostrils of Save Old Sheringford's Main Committee from the smoke of Deirdre's broadsides at the Public Inquiry was insufficient to isolate her in full but Charlie spelt out the position quite clearly. "She has used us, used us to promote her own political ambitions and those of the Labour Party in the forthcoming by-election." She was very angry indeed at Deirdre's behaviour but La Plant was conspicuous by her absence. She had not been seen in Sheringford since her appearance in the Town Hall, and as Gerald Sheldrake, who represented The Council for the Preservation of Rural England pointed out, she had in essence put over the Save Old Sheringford point of view as well as her own and looked at broadly, it may not have done their cause any harm at all.

Charlie was not convinced, however. SOS had promoted its aims through pressure and persuasion in the past but it had always done so knowing that its cause was genuine and its motives unselfish. In my view this was its major political weakness; it seemed to me that most causes bearing those two attributes ended as failures with their faces in the mud being used as stepping stones for stump politicians with overactive personal ambitions.

"These days," I reflected, "if you want to get action, make trouble." So much the better if you have a good case but that did not seem to me to be an essential ingredient. Thus I tended to side with Sheldrake's viewpoint, but Charlie was scornful.

"It's all right for you, it's not you that's going to have to try to get SOS out of this mess. That woman could have done us immeasurable harm locally, making out that it was only the socialists who cared about saving Sheringford. It's going to take me ages to limit the damage she's done to us and build up our credibility again."

I smiled cynically. "There you go again, using those funny words that are not in the politicians' lexicon – 'credibility'! What the hell has that got to do with persuading politicians? Look, the best thing you could do is to get the whole of SOS to tell the government that it will vote en masse for this Winlewis fellow unless they do something immediately to counter the acid rain threat or whatever you want!"

It was just an observation off the top of my head, tossed into the discussion without much thought but I suddenly realised that that could be the very lever that Save Old Sheringford needed to ram home the force of its argument to the government.

She looked at me quizzically, tapping her teeth with her pencil. "I must admit, Marcus, for all your twisted views on life there are times when I might concede that you have a point."

I grinned triumphantly. "You mean I'm right, don't you? Ah ha!"

"I meant nothing of the kind." She turned away with a wry smile. "But just assuming, assuming mind you, that there *is* something in what you say, it's a bit of a far-fetched idea. I mean there's no way most of the SOS members would vote Labour, not even New Labour, whatever that stands for. They would have their fingernails pulled out first. Certainly they wouldn't switch for that reason. They would continue to assume, despite you being the exception, that pressure and persuasion will eventually bring about change."

I grinned at her. "Oh, it's worse than that! Hasn't it

dawned on your lot yet that Winlewis is not New Labour? He's not even Labour. He represents this militant outfit that your friend Deirdre is mixed up in, called The Socialist Organisers Soviet Revolutionary Party. They're even more opposed to New Labour than they are to the Tories. They regard them as traitors to socialism, and likewise New Labour hate the militants almost as intensely. You saw the banners and placards at the Public Inquiry. 'Vote for SOS'. They've hijacked your SOS and made it into their slogan. A lot of people will vote for them under the mistaken impression they're supporting you!"

"My God, she's really used us, hasn't she?" Charlie cried bitterly. "Every single thing she has done has been for her benefit and not for Sheringford's. She couldn't give a hoot about the old town and preserving its fine old buildings, it's all been a sham."

"Don't think of it like that," I said sympathetically, "she has done a lot of good in consolidating SOS into a coherent pressure group. What you have to do now is take a leaf out of her book and use this by-election to hammer home your points.

I was serious when I said that you could threaten to support Winlewis en masse if the government didn't go some way to reducing atmospheric pollution in Sheringford. The last thing any of the political parties want is fiery left-wing penetration of parliament. The polls show the two main parties neck and neck so you only need to convince the government that Save Old Sheringford defections will produce a small swing to the left and bingo, brown trousers in Westminster and maybe some fast action." I grasped her by the shoulders and turned her to face me and looked into those deep violet eyes. "And what's more – and you're going to like this, in fact you're going to like it a lot – if you're quick about it you should be able to use the evidence of Deirdre Plant and her involvement to convince the government that SOS has gone left. You'll be using Deirdre to obtain Save Old Sheringford's ends."

A lovely smile began to crinkle her eyes. "You're not quite as daft as you look, are you?" she chuckled. "I like it, I like it." She laughed out loud at the Confucian justice of the neatly reversed position – if it worked. Well I liked it as well – and as I hadn't had it for at least a week, and as I was still gazing into deep violet, now smiling eyes with a firm hold of a pair of shoulders, and as the remark about 'not as daft as I looked' had a touch of receptive cheek about it, I struck.

I think if it hadn't been for the thought that action on SOS was required immediately – well, tomorrow – we would still be in bed. It was as if we both sensed a lightening of the sky in the west. The tensions of the past few months seemed to drain away and for a few hours all was back to normal, and serene.

* * *

Early in the week following the Inquiry, Barclay called a meeting at his office of all those involved in the Sheringford scheme. The Public Inquiry had eventually run on for five days and in Barclay's view had been inconclusive. The outcome was unpredictable – in the lap of the gods, as most of these things are when politicians are the ultimate arbiters of choice. Additionally, it was extremely unlikely that a decision would be announced for at least six months, probably longer, based on the Department of the Environment's track record, and that was far too long to wait with costs of construction rising and prospective tenants losing interest.

In subdued mood we all gathered in Barclay's Boardroom, assuming that an inquest would be held and then the scheme thrown out into limbo whilst the Secretary of State for the Environment, Food and Rural Affairs condescended to give judgement at some future unspecified date.

I cast an anxious eye over the assembled group. I was particularly interested to ascertain Fitzallan Percival's state of wellbeing and was gratified to be confronted with a face smiling like a split chestnut and a "Good morning, Moon" that had a distinct note of bonhomie in it. His gait was a little stiff and I noted with secret satisfaction that he lowered himself somewhat gingerly into his seat. However, there no doubting the vast change for the better in his demeanour. The man was almost benevolent, it was extraordinary.

Feeling slightly disappointed that Percival's injuries were not more obviously severe, but also relieved that whatever had happened to him he seemed to be enjoying it and was hanging in, I switched my attention to the taciturn Crabbe, he of the stultiloquent sophistry. Crabbe looked just the same as he always did; his hair still looked as if Ferdinand de Lesseps had parted it and his face like a metre of bad road. His eyes flicked about nervously and he was, as usual, picking his teeth, forking out large lumps of some brown fibrous material on the end of a plastic toothpick. I wondered what he did with this hard-won matter, and then decided that I didn't really want to know. One thing was certain, however; there was no chance of Crabbe suffering from anorexia nervosa with all the spare food he carried about concealed in his dental cavities. It was like observing an oversized chipmunk.

Fullerton was sitting there like Buddha – expressionless, so there was nothing to be learned from him. But Martin Holmes seemed excited.

Bob Barclay led off, face impassive, leaning back in his chair with both hands resting casually on the table in front of him. His voice was even and dry.

"I want to thank you all for your efforts last week at the Public Inquiry. I felt that we, as a team, put forward the best possible case based on the information available to us. In particular I thought Fitzallan here lived right up to his reputation in presenting his evidence as our architectural expert at that quasi-governmental hearing." No trace of irony entered his voice and not a flicker of an eyelid changed his expression. Nobody else moved. If they had I'm sure the place would have collapsed with laughter.

Percival beamed and more gamma radiations of well-being showered upon us. I was mystified by this; if we were to be put 'on hold' for six months, why was Percival so happy? It couldn't be all down to his relationship with Deirdre.

Barclay continued, his voice sharpening up. "However, as you are all aware the main objection to our scheme appeared to be that there was no positive plan for St Frideswide's. Sheringford Council, Save Old Sheringford Society and the local citizenry are all very concerned that even if we tart the place up it will still remain a pointless lump in the middle of the town. They don't have the money to do anything with it. However, there's absolutely no chance that permission would be granted to demolish it.

"So, after the Inquiry was over, I took the opportunity to have a long private discussion with the Planning Officer and the Chairman of the local Planning Committee, together with the Leader of the Council, to canvas their views. I took Fitzallan along with me to advise on any proposals they may put forward."

We all sat forward, sensing something of interest was about to be revealed.

"The upshot of that meeting is that, in addition to restoring the fabric of St Frideswide's, I have agreed to fund the fitting-out of the interior as a small theatre, combined with a function room and a centre for local crafts.

"Whilst we were there Fitzallan sketched out some ideas, which we discussed at some length. The outcome, I am pleased to say, and as you are no doubt pleased to hear," he added dryly, "is that they've withdrawn all their objections to the scheme and will notify the Secretary of State for the Environment of that fact. They will also advise him that the Council is giving full support to the whole project. We can continue with the design work and we should receive full planning approval in approximately six weeks." He continued before he could be questioned.

"Jane Treadwell and I went back to Sheringford the following day and visited the solicitors acting for Mr Jackson and the Misses Threadle to exercise the options I'd taken on their land to give us High Street access on either side of the chapel. Gentlemen, it looks as though we have a project."

A big grin spread across his face. "You'll also be amused to know that I also contacted Grime whilst I was there and he's agreed to put up a hundred thousand pounds towards the cost of fitting out the theatre in return for it being called 'The Ron Grimshaw Memorial Theatre'. Apparently his proper name is Ronald. He said it would be different to have a memorial and still be alive! He sends his best wishes and wants to go sailing with us again in the spring!"

"Bloody well done!" said Crabbe. "If Perce can give me an up-to-date site layout of the revised scheme, I'll let you have preliminary Cost Plan in three days."

Mixed emotions flitted across Percival's face. He was slightly irritated that the spotlight had switched from him to Barclay, but, on the plus side, he had a positive scheme now. However that meant totally re-planning and re-drawing part of the original scheme. It meant he would have to do some work. The drawing was no problem, the computer could easily be re-programmed to take care of that, but the planning required serious consideration. The High Street access changed the whole concept.

As Barclay seemed to be in a good mood, Percival decided that now was as good a time as any to broach the subject dearest to his heart – money.

"Whereas I'm delighted naturally that we have what looks to be a positive scheme, I'm concerned about – or rather there's the question of my er... the other scheme. The scheme that will be abandoned and I wouldn't like to think... that is, we did a lot of work on that, you will recall, for the Inquiry and I trust that perhaps you will... could rather, see your way clear..."

Barclay put him out of his misery with a well placed shot into the wallet.

"All the team will receive fees for the work on both schemes, Fitzallan. If you'll all let me have your accounts for the Public Inquiry scheme first, I will settle those immediately."

I knew that my firm was going to be paid in any case, but I was still pleased. Percival was overcome. His irritation vanished; the sun came out and angels sang. He was loved and wanted by the most beautiful woman in the world, his professional future was now assured with this large, prestigious project and the haemorrhaging of his bank account was to be reversed by an immediate transfusion. Oh, what transports of delight were from His celestial favours! For the first and possibly the last time in his miserable, arrogant, selfish life, he felt complete – and then spoilt it all by attributing this result entirely to his own efforts, personality and genius. However, this conclusion moved him sufficiently to invite the whole group of us to lunch, spontaneously and without his usual careful consideration as to the effect on his pocket. "To have a little celebration at my expense", as he pompously put it. It was a momentary weakness that was subsequently to reconfirm his previously unshakeable, but temporarily obscured convictions of man's cupidity.

Barclay beamed. Gave him the full Barclay, all-embracing, benevolent sunshine smile that under normal circumstances chilled the blood of those embraced and had strong men calling for their mothers.

"Good man, well, I'll go along with that for a start." He picked up the telephone. "Lucy, my poppet, book us a table for six at Le Gavroche for one o'clock in the name of Fitzallan Percival – and ask them to open three bottles of their '52 Lafite and decant it." He grinned at Percival. "Got to let it breathe a little to get the best out of a really expensive wine." Tuning back to the telephone, he continued, "And tell them to make sure the Baron d'L is nicely chilled. They know how I like it, if you mention my name. Thanks, dear." And he replaced the receiver.

Crabbe removed his toothpick and examined the pristine point. His normally impassive features cracked into a smile. His face now looked like a metre of bad road after an earthquake of force seven on the Richter scale. "Top hole." He expanded it further. "I like me nosh, don't I. You're a real classy gent, guv, you are. By God that's goin' to set you back a handful of notes, Perce."

The world had closed in again on Percival as the import of Barclay's instructions registered in his mental accounts department. Lunch at Le Gavroche with the supporting cast and wine as specified was going to set him back well over a grand, maybe fifteen hundred, and added to this that swine Crabbe, who was a notorious knife and fork artist, was obviously not going to help. He could have wept, and Crabbe...! Jesus H Christ, whether he was shovelling down faggots, chips and jellied eels or the finest French cuisine made not the slightest difference to him, it was like feeding a Sludge Gulper. Percival started to sweat. Talk about pearls before swine! Well, he would see about that...

And then the sun peeped from behind the clouds again. The old financial fiddling department, which occupied most of the numerical computing space in his brain, punched out an instinctive response. He could charge it all up to job expenses to be paid by the client; there was no problem.

A sigh of relief gently oozed through his lips, his heart stopped its financial flutter and the beads of sweat dried stillborn on his brow. He smiled effusively and expanded as a gracious host does when he believes he's not footing the bill.

"All great events should be celebrated, so let's get started."

It was a famous lunch. The final bill hit the two thousand five hundred mark. Percival signed his Diners chit with a flourish and at four-thirty in the afternoon, we poured ourselves out on to the pavement with protestations of mutual amity. It was definitely taxi time and Barclay, with a bellow that set the pigeons rising from Grosvenor Square, summoned three of the little yellow lights from the moving mass of vehicles. Crabbe and Percival moved unsteadily to the first. Percival was about to instruct the driver as to their destination, when Barclay's boom broke into his befuddled brain.

"By the way, Fitzallan, I don't want to see this lunch charged up to my job, this was on you, remember. Cheerio!" And with that, Barclay, Holmes and Fullerton boarded the second cab, leaving me and the driver of the third cab as the sole witnesses to Percival's throwing up all over Crabbe's trousers.

"There's over four hundred quid's worth of good living in that revolting mess," I observed casually to the interested driver. "You wouldn't think the human body

352

could devalue fine food and wine in that way." Still, with Percival's body I suppose it might.

The first cab driver, seeing the state of his prospective passengers, suddenly decided it was his teatime and shot off into a convenient gap in the traffic, leaving a weak, pale-faced Percival doubled up against the wall, and an enraged Crabbe trying to stand upright in his trousers without touching the insides, shaking pieces of chewed carrot to the ground like dandruff. I shook my head in mock disapproval, a movement which I regretted as the last few Armagnacs made their presence felt. So I concentrated on opening the cab door and sank back into the firm leather seat as the driver pulled away.

Chapter Twenty

God, I felt rough! Hugo had insisted on cracking a bottle of champagne when Barclay's substantial cheque hit the firm's doormat a couple of weeks after our team meeting. I still had to sort out Fitzallan Percival over the cyanide performance, but I was keeping that in reserve in case I needed a bargaining asset at some future date. Hugo even mumbled something about 'will be bearing your efforts in mind, Marcus, come the first of July' – that was the date when our annual salaries were reviewed. Well, he was right about that, it would be at the forefront of any conversation I held with him in June – even May!

Charlie had taken herself off smartly to Sheringford this morning to put what I modestly referred to as Moon's Political Plan into operation. Charlie, I might add, called it no such thing – she called it Prinknash's Political Plan. The point is, she would not be home to see what depredations the day, plus a long evening in The Frog and Nightgown, had wreaked upon her loved one. So it was with a happy heart and a spinning head that I hit the sack late that night.

When the phone rang at seven-thirty the next morning, I was not too pleased.

"Oh, it's you," said the female voice in reply to my curt opening.

"Yes, I know it's me," I responded testily, "but who are you?"

"I want to speak to Charlie, put her on."

I looked at the telephone sharply. I recognised the voice now, it was La Plant. I decided to give her a hard time.

"I'm sorry, who's speaking?"

"Look, put Charlie on will you, Marcus, and stop pissing about!"

Ah ha! The penny dropped. So she thought Charlie was here – which meant of course that she didn't know Charlie was in Sheringford at an SOS Main Committee meeting, which in turn meant that Deirdre wasn't! Not bad for a befuddled brain at 7.30am with a hangover!

"Oh, it's you, Miss Plant," I riposted, "how nice to hear from you so early in the morning. And Fitzallan, well is he?"

She hesitated, weighing this one up and then decided she didn't care who knew what about her and Percival. With exaggerated politeness she said, "Yes, he's well, I'm well, we're both well, now will you please put Charlie on the phone?"

"She's not here I'm afraid, Deirdre, she left early for work." A little white lie in a way, but I suppose 'yesterday' could be called early and 'SOS' work.

"Well, why the fuck didn't you say so before?" she bawled, doing my hangover no good whatsoever, and then slammed down the phone.

I rang Prinknash Keep and told Charlie about the call. She in turn told me that word of the militant left's penetration into SOS's higher echelons and their other political activities had already reached Downing Street and apparently caused more than a few ripples. She was going to make sure the brew was well stirred. I said that sounded like good news, told her I loved her and rang off before she could ask any other questions.

As I sank back exhausted, Deirdre sat biting her lip – a worried girl. On the one hand Winlewis was really putting the pressure on her to tie up the extra votes he needed in Sheringford but on the other, wonderful Fitzallan had asked her join with him as co-author of a paper to be presented to the Architectural Association Summer Symposium entitled 'Gender Differentiation in Local Authority Housing'. She was dying to get started and begin researching this project and found that she couldn't give a hoot about Winlewis any more. After all, there would be nothing in it for her any longer, she had proved her abilities, now all that was left was for Straker and Winlewis to take the undeserved credit – she was sufficient of a realist to know that that was exactly what was going to happen whether she accepted it or not. So stuff them.

On the other hand, the idea of putting her restless energy behind community architecture was very appealing. It had the double attraction for her of presenting an ideal medium for promoting the female dimension in a concrete way and was politically socialist and positive.

Fitzallan Percival was equally enthusiastic, he saw all this potential local authority work, which she should be able to pull in, as very socially desirable – for him and the bank balance. Local Authorities paid full-scale fees for nice repetitive housing, not like that tight-fisted haggling philistine Barclay, who wanted a pound's work for a pound. A few flashy sketches coloured up to impress the committee and some basic layouts, that was all that was necessary; the contractor could work out the rest, and for that he would get five percent of the cost plus a supervision fee. And by God didn't *she* turn him on as well! Perce really felt his ships were coming up the river.

The problem was, however, that although Deirdre would have been torn apart between wild horses rather than admit it, she was terrified of Straker. The 'brothers' of the Soviet Organisers Soviet were not known to tolerate back-sliders and, on more than one occasion that she knew of, the heavies had been brought in to provide incentives to the members who were not pulling their weight: Hence the early morning phone call to Charlie Prinknash; she wanted to find out what her current standing was in Save Old Sheringford but at the same time put over her position quite clearly. She was going to take the line that she had spelt out the SOS case exactly as they had directed to the Inquiry, glossing over the fact that that was not her original intention. She had felt that she should also put over the socialist viewpoint. No doubt some of the old farts on the Main Committee would fizz and froth a bit, but if she could get Charlie to accept this reasoning then her influence and control would remain.

She was still cursing 'that pig Moon' when the phone rang in Percival's flat – we had got that sussed out. It was Charlie.

"No, no problem, Deirdre, thought you put our case over very well – yes, Corrigan Croot and Mrs H-W were a bit huffy but all smoothed over – well, you know how narrow-minded some of these county folk are..." Then: "Now's the time for a bit more action – to cash in on the publicity." (Ignoring the fact that there had hardly been any.) "We want to hold a demonstration march and rally next weekend, you people are experts. Can you get down to Sheringford and put something together fast? And Deirdre, it's got to be multi-political, not just Labour."

A slow scornful smile spread across Deirdre's face as she put the phone down. How naïve, how stupid these people were! They deserved to be taken to the cleaners, they really did. Multi political! What on earth did they think she was going to do – promote the bloody Tories? Or, worse still, those wet, weedy, traitorous renegades in New Labour. No way! This was going to be it. When you get thrown a lifeline like that, you don't tie your sworn enemies to it, and the beauty of it was, it solved all her problems. Winlewis could lead the march, putting him right in the public eye. They would campaign under the SOS logo: blood-red banners with Socialist Organisers Soviet Save Old Sheringford. Straker would be placated, lots of local publicity – this should really stitch it up for Winlewis and if it didn't, well, it would be he who would shoulder the blame if she played her cards right. Put him right up at the sharp end, then he couldn't skate out of that. She seized a piece of paper and began drafting out her requirements. Printed hand bills, printed placards with poles, lapel badges, portable megaphones, get the local Socialist Organisers mobilized to pull in the fringe protest groups: Campaign for Nuclear Disarmament, Women Against the Bomb, Abortion for All, Jobs for the Boys, Free Wales, Down with Everything, The Wimmin's Movement – no, she would handle that with Suzie. The local Labour Party Committee would do as they were told, and she must find a marching band. There was a hell of a lot to do between now and Sunday but this was Deirdre's forte. Charlie had played a clever card.

Charlie replaced the phone with some trepidation; old adages like 'she who sups with the Devil needs a long spoon' sprang to mind. It was some gamble, but the intelligence reports brought back from Westminster were stressing the government's increasing nervousness about Sheringford. She smiled to herself at the 'multi-political' angle she had tossed in; without it Deirdre might have smelt a rat. She thought the matter through again. The Save Old Sheringford committee had taken some convincing of the plan to use Deirdre and her socialists to scare some action out of Westminster. Corrigan-Croot and Minerva Hartley-Worthington were 'damned if they would march with a bunch of Commies!'

The other members took a more pragmatic view and considered that the possible advantage was worth the risk. Besides, they were running out of ideas to put pressure on the government.

Charlie went down on the train on Friday night but Barclay had three stand tickets for the Arsenal Liverpool game, so he, Fullerton and I decided to do the match on the Saturday, have an easy Sunday morning, take in a pub lunch on the way down and make Sheringford in time for the three-thirty start to the demo. Not that we were going to take part, of course, but Barclay and Fullerton had meetings first thing Monday morning with some prospective tenants and I was going to drive Charlie back to London after the march. It seemed a sensible and possibly entertaining thing to make a day of it.

We were a bit late setting off, having had a quick beer in The Frog, and it was thus a few minutes before two o 'clock when we pulled into the car park of The Ancient Mariner at Deane.

"Bloody good," said Fullerton, rubbing his hands together, "a nice pint of Blackthorn Cider to wash down a healthy Wiltshire yeoman's lunch. Right up my street, that!"

The place was busy, but there were a couple of spare tables. Barclay headed for the bar.

"I'll get the drinks while you sort out the food, Marcus. Grab the table, Robin. What do you want? A nice glass of red wine will do me, some fresh ham, a large piece of game pie and a salad with some French bread and cheese."

I surveyed his gut. "I see – you're on your Weight-Watchers kick again!"

I wandered over to the vacant food counter which contained a variety of salads, coleslaw, pies, pasties cold cuts of meat and other delicacies.

"Afternoon, dearie," I nodded at the thin, harassed-looking girl behind the counter. "I think we'd like to sample some of your 'Wessex Fayre'. Three large helpings of game pie for a start and I think..." She cut me off in mid-menu.

'Sorry, the food's finished."

"You what?" I was totally taken aback.

"The food's finished," she repeated testily.

"What's all this then?" I indicated the display with a wave of the hand.

"Sorry, food finishes at two o'clock prompt. Them's the rules and we got to be stickin' to 'em."

"But everybody else is eating," I reasoned, gesticulating round the pub where crowds of happy munchers were cheerily chomping their way through mounds of 'Wessex Fayre'.

"Sorry, but rules is rules," she said. I looked down at my watch.

"Hang on a minute; it's not two o'clock yet, it's one minute to." I held out my watch for her to see, indicating that it was indeed one minute to two. I also noticed a clock above the bar and the big hand was quite definitely pointing at one fifty nine.

"Right," I said, "three large helpings of game pie, for a start. "Rules is rules', as you've quite clearly said: if the food's off at two and it is now one fifty-nine, then the food must still be on so get on with it."

She flushed and, without saying a word, disappeared through a doorway at the side of the food counter, reappearing twenty seconds later with a far more authoritative looking, heavy-faced woman. My heart sank, I felt a loser coming up here.

"Sorry," she said, giving me a look that could have sliced her own meat, "food's off."

"I'm sorry," I replied, "but it's still not two o'clock."

The woman looked at the clock above the bar and it was quite true; the minute hand had not yet leapt across the final, crucial gap to zero hour.

"All right," she said, "I accept it's not two o'clock, but

we've got so many orders on you'll have to wait thirty-five minutes before we can provide you with your food."

"But closing time is two-thirty," I protested.

The woman smirked. "Precisely."

"I mean can't you just cut us off some cold pie? It's not going to take ten seconds."

"If I start giving you your order before anybody else, there's going to be rioting, isn't there? Other people are going to want to jump the queue as well and I'm not prepared to upset my regulars." She folded her arms in finality. It was deadlock. I frowned thoughtfully.

"Stone me! Here, hang on." And I went back to the table.

"Right lads, the old bat behind the bar is just being bloody difficult and says we can't have any food for at least thirty-five minutes and the pub closes at two-thirty. What are we going to do?"

They glanced at each other, making a quick decision.

"Let's drink up and go on further down the road, there's another pub about a mile on the right-hand side," Barclay pronounced. I nodded and went back to the food counter where the heavy-faced authoritarian was lodged like a defender of the bridge, meaty forearms akimbo, face thrust forward and small eyes narrowed down to gun-slits. She was awaiting the attack.

I leant towards her confidentially.

"Then out spake brave Horatius
The Captain of the Gate
To everyman upon this earth
Death cometh soon or late
And how can men die better
Than facing fearful odds
For the ashes of his fathers
and the temples of his Gods."

The HFA was taken aback. "What's that?" she muttered.

"That, my dear Horatius, or should I say Horatia, is Thomas Babington Macaulay."

"What's he got to do with it?"

"He's asked me to tell you and Lars Porsena of Clusium there," I pointed at the thin bint twitching the background, "that you can take your Wessex Fayre and stuff it!"

I shook my head in bewilderment and turned and walked back to the others. We knocked back our drinks and drove up the road to an even smaller country inn which proclaimed itself to be The Black Horse, servers of, amongst other things, Bar Food and Snacks. As we got out of the car, Barclay looked across at me. "You'd better leave this one to me, Marcus, I have a way with these country people, you know.

This was news to me but I nodded. "Okay, fine with me."

There were only two other cars in the small car park. We parked beside a notice which read 'No Coaches' and walked towards the door past another notice proclaiming 'No Picnicking'. Barclay pushed open the low, dark oak-stained door and we followed. There were three notices pinned to the door by thumb tacks. The first said, 'No dogs allowed in the bar', the second said, 'No children under 14 allowed in the bar', the third said 'No Singing'. A real little hive of mirth and jollity we've got here, I thought, I bet inside are two more signs saying 'No Drinking' and 'No Talking'. I wasn't far wrong.

There were only three other customers present, all in a huddle at one of the bars, with the landlord, a small, strutty, game cock of a man making a fourth. Barclay breezed up to the counter like a galleon in full sail.

"Good day, jovial landlord, this is a very pleasant hostelry you keep here. We are three weary travellers from afar, parched by the dusty roads of our native isle, and we would like to enjoy your hospitality to the extent of three foaming tankards of your Blackthorn Cider, three large pork or game pies, some bread and cheese and possibly half a dozen pickled eggs."

The publican glanced up at the interruption, wiped his nose on his sleeve and then returned to his conversation with the three other shifty-looking coves that looked as though they were screwed to the floor. Barclay cleared his throat and upped his volume ten decibels.

"Excuse me, my good man, but we're faint with fatigue and three pints of your draft local ambrosia plus a good ploughman's lunch are necessary to restore us to a suitable state to continue our journey."

The publican glanced up again. "No food. The food finished at two."

"Surely for three starving travellers it should be possible to put together something as simple as bread and cheese?"

"I told you, no food. The food finished at two."

Barclay persisted. "But you have there some nice French bread and cheese and some Scotch eggs, I can see them." He pointed to where, at the back of the bar, were indeed the comestibles he had specified.

"How many times do you need telling?" snarled the landlord. "There's no food. Food finished at two."

Barclay turned a slow shade of crimson. "I'm bloody sorry," he ground out, "that we're embarrassing you, coming into your overcrowded establishment, bulldozing our way through the throng of merry drinkers, spreading plague and pestilence around the milling customers and trying to force our money upon you." His eye caught the notice nailed behind the bar that said 'Smiling Service Sells'. "I don't wonder that people go abroad for their holidays, if they've got to contend with the sort of service one gets around here. You want to take a good read of your own notice, sunshine." He reached over the bar, jerked it off the wall together with a fist-sized piece of plaster and slapped it down in front of the man. The publican reacted angrily but, seeing Barclay's size, and also the size of Fullerton and me, who had taken up positions on the flanks, controlled himself, deciding that discretion was without doubt the better part of two weeks in intensive care.

"You can have a drink," he muttered.

"What are you going to do about the three carloads that are following just behind us?" asked Barclay.

The publican sneered. "Pull the other one, it's got bells on."

A meaty forefinger the diameter of a German sausage rammed him in the chest bone, moving him back a couple of feet. Barclay smiled sadly.

"I didn't think you'd got another one, in fact I don't think you've got any at all." And with that parting sally, we all turned and left the pub before the landlord could think of a reply.

"When you're down and feeling blue, no matter what they say, give a little whistle." Fullerton pursed his lips and blew a couple of perky notes. "Give a little whistle. That's what my nanny used to say."

We registered absolute incredulity.

"Good Lord," said Barclay shakily, "is that so. Hey, Marcus, d'ye hear that? When you're down and feeling blue... How does it go, Robin? No matter what they say, give a little whistle," and he repeated Fullerton's whistle. "What do you think of that, Marcus? That's solved our frigging problems hasn't it? Starving we might be, and dying for a couple of pints of best West Country brew, and all the time Robin has got the solution."

"Amazing, incredible," I responded, "that's fantastic."

Fullerton eyed us both warily. He wasn't sure if the piss was being extracted.

"It's what Jiminy Cricket used to sing to Pinocchio when things looked a bit down."

Barclay gave an evil grin. "Is that so? And what did he used to sing when he was chucked in the village pond?" And we advanced on him.

"No, hang on a moment, I've got an idea!" cried Fullerton desperately. "The Star! The Star doesn't close till three o'clock, we can get there by two-thirty if we set off now."

He was right, I remembered now, The Star had some ancient dispensation as an old coaching inn to serve food and drink to travellers to a much later hour. So with a reprieved and relieved Fullerton, we made for Sheringford in double-quick time.

Feeling refreshed after a couple of pints of real ale and a good ploughman's lunch of crusty bread, pickle and fine English cheeses, we leaned back in our comfortable chairs in The Highwayman's Bar and watched through the windows as the Save Old Sheringford marchers gathered on the green outside. La Plant was in her element; strutting about with a megaphone bellowing at various groups to take their places. The marching band of the local Salvation Army blew the spittle from their instruments, showering it all over the local Brownie troop. Brown Owl threatened to knock the Sally Army's trumpet player's 'fucking head off' if he did it again, and, precisely on the dot of three-thirty, the blood red banners were unfurled.

The band struck up 'Blaze Away' and Winlewis, dressed in a borrowed Barbour jacket and tweed cap, strode out into Bath Road at the head of the march. Immediately behind him two burly SOS men carried a huge banner, which extended across the width of the road, bearing the legend 'VOTE SOS – VOTE WINLEWIS'. Other flags and placards proclaiming 'WINLEWIS FOR SHERINGFORD' and similar sentiments were scattered amongst the Fire Brigade, Scouts, farmers, shopkeepers, churchgoers, Voluntary Services, Sea Cadets, Air Cadets and the many ordinary folk who made up the two thousand people who had turned out believing that they were protesting against the destruction of their town.

Augustus Withers, the Tory candidate, was somewhere at the back with his large blue rosette. He hadn't been invited, and when he showed up and demanded to be given equal prominence with Winlewis, Deirdre and the two beefy banner carriers explained to him that the nearest intensive care beds were in Swindon, many miles away.

Charlie and her father were looking apprehensive as they marched past The Star with a group of local landowners whose expressions were those of the condemned rather than full of optimism. Chants of 'SOS Save Old Sheringford' were echoing in the narrow streets.

I had to admire the way Deirdre had manipulated things to link the Socialist Organisers Soviet to Save Old Sheringford and was presenting Winlewis as the saviour of the town. It was masterly.

I hoped it worked!

* * *

"Now let us turn to the forthcoming by-election in Sheringford." The Prime Minister flicked through the briefing paper his aides had prepared. "You've seen the reports on the demonstration there last Sunday. What's the current situation Dougal?"

The Chairman of the Party didn't refer to any notes, he knew the score exactly. "The Marplan and Gallup polls out this morning show a two percent shift to Labour in Sheringford. If that holds, Winlewis will take the seat."

"And is there any reason for this? It seems to go against the current national trend. It must be a local problem."

366

The Secretary of State for Industry began to ease his collar. This conversation had all the characteristics of a plank being run out on a pirate ship. That inborn sense of self-preservation at all costs was murmuring that perhaps a very quick course of manacled swimming lessons would be prudent. He listened anxiously as the Chairman continued.

"It is indeed, Prime Minister. Unfortunately the militant left, who have secured the selection of their candidate to represent Labour, have also penetrated and suborned that pressure group which has been giving us a problem – Save Old Sheringford. The outcome is that local Conservative voters have been put on Morton's fork. On the one hand they feel that if they vote Tory there'll be no pressure on us to do anything about the pollution issue, and we'll continue to ignore their demands to remedy the acid rain problem. On the other, they've seen the active socialist militants supporting their campaign – as evidenced by the demonstration you mentioned, Prime Minister, and they feel that by backing this man Winlewis, who is committed to continue campaigning vigorously to embarrass us, they stand a chance of our capitulation.

Even Save Old Sheringford, which, for all its pressure, used to be rock solid Tory, is now being led by some hard-left feminist. The whole shooting match is threatening to go over to the militants simply because we've not responded to their demands that we exercise tighter control over fume emissions. And, equally damaging – so they claim – we haven't agreed to move the proposed Nippon Kansun forge and foundry project elsewhere."

The cold blue eyes of the Prime Minister swivelled on to the fledgling handicapped swimmer, as he had anticipated.

"Not a very sensible idea to locate such a plant in the

first place right in the middle of a rural community, Frank?"

It was no good protesting that it hadn't been his idea but the PM's; you only ended up sinking with mouthfuls of saltwater. Far better to don the water wings and swim like Joe Buggery.

"We can easily and quickly relocate it to Bridgend, Cumbernauld or County Durham. My department has done all the studies and prepared the paperwork for each of these towns. Nothing has been signed with the Japanese and any of those three locations are quite acceptable to them." The blue eyes softened a little, Frank was an old campaigner, hard to catch out, not like that silly sod Sam.

"And do you have any funds for industrial grants we could make available to the existing firms in Sheringford to assist them in the installation of fume scrubbers and filters?"

That made Frank twitch inwardly. He didn't know whether he had or not, or even what a fume scrubber was, but he didn't bat an eyelid.

"Yes, we do."

"Very good, Frank, we'll leave it in the capable hands of you and your department to liaise with Environment and make the appropriate announcements – tomorrow!"

The Prime Minister tapped his teeth with his pen and switched his gaze on to Sam McAvoy, the Honourable Member for Glasgow Bridge and Secretary of State for Scottish Affairs. Sam had backed him when he had been in a tight spot a couple of months ago. He was still as thick as pig shit, though. "A nice little present to lay before your Scottish voters to celebrate your elevation to the peerage, Sam." It was the perfect opportunity to give Sam, sitting there goggling in bewildered ignorance at the realities of political life, the order of the elbow.

"Cumbernauld, I think," said the PM. "And five

hundred thousand pounds per factory in Sheringford. That should swing a few votes our way."

The PM paused for a minute; thinking that it would be advisable to cover all the angles. He turned to the Home Secretary.

"Hugh, see if there's anything that Special Branch can do about Winlewis!"

The Secretary of State for Industry sank back in his leather chair with relief. Handled right, this would mean kudos for him, plus exposure on some prime time television. If that ambitious little climber at Environment thought he was going to get a look-in, he had another think coming. The money was no problem, a few million at the most, his civil servants could find that. The relocation was a matter of political capital... reassessment of the employment position... benefit Scotland... no, better keep off that, he didn't want to upset his own constituents in Wales... good, hardworking labour force immediately available. Yes, that would be easy to put over. He'd get his staff to contact the Japanese this afternoon and see if he could screw something else out of them for granting them this advantageous move.

Of course the opposition would carp that it was blatant electioneering but they would have to tread carefully. All in all, a successful arrangement, and the plunge into the shark-infested waters of political oblivion neatly avoided.

The Prime Minister was saying, "The next item on the agenda is the forthcoming State Visit of the President of France. He'll arrive on Eurostar. It comes into Waterloo I believe – very appropriate, that should remind him of who won what and where!"

* * *

Charlie heard the announcements on the six o'clock television news. The Right Honourable Frank Morgan PC, MP, Secretary of State for Industry, announced today that the government was making ten million pounds available in grants to industry to assist factories in controlling the emission of harmful waste products. The first grants would be made immediately in a trial area in Sheringford in the West of England, and if successful, would be extended to other areas. Simultaneously a much stricter monitoring of emissions would be implemented, and prosecutions under the Clean Air Act instituted on defaulters.

It was also announced that the government was becoming increasingly concerned about the rising unemployment in Scotland and consequently had persuaded Nippon Kansun to relocate their forge and foundry project into Cumbernauld, where advantage could be taken of a good, hardworking skilled labour force that was immediately available. A financial aid package had been presented to the Japanese who, as a consequence, had agreed to increase their investment and in addition build a microchip plant at Sheringford as well.

A huge sense of relief flooded over her; it was over, and they had won. She sat for a few minutes, letting it sink in and then began to plan the celebrations. The big party could come later; tonight, she decided, was going to be small and private.

I knew none of this, having left the office late and struggled through the heavy traffic on the Fulham Road. I slid the key into the lock and eased open the door. The cry of welcome froze on my lips; I knew there was something wrong instantly. The aroma of succulent cooking wafted through the hall and I could hear Charlie singing in the kitchen. Pausing warily like a roe deer, I sniffed the air for clues – nothing. I quickly pulled out

370

my diary to check the date – March 5th, that didn't mean anything to me – and there was no entry under that date. Nobody due here for dinner; we obviously weren't going out; it wasn't Charlie's birthday, or mine; we had met in June, I couldn't remember the date but it was definitely June because Wimbledon was on, so it couldn't be that. What the hell was it? The date obviously meant something to her – a lot to her to go to all this trouble.

Christ! I hadn't closed the door so I quietly slipped out again and went to sit in the car. The last time I had forgotten a silly old date the Mark Two bollocking had left me somewhat chastened and bereft – the chastening I could take, it was the bereft bit that really hurt. I had been fancying my chances for this evening as well – increasingly as the day passed by, and unforeseen circumstances like this played havoc with those plans. Unease grew. I ran through all the possibilities, again to no avail. The other thing – it came to me now – I could smell candles back there in the hall. Jesus Christ, it *was* important!

I thought about nipping down to the shops for some flowers or chocolates but apart from Jamal's General Store on the corner, they would all be closed – and everything he sold me was either curried or spiced. Oh God, what is it? I thought. *What is it?*

There was nothing for it: it was either go down to the pub and get smashed then bollocked, or take it straight now like a man. I squared my shoulders, bracing myself, and was just about to head for the pub when the house door opened and Charlie looked out.

"Hi, Marcus, thought I heard the car door, come on in." She took me by the hand and pulled me thorough the door, closing it behind her and murmuring, "Hello, you gorgeous lover, you", and she gave me a big hug and a long, lingering kiss that under normal circumstances would have had the old trousers off in thirty seconds flat. My unease grew to extreme alarm, reinforced by her hand sliding inside my shirt and massaging round the ribs – just feeling for a spot to slip in the knife. The longer this went on, the greater the violent reaction when she found out I had forgotten whatever it was I was clearly supposed to have remembered. My various parts weren't co-ordinating either, I was not one of those people who, told by the pilot that all four engines have cut out and there are only three minutes before we hit the deck, could get his leg over the nearest bit of presentable crumpet. Scales claimed he would, but I had to have the right atmosphere – ambience – to perform satisfactorily. True, the specification for 'right atmosphere' had not been too demanding in the past: I remembered giving one to Annabel Mac somebody-or-other in the back of her old man's hearse – we moved the coffin to one side but it was a bit cramped. The handles had stuck in my ribs so I turned her with her back to it and that was more comfortable. Oh yes, ribs (mine) were likely to get more than a handle stuck in them if I didn't do or say something quickly.

I gently eased Charlie to arm's length and surveyed her solemnly, which was not easy because her hand now slipped down to navel level and was feeling around there. It looked like a ritual disembowelling then.

"Flower of the East, Lotus Blossom, I note with pleasure your ravishing appearance, my nose detects succulent aromas drifting from the kitchen, your touch is divine to my skin but 'mea culpa, mea maxima culpa,' the reason for these events has er... momentarily... er... slipped from my memory."

I didn't usually talk drivel like this and the rhetoric deserted me at the end but I was trying to break it gently. I waited.

"You bad boy, you mean you've actually forgotten what day it is today? You really have forgotten. Well I declare, that's the second time this year. It really is too bad, Marcus."

Her face was stern, her body rigid with indignation, and her voice reproving but strangely her eyes were sparkling wickedly. I couldn't work this out. I shifted nervously from one foot to the other but found I was being eased gently towards the stairs.

"What's all this for?" I mumbled.

"...so just you come upstairs with me my lad, and I'll give you what this is for, well and truly." And taking a firm grip on me, she set off up the stairs.

I was still totally in the dark as to the background for all this but the promise of being given 'what for well and truly', coupled with the novel and exciting mode of my progress up the stairs, convinced me that it couldn't all be bad. To paraphrase Herrick, rosebuds must be gathered whilst I may!

Chapter Twenty-One

The police car slid quietly down the dark street with siren switched off. It drew up outside the pungent entrance to Tolliver Grimshaw's Memorial Gentleman's Urinal. Uniformed officers eased out from each side of the car and carefully put on their peaked caps. One nodded to the other and they both moved quietly through the entrance into the interior. Two low wattage bulbs cast a pale light over the cracked cream tiles, the long line of urinal stalls on one side and the swing doors of the cubicles on the other. All but one of the cubicle doors was open. Holding on to his hat, one officer bent down to look through the gap underneath the solitary closed door. He straightened up and gave the thumbs-up sign to his companion. They stood on either side of the door. The larger of the two raised his fist and then hammered loudly on the door.

"Police! Come out please," he shouted. "Now!"

There was a gasp of alarm from within the cubicle and a sound of frantic activity. The policeman hammered on the door again. "Come out now or we'll break the door down!"

There was the sound of a bolt being withdrawn and the door opened slowly. A pale young man, no more than a youth really, his face covered in sweat, squeezed though the narrow gap between the door and the jamb.

"What do you want? Can't somebody have a crap in peace?" he blustered.

One of the policemen hauled him out of the way whilst

the other slammed his shoulder into the half-open door. The door hardly moved and there was a cry of pain from within the cubicle. The policeman reached round the door and seized a bare arm.

"Come out, sir," he ordered.

With an expression of total shock on his face, a half-naked Arthur Winlewis shuffled out into the urinal's lobby. He was wearing French knickers, stockings and suspenders; the rest of his clothes could be seen hanging on a hook in the cubicle.

"You're both under arrest," snapped the smaller policeman, and handcuffs were fastened on the wrists of both men.

The larger policeman turned to his companion and, pointing to the exit, growled, "Let's get them out of here quick, this place turns me over."

The feel of the handcuffs shocked Winlewis back to reality. He blinked in the feeble light.

"Look, officer, I'm sure this is all a mistake," he protested. "We weren't doing anything wrong. Can't we come to some arrangement?"

"What do you have in mind?" asked one of the policemen. "Neither George here, nor me, are into buggery, are we, George?"

Winlewis reeled back at the savageness of the observation, unsure whether to deny the buggery or carry on with the bribe. He decided to carry on with the bribe.

"I'm a wealthy man and not without influence," he began, and, sensing encouragement, proceeded to dig himself in even deeper by offering them a thousand pounds each to let him go.

"Make a note of that George. Attempting to bribe a police officer to be added to the charges."

"All right, five thousand!" Winlewis cried in desperation.

George put away his notebook and took hold of

Winlewis's arm. The two were taken outside and pushed unceremoniously into the back of the police car. Winlewlis's clothes were slung into the boot, despite his protestations that he should be allowed to dress.

The smaller policeman radioed through to the police station. "We caught them both at it – bare-arsed, so to speak. Be there in ten minutes."

"Drive slowly," said the sergeant with a chuckle.

* * *

The Sheringford Bugle reporter got the phone call as he was preparing for bed. Hastily pulling on a sweater and jeans over his pyjamas, he just made it to the police station, with his photographer as the police car drew up at the main entrance.

There were some beautiful shots in the morning papers of Winlewis, French knickers and all, being hauled out of the back seat of the police car and up the steps into the reception area. He was desperately trying to cover his face with one had and his nether regions with the other – both unsuccessfully.

The reporter's enquiry – "How does it feel to be arrested, Arthur?" – fell on very stony ground.

* * *

Deirdre was having breakfast and watching the morning television news when the story broke. Shots of Sheringford Police Station interspersed with stills of Arthur in ladies underwear, accompanied by an effete young man being hauled out of a police car, froze the transfer of Wheaties and soya milk from bowl to mouth.

Being charged with performing acts of gross indecency and attempting to bribe a police officer was clearly going to put paid to Arthur's, and thus Socialist Organiser

Soviet's, chances of winning the Sheringford seat well and truly. Deirdre's initial reaction was shock and disappointment that all her hard work was going to come to nothing but, as she reflected on these events, she realised that it got her off the hook with Denis Straker. What is more, she could now spend more time with Fitzallan doing their joint socialist projects. She gave a thin smile as she recalled the hard times Straker had given her. Bloody arrogant, chauvinistic pig. Now it was payback time. Revenge for all those indignities she had had to suffer. This must be handled carefully to extract maximum satisfaction and needed some thought.

She leant back in her chair and pursed her lips. Straker was clever, and would probably sense a trap, so he was to be avoided for the time being. Hugh Evans was supposed to be her contact, so Rat Face it would be for starters. She reached for the phone.

The hastily convened committee meeting of the Socialist Organisers Soviet met in the usual rundown terraced house at 23 Inkerman Terrace in South London, ostensibly to review the Sheringford situation and see if anything could be salvaged from the wreckage. Arriving a few minutes late by intention, Deirdre chained her bike securely to the rusty railings in front of the weed-covered front garden and pushed open the creaking gate. The response to her answerphone identification was immediate, and the small wispy grey woman scanned her smart two-piece suit and crisp white blouse before ushering her up the three flights of stairs to the top floor.

Clutching her prepared (and very brief) speech in her hand, she sat down, without invitation, in the vacant chair left around the table, noting that it was the place nearest the only door. This time the furniture had been arranged with chairs all round the table presumably to include her. The original five committee members had now been reduced to four following the political demise of Winlewis; Dr Michael Pruitt, the so-called party strategist, appeared to be the new Chair. Rat-faced Hugh Evans, Klipspringer and the smooth Denis Straker were the others.

The faint hope that lurked within her ample bosom that they might suggest that she try to take over as the SOS nominee as the Labour Party candidate for the Sheringford by-election was dashed by the Chair's opening remark.

"Comrade Plant, we are disappointed that you failed to protect Arthur Winlewis from what is obviously a cooked up plot to discredit him by this corrupt government. All our efforts over the past months in Sheringford have come to naught and, as you cannot be relied upon, we are going to have to look elsewhere to progress our cause in future."

The barefaced effrontery of it made her catch her breath and any residual sympathy she may have felt for their fallen cause evaporated like Scotch mist. That was the last straw. The prepared speech was abandoned. She inflated her lungs to the maximum, thrusting out her chest like an enraged bullfrog. She rose to her feet secure in her power dressing; she was now in charge of the situation, and, because she blocked the exit, she had a captive audience.

Denis Straker eased his chair back slightly and the sardonic smile on his face indicated that he had a good idea of what was coming. None of the others had experienced Ms Deirdre in full fulminate; it would be quite a surprise for them. He couldn't care less. She had served a purpose, it hadn't worked, forget her and move on to the next thing.

She paused to settle herself, fixed Pruitt with a glare that made him clench his buttocks tightly together. Then she let rip.

"You useless, incompetent, inefficient, fucking bastards! You couldn't organise a booze-up in a fucking brewery! How on earth could you put forward a known homo like Winlewis for this high profile position? You must have known his sexual proclivities, and to put him up for a constituency like Sheringford was sheer lunacy from the start. Jesus Christ, he was bound to be caught rogering somebody or something illegal before long! Are you thick or something? Have you no sense?" She paused for breath.

"All the work that I put in to Sheringford – yes, I not you – to get him nominated – and certainly he would have been elected – has been wasted! You idle fuckers sitting here, lolling about in your steam-heated office, chucking out orders but doing bugger all! And you, Doctor Michael Pruitt, so-called Party Strategist and Planner," she snarled, turning her anger on the Chair, "you couldn't plan your way to the nearest fucking bus-stop. Well, I've had it with you lot right up to here." She lifted her hand to the top of her head, and when Joe Klipspringer started to stand up to protest, she told him to sit down or she'd break his fucking arm – and they believed her.

"So, I'm out of here, and I'm going to do something where brain-dead, incompetent prats like you lot can't cock it up."

Casting a withering glance all round, she turned and swept out of the room, slamming the door behind her. The thin wispy woman, who had been listening at the keyhole, was brushed casually to one side and flattened against the wall as Deirdre thundered down the stairs and out into the night.

She was brought smartly to a halt in shock. All that was left of her bike was the front wheel chained to the fence; the rest of it – frame, back wheel, saddlebag and all – had gone. Calling down imprecations and curses from the sky on the perpetrators of this dastardly deed, she unchained the wheel, bent it in her bare hands and hurled it at the front door of number twenty-three. She then turned and headed for the bus-stop. Ten minutes later, having failed to find it, she hailed a passing cab to take her to the station. The irony was lost on her.

* * *

When Fizallan Percival opened his Guardian that morning and saw the photos of Winlewis, his first thought was to telephone Deirdre. He vaguely knew that she was involved with Sheringford Labour politics, but how deeply and in what way, he didn't know.

However, he had to go down to Sheringford next afternoon to see the local planners, so he decided not to phone but to call at Deirdre's flat after his meeting, and surprise her. They hadn't seen each other for a few days and he was feeling a bit horny and in need of a fettle-up. It seemed like a good idea. He didn't know that she would be up in London at the Socialist Organisers Soviet committee meeting.

He had never been to Deidre's flat in Sheringford before – all their trysts had taken place either at his luxury pad in London, or in hotels – but he had the address.

The gleaming Mercedes seemed out of place in Sheringford New Town and, as it slid to a spot outside the ground floor flat set in a low-rise, cheap brick building, quite a few net curtains twitched. One of them was in the flat itself.

Suzie Kassenbaum, alerted by the unaccustomed engine noise, glanced out of the window. She knew immediately to whom the flash wheels belonged and watched with increasingly furious savage jealously as Percival's bronzed hand carefully locked the car doors. This was the bastard 'man', she spat out the word to herself, who was stealing Deirdre's affection and attention away from her. Increasingly since the disastrous weekend Womyn's Wigwam, she had felt Deirdre's interest slipping away and she had noticed, with increasing heartburning, that whenever Fitzallan Percival's name had come up, Deirdre perked up. Now here he was, boldly coming up the path to invade their very private love nest itself.

The bell rang and Suzie opened the door with a winning smile. "You must be Fitzallan," she gushed, "the famous architect. I've heard so much about you."

This was grist to the mill for Percival, he liked people to 'hear so much about him', it was his due as a celebrity anyway.

"And you must be little Suzie, Deirdre's help," he replied offhandedly, thus sealing his fate. "Is Deirdre about?"

"Come in," Suzie invited, "Deidre's not here at the moment but she should be back soon," she lied convincingly.

He was put in the sitting room and asked what he'd like to drink.

"Bring me a Campari and soda," he ordered, "about half and half." He cast a glance round the place, it was very shabby. The maid obviously wasn't doing her stuff. He would mention it when she came with his drink.

She never did. She slipped into the bedroom and took her Swiss Army knife from the bedside table drawer. She tested the blade. It was still razor sharp from the honing it got after Womyn's Wigwam.

It was only the coincidence that a boy delivering flyers for SOS happened to come to the door, and heard Percival's screams through the letter box, that saved his life. The boy managed to drag an infuriated Suzie off Percival's twitching body before murder was done. The ambulance and police were called, and Percival carted off by the paramedics to Sheringford District Hospital with stab wounds to his lower abdomen. Suzie was taken to the local police station for interrogation.

Deirdre knew nothing of this. Her train arrived late in the evening at Sheringford Station. Cursing the capitalist lackey who had stolen most of her bike, she caught the night bus to New Town, arriving there to be met by a police cordon and crime scene tape stretched round her pad. Her first thought was that the Socialist Organisers Soviet had firebombed the place, but there was no outward sign of damage. She accosted a policeman standing guard at the door.

"This is my flat. What the hell's going on?"

"Wait there," he instructed, and disappeared inside, returning shortly with a sharp-featured woman in civilian clothes.

"I'm Detective Sergeant Tyler and you are...?"

"Ms Deirdre Plant, the tenant of this flat. What's going on?"

The DS took her inside, avoiding the sitting room and its bloodstained carpet, and went into the small kitchen. The DS asked, "If you are the tenant, then who is Suzie Kassenbaum?"

A look of alarm flashed across Deirdre's face. "Why? What's happened to her? Is she all right?"

Before answering any of Deidre's questions, the DS made Deirdre explain where she had been all day. Deirdre tried to control her exasperation at this ponderous procedure and explained that she had been at a meeting in London, and yes, there were people who could confirm that, and yes, she had come back on the last train, and yes, there were people who'd seen her on it.

"Now, what the fuck has happened here?"

"Do you know a Mr Fitzallan Percival?'

This jerked Deirdre to full alertness. A puzzled look

on her face, she said, "Yes I do. He's a good friend of mine. Why? How is he involved?"

The DS went on to explain how Percival had been found bleeding from knife wounds in the sitting room and was at the moment undergoing surgery in Sheringford District Hospital.

Deirdre grasped the whole thing in a flash. "Bloody Suzie!" she exclaimed, and, before the DS could respond, Deirdre was out the door. The policeman, who held out a restraining arm, nearly got a double fracture for his pains. She seized his bike, which was leaning against the fence, and set off pedalling like fury for Sheringford Hospital leaving the policeman's 'Hey you!' fading in her slipstream.

* * *

I propped myself in the corner and happily contemplated the scene through a silly smile – well, it was my party. After all, you don't get made an Associate Partner every day. They even moved me out of my broom cupboard up to an office on the first floor next to the bogs. "Three shits in a row" as some wit in the design office put it. I didn't know who – yet.

Charlie, surrounded by lascivious eyeballs, was her usual knockout in violet and black that matched her eyes and hair. She handled the offers of sexual paradise easily, accepting them as a compliment and turning them down without insult – I hoped! The turning down bit, that is; I couldn't give a monkey's if she insulted those randy buggers grievously – and they were my friends!

Deirdre wasn't there, she would have come with Percival but the Little Brown Turd wasn't there either. Although reluctantly invited – business is business, my boy, as the Senior Partner said – the LBT was at that moment lying in Sheringford District Hospital recovering from stab wounds to the lower abdomen inflicted by some demented woman attempting to disembowel him with a Swiss Army knife. Deirdre was constantly at his bedside, keeping a close watch on her investment and anxiously wondering if he would be able to father anything other than a selfish thought in future. She had wiped the floor with all the hospital staff over the stereotyped sexual roles they played, including the Chief Nurse. A clash of Titans that had been. Deirdre, out-bosomed by a good twenty centimetres, had won on volume and vocabulary and now came and went as she pleased, running off copies of her *Cervical Cap Fitters Handbook* on the Gynaecology Department's photocopier at will. I wondered how Percival explained his welts away when he had his bed-bath. Rumour had it that he was well striped, purple and red like a Brighton deckchair – belligerent but beautifully marked.

Grime had turned up in a smart blue suit and white shirt – "Gorra few quid thanks to you lads." His progress round the room could be followed by squeals, shrieks and raised men's voices threatening retribution of the "if you dare do that to my wife again" kind. He drifted over to me, clutching his usual bottle by the neck – no glass.

"Eh, Marcus the new threads don't pull the crumpet like the nautical gear."

"Is that so?" I murmured, thinking that as far as I could remember the only thing Grime had managed to pull in those filthy revolting clothes had been himself – even Madame had give him the thumbs-down before he set the whole of Honfleur Harbour alight.

I would have liked to see how Deirdre would've coped with Grime. I'd not included him in the runners and riders when I short-listed the 'providers of pecker' for what was to be the big bonking scene. I certainly wouldn't have picked Percival; the Little Brown Turd wouldn't even have made the subs bench. Just shows how wrong you can be.

A great guffaw of laughter showed where Barclay was holding court, he had signed up his anchor tenant for Sheringford today, hence the bottle of Louis Roederer Cristal I held firmly in my hand out of Grime's reach. It was one of the cases Barclay had brought to the party as a little token of his appreciation. Good living and Barclay were synonymous. As Scales put it, whenever Barclay rubbed his hands together you could never be sure whether it was a pint, a profit or a poke he had in mind.

Barclay had buttonholed me earlier and, sliding a beefy arm round my shoulders, said confidentially with a quiet smile, "By the way, Marcus, if you ever get round to making an honest woman out of the gorgeous Charlotte, I could end up as a neighbour of your father-in-law."

I raised an interested eyebrow. "Have you bought a house in Sheringford then?"

He grinned, "Forty acres of prime land at the foot of the Downs – going to build a nice country house there with spectacular views – my country seat."

"Really?" I exclaimed dubiously. "Well, you'll never get planning permission for anything like that in that area."

"Already got it. It went through the Planning Committee last night with the full backing of the Chief Planning Officer and the Chairman." He grinned and tapping his nose raised a triumphant finger.

"You didn't!" I gasped. "You haven't!"

"What the eye don't see the heart don't grieve, old son; but don't mention it to Percival cos he's definitely not the architect." And with that he strolled off, leaving me stunned.

Eleven months it had taken, eleven months of disturbance to my tranquillity before it had all eventually slotted into place. The government had capitulated, however they dressed it up as part of their environment programme; Charlie and her team had won. You had to hand it to her, she was a star.

Fitzallan Percival had cancelled out the Great White Shafting Shark and vice-versa.

Barclay had reconciled God and Mammon and would make a bomb out of it.

I had been promoted, and both my salary and prospects enhanced considerably.

The final irony of the whole saga was that seven days before polling, Winlewis, wearing French knickers, suspenders and stockings, had been dragged from the public lavatories in Sheringford fiercely resisting arrest. Charged with performing an act of gross indecency, he had been forced to withdraw as Labour's parliamentary candidate in the Sheringford by-election at the last minute. The Liberal/SDP no-hoper had streaked through on the rails to take the seat by sixty-three votes. He had been so overcome by his unexpected success that he had wet himself on the platform in front of five million television viewers. I felt his career in politics would be short – it was too easy to take the piss out of him.

And it all stemmed from that day last May when Moon, drifting in like a summer breeze, hammered a stone into the front wheel of Minerva Hartley-Worthington's bicycle.